BOOKS BY HELENA NE

Helena Newbury is the *New York Times* and *USA Today* bestselling author of sixteen romantic suspenses, all available where you bought this book. Find out more at helenanewbury.com.

Lying and Kissing

Punching and Kissing

Texas Kissing

Kissing My Killer

Bad For Me

Saving Liberty

Kissing the Enemy

Outlaw's Promise

Alaska Wild

Brothers

Captain Rourke

Royal Guard

Mount Mercy

The Double

Hold Me in the Dark

Deep Woods

BROTHERS

HELENA NEWBURY

FOSTER & BLACK

ISBN: 978-1-914526-21-3

DEDICATION

To my readers, who—like me—wanted to know what happened next.

WARNING

All of my romantic suspenses are standalones.

EXCEPT THIS ONE!

I wrote *Brothers* especially for my readers who've followed the O'Harras through four books. This book is *not* a good place to start. Not only will you have missed out on how all four couples got together but you'll also ruin the four O'Harra books for yourself.

So if you've somehow stumbled across this book and you haven't read the others, go and read them first. The O'Harra books are, in order:

Punching and Kissing (Aedan and Sylvie)
Bad For Me (Sean and Louise)
Saving Liberty (Kian and Emily)
Outlaw's Promise (Carrick and Annabelle)

Okay, back? Good. Let's go ;)

1

KIAN

I always keep a hand on her back. *Always.*

When I'd been her bodyguard, it had been about guiding her through the crowd and being able to grab her and pull her behind me at a second's notice. It had been about quelling her panic attacks, reassuring her that I was there, that she wasn't alone. That I'd never let anyone hurt her. And, in the days when we'd been trying to hide our growing, smoldering, unstoppable attraction, it had been the one way we could touch without anyone knowing. All of that emotion, all of our need for each other, focused into just the tips of my fingers and the press of my palm. Those moments of touching were what I looked forward to all day.

Everything was different, now. I wasn't her bodyguard. Her panic attacks were a fading memory. And everyone knew that we were together. But I still kept my hand on her back, every time we were in a crowd. I couldn't bear not touching her. It was reassurance for both of us that, after everything we'd been through, we were finally together for good.

"Bergier," whispered Emily, leaning close. "French ambassador."

I grunted and forced a grin as they guy approached and did the whole double-air-kiss thing with us. We'd only been at the reception a half hour and already my smile muscles were hurting.

"Lundgren," Emily whispered. "Danish ambassador."

How did she *do* that? All these people looked the same to me: politicians stuffed into dinner jackets. The names were gone from my head by the time the next one approached. The saving grace was that, each time she clued me in on who someone was, I felt the brush of her soft, mahogany hair against my neck and the heat of her breath in my ear. The scent of her, warm skin and big, open horizons and rocks baked by a desert sun...it made me instantly hard. I'd endure a thousand embassy receptions if it meant I got to be close to her. But I wished they built breaks into these things, away from the cameras, so I could pull her into a quiet room, push her up against a wall and—

Emily gently tugged my sleeve, guiding me towards a couple who were either connected to the British royals or Iceland, I wasn't sure which. I forced a fresh smile onto my face and shook their hands, trying to stretch my shoulders under the dinner jacket. Whatever I did, I couldn't get comfortable. Maybe it was too tight: it certainly felt ridiculous, stretched over my big frame. But it was tailored for me so I knew it wasn't that.

I ran a hand over my cheek as I thought about it, still thrown when I didn't find the expected stubble there. I had to look respectable for the press. Maybe that was it, maybe I still wasn't used to being clean-shaven. But I knew deep down that it wasn't that, either.

I froze as I saw something out of the corner of my eye. A waiter coming towards us, carrying a tray of champagne glasses...but there was something off about him. The chattering of the Brits or the Icelandics or whoever the hell they were seemed to fade away as adrenaline pumped into my system. The waiter was doing everything right: he had the walk and the polite, discreet presence and he held his tray rock-steady but—

But his eyes. His eyes were wrong. They were everywhere, flicking over the crowd, just like mine were. He'd nearly reached us, now, and he was looking behind us. Maybe checking on an accomplice....

I whipped around. A man in his thirties was approaching fast. "Miss Matthews?" he called out.

Emily began to turn around. Just as the guy wanted. Adrenaline was slamming through my veins, now, every muscle going tight and hard. I saw Emily's eyes widen as she recognized the look on my face: *trouble*. All old, familiar feelings surged up inside me: the gut-wrenching fear when she was in danger; that primal, all-consuming need to protect her. I reached for my gun....

My fingers closed on air. *Shit!* I didn't carry a gun anymore.

The waiter was almost on top of us and now I thought I could see a bulge under his jacket. And the guy who'd come up behind us was reaching under *his* jacket—

The fear was subsumed by something stronger: the need to destroy those who threatened her.

Time seemed to slow down. I used the hand on Emily's back to shove her to safety. Then I grabbed the waiter's shirt and yanked him towards me so hard his feet left the ground. I drove my fist into his face and he slumped to the ground, champagne glasses falling like rain and shattering all around him.

I grabbed the metal tray, spun around and slammed the edge of it into the nose of the guy behind us. It wasn't enough to knock him out but he went down on his ass, blood spurting from his nose, and it made him pull his hand from under his jacket. All around me, people were screaming but I ignored them.

I turned back to the waiter and checked under his jacket. Jesus, I'd been right: there was a handgun in a holster there. I pulled the gun and shoved it in the face of the guy on the ground. "Stay down!" I yelled.

He lifted his hands from his broken nose, his face white with fear.

Suddenly, Secret Service agents were all around me. I was pleased to see that Jack, the agent who'd taken over from me as Emily's bodyguard, had already pulled her to the edge of the room. Others were hustling away the guests, leaving me in a widening circle of space.

"Check him," I ordered, nodding at the guy with the broken nose. "He was going for something under his jacket."

One agent patted him down and pulled something from his inside jacket pocket: a Dictaphone. *Maybe it's a bomb.* They could be that small, these days, and it would explain how he got it past security.

Emily managed to get to the edge of the circle, even though she had to drag a reluctant Jack with her. "That's Warren Banks!" she said. "He's with the *Washington Post!*"

Shit.

"I was just going to get a quote," said Banks, his voice distorted by his broken nose.

Shit! I spun to point my gun at the waiter, still unconscious on the ground. "What about *him?*" No way was he innocent. He'd had a concealed gun, for God's sake.

At that moment, Miller, the head of the White House Secret Service detail, pushed through the crowd. He waved for his agents to lower their guns and I lowered mine as well. He looked at me, looked at the waiter and sighed. "He's NCIS," he said. "He was here undercover."

Navy intelligence? He was an *agent?* A creeping sense of dread wound its way up through my legs, tightening around my torso like cold, clinging vines. *Have I just—Oh God....* I looked around the room at the two injured men, the shattered glass, the shocked guests. Yep: I'd messed up on an epic scale.

I dropped the gun on the floor and put my palm to my face. *"Feck,"* I said loudly.

Much later, I lay on Emily's bed, staring up at the ceiling. I'd been spirited out of the reception while the Secret Service "secured the scene." Which I knew was code for *cleared up my mess.*

I heard the door open and close, then Emily's soft footsteps padding across the room. But I didn't look up, even when I felt the bed sink under her weight. I was brooding too hard. Only when she swung a leg over me and brought her face over mine did I focus on her...and immediately, everything felt a little better. God, the sight of her: the perfect, wide mouth, those eyes filled with warmth and compassion and the soft waves of hair that hung down between us to brush my cheeks. *I love this woman.*

"So," said Emily. "An update." She took a deep breath. "The NCIS agent is fine and said you have a hell of a right hook. He's on his way home."

"I blew his cover, didn't I?" I muttered.

"He didn't say," said Emily diplomatically.

I winced. I'd probably cost the NCIS weeks or months of work and tipped off whoever they were investigating. "And the reporter?"

"I've promised him an exclusive interview." She straddled my waist. "No one wants to press charges. It was a misunderstanding. Everything's okay."

I sighed. I wanted to believe it, wanted nothing more than to pull her down to me and kiss her and forget about all this. But I was mad at myself.

"You couldn't have known he was undercover," said Emily, her voice soothing.

Of course I couldn't. I hadn't been briefed, unlike the Secret Service. And that was the whole problem: I'd behaved like her bodyguard when it wasn't my job anymore. Protecting people was what I *did*. I didn't know how to do anything else. That was why I'd felt so uncomfortable all evening, why I always felt uncomfortable at these events. It wasn't the bowtie or being clean shaven. It was not knowing who the hell I was, anymore. Emily was born to this life: effortlessly charming, completely comfortable making small talk with foreign princes and prime ministers. But that was my idea of hell. I'd always been about *doing* things: as a Marine, tell me who to fight and I'd fight them. As a Secret Service agent, tell me who to guard and I'll protect them with my life. Now I had no purpose other than to be on Emily's arm.

I turned my face away from Emily's—I didn't want her to think I was mad at *her*—and glared at the door.

A second later, I felt her cool, soft fingers on my cheek, gently but firmly turning me to look back at her. "What?" she asked.

I didn't want to talk about it but, as soon as I looked into those big green eyes, I knew that wasn't going to fly. Emily had her mom's diplomacy but her dad's Texan stubbornness. I could scowl and brood as much as I wanted but she'd get it out of me eventually. "I just feel like a fifth wheel around here," I told her.

"Kian, there are people lining up to give you a job. Say the word."

It was true: ever since what had happened with Kerrigan and his attempted coup, all sorts of CEOs had been asking if I wanted to be their head of corporate security. But I knew it would be a publicity stunt: I didn't know a thing about corporate espionage. They just wanted to be able to tell the press they had the guy who saved the president on their staff. And, even worse, they wanted my influence on Emily and her father. No. No way. I wasn't going to put Emily and her dad in that position. Besides, I'd go crazy, sitting in meetings all day. I had to find something that actually suited me. But I couldn't go back to being a bodyguard: as long as I was with Emily, I'd be a liability, more of a target than the person I was protecting. Besides, it would mean too much time away from her and DC. I sighed and rubbed my cheek, still missing my stubble. "I'll figure it out," I muttered.

She lay down on top of me and rested her head on my chest, using my much bigger frame like a bed. The warm press of her body, all the way from shoulder to ankle, made me groan and the stress slowly oozed out of me. I gazed up at her, totally enamored. She always knew exactly how to make me feel better. "How the hell did I land a woman like you?" I asked, the words buzzing in my chest against her cheek.

"I don't know," she said, deadpan. "You're definitely shopping way above your station—*Ow!*"

The last was a yelp as I swatted her ass. Then I was growling and twisting, rolling us over on the bed so that she was beneath me. Her dress was suitably demure for the president's daughter but it had ridden up on one side and my thigh was pressing against smooth, bare skin. I felt myself hardening against her. I leaned down and kissed her hard, capturing her mouth and teasing it then plunging in, unable to stop myself. The blood started to pound in my ears. God, I got *drunk* on this woman. I was addicted to her, even more now than when we first met. She returned the kiss eagerly: that mix of innocence and desperate heat that I'd always found such a turn on. I reached down, grabbed the top of her dress and pulled it down, delighted to find that the bra was built-in.

Our lips parted for a second. "Oh, it's like *that,* is it?" she panted.

"Damn right it's like that," I panted back, my troubles forgotten. I cupped one breast, lowered my head and—

There was a knock at the door. We both froze. Then, "No one here," I growled loudly, the Irish strong in my voice from my lust. "This is a recording. Leave a message."

Emily patted my cheek, slipped out from beneath me and hurried over to the door, pulling her dress back into place at the same time. When she opened it, Jack, her bodyguard, was standing there. If he hadn't guessed what he'd interrupted by Emily's flushed face, my glare filled him in. He had the decency to look sheepish. "Sorry, ma'am. Sir. But...your brother's here, Mr. O'Harra."

I blinked at him. My *brother?* Here? Now? It had been weeks since I was reunited with Sean in Anacostia Park. He knew better than to come here: the last thing Emily needed was for the press to find out that her boyfriend's brother had grown a massive crop of weed. They wouldn't care that he'd had a good reason to do what he did: they'd make a scandal out of it and Sean and his girlfriend Louise would probably wind up in jail. It must be an emergency.

I turned to Emily. "Sorry," I mumbled. "I have to—"

She nodded quickly. "Go!"

I leaned down, gave her a quick kiss and went. I was still wracked with guilt that I hadn't been there to help Sean during everything he'd gone through. He was the youngest of us, my baby brother: I was meant to protect him, for God's sake. Well, whatever he needed, I'd help him now.

The Secret Service had put him in a quiet side room, well away from the press. The room was dark except for a few table lamps and it took me a second to find him in the shadows.

It wasn't Sean.

"Hello, brother. Been a long time," said Carrick.

2

KIAN

Carrick?

I stood there frozen but my brain was going full speed, trying to catch up. *Carrick? Here? Now?*

It had been so long since I'd seen him. For a second, my mind rebelled: *it can't be.* This was a man, as big as I was. The image I had of him in my mind was still a teenager. But there was no mistaking that face...even when it was coupled with *that* outfit.

He was wearing faded jeans and a biker's leather cut over a white t-shirt. His arms were loaded with muscle, the skin a rich tan. I could see the top of a back tattoo peeking out just above his t-shirt, the ink black and vicious. There was another tattoo on his bicep, much more colorful. A butterfly with a name emblazoned across it.

I finally stumbled forward, still taking it all in. *My brother is a biker?*

He stepped forward as well and we met in the middle of the room. Cars on Pennsylvania Avenue lit up our faces with faint white flashes as they passed the window. "Jesus," I said, my voice thick with emotion. "*Carrick?!*"

He gazed into my eyes and I saw the pain there, the momentary hesitation. *What's he scared of?* And then he spread his arms wide and we pulled each other into an embrace, my arms locking around warm leather. Under my palm, I swore I could feel the shamrock tattoo on his back throbbing, just as the one on my own back was. I felt him relax: whatever his fear had been, it was gone, burned away by the hug.

I let him go, but kept my hands on his shoulders. Saw him glance away into the corner of the room for a second and blink a couple of times. I didn't want to admit it, but I was the same.

I was still trying to take in what was happening. Ever since Sean had come to DC to find me, I'd been trying to find Carrick and Aedan but with no luck. I'd been so focused on looking for them, I'd never considered that one of them might come looking for me. Now I realized how stupid I'd been. Since the coup, my face was all over the news. And I lived at the best-known residence on the planet.

I fumbled with the nearest light until I found the switch. Now I could see him properly and it was almost like looking in a mirror. We had the same jet-black hair and the same jaw...but his was covered in dark stubble, the way mine used to be. I could see the butterfly tattoo better, now. The name on it was *Annabelle.*

"How are...are you *okay?*" I just blurted it out. That was what I had to know before anything else. I'd been living with the possibility, all these years, that I'd find out he was dead. Now that he was before me, out of the blue, I had this sudden, crazy fear that he was going to say he was dying of cancer or something—

He nodded. "I'm fine." Like me, he'd kept his accent, although his was blended with a good helping of Californian gold. He glanced down at his leather cut. "Found myself a family. Thought it was all I needed, for a while. Then someone made me see sense." My hands were still on his shoulders. He reached up and put one of his on top of mine. "It's time we got our family back together."

I stared at him. He was the eldest but not by much, then there was a bigger gap between us and the younger two: Aedan and finally Sean. It had always been a battle for leadership, between Carrick and me. Him the risk taker, getting us into trouble. Me the responsible one, getting us out of it.

"I know where Sean is," I said.

I saw his chest fill. "You do? I couldn't find him."

"Yeah, they're...trying to stay off the radar."

"They?"

"He got himself a girl. Louise. He came out here a few weeks ago. They live in LA."

Carrick's voice rose in disbelief. "Sean's in *Cali?*" He shook his head. "*I* live in Cali. Jesus, all this time and he was a few hours' ride away. He okay?"

"He and his girl had a rough summer. Had to get involved in some bad shit, but they got out clean. They're all okay. And the kid."

"He has a *kid?!*"

"No. The kid's Louise's. And it's her sister, but she's like...fourteen. Anyway, they're fine." My chest tightened. "What about Aedan? You any idea where he is?" We were three for three so far. *Please don't let him be dead.*

"Chicago. He was boxing in New York for a while, then he and his girl had to bail. They're okay."

I let out a long breath. *Four for four.* A slow warmth started to fill me. I hadn't realized how much I'd been dreading bad news. All sorts of plans started to swim in my head: I could fly out to Chicago in a few weeks and meet up with Aedan, then maybe take a trip to Cali and—

I stopped. There was something in Carrick's eyes.

"This isn't just about getting back in touch," he said.

And suddenly I knew why he hadn't just called. I'd been wrong. We *were* four for four. But there were five of us.

"We don't even know if he's alive," I said.

"Then it's time we found out."

"You think I haven't tried?" I'd tried to find out what happened to Bradan many times over the years, even hired private detectives a couple of times. No one had gotten anywhere.

"So have I," said Carrick. "But we haven't tried together. All of us."

"All of us?"

Carrick lifted his chin and looked me right in the eye. It was just like when we were kids: he was the oldest so he was giving the orders. "We're going to Chicago right now to get Aedan. You can call Sean, get him to meet us there. And then we're going to find our brother."

I opened my mouth. I was about to ask what the urgency was: why *now?* But the words never made it out because I looked into his eyes and I understood.

The urgency was that it had been far too long already. We all felt it: Sean had come looking for me, I'd been looking for the others, Carrick had found Aedan...after years apart, we were all finally doing what we should have done long ago. In my case, it was Emily who'd finally made me see it. Maybe it was the same for the others.

And looking into Carrick's eyes, there was something else. I was mad at the cult for taking Bradan, mad at my dad for killing our mom. But Carrick was mad at *himself.* I felt guilty about not trying to reunite us sooner but Carrick looked as if he was tearing himself apart inside. It made my chest ache to see him in so much pain.

"...okay," I said at last. "I'll pack a bag. But it'll be a while, I have to let people know I'm going. Let me take you somewhere you can wait—"

"I'll meet you down the street," he told me, and named a bar. "I think I make your security guys nervous."

I nodded reluctantly.

"You, though," he said. "You fit in just fine here."

I looked down at myself. I'd completely forgotten I was in a tuxedo. Fancy clothes felt almost comfortable, now. "Yeah," I muttered. "Well."

"You did good, you know. President's daughter. Saving the country."

I gave him a look. "It wasn't like that. I just did my job. A lot of other people deserve credit. Emily, for one."

"Well," said Carrick as he opened the door. "I'm proud of you."

It's funny. After the coup, the papers had been backpedalling so furiously from supporting Kerrigan that they tried to turn me into some sort of hero. They'd come up with all sorts of bullshit praise, but none of it had really meant anything to me. This did. "Mmm," I muttered, looking away. I felt my neck going hot. "Thanks."

Carrick smirked and nodded at my tuxedo. "Even if you do think you're James Bond."

And suddenly it was just like old times. We could have been kids back in Ireland, again. "Oh *feck off,*" I muttered, grinning. "I'll see you in a few hours."

Miller was waiting for me down the hallway. "That's your brother?" he asked, watching Carrick walk away.

"One of them."

"And I thought *you* were a reprobate. Still on for poker?"

The weekly poker games with him and a few of the Secret Service agents had become a thing, since the coup. I enjoyed it, especially because it felt like I had a lot more in common with those guys than with the bigwigs I met at cocktail parties. "Maybe not this week," I told Miller. "I'm going to have to go away for a while."

"Everything okay?"

I knew I couldn't get him involved: however much I loved Sean and Carrick, one was an ex-drug grower with links to the Mexican cartel and apparently the other was an outlaw biker. If some story appeared in the press about how the President's daughter's boyfriend came from a family of criminals, I wanted the White House to have deniability. "Just family stuff. I can handle it." Then, thinking out loud, "I'm going to need to rent a car."

"I can do that for you. What do you need?"

I added it up in my head. Me, Carrick, Sean, Aedan...and it sounded like the others had girlfriends, too. "Something big," I said.

"I'll take care of it."

I slapped him in on the shoulder in thanks. Funny how we'd wound up friends, after being at each other's throats for so long.

I went back to our room but Emily wasn't there. Probably off with her mom somewhere and I really didn't want to have to have this conversation in front of the First Lady, so I stayed put and started throwing shirts in a bag. I had no idea how long I'd be gone for. But now that I'd made the decision, my whole body was buzzing with excitement. *Carrick! And Sean! And Aedan!* All of us back together again. And maybe, just maybe, Bradan, too.

My hands tightened on the bag's handles. The last image I had of Bradan was of him in the back of our mom's car, hands banging on the glass so hard I thought he was going to break it, *begging* her not to take him to the cult. My chest closed up. *The bastards.*

Alive or dead, we were going to find him. And we were going to make them pay for taking him.

I'd just changed into a suit when Emily opened the door...and stopped in the doorway as she saw my bag sitting on the bed. "What's going on?" she asked immediately.

I sat her down and told her. Before I'd finished, she was on her feet: closing her laptop and grabbing the power cord, plucking dresses off hangers to throw into a suitcase. Then she caught the look I was giving her and her expression darkened. "I'm coming with you," she said in a voice she'd inherited from her father.

"No."

"Don't 'no' *me,* I'm coming with you! That's not up for debate!"

I stood up and gently put my hands on her waist. "Emily—"

"No!" She shook her head, long hair flying. "Uh-uh. Not even a question."

I stroked my hands gently up and down her sides. I could smell her scent and it made me crazy: it made me think of warm Texas sun and wide open spaces. I was raging inside at the unfairness of it: I'd finally found the woman I wanted to spend the rest of my life with and now I had to tear us apart? I wanted to take her with me but— "I can't," I said at last.

"You *can!* If you're looking for Bradan, you need me. I'm good at tracking things down."

"It might be dangerous."

"Then you *definitely* need me. Have you forgotten who saved your ass in the hotel ballroom?"

I sighed. She had me there. But: "You can't come. Emily, you know what Sean and Louise were involved in."

"They got away with it!"

"But they still did business with the cartel. The press watches everything you do. If I meet up with Sean, hopefully no one will care. But if you're there, it's a story. Someone in the press will dig up Sean's history, or find out about Kayley's medical treatment and how they paid for it, and suddenly it's a scandal. *President's daughter linked to drug farmers!* It could ruin you. *And* your dad."

She took a deep breath but bit back whatever she was going to say. Instead, she stared off into the corner.

"Emily."

She wouldn't look at me. She knew I was right but that didn't make it any easier. We'd barely been apart since we got together. She'd always had my hand on her back. She needed that and I needed to protect her...but this time, protecting her meant keeping her away.

"Emily," I said softly.

Even in her heels, she was smaller than me. When she finally met my gaze, she had to look up at me to do it. The defiance on her face made my heart melt.

"We have to do it this way," I told her. "For everyone's sake."

Her shoulders sank as she relented. She took another deep breath and this time I heard the tremor in it: she was just barely keeping from crying. "You'll call me *every day,*" she told me.

I bent down and kissed her lips. "Yes ma'am."

I backed out of our room, bag slung over my shoulder, and nearly walked right into the President. "Sir!" I straightened up fast.

"Walk with me," he said and led the way.

I fell in beside him. He was still in his tuxedo but his bow tie was hanging unfastened around his neck. I'm a big guy—physically, I'm bigger than him. But he still towered over me, his presence filling the hallway, members of the Secret Service coming to attention long before he came into sight. He was *the President.*

I swallowed when I realized we were heading for the Oval Office.

We swept in and the President nodded for me to close the door behind me. He poured himself a whiskey and then walked around to stand behind his desk.

I slowly put my bag down on the floor, more than a little freaked out. I had no idea what he wanted: we'd talked plenty of times but this felt different. I nodded to my bag. "Sir, I've got to...ah...go away for a little while."

"I know," he said. "I heard about your brother visiting."

I nodded. So that was it. I thought about lying to him, telling him that it was just a happy family visit. But the thought went out of my head as soon as I looked at him again. You don't lie to the President. "Sir," I said at last, "there's some stuff that maybe I should have told you. About my family. One of my brothers, Bradan—"

"I know," he said, cutting me off.

I blinked, dumbstruck.

The President tilted his head to one side. "You really think I didn't do a full background check on you before I let you guard my daughter...much less *date* my daughter? I know about Bradan. I know about your mother." He sighed. "That's why I have to ask you not to go."

"Because you're scared of the fallout, if the press find out?"

He shook his head. "Because the cult is more dangerous than you can possibly imagine."

3

KIAN

The President sat and nodded me to a chair. "What I'm about to tell you doesn't leave this room," he said. "It's known to me, a couple of intelligence staff I trust and that's it. Even the joint chiefs aren't aware of it."

I slowly sat down. *What the hell is going on?*

"When I took power, my predecessor warned me about three things," said the President. "A military project that was threatening to damn near bankrupt us; some guys at State who he suspected were on the take—they were—"—he drew in a deep breath—"and the cult."

I shook my head. "I know they're bastards—"—I caught myself—"sorry, Sir. I mean: I know they're evil but I didn't think they'd be on *your* radar. Or on anyone's radar. When they took Bradan, no one even believed us or took us seriously."

"That probably saved your life," the President said.

"*What?!*"

"They'd already pinned your mother's murder on your dad. They knew no one would listen to a bunch of kids so they let you go. If you'd been adults, if you'd pressed a little harder...we wouldn't be having this conversation." He picked up his glass, staring at the amber liquid inside. "These people," he said, "are merciless. They are relentless. They will do *absolutely whatever it takes* to protect themselves. They didn't let you live out of any sort of mercy for children. They did a goddamn calculation and figured killing you wasn't worth it." He looked at me over the rim of his glass. "How many people do you think are in the cult?"

I shrugged. Surely not that many...they weren't *known:* I mean, you never heard about them on TV or saw advertising for them. I didn't even know their official name. "I don't know...thirty, forty people around Chicago?"

The President took a sip of his drink, then marched the glass around and around between his fingers. "The best estimate I could get," he said, "was five or six thousand."

"*Thousand?!*"

"And it's not how many there are, it's *who* they are. These people are woven right into the goddamn government, Kian. CIA, FBI, DEA. I suspect they're in the NSA which means they're into our computers, into our emails. Maybe even *my* emails. Judges. Senators. At least one justice in the Supreme Court. You don't need millions of people to make a difference. A few thousand will do it, in the right places."

The room was spinning. I'd thought I'd known what we were dealing with: when I thought *cult,* I thought of a group of fanatics in white robes, worshipping some conman. I'd had no idea.

"Every time I tried to probe them," said the President, "*Every* time, however delicately I did it, there was a warning. They didn't dare take me on personally but they got to the people I sent. I made the mistake of talking to a DA about it and he started making enquiries. A week later, he was dead: drove his car into a tree...on a clear, dry stretch of road. A woman at State started an investigation: she died in a boating accident. " He leaned across the desk to me. "Now you know me. You know I never walked away from a fight in my goddamn life. But I wasn't going to send more good people to die. I dropped it, even though it killed me to think of the cult out there, uncontested." He shook his head. "I don't know who's leading these people. I don't know what they want. But I know that if you try to go after them, they'll kill you."

We sat for a few seconds, his words hanging in the air between us. He drank a little more of his whiskey, the rattle of the ice cubes loud in the silent room.

"When Emily first hired you and I checked you out and found the connection to the cult, I nearly vetoed the whole thing," he said. "I thought maybe it was all a setup, maybe they were trying to sneak someone into the White House. But when I looked closer, saw how they'd split your family apart...I knew we were on the same side. When you and Emily started seeing each other—and I knew about that long before you think I did, I'm not a goddamn idiot—I hoped this day would never come. Because I like you, Kian. And I know what these people will do to you and your brothers if you try to take them down."

I sat there reeling, my eyes unfocused. Now I knew what we were up against...*what chance do we have?* If the President's best people couldn't even penetrate the cult, what hope did four Irish brothers have?

Then I remembered Bradan's face, in the back of that car.

I looked at the President. "I'm sorry, sir," I said. "But he's my brother. I have to try."

The President closed his eyes and nodded. "Yeah," he said with a sigh. "I had a feeling you were going to say that." He knocked back the rest of his whiskey, rubbed his eyes and then looked at me. "I don't know who's part of the cult. If I try to bring the authorities in to help you, I'm liable to just tip them off. But there *is* one guy at the FBI I do still trust. Bit of a rule breaker but he's a good man. He knows the cult and he might be able to help."

He wrote a phone number on a scrap of paper. When he passed it to me, he took my hand in a warm, firm grip. "You come back alive, you hear?"

I nodded. "Yes sir, Mr. President."

I walked down to the White House garage to pick up my rental car...and found Miller standing next to a huge black SUV. It was unmarked but I recognized it as one of the ones the Secret Service used, the kind with discreet armor plating and bulletproof glass. "I can't take this," I protested. "What I'm about to get into...you don't want the White House anywhere near it." I was pretty sure that, to find Bradan, I'd have to break some laws.

Miller shrugged. "It's fine. Anyone asks, I'll say you stole it." He moved closer and lowered his voice. "I don't want you getting shot, O'Harra," he said gruffly. "It'd break Emily's heart."

It was as close to an emotional outpouring as the two of us got. "Yeah," I said. "Okay. Thanks."

I climbed in and put the SUV in gear. God, the thing was ridiculous: it seated eight with luggage and looked as if it would go through a brick wall. But after the President's warning, it made me feel a little better. I gave Miller a wave, drove up the ramp to the security barrier and set off.

Carrick seemed to have sought out the darkest, grimiest bar he could find: maybe it was the only one that would serve a biker. I couldn't even believe the place existed within a few streets of the White House. The SUV looked conspicuous as hell parked outside but, fortunately, Carrick came out as soon as I pulled up. His arm was around—*wow.* She was stunning. Hair the color of the sun just as it drops below the horizon and so long it almost hit her waist. Gorgeous, delicate features and soft, pale skin: she didn't look like a California girl. She had curves that made you stop and look, too, especially in tight jeans and a fitted leather jacket.

"This is Annabelle," Carrick told me as I lowered my window.

Holy shit. My brother had hit the jackpot. I mean, she wasn't Emily, but.... I shook her hand through the window and she gave me a smile that lit up the whole street. I nodded to the rear seats. "Jump in. There's plenty of space."

Carrick looked from me to the SUV. His expression said, *are you kidding?* "We'll ride."

I blinked. "You'll...?" I watched as he swung a leg over the Harley that was parked alongside me. "To *Chicago?!* That's like *ten hours!*"

He ignored me and put on a helmet. Annabelle slid onto the bike behind him, her body pressed close to his.

I sighed and started the SUV. The roar of Carrick's Harley shook the buildings around us, making people turn and stare. When he pulled out into traffic, I fell in behind him.

"Okay," I muttered. "Let's start putting this family back together."

4

BRADAN

I woke into darkness.

That made no sense. Whenever I opened my eyes, it was to the flashing blue light and gentle chime that meant it was time to get up. Whenever I went to sleep, it was with my eyelids bathed in the pulsing red light that meant it was time to rest.

I've heard that other people dream. They wake up having slayed dragons, or been to school naked, or kissed their best friend. I've never dreamt. Between the red light and the blue light is deep, seamless black. Maybe I dreamt Before. But I don't remember much about Before.

I slowly sat up, grunting as my spine protested and my legs cramped. Your body isn't designed to be in one position for hours. That's the other thing about me: I sleep absolutely still. Motionless. I think we all do, at least all the Primes, who were trained as I was. It's a side effect of Room Nine.

Room Nine is in a disused water treatment plant, one of the many properties Aeternus own. Room Nine used to be an observation gallery. There's this huge space inside the plant where millions of gallons of water used to fall in a continuous, crashing waterfall. There's a walkway that runs around the edge of the space where staff could look up about fifty feet to the top of the drop and down a few hundred feet to the bottom, as water rushed by inches from their noses. It must have been a pretty scary place to stand, even in those days.

When Aeternus took it over, the water had long since stopped running and all that was left was the drop into inky blackness. They got angle grinders and sawed off the metal fence that stopped you falling off the walkway. The result was Room Nine: a ledge less than three feet wide, running around the perimeter of a huge, dark hole.

That was where I slept. That was where all the trainees slept, stretched out on our backs along the length of the walkway. If we rolled over in our sleep, we'd wake up screaming, midway through a two hundred foot fall.

When it was time to sleep, we had to file in one by one and fill up the ledge in order from furthest-from-the-door to nearest-to-the-door, because once people were lying down, there was no room to get past and change position. At first, none of us dared to go to sleep. But you can only keep that up for a few days. We had to will ourselves not to move, imprint it on our minds so hard that we held our position all night. That's what they wanted us to learn: that resolve.

I was fourteen, the first night I slept in there. I cried my little heart out—silently, because they would beat you if you made a noise. In the morning, the kid next in the line, the one who should have been lying by my feet, was just...gone.

I slept in Room Nine for four years. I don't move in my sleep anymore. I don't think I ever will again.

The blue light finally came on, lighting up my tiny room. I'd awoken maybe thirty seconds before the alarm: that *never* happened. It was bad: wasting sleeping time was inefficient. I wrinkled my brow. What would wake me? The mansion was silent. I couldn't recall a noise. It felt more like something had happened. Like a change had begun, far off in the distance, and the ripples it had thrown out had just reached me.

I shook my head. Superstition. And there was no place for that in Aeternus.

Angry, I dropped to the floor and started my push-ups, pumping them out mechanically as I replayed last night's job in my mind. It made me feel better. I'd done well, last night, sneaking undetected into the grounds of a house belonging to a judge. He'd been one of us for years but his new wife had been trying to separate him from us. So I'd snuck into the garage, found the little red sports car he bought her and cut almost through the brake cables, filing down the casing so that it looked like the cable had been rubbing on exposed metal for months. She drove too fast anyway and the area near the judge's home was full of long, sweeping downhill bends, many of them running alongside the cliffs overlooking the sea.

I didn't feel any guilt about it. We are a family and she'd tried to separate him from us. There is no greater crime.

I finished exercising, showered, dressed, and hurried downstairs. I was hoping he would still be eating breakfast and he was. A grin spread across my face as I saw him: bald now on top, his hair just two neatly trimmed lines of white extending back from his temples. But he was still a strong, muscular man, still started off his day with the same exercise routine he'd taught me, still dressed in shirts pressed with military precision.

Aeternus extends to fourteen countries that I know of and there are thousands of us just in the US. Very few people get to know the man who's taken on the difficult burden of leading us. But me? I get to live with him.

Everyone else calls him Mr. Pryce. I am forever grateful that he allows me to call him by another name, accurate in sentiment if not in blood.

"I heard about last night, Bradan," he said. "Well done."

I beamed. "Thank you, dad."

5

SEAN

There was a faint whistle as the sledgehammer swept through the air. Then that split-second of resistance as the cinderblocks fought my resolve, trying to slow the unstoppable force of the leaden head. The satisfying sound of crumbling, splintering stone as I smashed them. And then, with a twist of my waist, I reset to swing again.

Time was, it would have been the hood of some guy's BMW crumpling under my hammer. Or priceless oil paintings and vases as I smashed up an upscale apartment. Scaring people and smashing their places. *Simple.*

This new life was complicated. Who knew that going straight involved so much paperwork, so much talking? Medical insurance and Kayley's grade point average and 401Ks. A billion things I had no idea about. The only thing I knew was, I couldn't solve them with a sledgehammer. When it all got too much, I asked my boss on the construction site if there was anything that needed destroying. *This,* I understood.

The smooth rhythm was interrupted by my phone ringing. Muscles aching, sweat running down my chest, I pulled it out and answered. And instantly, the din of the construction site died away.

Kian. And he'd found Carrick. Wanted me to come to Chicago because they'd found Aedan, too. My whole family. I stood there, the sledgehammer still dangling from one hand, my eyes closed as years of memories swept over me.

Kian asked if I wanted to speak to Carrick: he was *right there,* standing next to him. I swallowed and mumbled something about wanting to wait until I could do it face-to-face. I told them I'd get a flight and then quickly ended the call. Then I opened my eyes and just stared at the half-demolished wall as the noise of the site filled my ears again. I took a long breath, the scent of scorched wood from the saws filling my nose. *Carrick! Aedan!* It had been so many years. I hadn't even been sure they'd been alive.

I felt my eyes going hot and blinked quickly. *Feckin'* sawdust in the air.

I called Louise and told her what was happening. I told my boss I was going to need to take some time off. Then, for the rest of the day, I obliterated the wall, letting the emotion that was boiling up inside me power my swings. It all came back to me: my mom being drawn into the cult; Bradan, locked in the back of the car as she drove him away; she and my dad fighting on the kitchen floor; the flash of a knife.... Aedan and Carrick had seen my dad's side of it but Kian and I had never been able to forgive him for killing our mom—

I swung the hammer hard enough to send a lump of wall flying twenty feet. I heard muttered, awestruck curses from the workers around me. Even now, I still scared the others. I might be reformed but I was still the big Irish fucker who destroyed stuff.

My new life had already been too complicated. To suddenly be thrown back into the middle of a family again, to revisit the past I'd so firmly locked away...*I don't know if I can do this.*

Someone yelled *Time* and the others threw down their tools. But I stood there, hands still gripping the shaft of the sledgehammer, unwilling to put it down. As long as I was smashing stuff, I could make sense of the world.

And then I heard the familiar growl of a V8 engine and I let out a long, shuddering sigh and placed the hammer down. Because suddenly, everything was okay.

As I stalked across the construction site, I felt myself growing lighter, felt the clouds of rage retreating. Every guy there had turned towards the street as the engine noise increased. I saw their jaws drop as my 1960s Mustang pulled up and Louise jumped out.

Despite everything, I felt a big, dumb grin break across my face.

No matter how many times I saw her, she still cast a spell on me. It didn't matter if it was first thing in the morning, rolling over to see her sleeping face as the light came through the drapes, or when she came out of the bathroom, hair dripping and a towel snugged around her breasts. Every time, I remembered I was the luckiest goddamn guy alive.

The construction site was all hardness and brute force: iron nails hammered into sharp-edged planks of wood, cold steel split by jagged-toothed saws. When Louise arrived it was as if a portal had opened to some other world and the goddess of plants and nature had stepped through. That copper hair, long and shining and blowing in the breeze. That gorgeous, bountiful body with an hourglass figure, like some Greek statue come to life. Those full, soft breasts, their tops displayed by the vest top she wore. And best of all, that smile that made it feel like the sun had just come out. I remembered the days when she'd been haggard and drawn, when Kayley had been ill. She smiled a lot, these days.

I knew that, behind me, every guy on the construction site was looking at her as they filed out. No one dared wolf-whistle because they knew I'd punch them out, but every time Louise stopped by—to pick me up or to drop off the lunch I'd forgotten or, once, to bring a basket of homemade cakes for the whole site—all of them had told me how lucky I was. *What kinda leprechaun magic did you use to snag her, O'Harra?*

I didn't have an answer. I just knew I loved her. She was the person who'd helped me to change: the only one who could have done it.

I barely let her get out of the car. The door was still swinging closed when I slipped an arm around her waist and lifted her into the air, pulling her against me so that her legs slid around my hips, those luscious breasts pressed against my chest and her groin nestled warmly against my abs. I breathed in the scent of her and sighed, immediately at peace with the world.

"I've booked us on an overnight flight to Chicago," she said as I studied her, lost in those big, moss-green eyes. "Kayley's psyched because she gets to stay at Stacey's apartment for a few nights." Stacey was Louise's best friend. She lived downtown, roared around in a Mercedes visiting all the bakeries she managed and could hold about twenty different conversations at once on her hands-free phone while training for her next triathlon. She was great, even if just watching her made me feel tired. And compared to the calm, slow-paced life we'd settled into, Kayley thought "Aunt Stacey" was incredibly cool.

"There's a bag of clothes for you in the trunk," Louise continued. "I wasn't sure how long we'd be in Chicago so I haven't booked anything yet, but I've scoped out some hotels. Oh, and I brought you a sandwich because I'm not sure we're going to get chance to eat before we get on the fligh—*MMF!*"

I'd pulled her closer and covered her lips with mine. A few of the braver guys passing behind me cheered. Christ, I loved this woman. This is how she'd been able to make the grow house work: she organized like no one I'd ever met. And she'd dropped everything to come with me, to support me, no questions asked.

She groaned in pleasure as my tongue brushed the inner edge of her lip, and opened to me. We twisted and moved, my hand sinking into that glorious copper hair, silken strands tickling between my calloused fingers. My tongue found hers and she drew in a breath, pressing herself closer. I felt a ripple pass through her body as I kissed her: she was coming alive in my arms, everyone watching us forgotten.

It was more than just lust. Sure, I wanted to just put her down on the hood of the Mustang and peel those jeans off her, but there was a different kind of urgency, every time our lips met. Like a day was too long apart. Like an hour was too long apart. We'd found our other halves and now we weren't complete unless we were together. I honestly couldn't figure out how I'd managed before I met her. The kiss changed, growing deeper and slower. My hands moved down her back, cupping her ass and squeezing, and she moaned against me.

When we finally broke the kiss, we moved back very slowly and just gazed into each other's eyes. The sun was sinking fast, red and gold light making her hair gleam and blaze. "We should get moving," she murmured, not moving.

"Uh-huh," I said, not moving either. I kissed her again, then bit gently at her lower lip and she writhed, her groin pressing hard against me. We stayed there for another few minutes, until we had to go or we'd miss the flight.

"You feeling okay now?" I asked as I climbed behind the wheel. She'd had to suddenly run to the bathroom, early that morning, to throw up.

She nodded. "Probably just something I ate."

I threw the car into gear and we roared off.

6

CARRICK

Washington DC to Chicago is almost exactly seven hundred miles. Seven hundred miles, at night, with the temperature down in the forties and a vicious wind whipping across the interstate.

I loved it.

A Harley, when it's properly tuned and cared for, settles down into a low throb at freeway speeds, a vibration that's almost a heartbeat. My bike had been with me for years and, since Annabelle came along, it had two of us giving it love and attention. She'd tended to its pipes and pistons like a master surgeon and now it *sang*. The heat from the engine rose up through the saddle and warmed me and my leather cut kept the worst of the wind at bay. Behind me, Annabelle was tight against my back, the soft press of her breasts making me smile every time I shifted or moved. She had her arms around my waist with her hands snuck up inside my cut to keep warm. Every few miles, her hands would explore my abs and then give me a little squeeze.

Best feeling in the world.

Beside us, Kian in that ridiculous SUV. He was sitting in a heated leather seat that probably massaged his back at the push of a button.

He was sitting in there cocooned from the world: hell, he probably had the radio on. I shook my head. *You don't know what you're missing.*

And he wore a suit. A *suit!* I couldn't get over that. I wasn't kidding about being proud of him. But a suit? And dating the President's daughter? I'd seen Emily on TV and she was beautiful and sweet but she was also sophisticated and moneyed. It was hard to wrap my head around the idea of her snuggling up to the Kian I remembered, a guy who'd gotten into a thousand schoolyard fights alongside me.

Not unless my brother had gone soft.

And that got me thinking about my other brothers and how they might have changed. For the first time, the cold started to creep in through my cut.

We stopped for gas for the bike and the much thirstier SUV. We also refueled ourselves, gorging on frosted donuts and huge paper cups of steaming coffee to keep our eyes open. But even inside the heated gas station, even with my hands wrapped around my coffee cup, I couldn't seem to get warm.

Ever since that day I'd run away, I'd been twisted up inside, convinced I'd done the wrong thing. I was the oldest. I should have stayed and somehow kept everyone together, protected everyone. That was what had made me give life and soul to the MC all these years, trying to pay back the debt I felt I owed. Annabelle had lifted some of the guilt and seeing Aedan again had helped. I knew now that he didn't hate my guts for leaving. And Kian seemed okay with me, too. But soon I'd have to face the hardest one of all: Sean, the youngest of the family.

I knew he'd been taken into foster care after I left. I didn't know what sort of family he'd wound up with and I didn't

know if he blamed me. I just knew that, tomorrow, when

his plane landed, I'd be facing everything I feared. That's why I was pushing this so hard, that's why I'd gone to Washington to get Kian, why I was determined to find Bradan. We all wanted to put our family back together but I felt I had the most to make up for.

It was morning by the time we neared Chicago. The traffic grew heavier and we slowed down. Drivers started to look at us: first they'd see Annabelle's long red hair whipping in the wind. Then their eyes would track down to that ripe, perfect ass, its curves shown off by the tight denim.

And then they'd glance forward to see who she had her arms wrapped around and see me glaring at them. They'd turn pale and suddenly become very interested in the car in front.

Kian waved for me to come alongside. He lowered his window and I could feel the warm air bathing my frozen face. I would never admit it but, just for that second, the SUV didn't seem so dumb.

"Where are we heading?" Kian had to raise his voice over the slipstream. "Does Aedan have an apartment here or what?"

"He does, but he's never there," I yelled. "But I know where he'll be, this time of the morning."

I twisted the throttle and roared forward and he followed me. Soon we were moving through the city and I had to wait for him every time we hit traffic: I could thread my way through small gaps but he couldn't. I tried not to smirk at him in my mirror.

I pulled up outside a gym. Not the sort of place bankers go to pound on a treadmill for an hour; the sort of place men spend all day in, thumping bags and lifting iron. I went straight inside, still taking off my helmet, Annabelle and Kian falling in behind me.

We pushed through the doors just in time to see Aedan punch Sylvie right in the head.

7

SYLVIE

My head rang like it was a bell and someone had whacked it with a hammer. I was wearing my padded head protector but I still wavered for a second. Aedan's eyes lit up with concern: he'd only hit me with about a tenth of his power but still, his brows lifted: *are you okay?*

I glowered at him and struck back with a quick one-two, then ducked under his hands and landed a hook on his side. He *oofed*, frowned and then gave me *that* smile, the one that said I was in trouble now.

I danced around him. He stood like a colossus in the center of the ring, stripped to the waist, his muscles gleaming with sweat. I felt like a hummingbird buzzing around a bear. I was getting in three hits to every one of his but *wow* his hits were hard, even with him pulling his punches. I was sweating too: we'd been at it for two rounds already, each of us holding our own. We were spiraling toward the conclusion but neither of us knew which way it was going to go: he couldn't take much more of my dodging and sharp, quick blows but I couldn't take many more of those big hits, either.

Both of us were drunk on adrenaline. We'd lost track of everything outside the ring: I could distantly hear people cheering

but they might as well have been on Mars. My entire world was those
blue Irish eyes. We were connected on a level most people never
know, communicating without words, daring each other to attack,
drawing each other out. He suddenly lunged forward but I darted out
of the way and my glove hit those iron-hard abs with enough power
to wind him. He wheeled around and I grinned at him...and
unconsciously, I pressed my thighs together beneath my shorts. We
had rules for what happened in the bedroom, if I won a fight.

Movement in the crowd caught my attention for a second. Some
woman shaking her head, aghast. She didn't understand, didn't know
the adrenaline rush you get from fighting someone you're truly in
love with. All she saw was a muscled, scarred fighter. She didn't
understand that I loved every part of him, even those scars: they were
evidence of everything we'd been through to be together. Once, I'd
sought him out because he was the scariest fighter around, a man
everyone thought was a monster. I hadn't been ready for what I
found, or how meeting had changed both of us. He'd lost his coldness
and let me in. I'd gone from being scared to holding my head up
high: I didn't shy away from a fight anymore, in or out of the ring.
And now, months after it all happened, Aedan and I had never been
closer.

An incoming punch from Aedan snapped me back to reality. His
gloved fist seemed as big as my head and it was driven by a body that
was nothing but muscle, from that rock-hard midsection to the wide
shoulders and thick biceps. I ducked just in time, the rush of air from
his fist lifting the hairs on the back of my neck. A shot of primal fear
sluiced through my system...and soaked down to my groin.

There were rules for what happened in the bedroom if I lost a
fight, too. Losing was just as much fun as winning.

I backed away, panting. I was having the time of my life and I
wouldn't trade this for anything. Even though Chicago still
felt...*temporary.* It still felt like we were treading water here. Maybe it
was because, in New York, my brother Alec and I had lived in our
parents' old apartment: it had felt like home in a way Chicago didn't.
And I didn't have a single friend here. Everyone I'd known was in

New York and I couldn't even visit them, given that I was meant to be dead.

I saw Aedan ready himself: that slight narrowing of the eyes, the infinitesimal lifting of his fists. This would be it: a final charge and either he'd take me down or I'd take him down. Then we'd kiss and he'd drag me off somewhere and...the heat that had been building inside me all through the fight tightened and compressed even more.

He charged. I darted forward, trying to judge which way to dodge to get under his attack: left or right? High or low? And then—

And then he dropped his hands. *What?* Aedan *never* dropped his guard. It's one of the first things he taught me. And he was staring off into the crowd. He never did that, either.

As he came to a halt I dropped my fists, too, and tried to pull up short, but I was going too fast. I skidded on the canvas and whumped into him. Even distracted as he was, he folded his arms around me and gathered me into his chest...and I just melted inside. It felt even better than victory.

I followed his gaze to see what the hell had distracted him so completely. His brother, Carrick, was standing there and Annabelle was beside him. I'd seen them both a few times since they'd come to Chicago to find us. But that alone wouldn't have drawn Aedan's gaze, not in the middle of a fight.

I looked again...and this time I saw the other man. I hadn't even glanced at him the first time because he was in a suit: I thought he must be someone who'd wandered into the wrong sort of gym by accident. But now I saw his face, one I'd seen on TV. *Oh my God! That's—*

8

AEDAN

Kian. I'd seen him on TV: for a good while following the attempted coup, he wasn't off the screen. I recognized the expensive suit, the quiet confidence: a man who could blend into a crowd but could put you down with one punch. He looked every inch the Secret Service bodyguard.

What I couldn't believe was that *this was my brother.* Right here. In the flesh.

I grabbed the ropes and swung myself out of the ring. Behind me, I heard Sylvie doing the same. The crowd of people who'd gathered to watch our fight turned to follow us as Kian moved in front of Carrick. *"Holy feckin' shit,"* I muttered under my breath. We stared at each other....

And then we grabbed each other at the same moment and pulled each other into a fierce, bone-crushing hug. The emotion hit me all at once: something about the closeness, the feel of someone you love *right there* against you. I was blinking, the room blurring. *Jesus....*

When we finally moved back I stood there shaking my head, trying to take it in. He'd changed so much...I hadn't seen him since I went back to Ireland, well before he joined the military. *And now he's with the President's daughter....* A flush of shame went through me. *And*

I'm still boxing. Just like when I was a kid. Hell, just months before, the fights weren't even legal. I'd started to make some money at it, since we came to Chicago and I went legit, enough that I'd been able to quit working at the docks and train full time. We were getting by but it didn't change the fact that I was still earning my living with my fists. Always would.

And that brought me back to what had been weighing on my mind for weeks. I automatically glanced at Sylvie, then quickly looked away. She already knew something was up and I didn't want her asking questions.

"Nice suit," I managed at last.

Kian looked down at himself, frowning, as if he'd forgotten he was wearing it. For a second, he looked as embarrassed by the gulf between us as I was.

Sylvie stepped forward and embraced Kian. Then Alec stepped forward. "Sylvie's brother," he said by way of introduction. He nodded at me. "Your brother saved my sister, this summer. Any brother of his...." Then he slipped his arm around the waist of a curvy woman in long blonde hair. "And this is Jessica," he told Kian, snugging her close to his side. "My girlfriend."

We'd had to flee New York after Sylvie faked her death. But Alec still needed physiotherapy: the bones in his shattered leg had mostly healed while he'd been in the coma but he'd been immobile for a month and that had left his joints and muscles in need of attention. When we came to Chicago, I took a job at the docks and Sylvie helped Alec find a physiotherapist.

I'd driven him to his first appointment and, from the very first time he met Jessica, I could see it. I saw it in the way his jaw dropped when she straightened up from her position beside some kid's wheelchair to look at him, tossing back that long golden hair. I saw it in the way she blinked and swallowed as she laid eyes on the blond, muscled boxer. I knew exactly what was going to happen.

Jessica had spent long daily sessions with him, his arm around her shoulders and his teeth gritted as he'd struggled to walk without crutches. When we ran out of money and couldn't pay the bills,

Jessica started helping him outside of hospital hours for free. Alec had been frustrated by his slow progress, even grumpy: he was determined to get back in the ring. But every time I dropped him off at the hospital and he saw Jessica, his face lit up. Jessica had been patient and gently firm, catching him when he stumbled, encouraging him when he wanted to give up. She was cautious, full of nerves about getting

involved with a patient, even if it was all happening off the books. The tension between them grew until every touch of his hand on her arm and every brush of her hair against his shoulder made them both tense.

Then the day came when Alec pushed himself too far and fell. Jessica tried to catch him, his muscled bulk pushed her to the floor and he wound up on top of her, his legs between hers. The way Alec tells it, they stared into each other's eyes for all of three seconds and then they were kissing.

After that, they were inseparable. Alec slowly progressed to walking unaided and then to running and they'd go on punishing runs together around Chicago's streets. Not long after that, he moved into her apartment. By then, I'd quit my job at the docks and was training full time, and Alec started to spar with me. He wasn't quite ready to join the fighting circuit yet, but instead he'd done a course in personal training and started taking clients at an upmarket gym: the business executives loved the idea of being trained by a real-life fighter.

Sylvie had done a similar course and then applied for a job teaching a boxercise class at the same gym. Some of the staff had laughed when they saw her slender form: right up until the point when she kicked their asses in the ring. She got the job and, after all the hardcore boxing training I'd put her through, she took no prisoners when it came to her class. It quickly became notorious for being the toughest class the gym offered, with the most calories burned. People loved it: the class now ran three times a week and the waiting list to join was up to two months and counting.

As Alec and Jessica stepped back, Carrick stepped forward. He clapped a hand on Kian's shoulder and looked me in the eye...and that's when I knew this wasn't just about Kian paying a visit. I drew in a long breath. Carrick had told me his plan when he went to get Kian but I hadn't believed it could really happen.

"We're putting our family back together," said Carrick.

I swallowed. "Sean?" Just saying the name made my throat close up. The thought of all of us together was too much.

Kian nodded. "I'm in touch with him. He's flying in from LA. He'll be here in a few hours."

Sean! He'd been in LA all this time? I had about a million questions.

Carrick's next words drove them all away. "Once we've got everybody, we're going after Bradan."

In a split-second, I was a kid again. Bradan's young, pink hand pressed against the car window, its warmth soaking through the glass and into my own palm. My mom yelling at us to get out of the way, revving the engine—

I closed my eyes and felt myself rock back on my heels. The sweat on my body turned to ice water. *Jesus.* I didn't want to face all the possibilities this opened up. *What if he's dead?*

What if he's alive and they've had him all this time and I've been living my life with Sylvie while those bastards—

I felt a hand grip my arm, soft and comforting. I opened my eyes to see Sylvie looking at me with concern.

"What makes you think you can find him?" I croaked. "I looked for him for years."

"We all did," said Kian. I could see it in his eyes: he was thinking the same thing I was. "None of us got anywhere."

"Because we were doing it wrong," said Carrick, his voice like iron. "We were doing it on our own. This time, we'll be together. And we're not quitting until it's done. Until we know he's dead or until he's back with us."

I nodded. Knowing they'd been through the same process: the looking, the giving up, now the guilt that we might have given up too easily: that made me feel better. And knowing that we were in this together, whatever we found...that gave me the strength to do it. "Okay," I said. And turned to Sylvie.

When she saw what was in my eyes she tilted her head to one side and narrowed her eyes. "Don't even think about it. I'm coming with you."

I should have known better. "Okay," I said at last. "But what about your classes?"

"I'll take them," said Alec. "I've filled in for her before." He looked at me. "It's the least I can do."

Sylvie nodded. "People love it when he fills in. The women go *nuts.*"

Jessica gave Alec a sidelong look and he flushed. To cover his embarrassment, he stepped forward and wrapped Sylvie into a hug. "Go," he told me over her shoulder. "Do what you need to do." He squeezed his sister hard. "But take care. And just call if I can help."

I nodded and took Sylvie's hand. "Alright," I told my brothers. "Let us grab a shower and stop by our apartment to throw some stuff in a bag. And then let's go get Sean."

9

SEAN

The automatic doors to the arrivals hall slid open...and I stopped. I felt the other passengers pile up against my back and heard a few curses. Then, as they looked up and saw my size, they mumbled apologies and quickly walked around me.

I didn't respond. I was staring at my family.

Kian I recognized from when I'd gone to Washington. But standing beside him were two more men with jet-black hair and blue eyes that matched my own. I knew their faces, even across all the years. One was a little older, wearing a biker's leather cut. *Carrick!* One was more my age and had that unmistakable athlete's build, broad chest narrowing to a tight waist. *Aedan!*

I finally got my feet moving again and took a stumbling step towards them. I didn't know what Carrick and Aedan had been doing but likely they'd done better than me: enforcer for the drug gangs, now a construction worker. My step-dad's words echoed in my ears again: *wrecking stuff's all you're good for*. My next step was smaller, the next one smaller still—

And then all three of them were stepping forward, closing the distance between us in huge strides, reaching forward as one to pull me into their arms. I wound up crushed into Kian's chest with Carrick's arm and Aedan's arm around my back.

And I suddenly wondered what the hell I'd been worried about. Because these were my brothers and nothing else mattered.

"Welcome home," said Kian, his voice thick with emotion, and we all nodded because we knew what he meant. The arms around my back might as well have been made out of girders. I wasn't getting out of that hug anytime soon.

When they finally decided to let me go, I introduced Louise. Carrick introduced Annabelle and Aedan introduced Sylvie. And then there was an awkward moment when Kian was left there on his own. "Emily can't be involved in this," he told me.

"In what?" I asked.

The others looked at each other. And that's when I realized what Kian hadn't told me on the phone. "We're going after Bradan?" I asked. Even as I said it, I could hear a little more of the Irish coming through in my voice, the effect of being around them. "Do we even know where to start?"

Kian nodded. "I might have someone who can help. We'll need to go to New York. I've got a car that'll take all of us."

But Carrick shook his head. "There's something we have to do first, while we're in Chicago."

Kian frowned at him, confused. Then I saw realization dawn and his face fell. "*No!*" he snapped.

Carrick ignored him and turned to the women. "You girls okay grabbing a bite to eat together? We'll be gone a few hours, then we can meet back here." I saw Kian glare at him. Just like when we were kids, there was always a battle between them for who was leader.

Sylvie shook her head and took Aedan's arm. "I want to come with you."

Aedan put his hand on her arm and stroked gently down its length. "No," he said slowly. "This is something we have to do alone."

"It's something we don't have to do *at all!*" said Kian, his voice jagged and bitter.

I looked from one face to another. "*What?*" I asked, feeling stupid.

"What are we talking about?" And then I got it and I felt my chest close up tight. "Oh." I swallowed. "Oh, shit."

Louise pressed close to me. "What? What is it?"

I took a deep breath, trying to quiet all the memories that were rushing up inside. "We've got to go visit my dad."

10

KIAN

After years apart, you'd have thought we wouldn't be able to stop talking. But the drive to the prison was almost silent, all of us caught up in our own thoughts. Through the windshield, I could see Carrick hunched over the handlebars of his Harley, powering through the gray morning rain. Beside me, Aedan sat in the passenger seat, staring out of the window. Behind me, Sean, looking out in the opposite direction. It was bitterly cold in Chicago and I had the heater going full blast but I couldn't seem to warm up.

I hadn't seen my dad since the day I'd silently handed him the form to get parental consent to let me join the Marines. Aedan had muttered that he'd visited the jail a few times and I knew he was like Carrick: he didn't blame our dad for what he'd done. Sean I wasn't sure about but from the look on his face he was more like me: he couldn't get past the sight of our mom lying on the kitchen floor.

I understood why we were going. I knew Carrick was right: with all four of us only a short drive from the prison, we couldn't *not* visit. Plus, we needed all the information on the cult that we could get.

But that didn't mean I had to like it. And this was going to be tough on all of us. I was meant to protect my brothers: was I doing that, by letting this happen?

At the prison, we signed in, submitted to a pat down and then took our seats facing the thick sheet of Plexiglas, behind which sat a solitary chair.

I looked around. Thick, unpainted walls, no sound or daylight from outside. Shambling men in chains, their spirits broken. Guards with batons in hands, waiting to hand out a beating at the slightest sign of dissent. And always that *fear,* the way the prisoners never stopped checking their surroundings, anticipating the touch of a homemade blade at their throat that would signal a quick death or the first quick stab into their kidneys that would signal a slower one. When I'd come here as a teenager to get him to sign my enlistment papers, I hadn't taken in just how bad the place was.

Good, I thought savagely, pushing back my sympathy. *It's what he deserves.* I looked over my shoulder, towards the parking lot. *I could go. Just tell them I'm not doing it, wait for them outside.* But then I caught Carrick's eye and he gave me a curt shake of his head. I glowered, hunched my shoulders and turned back to face the glass. I wished Emily was there. She was always good at calming me.

And then *he* appeared.

My stomach seemed to fall through the floor. I'd been ready for the anger, for the rage that had been burning in me ever since that day, but I hadn't been ready for the shock of seeing *him.* For that indescribable feeling of being in the presence of absolute authority. That feeling only your dad can give you.

More of his hair had turned silver but it was still thick and lush and he still carried most of his muscle. A quiet man but I had no doubt he'd been able to hold his own, even in this hellhole. We shared the same looks: everyone had always said how much we looked like him, Carrick and Aedan especially. Sean and I were meant to have a little more of our mom in us.

He didn't sit. He met my eyes: maybe he could see it coming before I did. But suddenly I was up out of my seat and turning towards the door, chest so tight it felt like it was going to explode.

His voice caught me before I'd taken two steps. "Kian." He had to shout to make himself heard through the Plexiglas and the whole room turned to look. The sound of my name rolled through me. I closed my eyes and I was a kid again. My dad had just come home from work and he was calling me to go outside and play and then we'd all run in for tea with my mom—

My hands had formed fists. I stood there sucking in deep lungfuls of air, trying to calm myself.

"Sit down." That voice, the river of Irish silver that our accents merely tap into. Strong enough that some Americans had trouble understanding him, when he spoke fast. The sound of it could be fast and savage as an axe blade when you'd done something wrong, but soothing as a cold compress on your head when he told you he loved you.

"...I've got nothing to say to you," I managed at last, still not turning round.

"You've got plenty," he said.

I whirled around to face him, mouth opening in a snarl. But when I saw the sadness in his face I just...stopped. A fierce anger had been burning inside me all these years, roaring higher every time I gave it the oxygen of his memory. Now the flames seemed to freeze in place, becoming ice and stone.

He missed my mom even more than I did.

My legs were shaking so I sat, taking the chair closest to the glass. And then, because I saw him doing the same on the other side, I picked up the phone. But I couldn't look at him, had to focus on my own reflection in the glass or I was going to lose it completely. My brothers shuffled closer in their chairs and I held the phone's mouthpiece away from my mouth so they could hear. But I couldn't speak.

"Talk to me, Kian." The same voice he'd used when I messed up in school, or when I'd split up with some girl. He wanted to draw what was causing me pain out of me, even if it was so poisonous that it would hurt him.

It boiled up inside: all my memories of her, all the memories I never got to make with her. All the times I'd needed a mom and didn't have one, all the times in the future I'd want her and she wouldn't be there. Emily. Our kids. They'd never even know her.

"You took her away from us," I whispered, my voice shaking.

He leaned closer and I could feel his eyes on me, pinning me with one of his looks. "*They* took her away from us."

I finally looked up at him.

"They took me away from you, too," he told me, his voice thick with emotion. "Locked me up in this feckin' place so I missed all of you growing up." He glanced around at all four of us. "I missed...Christ, I missed *everything*. I don't know who you are, what you're doing, except Aedan, a little." He looked right at me. "But I saw *you*. Saw you on TV. And I'm proud of what you did, Kian."

I felt something give and move deep inside me. The dam was bursting and the bigger the hole got, the less I could fight it. My hands bunched into fists, knuckles whitening where they held the phone's handset. My eyes were hot. And then I was up out of my chair, pressing towards him—

And I couldn't.

I couldn't hug him. There was no way to gather him into my arms and show him how I felt because all that was under my hands was cool, solid Plexiglas, scarred and misted by the fingernails of thousands of visitors who'd done the same. My dad and I stared at each other through the glass, both close to tears. I felt all the years pulling at me. God, he'd gotten *old*. He'd been stuck in here and I hadn't even visited, not once, because I'd had so much anger. All this time, wasted.

I looked into his eyes and nodded and he nodded back in understanding. It was all we could do. Then I moved back and Carrick took the phone. As I watched them, the anger came back, but this time the fire swirled and reshaped, forming a ring of iron around my heart, a resolve nothing could break. We were going to have our revenge for what they did to us. The cult was going down.

Carrick and Dad had a long conversation, muttered and low, Carrick's Irish accent thickening the more he talked. After a while, he placed his palm on the glass and my dad did the same. Like me, he was feeling guilty we hadn't done this sooner.

Then Sean. He was hesitant at first, turning away as I had done. But as they talked he began to nod, his lips pressed tight together. Then he suddenly stood and walked out, but not in anger. I could see him blinking as he pushed through the door to the restrooms, determined not to let it out in public.

Aedan went last. Unlike the rest of us, he'd visited a few times but he still had a lot to catch dad up on. By the time he'd finished, Dad wanted to meet Sylvie...and Louise, Kayley, Annabelle and Emily. We all nodded but I found myself looking again at the cinder block walls, the orange jumpsuits, and when I looked back to Dad, he caught my eye and nodded. He wanted to meet them...but not here, not like this.

I took the phone and sat down closest to the glass again. I had to take a few deep breaths and just get used to it for a moment: after so many years, not feeling that raw, hot anger when I looked at him or thought about him felt strange. Dad waited and then, when he saw my eyes focus, he asked, "Why now?" He looked around at the four of us. "Why come together now?"

I took one final, slow breath. "Bradan," I said. "We're going to find Bradan."

Dad's face fell. The hand holding the phone dropped to his side and when he spoke, it was through the Plexiglas.

"No you're fucking not."

11

CARRICK

When he was angry or worried, Dad's voice became a weapon, quick and razor sharp. When we were kids, it was always enough to pull us up short when we were about to run into the street or get into trouble with the law. Now, in a maximum security prison, it still cut through the air like a knife. He was surrounded by men who'd committed multiple murders, guys from street gangs right up to men with links to the mob. But *that voice:* granite-hard and coated in silver so cold it would freeze your skin...every man in the room glanced up and then studiously looked away. I saw the guards shift uneasily, ready to intervene but praying they didn't have to.

I stared at him, my mouth open. I'd thought he'd be *pleased....* I took the phone from Kian. "We have to," I told Dad.

He shook his head. His skin had gone pale. God, he was scared—no, *terrified.*

Terrified for *us.*

"He's out there, somewhere," I said. "We're not leaving him."

My dad's chair creaked as he leaned forward and brought the phone to his ear again. "*Listen,*" he spat. "Listen to me. Those bastards took your mother from me. They took *you* away from me. They got me locked up in here. I'm not letting them take the one thing I have left."

"He's our brother—"

"*HE'S MY SON!*" Dad exploded up out of his chair, both fists slamming down on the table. His chair flew out behind and bounced off the wall.

"*Hey!*" yelled a guard, one hand going to his baton.

Dad stood there shaking and furious, his face inches from the Plexiglas. I took a deep breath and stared at him pleadingly, willing him to calm down before they dragged him away.

I saw his hands grip the table as if he wanted to rip great chunks of wood out of the surface. Then he turned, grabbed the chair and sat back down, glowering at the guard. When he spoke, his voice shook with the effort of restraining his rage. "You have *no idea* what they're like. How vicious they are. They'll think nothing—*nothing*—of killing you and everyone you hold dear. Don't do this!"

I sat there staring at him, shell-shocked. Over the last few weeks I'd played this meeting out a thousand times in my head and it had never gone like this. I'd been expecting him to give us his blessing, to tell me *attaboy, go get 'em.* I had to do this, to make things right.

Stubbornly, I reached into the pocket of my cut and drew out a photo. Unfolded it and then smoothed it flat against the glass. Me, Kian, Aedan, Sean and Bradan as kids, arms around each other in a line, with dad beaming proudly behind us. It had been taken on a hillside just outside Belfast, just as the sun was setting. We'd been playing half the day, shins muddy and knees grazed from football and wrestling and chasing around.

Dad shook his head and looked away.

"*Look at it!*" I was struggling to keep my voice under control. I wasn't angry with him, exactly: I just wanted him on our side. And I wanted to be wrong about the fear I saw on his face. Nothing, should scare our dad like that.

He looked. I felt my chest tighten, praying this would be it, that now he'd support us. But instead he raised big, sorrowful eyes to Kian and me. "You two are the oldest," he told us. "You have to look after your brothers." He raised his chained hands. "I can't do anything in here. I can't protect you. You've got to do the right thing. You've got to let Bradan go."

He was so scared for us that he was prepared to give up on his missing son. My stomach lurched. For the cult to scare a man like our dad that much, they had to be far more dangerous than I'd thought. *What the hell am I leading us into?*

A few hours later, we were back at the airport. The ride back gave me a chance to think. From the look of Kian's face in my mirrors, he was doing the same thing. I knew we needed to talk but, when we arrived back at the terminal, I saw something that made me forget all my troubles for a second.

I'd been worried about the girls. I mean, Annabelle had only met Sylvie a few times and Louise didn't know either of them, but we'd just sort of dumped them together and run off. I'd gotten it into my head that it had been one long awkward silence since we'd been gone.

But when we found them, they'd taken up residence in a booth of a diner, one of those places where the Americana is cranked all the way to eleven. They were munching fries and hot dogs under a Route 66 sign while waitresses in striped shirts brought them cocktails. They were all chatting away happily and looked as if they'd been friends for years. They didn't notice us and all four of us stopped for a second at the edge of the open-plan restaurant to just...*look.*

Annabelle first, of course, her pale skin gleaming under the perpetual twilight of the diner's mood lighting. I wanted to slide my hand deep into that silky red mane and draw her to me, kiss all the way down that elegant neck.

Facing her, Louise, her copper hair equally eye catching. And all those curves.... She put me in mind of some medieval maiden, some wench all the knights would bring roses to. I wouldn't say any of that to Sean because he'd think I was going soft. But it was easy to see why he'd fallen for her.

Then Sylvie, small and slender with a quick, urgent energy, the perfect counterpoint to Aedan's brooding and raw power. She grabbed your attention and you didn't want to look away and with those pert little breasts and tight ass.... I flushed, feeling bad thinking it because she was my brother's girl, but *damn,* I bet she was a handful in bed.

All three of them were gorgeous. I mean, obviously Annabelle was the best but...I said out loud what I knew all of us were thinking. "We all did bloody well."

Sean and Aedan grinned. Too late, I remembered that one girl was missing and quickly looked across at Kian. He was smiling gamely but he caught my eye. "Wait 'till you meet Emily," he told me firmly. I nodded.

The rest of us embraced our women and then we took over a second booth beside the first and joined them for dessert and coffee. The waitresses did a double-take at the weird mix: me in my biker gear, Kian in his suit, Aedan in his hooded top and Sean in his tank top and jeans.

None of us had slept the night before and we all needed to refuel and recharge before whatever was next. Food and caffeine made me feel better but what happened at the prison was still going around and around my head and I caught Aedan and Sean looking at Kian and me. Just like Dad had said, we were the oldest and they were looking to us to lead.

While we waited for the check to come, I pulled Kian into a quiet corner of the restaurant. "What do we do?" I muttered. It was the first time I'd questioned my plan since I'd settled on it, way back in Haywood Falls. "Dad was...he was *scared.*"

Kian nodded. "He's not the only one. I talked to the President about the cult, too."

My brow knitted. "You told the President about—"

"*He* told *me.* He knew all about them. The cult's bigger than we thought, *much* bigger. And they're into everything: they've got people in the police, the FBI, the courts. He said the same as Dad: they're dangerous. They kill people who mess with them." He looked towards our table. Annabelle was splitting a huge fudge brownie sundae with Louise. Sylvie was devouring a stack of pancakes bigger than her head.

My heart suddenly ached like someone was squeezing it in a vice. I was *happy,* dammit. I'd finally found a woman I loved and I had the sort of peace I hadn't even been able to imagine a few months ago. And it seemed like Kian, Aedan and Sean were the same. When I'd set off to find Aedan, it had all seemed so simple. But now, looking at my brothers...what if we went after the cult and not everyone made it back alive? Bradan might already be dead. I could get all of my brothers killed for no reason. I tried to imagine explaining to a grieving Sylvie, or Louise, or Emily.

I suddenly didn't want to be the oldest. I didn't want to be the one to decide. I looked across at Kian and I could see the grim tension in his face. He'd always tried to protect us, as kids, and I knew his instinct was to do the same now...and drop this whole thing.

I took out the photo again and stared at it. I could feel Kian's eyes on it, too, on that boy with the shy smile and the solemn eyes. Bradan had always been the good one, the least likely to get into trouble....

I glanced across at the table, at the other brothers and their women. And that's when I made up my mind.

"He should be here," I said quietly. I glanced at Kian, then back at the table. "He should be sitting right there. With a girl. In love or maybe married or with kids. He's—" I struggled for the words. "He's *missing,* Kian. He's missing from this fucking world. He was a good kid and they just *took him* and—"

My voice broke and I had to stop. Kian and I just stared at each other for a second. "We have to *put him back,*" I said at last, wondering if I was making any kind of sense.

And Kian slowly nodded, reached across and grasped my hand in a death grip.

And I realized I wasn't making the decision alone. The two of us had always tussled for leadership but, right now, it was *us,* together, making the call. And I was glad of that.

I let out a long breath. "Where do we start?" I asked.

Kian leaned close. "The President gave me a name. A guy who knows the cult. I called him and he'll talk to us, but it's got to be in person, off the record."

"What do you mean, *off the record?* Who is he?"

"He's FBI."

I felt my eyes bug out. "A fucking *fed?*" Everything that had happened in Haywood Falls came back to me. I and the rest of the MC hadn't trusted feds even before that, with the possible exception of Hunter. Now, I'd sooner stuff a rattlesnake in my boot and ride fifty miles than put my faith in anyone bearing a three letter acronym.

"The President trusts him," said Kian. "So I trust him. If we want to find Bradan, we've got to take whatever help we can get."

I cursed under my breath and looked across at Annabelle just as she let out an easy giggle that bubbled up to the ceiling like goddamn music. Louise had whipped cream on her nose and everyone was conspiring not to tell her. "*What?!*" she asked, bemused. Annabelle started full-on laughing, bending over the table and hiding her face, and I just wanted to wrap her up in my arms, throw her on my bike and drive her away from all this. She was so precious to me...more than I knew how to tell her. The thought of bringing her anywhere near a fed, after what that bastard Volos did to her, made me want to reach for my shotgun. But if the cult was as dangerous as everyone said, I had to protect Annabelle from them, too. And for that, we needed help. "Okay," I spat. "Fine. Let's talk to him."

"Alright," said Kian. "He's in New York."

12

CARRICK

We were in Central Park and Annabelle couldn't get enough of the New York skyline. As we walked, she kept taking a few quick steps ahead of the group, going right out to the limits of our joined hands. Then she'd stop and turn in a slow circle, staring in amazement, until the rest of us caught up. Then she'd do it all over again. "It's just—" She had this grin on her face, like a kid at Disneyland. Each time she looked at me, she'd shake her head in amazement that I wasn't blown away by it, too.

Of course, I'd been close to cities most of my life: Chicago and then LA. Annabelle had grown up on the outskirts of a tiny town and she'd never even seen New York City until I'd brought her there to look for Aedan. And the truth was, I loved seeing it through Annabelle's eyes and experiencing her wonder. I acted grumpy and unimpressed because I didn't want to blow my hardass reputation in front of my brothers but, every time she grinned, I had a big grin inside me, too.

This girl was good for me.

We'd figured we shouldn't all go to meet the FBI guy, because that might freak him out. Kian had to go, since he was the one the guy was expecting. I had to go because I didn't trust a fed and I wanted to be there if it all went wrong. And that meant Annabelle had to be there because she wouldn't leave my side. We were still at that stage where we never wanted to be apart. Maybe that would pass, eventually, but I didn't want it to. I'd happily be right next to this woman for the rest of my life.

Aedan had come because he knew New York better than any of us. Sylvie couldn't come: as far as Rick, the crooked fight promoter, knew, she was dead. If word spread around the New York underworld that she was alive, Rick might figure out that she had something to do with him getting arrested and he might try to take revenge: even behind bars, people like him still have power. So Sylvie had stayed in the SUV, having made Aedan promise to bring back bread from their favorite deli, coffee from their favorite coffee stand and pizza from their favorite pizza parlor. Sean and Louise stayed to keep her company.

"You miss it?" I asked Aedan as we walked.

He was looking around, too. Not wide-eyed, like Annabelle, but with a wistful look. "Yeah," he said after a while. "I spent so long here. It felt like home." He shook his head ruefully. "Chicago still doesn't." He slowed to a stop. "We're here."

We were at the intersection of paths, somewhere near the middle of Central Park. Four musicians were sitting on chairs, wrapped up in thick coats against the cold. There were a couple playing violins, one on some sort of bigger violin and then a tiny woman, even smaller than Sylvie, with her legs astride one of those fuck-off giant things: a double bass? A cello? I wondered how the hell she'd got it there: it looked far too big for her to carry. They were playing classical music: some sad, slow piece that made me want to grab hold of Annabelle and never let her go. Not the kind of thing I'm usually into at all, but they were really good.

"You like it?" asked Aedan. I'd forgotten he was standing beside me. He must have seen me staring at the musicians.

I coughed. "No," I lied. I nodded to a spot a little further down the path, where a couple of dancers in leotards were doing ballet steps to the music. "But *they're* alright." At that, Annabelle turned and gave me a look of mock outrage. *Dammit. I can't win.* I pulled her close and nuzzled her neck. Beside me, Aedan smirked.

Then I saw something that made me sober up. A woman dressed for running, her dark hair drawn back in a tight braid that bounced against her neck. She was soaked in sweat as if she'd just finished a run and she was just reaching up to a coffee cart to pay for her coffee, head cocked to listen to the music. All fine and normal except—

I nudged Kian. "He's definitely a guy, right?"

Kian turned to me. "Yeah. Why?"

I shook my head, worried. "Then this is a setup, because there's a fed over there."

"*What?*" Aedan followed my gaze. "Her? How do you know she's a fed?"

I tried to put it into words. It's hard to describe but investigators just have this...*way* about them. The woman's eyes were never still: even as she picked up her coffee cup and started sipping, she was scanning the crowd, looking for trouble. I'd seen that look too many times, when the FBI and ATF had been sniffing around the Hell's Princes. They looked the same on duty and off duty: it was just the way they were wired. "She *is*," I insisted, staring at her.

"Your brother's right," said a voice behind us. "But she's not with me."

We all whirled around.

The man who'd walked silently up behind us fitted every image of a fed I had in my head. His gray suit and overcoat might as well have been manufactured by them and he fitted it the way I fitted my leather cut. And he had all that chiseled jaw shit going on: he looked like a goddamn model. "I'm Calahan," he told us. Then he nodded at the runner. "Lydecker. She's from my office. Step back a little until she's gone, I don't want her to see us."

He retreated a few steps until he was in the shadow of a tree and we did the same. The woman—Lydecker—drank her coffee as she listened to the string quartet.

"Is she in the cult?" asked Kian.

Calahan made a disbelieving noise. "*Lydecker?* Jesus, no. Kate's a straight arrow. But that's the problem, if she sees me talking to a biker, a boxer and the President's daughter's boyfriend, she's going to have about a million fucking questions and once she gets a hint of something she's like a goddamn dog with a bone." Then he let out a sigh of relief. "*There!*" Lydecker had tossed her cup—into a recycling bin, I noticed—and was walking off. "She's alright," Calahan said to himself. "She just needs to find a guy."

We all turned to face him. He looked from one face to another and then shook his head. "Jesus," he said at last.

"What?" asked Kian.

"*You.* You really think you're going to take on Aeternus?"

"What?" I asked.

"It's what they call themselves." He shook his head again. "You don't have a fucking clue what you're getting yourselves into, do you?"

I felt the anger start to smolder in my chest. "Everyone keeps telling us that. Be nice if someone actually told us something useful."

Calahan looked at me. "Useful? Okay: turn around, go home and forget about these people."

I looked at Kian. "He's wasting our time."

"The President said you'd help us!" snapped Kian.

"I *am* helping you! Jesus, do you know what I'm risking, just talking to you about this shit? I only agreed to meet you because President Matthews says you're okay. And the best advice I can give you is to drop this whole thing, right now!"

"Not happening," I said.

"*Reconsider,*" Calahan grated, getting in my face. "You are way, way, *way* out of your depth."

"Let us worry about that," said Kian. "I'm tired of this. The President tried to scare us off. Then my dad, now you."

I nodded. "Maybe it's just *you* who's scared of these bastards."

Calahan froze at that. He walked right up to me and lowered his voice until it was a thin, cold whisper. "Scared?" he asked. "You think I'm scared?" He leaned even closer. "You're *goddamn right* I'm scared." And something in the way he said it cut right through all my bravado. "I've gone up against the mob. I've been tied to a chair in Texas, waiting for someone to put a bullet in my brain. I've tracked down serial killers who made me seriously question if the devil was walking the earth because I didn't think any human could do the things that they did. I've seen shit you and your little punk-ass MC friends can't even *contemplate*. I've been scared plenty of times because I'm not an asshole. But nothing has ever scared me like *they* scare me."

We shut the hell up and listened.

"You've got to forget what you think a cult is. This isn't some kooky people in white robes praying for a UFO to take them away. This is...*changing people*. Normal people, smart people. They can do it to anyone, I don't know how but they can." He turned to Kian. "The President tell you about how deep they are?"

Kian nodded.

"My fucking *boss* is one of them," Calahan spat. We all gaped at him. "Yeah, get your head around that. The President asks me to start looking into them, because I'm the only one he trusts at the Bureau. I get six months in before I work out that the guy I've known for over eight years is in the cult. Where the hell do you go from there? Who do you trust?" He shook his head, remembering. "I was already keeping the investigation under wraps but...*Jesus*. When I think about how many times I nearly talked to my boss about it...."

Calahan sighed and rubbed his eyes. "I worked on it for nearly a year. Hit a brick wall. Had to take bigger and bigger risks to progress, calling in favors at different agencies." He paused and, when he started again, the words came slow, as if he was having to pry them out like barbs sunk deep into his flesh. "I guess somehow, they got wind of me."

He stopped. We all stood in silence for a second, a chill wind blowing through our little group, Annabelle's hair streaming out into a silky red mist. I slipped my arm around her waist and pulled her close.

"I'd been seeing this woman," said Calahan. "Becky. We'd only been together a few weeks but..." He stared down at the path for a second and, as he looked up, I saw it. He didn't have to say a word:

something passed between us and I understood. He'd felt the same way about Becky that I had about Annabelle.

"Anyway, I wake up one morning and she's lying kind of half on my arm. I try to reach across her to get a glass of water but I can't quite reach. So I try to wake her. She won't wake up. I try shaking her: nothing. I start to panic, roll her onto her back. That's when I feel how cold she is."

Calahan drew in a long, shuddering breath. "I call it in. There are a lot of questions: were we doing drugs: no. Were we drinking: no. With there being no known cause of death, of course there's an autopsy. They say it was a heart attack. That she must have had some sort of undiagnosed condition, but they can't lock down exactly what."

"I go home. I'm a mess. Drink myself into a stupor, wake up the next morning, look around...." He bit his lip. "And something's not right. I'm hungover and my heart's brea—"—he caught himself and took a deep breath—"and I'm *messed up*. But I have this feeling, looking around my room, that something's not right. I know I'm probably just going crazy. But I can't ignore it. And after almost an hour, I finally figure it out. My water glass is missing."

He looked around at the four of us. "I find it in the kitchen: someone's carried it through there and washed it up. And yet I *swear*, it was on the nightstand when I woke up and found Becky dead, because that's why I had to wake her, to get to it. So someone moved it, while they were taking Becky's body away. Someone moved it from the scene of a suspicious death. Why would they do that?"

We all stared at him, barely daring to breathe. I pulled Annabelle closer to my side and glanced down at her. She'd gone pale.

"I pick up the glass. All washed up, no evidence there. I go back to the bedroom and, on the nightstand, I find a few tiny drops of something, some liquid that's been dripped there and then dried. I get out a field kit, scrape a little off and take it to a buddy in the lab, all off the record. My buddy analyzes it and you know what he finds?"

He stopped. Took a long, shuddering breath. "Insulin. Someone had come into my apartment and dosed my water glass with it. A big dose of insulin will stop your heart and it won't leave a trace unless the coroner knows what to look for. They meant me to wake up, take a drink and that'd be the end of me. Only, sometime in the night, Becky drank it first. Then they had one of their people—someone with the coroner's office, probably—wash up the glass to get rid of the evidence."

"What'd you do?" asked Kian.

"I buried Becky," said Calahan bitterly. "Then I waited to die. Figured I was a dead man walking. Kept waiting for my brakes to fail, or someone to stick a knife in me. But nothing ever happened. I guess they decided they'd sent me a message. I stopped looking into the cult: I'd got as far as I was going to get, anyway. Worked other cases, life went back to normal. Except...." He looked off into the distance for a second. "Without Becky."

"Jesus," whispered Aedan.

"That's what you'd face, if you went after the cult," said Calahan, his voice suddenly savage. "They'll kill the people you love: not just collateral damage, like Becky. They'll do it to get to you. To hurt you. To make you stop. You want to wake up and find *her* dead?" he asked me, nodding to Annabelle.

I wrapped both arms around Annabelle and drew her into a bone-crushing hug. The President, our dad...they'd both given the same warning but Calahan's story made it real. When I looked across at Kian, I knew he was thinking the same thing.

I'd thought that nothing could keep me from looking for Bradan. *Nothing.* But Calahan had just met irresistible force with an immovable object. I couldn't abandon my brother. But I couldn't put Annabelle in danger, either.

We couldn't go any further. Our search was over before it had begun.

13

LOUISE

It was a *traditional-style* Irish pub a few streets away from Central Park, the fixtures and fittings designed to look like something from a hundred years ago, but the place had only been open five. Our men were by far the most Irish thing in there. But the place suited our mood: quiet and dark, and they served Guinness. It was a good place to hide, private enough that Sylvie could join us. Aedan had her hand tightly in his: he needed her. I knew Sean needed me, too. But helping our men wasn't as simple as being there for them. Sean's shoulder was pressed to mine, I could feel the warmth of his body...but he still felt a million miles away.

There was utter silence. Not just quiet but a kind of pressure caused by what the FBI agent had said. Kian had filled us in on the drive here. We sat staring into the black of our Guinness: we'd all ordered them but no one was drinking.

None of us could believe it was over.

I could see the men throwing glances at each other. Beneath all the sullen despair there was a white-hot anger, building and building as it reflected from one brother to another. I could feel it coming and looked at Annabelle and Sylvie but they looked as helpless as I felt: what could we do? What could we say?

The tension grew until it became unbearable. The men's breathing got tighter and tighter. Sean's arm muscles flexed as he hunched forward over the table. Every creak of Carrick's leather cut, every whisper of Kian's suit jacket made everyone stiffen—

"We can't—" started Carrick, shattering the silence. But he broke off, staring at Annabelle.

We all knew what he'd been going to say: *We can't just leave Bradan out there.* Annabelle looked as if she might burst into tears and Carrick grabbed her hand and squeezed it.

"I could go," said Kian.

We all looked at him.

"Emily's just about the best protected person on the planet. If there's anyone who's not at risk, it's her. I could go after the cult alone."

"Fuck that," snapped Sean. "If one of us is in, we're all in. We've been alone too long."

"And the cult's not going to care that you're doing it on your own," said Aedan. "You're our brother. The girls are still at risk." He looked at Sylvie, Annabelle, and me.

I looked at the other two women. We hadn't known each other long but I knew they were thinking the same thing. We could see it, even if the men couldn't: this is how the cult won. It took love and turned it into a weapon: the more you cared about the people in your life, the less likely you were to go after the cult.

And it was worse than that. Sean and his brothers had been without Bradan for years but they'd almost accepted that. Now that they'd tried to go after him and then had to give up because of us, because of Annabelle and Sylvie and me...the knowledge would be a poison injected into our relationship. Every mention of Bradan, every time we talked of family, there'd be sadness and anger, and that would turn to resentment and eventually to hate. I wanted to weep. The brothers had tried to do a good thing and, instead, this was going to wreck everything we had.

And suddenly, I knew what I had to do.

I looked up from my glass. "You're all a bunch of self-centered bastards," I said.

Everyone stared at me. "*What?!*" asked Sean.

My voice had started to shake with rage and fear. "You decide this," I said. "And *you don't even ask us?!*" I looked at Annabelle, then at Sylvie.

"This is about family," said Kian.

"You're goddamn right it's about family," said Sylvie. Everyone turned to her and I felt my heart soar: I had support. "Louise is right. We're with you. Bradan's our family, too. If we're the ones at risk, we have a right to decide. And I'm in."

Aedan glared at her, leaning across the table. "You didn't hear what the guy said. They will *kill you!*"

Sylvie's eyes were flashing. She leaned to meet Aedan. "*Let. Them. Try.*" Aedan went to speak but Sylvie put a finger to his lips. "You're scared of me dying?" she asked. "I would be *dead* right now. Have you forgotten that? I would be *dead!* I needed someone to teach me how to fight and you stepped up. Well, I'm stepping up now. Go get those bastards. I'm with you all the way."

I nodded, tears in my eyes. "Me too." I looked at Sean. "You were there when I needed someone. I'm sure as hell going to be there for you."

I could see the battle going on in Sean's eyes. "It's not just you," he said. "Kayley."

I nodded quickly. "You know how I feel about Kayley," I said, my voice cracking. "But she wouldn't be here today if it wasn't for you." I looked around the table, then back to Sean. "When I fell for you, I joined a family. And families will do anything for each other."

There was silence for a few seconds. Then we all turned towards Annabelle, who hadn't spoken yet. She was flushing, uncertain.

Carrick shook his head. "*No!*" He was trying to hide it but I could hear his voice fracture. "I nearly lost you in Haywood Falls! I'm not losing you again!"

Annabelle took a deep breath. She looked so scared, so shy: and yet so determined to get it out. "Look," she said. "I know I'm not the best with…"—she looked at her lap—"people and stuff." She looked at Carrick. "But I can feel something missing from you. From all of you. Brothers need each other. You've needed each other all these years. And the machine doesn't work if there's a part missing. You need to find him. Or you'll never be…complete."

Everyone looked at each other. Then we looked at Kian.

"You need to call Emily?" asked Carrick.

"No," said Kian slowly. "I already know what she'd say." He pulled out his phone and stared at it for a moment, deciding. We all held our breath. At last, he dialed. "Calahan?" he said. "We need to meet again. Battery Park. Right now."

He put the phone down. "And this time," he said, "we're all coming."

14

KIAN

The sun had set and the waters of the bay were like black tar, each gust of the icy wind sending slow waves rippling across them. The Statue of Liberty's reflection stretched out towards us, a smudge of green and gold. Next to me, Louise was cuddled into Sean's side. Carrick had Annabelle in his arms, her cheek pressed to his chest. Sylvie and Aedan had their arms around each other's waists, their heads together. It was too cold to stand there: we all should have huddled in the SUV to wait. But nobody felt like quitting.

Headlights lit us up from behind and we turned to see Calahan climbing out of his car. "Did you not hear what I said?" he raged as he stalked towards us. "Did you not hear a fucking word I said?"

"We heard," said Sylvie. "And we're not stopping."

Calahan glared at her for a moment and then sighed, rubbing a hand across his face. "Even if you're crazy enough to risk your lives, you're not going to be able to do this. Do you know how many people have escaped the cult, over the years?"

We shook our heads.

"None. Not a single living soul. That's why we know so little about them. Either they command absolute loyalty and no one ever turns or they kill anyone who even looks like they might leave. Maybe some of both. The cult is impenetrable. Nobody knows how it really works or who's in charge or *anything.*" His voice was strained, his own years of frustration showing through. "How the hell do you fight something like that?"

His shoulders dropped and his voice grew softer. "Look. I get that you want your brother back. I really do. But the cops have tried to investigate the cult. The FBI have tried. Even the CIA. Look at you." He waved his hand at our group of seven. "What chance do you think you have?"

Louise looked at Sean, then back at Calahan. "You'd be surprised what we can do, when we're motivated," she said firmly.

I spoke up. "The President said you'd help us."

"I *am* helping you!" snapped Calahan. "I'm trying to save your damn life! *Walk away!*" And he turned and walked back towards his car.

"No." My voice cut through the night air, halting Calahan just as he touched the door handle.

"No?" Calahan turned, the wind from the bay ruffling his hair.

"No," said Annabelle. We all stepped forward, surrounding him. For the first time, we felt like a team...and that felt really, really good.

Calahan drew himself up to his full height. "You can't beat the cult with stubbornness."

"That's *exactly* how we're going to beat them," said Sean. "You're right, we're not cops. We're a blunt fuckin' instrument. Look, you failed because the cult got wind of you: they have people in the FBI. Same with all the authorities. But we don't have that problem. They won't see us coming."

"You're going to get yourselves killed," said Calahan.

"Maybe," I said. "But we're doing this with or without you. If you really want to hurt the cult...." Calahan's head jerked up to glare at me and I knew he was thinking of Becky. "Then you'll help us make an impact. Tell us where to start."

Calahan turned away. For a second, I thought I'd blown it, that he'd climb back into his car. But he tilted his face up to the stars and let out a long sigh. "Shit," he said at last. "And I thought that cowboy was stubborn."

He turned back to us and dug in his pocket, pulling out a USB stick. "That's everything I know," he told me, pressing it into my palm. "All the files, all my notes. As for where to start: the cult started on the West Coast. If you want to find the center, the leader...I'd start in LA."

He opened his car door, then stopped. Without turning around, he said, "If by some miracle you pull this off and you find the leader...."

We waited.

When he spoke again, his voice was choked with emotion. "You kill that son of a bitch."

He got into his car and roared off. I closed my hand around the USB stick: a tiny little thing, but reassuringly solid.

"Our place has plenty of rooms," said Sean. "We could all stay there, while we do this."

Going to LA meant being even further from Emily. We'd be on opposite sides of the country. But I wasn't going to stop until I found Bradan. I turned to look at the others and found their faces as determined as mine.

"Alright then," I said. "Let's go find our brother."

15

ANNABELLE

We got an overnight flight to LA. I was behind Kian as we boarded. When he suddenly stopped in the aisle, I almost crashed into his back.

"What's up?" I asked.

He looked left then right, as if lost. "Nothing," he muttered, and finally marched off in the direction of his economy-class seat.

As the rest of us followed, Carrick leaned forward from behind me, his stubble brushing my cheek and sending a shiver down my spine. "He got used to Air Force One," he said with a smirk.

I saw Kian's shoulders rise: he'd heard the comment, but ignored it.

Once in our seats, I pulled the blanket over me, fluffed my pillow and settled in to sleep: Sylvie and Aedan weren't so bad but the rest of us hadn't slept for two days and we were ready to drop. I was very glad Kian had persuaded Carrick to have his bike shipped by van to LA instead of trying to ride it there.

Carrick, though, wasn't pleased. "They better take care of it," he muttered as he got comfortable.

"They will," I said gently.

"They better strap it down tight. If it comes out in LA with a scratch or something's bent—"

"They'll strap it down *really tight*," I told him. I leaned across and kissed him, my hair falling across his face, and his grumbling died away. He was asleep in minutes: he was even more exhausted than me.

I looked up and caught Kian's eye. He must have overheard the conversation because he was shaking his head in gentle disbelief...but he was smiling, too.

And I was proud of my man. The fact he'd agreed to ship his bike, however reluctantly, spoke volumes about how determined he was to find Bradan. I nestled my head into the warm space between his shoulder and cheek and by the time the plane's wheels left the ground, I was already asleep.

With seven of us, we had to get two cabs from the airport: Carrick, Kian and me in one and Sean, Louise, Aedan and Sylvie in the other. Louise gave me the address but, when the cab pulled up, I bit my lip and double-checked my phone. "Maybe there are two streets with the same name," I muttered.

"How do you know this isn't it?" asked Kian, looking through the window.

"Look *up*," I told him.

He was so much taller than me, he had to lean all the way forward in his seat and twist his neck to look up through the cab's window. Then he saw it. "Oh."

There was a tree growing out of the roof.

"I'll call Louise," I said. But just as I dialed, their cab pulled in behind ours and Louise jumped out.

"It's okay!" she told me, pulling my door open. "You *are* in the right place. Come on, I'll show you around." She was grinning and so was Sean, that bouncy, happy pride couples get when they show you the home they've made together. I wondered if Carrick and I would be like that, one day.

We stepped out into bright Californian sunshine. For me, the sun on my skin felt like coming home. But Sylvie and Aedan looked up at the sky in astonishment. Sylvie peeled off her thick coat, tipped back her head and let the warmth soak her neck. "Oh *wow!*"

A figure was hurrying down the path towards us, a whirlwind of energy in ripped jeans and sneakers, her blonde hair cut short. "Everybody, this is Kayley," Louise told us. "Kayley, this is...." She ran through the names. Kayley gave us all a big, wide grin and then grabbed Sylvie and me by the hands and we started the tour.

I'd assumed at first that it must be some sort of optical illusion but no: there really *was* a tree growing right through the old, mansion-style house. The trunk emerged from the floor in the hallway, tiles carefully removed to form a neat hole for it, and the branches soared up through the double-height space. Part of the roof had been replaced with skylights to give it light and there were strategically-cut holes to let branches thread their way out to the sky, with overhangs so that rain didn't get in. I could feel the breeze from above: it was like being outdoors while being indoors. I loved it.

Louise led us up the old-fashioned, wooden staircase. Kayley, though, took her own route, swarming up the tree with the speed of long practice and the confidence that comes from being fourteen and therefore indestructible. As I watched her work her way up the branches and then swing herself over the handrail, I caught my breath...but she landed safely on the galleried landing. As I relaxed, Louise turned and caught my eye. Her look said *I know, right? She scares me, too.* But there was joy there, too. Relief. I frowned, confused.

The house was huge, a maze of long, dark hallways that all looked the same. Sean hadn't been kidding about there being plenty of rooms. Louise pushed open the door to the one they shared and couldn't stop myself letting out a delighted little *oh!* when I saw the four poster bed. Carrick leaned into the doorway beside me and nuzzled my cheek. "Now you're going to want one of those, too," he said, mock-grumpily.

I nodded madly.

Sylvie stood on tiptoes to see past us, then grinned. "That's not a bed, it's a thing maidens get ravished on."

Louise said nothing but I saw her flush beet red.

Kayley grabbed us and dragged us along the hallway to show us the smaller version Sean had made for her, hers adorned with fairy lights and purple drapes. Her room had a window that looked out over the garden and roses were growing up trellises towards it. From what I was seeing of Kayley, she was going to be climbing down those trellises to secretly meet boyfriends anytime now.

Louise led us downstairs. I saw worn but very comfortable-looking couches that they'd bought from thrift stores and recovered, a TV and a big table I could imagine them all eating dinner at while Sean asked if Kayley had done her homework. Plants were *everywhere:* on window ledges, in pots, hanging from the ceiling...the kitchen had its own herb garden and outside there was a vegetable patch. Flowers climbed the ropes of a wooden swing Sean had hung from a tree and there was a big patch of long grass sown with wildflowers: almost a meadow. It made me wish I understood plants: I'd never been any good at getting things to grow.

Louise started to prepare some food and I wanted to help but I wasn't quick enough: Kian, Sylvie and Aedan got in first and four was enough to fill the kitchen so Louise chased Carrick and me out. While Kayley cornered Carrick with a thousand questions about being a biker, I went exploring. Following a faint smell of engine oil, I homed in on the garage, slipped inside...and stopped.

It was beautiful. As beautiful as Carrick's Harley but different in a way that made my mind skip like a needle on a record and then settle into a new, unexpected groove. The Harley was all about raw power and danger, the throbbing between your thighs and the thrill of leaning far over in a corner, your knees almost brushing the pavement. But *this*.... I ran my palm over the hood. This was all about style and speed. Black paint so shiny I could see my own awestruck face. Huge wide tires to grip the road and blast it into the rear view mirror. And...I ran my hand over the bulge in the hood, following its lines. That engine. So. Much. Power.

"Like it?"

I snatched my hand back and spun around. "Yes. Sorry. I was just exploring."

Sean was standing in the doorway, grinning. "It's a '69," he told me. "V8."

I looked back at the Mustang, trying to act normal. But when it filled my vision again, I couldn't help but let out a little sigh. "It's *beautiful!*"

Sean lifted the hood and I gave a little groan of pleasure as I drank in the engine. "She's running pretty well right now, but she needs a lot of love." He glanced at me. "I was thinking about changing out the carb...."

"*I'll help.*" I said it so fast it was almost one word. Then I caught myself. *I'm being weird again.* "I mean, if you'd like me to."

He chuckled. "That'd be great."

That night, when we'd all unpacked and settled in, Carrick and I helped Louise prepare a lasagna big enough for seven, with sauce made from tomatoes from the garden. Tomorrow, we knew we'd be going to work to find Bradan. But for just one evening, we had a chance to get to know each other.

Once Kayley was in bed, we took over the living room. Louise poured wine and we spread out over the couches and chairs: with seven of us, we used every available seat plus the couch arms. Wine was a new experience for me: at the MC, it was always beer. Perched on the couch arm, leaning to my right so that I could cuddle up against Carrick, sipping a glass of Merlot...it was heaven, and I felt all the stress of the last few days drain out of me.

We filled each other in on our stories. Louise and Sean had told us about Kayley's illness and growing the marijuana to pay for her treatment. As Louise described Kayley in the hospital and the race against time to save her, I suddenly understood that look I'd seen on the stairs: she was beyond relieved that Kayley was back to being a normal teenager.

Aedan and Sylvie told us about New York and how he'd trained her. Carrick and I told the story of how we'd first met when I was just a kid, and how he'd returned to my tiny town to save me from being sold to Volos, the human trafficker. Sylvie and Louise went white as I described the auction. I heard my voice go slower and slower as I recalled being up on stage, how the men had bid on me. My voice caught and then I stopped completely and I couldn't seem to continue. I looked around the room, panicked: ashamed that it still got to me.

Then, suddenly, Carrick's arm was tightening around my waist, pulling me to him. "It's okay," he said. And in those two words I could hear so much: the anger for what had happened to me, the need to protect me, the tenderness that made me go warm inside.

He put his lips to my cheek and for a second I just stayed there, eyes closed, as the memories retreated to a safe distance. Then I turned and we were kissing, slow and soft, a kiss that told me he was still there: would *always* be there. When he broke it, he tracked kisses up my nose and to my forehead, one big hand holding me there for a second before he let me escape. He glanced at the room for a second and then back at me, his heavy brows giving me a warning frown. *You know it's okay, right? You don't have to tell them if you don't want to.* He squeezed me again, his thumbs rubbing gently over my hips. *You don't owe anyone a damn thing,* his eyes said.

I nodded that I understood but then shook my head. "It's okay," I said. And when I turned and looked shyly at the others, it *was* okay. All of them were looking at me with total sympathy: I didn't need to be embarrassed. I was amongst friends, here.

Together, Carrick and I told the rest. Then we all turned to Kian as he told his story. We'd heard about Kerrigan and the attempted coup in the press but now we learned all the missing pieces. But even though the story had a happy ending, it was somehow sad because Kian was the only one who had to tell his story alone. I could tell, listening to him, just how much he cared for Emily, how strong his need to protect her was. And yet he'd been forced to leave her on the opposite side of the country to come and find Bradan. I wanted to hug him.

With everyone up to date, the talk turned lighter. I looked around at the other couples: of all of them, Carrick and I were by far the newest. Louise and Sean and Sylvie and Aedan had been together months, now. And Louise and Sean were so *domesticated*. I wouldn't change my life with Carrick for anything: parties at the clubhouse with the MC, weekends at the cabin, waking up to the sound of the chipmunk scurrying over the roof...I loved it but it was chaotic compared to their settled life. Would we be like that, in six months?

I felt a stab of fear and turned to Carrick. We *would* last, wouldn't we?

He caught my sudden movement and looked sidelong at me...and the look in his eyes made all my fears fall away. He had this way of gazing at me that always made me feel special, even when I was at my most awkward. He looked at me as if I was the most amazing thing he'd ever seen and that made me heart swell. Yes, of course we'd last.

Sylvie leaned over to me. "Have you noticed," she asked, "that the more time these four spend together, the stronger their accents get?" She looked at Aedan. "I give it a week and then we're going to need subtitles."

I burst out laughing and Louise and Sylvie joined me. The men looked at one another, suddenly sheepish, but it was true. The Irish in Carrick's accent had started to rise to the surface, breaking through the California sunshine. The rock in his voice seemed rougher, rasping against my ears in a way that made me squirm and the silver had grown sharper and yet smoother: it seemed to race right down my spine and vibrate through my groin. From the way Louise was looking at Sean, the change was having the same effect on all of us.

Some time later, I wandered upstairs to the bathroom. Sylvie had already complained about getting lost but one advantage of my weird mind was that even the old house's winding hallways formed a clear map in my head. When I got to the bathroom, though, the door was closed and I could see light coming from under the door. I leaned against the opposite wall to wait.

And that's when I heard a muffled shriek of horror from inside.

16

LOUISE

I*t's just a trick of the light.* But no matter how much I twisted and tilted the thing, it still looked the same.

I'm seeing double. But I hadn't even touched my wine: couldn't stomach it. And now I knew why.

No! That's crazy. I can't be. I'm misreading the instructions. Relief sluiced through me. Yes, of course. That's what it was. I re-read the leaflet, heart pounding, then stared at the little plastic window again.

Two lines. *Pregnant.*

I clapped my hand over my mouth just in time to muffle my shriek of horror. *What?!* I'd only done the test to put my mind at rest, after all the morning nausea, after not even tasting my Guinness in New York or my wine this evening. I thought I was just a little late! I was just *ruling it out!*

Someone knocked at the door and I jumped so much I swear both feet left the ground. "Louise?" Annabelle's voice. "Are you okay?"

"Yes," I lied in a strangled voice.

"I thought I heard you scream."

"I dropped the soap," I said. Then, "On my foot." I turned on the faucet to make it sound like I was doing something other than staring slack-jawed at my future. Then I stuffed all the pregnancy test packaging into the pockets of my jeans, hid the test itself under the hem of my top and opened the door, giving Annabelle what I hoped was a placid smile.

I went straight to our bedroom, pulled out the pregnancy test and sat down on the bed staring at it. But before I could even start to process, Sean came in and I had to whip the little plastic stick behind my back.

"You okay?" He sat down beside me, the bed sinking under his muscled bulk. "You went to the bathroom and never came back. You didn't drink your wine."

Behind my back, I rolled the pregnancy test in my fingers. It felt red hot: I couldn't keep it still. "Fine. Just feeling a little...off."

He frowned and laid a big palm on my forehead to check my temperature. "You've been feeling sick for days. I think you should see a doctor."

I wanted to kick myself for being so stupid. How could I have missed this? "Mmm. You're right. I'll make an appointment." ...*with an obstetrician,* I mentally added. My mind was shredding: my entire future was reshaping before my eyes and I was desperately trying to cling on. *Tell him,* I was screaming at myself. But I hadn't even figured out how I felt myself, yet. It was just too much: diapers and strollers and grade school ,and he or she would need a car and college and oh holy shit I have to *give birth*—

I want my mom, I thought suddenly. And the fact she wasn't here, anymore, made me collapse inside like a failing tower of cards.

"You really okay?" asked Sean, his eyes narrowing.

I swallowed and hugged him. "Sure," I said into his shoulder. "Everything's fine."

17

CARRICK

We started work the next morning and we didn't stop for a week. We took over the big hallway where the tree grew, since that was the biggest space, and for the first day Louise's printer ran non-stop, turning the data from Calahan's USB stick into a forest of paper that we could pin to the walls.

Calahan's information was full of anecdotes and specifics but he'd been unable to link it all together with a structure. Unlike a normal cult, Aeternus didn't have a website or any sort of publicity. *They* found *you*. There wasn't even much information about what the members believed: it certainly wasn't anything clear-cut and specific. There was no talk of aliens or UFOs or gods. There was talk of loyalty and family and needing one another. But there didn't seem to be a tier structure of leaders, with the money flowing upward in a pyramid, like I was expecting. In fact, we were having trouble finding a leader at all. Someone must have started the cult, someone must be controlling it...but whoever it was, they sure as hell weren't in this for the adoration; no one knew who they were.

Annabelle bought a big map of California and started mapping cult activities. Sylvie printed photos of every cult member Calahan had identified and pinned them up as a rogue's gallery so we knew who we were up against. He hadn't been kidding about the cult's grip on society: there were judges, two DAs, a mayor, even a senator. I started to get a sinking feeling. We really were up against it.

The hallway buzzed with activity, people hurrying back and forth with bits of paper or sitting on couches with laptops looking stuff up. Emily was helping back in Washington, too, sifting through the front companies Calahan had identified. We didn't have his FBI training but we made up for it in numbers: even Kayley helped, when she wasn't at school. She was also loving having three new older brothers around and we, who'd never had a kid sister, quickly became fiercely protective of her.

The house was huge. I was used to the tiny house I shared with Annabelle back in Haywood Falls. Sure, it was small but at least I didn't get lost. Sean and Louise's place was all dark hallways lined with a million identical wooden doors. Twice, I thought I was heading back into our bedroom and walked in on Sylvie and Aedan (once they were kissing up against the wall, her legs around his waist, once hotly debating who would win in a fight between Alec and Aedan).

There were advantages, though: Annabelle was already in love with the huge bedroom with its dark, intricately carved wood furniture and the bed you could live in. When we got back to Haywood Falls, I could see a bigger place in our future. When I first rescued Annabelle, an idea as civilized and normal as buying a place together had been utterly alien to me: you don't plan long-term when all you live for is the next job and you know there's a good chance you won't come back. But she'd changed me for the better.

From the noises coming from the other bedrooms each night, all the couples were inspired by the old, romantic house. Except Kian, of course. His room was silent and we all felt bad for him: Emily was a long way away.

Not all of the rooms had their own bathrooms so the mornings turned into a parade of topless Irish men shuffling through the hallways, towels wrapped round their waists, while women in bathrobes with towels around their heads scurried from room to room borrowing hairdryers. Breakfast was chaos, too, a production line of eggs, bacon, coffee, and toast. Between the eight of us, we ate a lot (I didn't know if it was because she was a teenager or because she was making up for lost time but Kayley seemed to eat more than any of us). There were so many of us, we had to extend the dining table out to its maximum length, and even then we were touching elbows. But it felt good. It reminded me of the MC. Or maybe it's that the MC reminded me of this: what I should have had all along.

After a week, the walls rustled every time a breeze blew through the house, the paper three sheets deep in some places. We were caught up to the point Calahan had reached...but just like him, we'd hit a dead end. Progress slowed right down: people walked instead of hurried, typed a little slower on their keyboards. We didn't want to run out of stuff to do but, with so many of us chasing things down, it was inevitable. Work ground to a halt.

Calahan was a fed so I still hated him on principle but I was starting to understand how he'd gotten so bitter about the whole thing. Trying to get a handle on the cult was like trying to catch smoke. We couldn't find a structure, a shape. It felt like we were missing something.

Everyone else went out into the garden to take a break. Late fall, here in California, meant warm winds and just enough sun to be pleasant without it baking you: Annabelle, with her pale skin, loved it. I stayed behind and sat down on the floor, staring stubbornly at the walls as if the answer was going to just suddenly leap out at me.

Then I realized I wasn't alone. Sean was under the tree, leaning on a branch. "You don't want to be out there with Louise?" I asked.

Sean shook his head. "Something's up with her," he said. "She keeps pulling me aside, like she's going to tell me something, and then she clams up. How's Annabelle?"

I sighed and rubbed a hand over my stubble. "Getting frustrated, same as me." She'd already spent hours poring over Calahan's notes, her delicate brow creased in concentration until I just wanted to kiss the frowns away. I could tell she was feeling lost in all the talk of loyalties and blackmail, manipulation and secrets. She'd always been better with machines than with "people stuff" and this was as *people stuff* as it got.

Sean sighed and came to sit beside me and we sat there staring at the walls. It looked as if we'd decorated with the damn stuff: there wasn't a square inch that wasn't covered with printouts and it was near impossible to find a light switch. "You think we can figure this out?" said Sean, his voice tight. "Because I've got this feeling...I mean, Calahan couldn't. No one could. How can *we?*"

I turned to him. "We will," I said grimly. "Because if we don't...we've lost him forever."

Sean nodded. We fell silent and he leaned forward, chin on his knees, to think. And that's when I saw it.

He was wearing a thin white t-shirt and, as he leaned forward, the muscles of his back stood out, stretching the material even more. I could see the dark ink of the tattoos that covered his back...but that wasn't all. I could see the way the fabric rose and fell to follow lines that shouldn't have been there. Scars, hidden by the tattoos.

I'd been around violence enough that I knew those sorts of scars. They weren't recent and they weren't from a one-off fight. They were from a long time ago...and they'd built up over years.

My first reaction was fury, an incandescent crimson glow lit my chest, shuddering down my arms to form my hands into fists. Someone had hurt my little brother and I was going to *kill them*.

And then the guilt hit, punching me in the gut and turning all that anger in on myself. It had happened to him because I'd left him alone and vulnerable. I'd abandoned my family and Sean had gone through hell.

The temptation was to run. Sean didn't know I'd seen: I could get up, march out of the house, climb on my bike and ride off to some bar. Drink like I hadn't drunk since I rescued Annabelle, drown all that guilt in whiskey.

And then I remembered that my bike wasn't here yet: the damn delivery company had been stalling for days, saying their driver was sick. It was like a message: I'd run for long enough.

Without words, I reached down, gripped the hem of Sean's t-shirt and dragged it up. Sean jerked and then started to twist around to stop me but then our eyes met and he saw how determined I was. He stared at me, angry and then ashamed. And then he simply looked away, staring fixedly into the distance: *go on, then. Look if you want to.*

I peeled the t-shirt up, every inch causing a new stab of pain in my chest. *Aw shit!* The tattoos did a good job of hiding the damage but close up, in the right light, I could see how someone had gone to town on him, worked him over day after day. The rage glowed white hot: I drew in a deep lungful of air, then another and another. I needed to be able to speak, not yell. *"Who?"* I got out at last.

"My foster dad," said Sean. He stared at the floor.

I wanted to tear my eyes away from the scars. Couldn't. "How long?"

"A few years."

My biker boots squeaked on the wood floor as a tremor went through my legs. Every muscle was hard with fury, my heartbeat echoing through every straining sinew. "I'll kill the son of a bitch."

Sean shook his head. "He's an old man, now. And I put the fear of God into him a long time ago." He turned to look at me and what he saw in my face made him freeze.

I've never been good at talking but now it was like dredging the words up out of thick black tar. I'd been wanting to say them for so many years and yet I could barely draw them to the surface. *"I'm sorry,"* I finally croaked.

Sean frowned. "You think I *blame you?*"

The house was very quiet. "I ran away," I said, staring at my boots. "If I'd stayed...."

"If you'd stayed, it wouldn't have made any fucking difference. They wouldn't have let you be my guardian. You were only a kid yourself."

I shook my head. "I could have stayed close. I could have stopped that bastard from hurting you."

Sean gripped my arm hard. I looked down at his hand, then up at his face. "The only person it's on is my foster dad," said Sean firmly. "Okay?"

I stared into his eyes for a long time, my own eyes getting hot. Then I nodded and quickly stood. Sean started to get to his feet too and I reached down, giving him my hand and pulling him up. He stood in front of me and—

Suddenly I was pulling him into a hug. I didn't say a damn word, just wrapped my arms around him, and held him there like I never wanted to let him go again.

18

SEAN

I blinked as I emerged into the sunlight, still reeling from what I'd shared with Carrick. Jesus, the poor fucker had been blaming himself, all these years? Eating himself up inside because he had the good sense to get out when he did? I felt better, though, for telling him. Until now, I'd only ever shared that with Louise. It didn't solve the other problem, though: we were still stuck in our investigation and the longer we were stalled, the more I felt like a big, dumb lunk.

Then I slowly smiled as I saw the one person who I knew would make me feel better.

She was sitting in the long grass, some of the stalks almost over her head. The sun was low in the sky and it was making her glorious copper hair shine and blaze. She'd put on a loose white blouse and, as I walked up behind her and looked down, I had a view straight down the front of it to that soft, perfect cleavage. *Damn!* I swore her breasts looked even more fantastic than normal, this week.

Or maybe I was just extra-horny because we'd barely touched each other since everyone had arrived.

Sure, it was difficult to grab time alone with the house so full but it had been a full week since we'd had sex and that was a long time for us. She drove me just as wild as she had when we'd first met and it wasn't unusual for me to carry her straight upstairs when I got home from the construction site. And however shy she acted, as soon as we started kissing, Louise's other side came out and she'd be just as breathlessly eager as me.

I stared down at those creamy breasts and the lacy edges of her bra and felt myself getting hard. Sex, I reasoned, might be just what she needed to relax her and get her to tell me whatever was bothering her. I sat down behind her, pressed my chest to her back and wrapped one arm around her waist. She gasped: she'd been too deep in thought to hear me approach. I cupped her chin and gently tipped her head back for my kiss.

She looked up into my eyes and I saw the worry there. She'd been sitting here stressing over something, just as she had been all week. Well, fine, I'd kiss that stress away.

But then, as she focused on me, something happened that made me freeze. Just for an instant, I saw the fear and tension in her face *increase.*

Her eyes closed and for a second we just stayed there: her face upturned for my kiss, my heart slamming in my chest as I tried to decipher what I'd just seen. She was worried about something...and seeing me made it *worse?* My stomach twisted. Something *was* going on with her and I had no idea what. Was she sick? Worried about Kayley or my brothers being here, or something else? Whenever I asked her, she claimed everything was fine.

I cursed inwardly, feeling clumsier than ever. With everything we'd been through over the summer, I'd learned to communicate a little better. But I still wasn't exactly silver-tongued. I'd never *been* in a long-term relationship until Louise.

All I knew was, I had to make her feel better. I'd kiss her and then, once things got heated, we'd slip away upstairs. And then, after sex, I'd somehow convince her to talk to me.

My lips came down on hers and she let out a little moan of need. My lips twitched into a smile. *There she is!* That was the Louise I remembered. I kissed her slow and deep and she responded, her body relaxing. My hands moved to her breasts—

She gasped, broke the kiss and pushed my hands away. "Don't!"

I frowned at her, wondering if she was playing. *Does she want to do the ravished princess thing again?* My hands cautiously closed on her breasts again but, before I'd even touched them, she squirmed out of my grip and crossed her arms protectively over her chest.

I stared at her. *What did I do?*

She bit her lip. "They're just really sensitive right now."

I ran a hand through my hair. Now she didn't want me touching her? I wracked my brains for some way to cheer her up. Something romantic. "How about, tonight, we let the others fend for themselves and you and me eat out here?" I said at last. "A picnic. I could get us a bottle of wine."

Her eyes went big. "I don't, uh...feel like wine," she said weakly.

I sighed. "Did I do something to piss you off?"

"No!"

I reached for her hand. "Then what—"

She sprang to her feet. In the space of just a few seconds she'd gone from horny to stressed: almost *panicked.* "Nothing! Just...." She pushed at the air with her palms.

Just stay here.

Just leave me alone.

And then she was gone, running off into the house. *Feck!* What the hell was going on with her? I swore I could see tears in her eyes and that made my chest lock up tight. She was never normally moody like this.

What the hell is wrong with my girl? And how the hell do I fix it?

19

KIAN

I stalked into my bedroom and shut the door behind me. I'd been trying to understand the cult for so long, my brain felt like lead. We were all feeling the same: everyone else was taking a break outside in the sunshine but, when Sean and Carrick had emerged from the house to join us, everyone had coupled off. I didn't want to stand there looking awkward so I'd come here.

But the bedroom didn't feel right, either. I couldn't relax: I started pacing like a caged animal. I sat down on the bed but almost immediately jumped up: the big four poster was too romantic, too obviously built for a couple.

I needed *her*.

This was the first time I'd had to do without her: we'd barely been apart since we got together. I wasn't used to this, to this...*tugging.* I'd spent so many years on my own, had my first family ripped away from me and then, in Iraq, lost a second one when the rest of my unit had been wiped out. I'd sworn I wouldn't let myself get close to anyone again because it hurt too much. And yet, when I met Emily, I couldn't resist. Not that face, not that pert, energetic body, not her soft Texan voice or her caring ways. I'd opened up and let her in and....

And now it felt like there was a part of me missing, every hour I was without her. I'd never felt like that about anyone before.

I cursed and paced some more. I shouldn't be like this, shouldn't be weak like this. I was meant to protect her. I was the big one, the strong one. I loved to fold her into my arms and hold her close but now...I guess I hadn't realized how much I needed her smallness, her grace, to balance me out.

I finally broke, fired up my laptop, and called Emily. A few seconds later, her face appeared on the screen...and it was like I'd thrown open the windows and fresh, clean air had filled the room. I drew down a deep lungful. I could *breathe* again.

"What?" asked Emily, immediately.

"Nothing," I muttered. I sat down on the edge of the bed and put the laptop on my knees. Emily was wearing a dress I hadn't seen before, navy blue and made of some soft, clingy material. It left her shoulders bare but she had a knitted gray shawl around them: the President's daughter can't show too much skin. It was all very modest but that didn't make it any less hot. My eyes traced her soft curls of mahogany hair: I wanted to sink my fingers into it and feel it against my knuckles. I wanted to stroke my thumb over her cheek and feel the softness of her skin. I wanted those big, liquid eyes to be locked on mine face-to-face, not over a damn camera.

Dammit, I was falling in love with her all over again.

"You're staring," she said.

"I know."

She blushed.

"What are you all dressed up for?"

"Garden party, this afternoon. One of mom's fundraiser things."

I looked at the clock in the corner of the screen. It wasn't even noon yet but of course there was a three hour time difference. It made her seem even further away. "You find anything out?"

She shook her head and the way her hair tossed made me want to reach right through the screen and kiss her hard. "It's making me mad. I've looked into plenty of companies that were trying to hide what they were doing. But this isn't like Rexortech. It's too loose, too chaotic. That *should* make it easy: I mean, if these people are just a disorganized rabble, they should be easy to track down. But when you try to grab onto something—"

I nodded. "—it's just not there." I felt my overworked brain start to cool down: Emily's voice was like a soothing balm. It helped, just having someone to vent to. "I know exactly what you mean. I thought I'd found something this morning. Started to follow it up...and the leads just went nowhere, like this little group of cult members weren't attached to *anything*. Which makes no sense. Makes me want to punch something." I frowned. The whole thing reminded me of something but I couldn't figure out what.

Both of us sighed and sat back from our screens. Then Emily's camera suddenly jerked and her eyes went wide in panic. My view seemed to tumble, I saw her lean forward and then the camera righted itself. "Sorry," she said. "Knocked the laptop with my knee and it fell off the desk."

But I was just staring at the screen. When the laptop fell, I'd seen: *"What are you wearing?"*

Emily looked bemused. "Nothing! A dress."

"Tilt the camera down again!"

The camera wobbled as she picked up the whole laptop and then my view tilted as she panned down. She was sitting in a desk chair, knees a little to one side and legs crossed. The dress was modest on top but it finished above the knee and it must have ridden up a little as she sat down. Her legs looked *amazing*.

"Your legs look amazing," I said out loud.

"Oh!" she reached down and started to tug the hem down.

"No!" I said sharply. "Don't."

She looked up into the camera and her eyes widened as she saw the look in my eyes.

20

EMILY

God, I missed him. Ever since his face appeared on my screen, I was trying to figure out how to tell him how much, without triggering him to rush back home to Washington. The last thing I wanted was to come between him and his search for Bradan. I just felt so useless, sitting there in DC. Sure, I was helping but I wasn't *there*. And he needed me.

And then I looked into the camera and saw *that* look in his eyes and I realized he needed me in different way, too. The heat in his gaze blazed across my skin, my clothes becoming insignificant wisps of cloth, scarcely there. It soaked into my flesh and coalesced in my core. I swallowed and pressed my thighs together. An idea had jumped into my head and I knew he'd had the exact same one.

I silently shook my head. *We can't.* I was sitting in the White House, for God's sake. There were people around. But it had been over a week. And just the idea, just holding it in my head for a brief second before dismissing it, had left me wet.

We can't.

But what if we did?

I bit my lip and looked over my shoulder. The door was closed. I looked back at Kian. He still had the same look in his eyes. I could see his muscled chest rising and falling smoothly under his white shirt as he watched me, a beast ready to pounce....

"Move the camera back, so I can see all of you," he said.

I did it.

"Lose the shawl," he said. I swore his Irish accent had grown stronger. It had always been beautiful but now it seemed to resonate through me, a magic frequency that made every hair on my arms and neck stand on end and my breathing grow quick. I shrugged off the shawl and it slithered to the floor behind me, leaving my shoulders bare. Kian's eyes narrowed in lust. I could see his gaze trace down the length of my neck, swore I could feel it as it burned its way across my naked shoulder and down to the neckline of my dress. "What are we going to do?" I asked. My voice sounded almost drunk: I hadn't admitted to myself how much I'd been needing him and now it was all coming out at once.

"I'm going to make you come." His voice had dropped to a low growl and this time the vibration of it seemed to throb right through the floor, buzz up my legs and explode in my groin.

"But you're not here," I whispered.

"I can be," he said. I saw him lean forward: he was gazing more intently into the camera than I'd ever seen anyone gaze at anything. And then I realized he was gazing at *me* and it was like a hot bomb going off inside me. "Close your eyes, Emily."

I closed my eyes.

"Stand up and hoik up that dress for me, beautiful."

I drew in my breath and opened my lips to tell him that I couldn't do this, wasn't confident enough to...*perform* for him on webcam. But he knew what I was going to say before I said it.

"Yes you can."

And suddenly, hearing his voice...it was like he was right there with me in the room, sitting across from me. As if I could reach right out and touch my fingers to his.

I stood, reached down and slowly lifted the hem of my dress, inching it up my thighs. He was silent as it rose up over my ass, up to my waist.

"I like your panties," he growled. I tried to remember what I was wearing. I didn't want to open my eyes, didn't want to break the illusion—growing stronger each second—that he was there. He went silent for a moment and I could feel his gaze caress me like heated silk: sliding around my ankles, rising up my calves, my thighs, my hips, toying with the edges of my panties. "God, I love your legs," he said at last. It was so simple, so *him,* but better than any poetry because of the passion I could hear in his voice, the Irish silver turned molten. "Now push your panties down."

I swallowed and hooked my thumbs into the waistband of my panties. *I can't do this,* I thought, but the blood was rushing in my ears and, as I toyed nervously with them, thumbs stretching the elastic, suddenly I felt him pressing up against me from behind. It was so real, I almost spun around. I could feel his hard chest against my back, the hot weight of his cock between the cheeks of my ass. "Push them down," he whispered and I gasped: his voice was right in my ear, hot breath making loose strands of hair tickle my cheek.

I pushed my panties down. Felt the cool air of the room lap at my sensitive flesh, felt the shock of being naked in the middle of the day. And yet his gaze was there to warm me, making me writhe and twist around that part of me, gently swirling my hips. The panties fell around my feet and I kicked them away, my dress still held up around my waist. I felt his big, warm palms cover my ass, sliding over my cheeks, squeezing gently, and—

"Play with yourself," he said, his voice low so as not to make me jump. My hand had started to move there just before he said it: I couldn't stop myself. My fingers found my wetness and started to glide up and down, my hips rocking to meet my touch. It was soft and gentle at first but the heat built rapidly, spiraling up my legs, weakening them.

I sank a little, knees bending, as the heat crept inward and concentrated. My ass dipped, my thighs starting to clamp together on my hand, and I stroked faster, faster. My ragged breathing filled the room. Behind my closed eyelids I could see Kian's blue eyes staring right at me, eating up every detail and the heat grew brighter, heavier, drawing everything into its core. It was happening much faster than normal, the effect of being apart for a week. I could hear him breathing hard, too, that tight, quick panting that means a man is close. *God, he must be— While he's watching me....*

I was rushing towards it now, out of control. My thighs crushed together, my fingers rubbing hard as my thumb circled my clit. My ass was clenching and circling, grinding up against Kian as he wrapped his body around mine from behind, his hand covering mine, pressing against my slickened fingers—

I came with a cry, bending almost double, riding it out. I heard Kian give a groan of pleasure and heard the staccato gasps of his own release. When I finally opened my eyes and slumped down in my chair, legs shaking, he was grinning at me.

We ended the call a few minutes later, promising to stay in touch, promising to be careful. But when he was gone, I sat there staring at the empty screen, wishing I was in LA with him.

I knew how tough he was. And combined with his three brothers and the girls they were a force to be reckoned with.

But I couldn't help thinking that they were in over their heads.

21

ANNABELLE

I'd rediscovered swinging.

Sean had walked off with Louise towards the greenhouse. Sylvie and Aedan had gone to sit in the long, meadow-like grass. Kian had disappeared indoors. So Carrick and I were alone and everything was quiet except for the creak of the ropes and the sound of the wind in the leaves above me.

The swing was built big enough that an adult could use it without feeling silly. It was an oak plank polished until it shone like dark taffy: Sean said it was a floorboard he'd ripped up when he renovated the place. He'd punched two holes through the ends and hung it from ropes from a tree. Then Louise had somehow trained a climbing plant—I had no idea what it was called but it had little purple and white flowers—along the branch and down the ropes. You could sit there facing one way and see nothing but nature and the old, wooden house. Or you could face the other way and look at the city spread out before you like a map. I loved it.

Carrick was pushing me gently, just enough to make my hair billow out behind me on the upswing. The wooden seat was warm through the thin material of my dress and the gentle motion was incredibly soothing. *I haven't done this since I was a kid.* "We need one of these at the cabin," I told him.

"Um-hum."

Something sounded different. I looked over my shoulder: yep, he was smiling. I hadn't seen that in days. *Maybe he figured something out about the cult.* "How's it going?"

"Terrible," he smiled. "Still hitting a brick wall. Maybe that fed had a point: this thing is impenetrable."

I nodded. "I'm stuck too. We all are." Then I frowned. "Wait: so why are you smiling?"

He grinned even wider. "I dunno. I sorted some stuff out. Stuff I should have cleared up a long time ago.' He looked around at the outdoors and took in a deep lungful of air. "Feels good."

I nodded and felt something relax inside me, too. Carrick had always carried so much weight: for the MC, for his brothers. If anyone needed to find peace, it was him.

At that moment, a horn beeped. We looked up to see a truck pulled up outside the house. The same company we'd shipped the bike with.

Carrick's strong hands caught the swing and easily brought it to a stop. Then he drew it backward until my back and ass were pressed against his hard thighs. He moved his hands to my shoulders, covering them in warmth, leaned down and kissed the side of my neck.

"Do you want to go for a ride?" he asked.

Less than ten minutes later, we were roaring down the road towards the shore. The delivery driver had gone pale upon seeing Carrick's leather cut and had stood there twisting his hands together as he apologized for taking so long. Carrick had ignored him, bending to examine every inch of the bike for scratches and dents. To everyone's relief, it was in perfect condition and Carrick simply thanked the driver and wheeled his pride and joy out onto the street, stroking the handlebars as if calming a nervous horse.

I understood that. That's why he and I got on so well, best friends as well as being in love. But as I swung my leg over the bike and nestled up against Carrick's back, I had another of those momentary panics. It wasn't that there was anything wrong. It was that everything was so *right*. I'd been so unhappy, trapped in that house with my step-father for all those years...now that I'd found happiness, I was waiting for the other shoe to drop. *What if something takes him away from me?*

I tightened my arms around his waist and the press of his muscles against my chest calmed me. *Nothing's going to happen.* The engine fired and its roar split the air. It settled down to a steady thump that vibrated through the saddle into both of our bodies. We both sighed at the same instant, then chuckled. We'd missed this.

We rode through Beverly Hills and along Rodeo Drive, the bike's vibrations setting off car alarms in the parked Ferraris and Lamborghinis. We drove out to Venice Beach, parked, and walked along the boardwalk, watching the skaters, ballers and the guys lifting weights at Muscle Beach. By the time we got down onto the sand itself, the sun was going down.

I made straight for the water, letting go of Carrick's hand so I could hop along and pull my sneakers off one by one. A silly grin spread across my face as I felt the sand under my toes. Even though I'd lived in California my whole life, I hadn't been to the beach since I was a kid: my step-father had never taken me, after my mom died. I stepped into the water, gloriously warm even in November. In fact, November was perfect for me: I could enjoy the sun without it burning my pale skin. I rolled up my jeans and went a little deeper. Paddling and swinging in one day: Los Angeles was giving me back the childhood I'd missed.

Then my stomach tightened and I flushed. *I'm being weird again.* All around me, girls with perfect, stick-thin bodies and California tans were prancing around in bikinis and here I was, pale and geeky and acting like I'd never seen the sea before. What if Carrick came to his senses and realized he should be with one of them instead?

A big, warm hand suddenly enclosed mine. I looked up to see Carrick standing beside me, his leather biker boots in one hand, his jeans rolled up just like mine. He didn't say anything, just squeezed my hand.

All my fears dropped away. I slid my arm around his waist and cuddled in closer. We stood there watching the sunset, the waves turning orange and then red as they broke around our ankles, until it was dark. I turned to go but he grabbed me and pulled me back.

The boardwalk lights threw just enough soft white glow to light up those high cheekbones and strong, stubble-dusted jaw. But most of all, they let me see the blue of his eyes. The tenderness and vulnerability I saw there took my breath away. "Can't believe I found you," he rumbled.

I blinked. He couldn't believe *he* found *me?*

He gripped both my arms. "Today's made me think..." He looked away and sighed. "I'm not good at this. But that's kind of the problem. Today's made me realize...maybe I need to get better at saying stuff that's on my mind. Or things can go wrong. Time gets wasted and you can't get it back."

I stared up at him. What had happened between him and Sean? Something had changed. I'd never seen him so open.

He squeezed my arms and then moved his hands to my cheeks, cradling my face. "I want to make sure you know that I love you, Annabelle."

The words went straight to the very center of my heart and I just melted. I tilted my head up just as his mouth came down to meet mine and we were kissing, feet splashing in the water as we shifted position, mouths chasing and exploring, my fingers rasping over his stubble, his hands buried in my hair.

By the time we arrived back at the house, everyone had headed to bed. We crept in like teenagers out past our curfew. I felt bad about disappearing when we should have been working...but when we walked through the hallway and I glanced at the walls, nothing had changed. Everyone had hit the same brick wall we had. Carrick sighed and his grin disappeared.

"What if this is as close as we get?" he asked, reaching out to smooth a piece of paper against the wall. "The *President* tried to look into this, with the help of the FBI. We're just...us."

I put my hand on his. "We'll do it. We'll figure it out." But it didn't sound convincing, even to me. He turned to me and I saw the stress that had been missing all day come flooding back. And beneath it, something I didn't fully understand. Something worse, something that chilled me to my core.

That moment on the beach had laid a lot of things to rest, reassured me about stuff I hadn't even realized I'd been nervous about. Now I needed to make *him* feel better. I took his hand and led the way up the stairs.

In our bedroom, I didn't turn the light on but I kept the drapes open, too. Bathed in moonlight, breaking for kisses, I slowly stripped him, sliding my hands under his leather cut and pushing it off him, then pulling his t-shirt up over his sculpted abs and kissing my way over each hard ridge as it appeared. By the time I got him topless, he was growling with need. He grabbed my top and almost ripped it getting it off me. My bra followed and then my nipples grazed his naked chest and I went weak, crackling pleasure rolling down through my body.

We shoved each other's jeans down our thighs and fell onto the bed in a tangle of legs and denim, racing to see who could get free first. He won and helped me kick mine off my ankles, his eyes lighting up as he saw the flash of copper hair between my thighs. The moon felt like it was right outside our window and, now our eyes had adjusted, it seemed bright as day as he pushed me back on the covers and lowered himself atop me. I moaned as he slid smoothly into me, drawing up my legs and wrapping them around him. He captured my hands, our fingers knitting as he began to thrust.

For the next hour, neither of us thought about anything but each other. It was slow and smooth, his firm ass flexing as he drove into me again and again. Then it was intense and urgent, me riding him, our eyes locked on each other's as the sounds of our pants filled the room and the spiraling pleasure whipped us to go faster and faster. And finally it was primal and savage, him behind me as I knelt, back arched and cheek pressed against the bed sheets, our cries rising together to a peak.

When it was over, he drew me on top of him and we lay there, sated and exhausted. After a while, he dropped off to sleep. I nearly followed...but then I saw the frown creasing his forehead. The sex had been a temporary escape but now the stress was back.

It was so frustrating. Whatever history he'd finally buried with Sean that morning, it had made him happy. If that part of him could be healed, it meant that the much bigger wound, the one he'd suffered when Bradan was ripped from him, could be healed too...if we could only find him.

And then I took a closer look at his face, at the deep lines of worry and pain. This was more than just frustration at being stuck. Much more. I frowned, turning it over and over in my mind. When I finally figured it out, my stomach seemed to drop through the floor.

All these years: the time Carrick had spent in Chicago, the years he'd ridden with the MC... knowing Bradan was out there had been driving him crazy with guilt but at least he'd had hope. If we gave it our best shot and still couldn't find him, that hope would be gone. And that would freakin' *destroy* him. He wouldn't just *not be healed*. He'd never be the same again.

Something new stirred inside me, a steely determination. I had to do something.

I slid out of bed, pulled on my clothes and padded barefoot down to the hallway. Then I sat cross-legged on the floor, staring up at the paper-covered walls.

Carrick was right: we'd hit a brick wall. We had all the information from Calahan but, just like him, we couldn't figure out how to put it together. It just didn't make any sense. The cult felt like a smooth glass sphere in my mind: the harder I gripped it, the more it slid through my fingers. And I knew part of the problem was me. This stuff was all about people: manipulating them, controlling them. It was precisely the sort of thing I didn't understand. What hope did I have?

It started as a feeling, a distant drumbeat I could easily crush. *We've failed.* But the longer I sat there, the louder it got. *We've failed.* *We've failed.* I started to feel nauseous, then full on sick. We were going to have to give up, go back to Haywood Falls and accept that the cult had won. And that would crush the brothers forever.

Tears filled my eyes and I blinked them away. *Why am I so stupid? Why can't I understand this stuff?* Carrick had done so much for me, saved my life again and again. All I wanted was to do this one thing for him. The pages blurred in front of me, becoming one amorphous white blob. I wanted to scream and rage but I hugged my knees instead, trying to choke down the sobs so that I didn't wake anyone—

And then, as I stared at the blurred, swimming scene, I saw something. Felt it, more than saw it. That same feeling I got in New York when we looked up at the skyscrapers and everyone else saw glass and smoothness and beauty but I saw lift shafts and air conditioning ducts and support beams.

With my tears smoothing away the surface stuff I didn't understand, I could see...not a shape, not yet, but the hint that a shape was there. I blinked and it was gone again. But I was sure it had been there.

I stood up and turned in a slow circle, looking at the mass of information. I didn't understand people, or psychology, or any of that stuff. But underneath it all, the cult still had to *work*. And that made it a system. And a system was a machine.

I thought for a while, wiped my eyes, and padded up the stairs. I softly opened the door to Louise's room and crept over to the bed. She was lying half on top of Sean, her long copper hair gleaming in the moonlight. I hesitated, not wanting to wake her. But then I saw her twitch in her sleep, and she was mumbling. A nightmare?

I crept closer and put a hand on her shoulder, intending to shake her awake. But as soon as I touched her, she sat bolt upright. "Mom?" she asked, her voice terrified.

We stared at each other. My mouth worked for a second without speaking: I didn't know how to cope with this. Louise was so organized, so mature, but in that second she'd sounded like a scared little girl. I threw my arms around her and she clutched me back even harder. She was sweating and shaking. "It's okay," I whispered. "It's okay. Just a dream."

Her breathing gradually slowed. Eventually, she moved back, then slid out of bed and led me over to the doorway so we could talk without waking Sean. "Thanks for waking me," she said. Her voice was still ragged with fear. Whatever she'd been dreaming, it had been bad. Was she ill? I only ever got nightmares that intense when I was running a fever. And twice that week, I'd heard her being sick in the bathroom. "Did I call out and wake you?" she asked. "Is that why you came in?"

I shook my head. "No. I needed to ask you for wool."

Louise stared at me as if wondering if she'd misheard. "Wool?"

"Wool."

"In the middle of the night?"

I flushed. "Yes. Sorry. It's an emergency."

Anyone else would have told me where to go. But Louise stumbled sleepily downstairs and started rooting through drawers. "I do have some...I had some crazy idea of knitting something for Sean but I never even got started. Ah, here it is." She handed me a whole bunch of balls of yarn, in different colors.

"Thank you."

"No problem." She yawned. "Happy knitting."

I waited until she'd gone back upstairs. Then I took a deep breath...and began.

22

AEDAN

S he was so...small.

It wasn't often I got to look at her like this. As soon as she realized I was looking at her, she'd ask me what was up, or she'd come over to me, put her hands on my chest, and it would turn into kissing. But now, as she lay there on the bed asleep, sunlight streaming through the window to soak her body in gold, I could just enjoy looking at her.

She lay on her back, utterly trusting, one arm up above her head and the other out to her side. She looked so fragile, so vulnerable...it reminded me of the first time I'd ever set eyes on her, in The Pit: I'd thought she was fragile then, too. Then I'd learned just how tough she was on the inside. And now I stood there next to the bed, my muscled, scarred body hulking over her. *Beauty and the beast.*

I silently crouched down, still watching, my face only a foot from her sleeping one. I'd woken early. Something about California agreed with me: the climate, definitely, but it was more than that. It felt as if there was space to breathe, here. We both had more energy, waking refreshed in a way we never had in Chicago.

Sylvie's dark hair was fanned out across the pillow and the tank top she'd slept in had ridden up to expose a slice of smooth skin just above her navel: it was hard to resist the temptation to dive straight back into bed. But I just crouched there, drinking her in. I needed this time. I needed to think.

I reached carefully under the bed and retrieved the little box I'd hidden there. Popped the top open and looked at the ring. A slender silver band that sort of reminded me of her: slender but strong, graceful and beautiful. And the biggest rock I could afford, gleaming in the morning sunlight and throwing points of light across her sleeping face.

I'd been meaning to ask her for weeks. But it never felt like the right moment. I'd nearly been ready back in Chicago but then Carrick had showed up. Then I'd been going to do it that night, after we'd sparred, and Kian had shown up. Now we were in LA in a house full of people and....

And even if I *could* find the right moment, I didn't know what to say. I've never been good with words. Carrick might be gruff but even he's better at that stuff than me. The others used to give me hell, in school, because I couldn't even mumble my way through a chat-up line. How the hell was I going to ask a girl to marry me?

I loved her. It hurt, actually *ached* when we were apart. She was the strongest, kindest, most beautiful woman I'd ever met. I knew I wanted to spend the rest of my life with her. But what if she wasn't ready? What if I scared her away? *What if she says no?*

She mumbled in her sleep and opened her eyes. Just in time, I jammed the box back under the bed and stood up, then leaned down and kissed her. "It's okay," I whispered. "Sleep a little longer. I'll hit the shower first."

I showered and dressed, gave her another kiss and started down the stairs.

And stopped.

Alien spiders had come in during the night, trailing colored strands from the bodies, and woven an intricate network that covered the entire hallway. The walls were covered in firework-like spray patterns that connected and shot out again in new colors. Some strands spanned the room, stabbing out diagonally from knee height right up to head height, while others formed tight little patterns you had to get right up close to, in order to make them out. I stood there for long minutes, staring so intently that I barely noticed when Carrick and Sean stacked up behind me.

Together, we walked slowly down the stairs and plunged into the dense mesh of threads. Crossing the hallway was like trying to negotiate one of those rooms full of lasers you see in heist movies. We climbed, ducked and side-stepped our way to the tree in the middle of the room. Annabelle was sitting astride a branch at head height.

"What did you *do?*" asked Carrick, looking up at her, awestruck.

"Red is influence," said Annabelle. "Yellow is logistics. Blue is recruitment. Purple is links to front companies. And the garden twine is communications." She glanced at Louise, who'd just appeared at the top of the stairs. "Sorry, I had to raid your gardening supplies. I ran out of colors."

"*You mapped the cult!*" breathed Carrick.

Annabelle looked down at us. "It isn't a cult."

23

LOUISE

My mind couldn't grasp it, at first. I was still half-asleep and the image of my mom from my nightmare was still there every time I closed my eyes, smiling at me just before she and my dad got into their car, the last time I ever saw them alive. *What if that happens to me? What if I have the baby and then....* The baby *and* Kayley would be left on their own. Even without that kind of disaster, I wasn't sure I could be a mom. Sure, I'd just about coped with Kayley —although I was far from perfect—but she was already twelve when I'd taken over, already shaped into a great kid by our parents. A baby was a blank slate and utterly dependent on me. What if I messed it all up? And how the hell would Sean feel about it all? He'd already welcomed Kayley, becoming like a big brother to her, but he hadn't asked for *this*. I needed to tell him but I still hadn't found the right moment. With the house so full all the time, there was precious little time alone...or maybe I was just making excuses.

So it took me a few seconds, after hearing Annabelle say *it isn't a cult*, to say, "*What?!*"

"It isn't a cult," repeated Annabelle.

There was silence. Kian had appeared at the top of the stairs just in time to hear her and I could see him exchanging glances with

Sean, Aedan and Carrick, trying to figure out a way to tell Annabelle she was wrong. I mean, they'd seen the cult up close, they'd seen what it did to their mom.

"I know it looks like a cult," said Annabelle. "But that's the trick. That's what you're meant to think." She jumped down from her branch. "The techniques they use are straight out of a cult: the close-knit groups of followers, the use of drugs, the isolating of people from their families. But that made everyone assume that it was structured like a cult, too. All of us—Calahan, too—we've all been trying to work *upwards*. That's how you always break these things open. In a cult, you'd find the priests and they'd lead you to the high priests and they'd lead you to the overall leader." She turned to face Sean. "Or in a drugs network, the street dealers would lead you to the mid-level dealers who would lead you to the kingpin. Right?"

Sean nodded.

Kian had his phone up and was panning it across the scene. "You getting this?" he said, and I realized he was talking to Emily in DC.

Annabelle continued. "We all thought we were stupid because we couldn't find that command structure. But we couldn't find one because *there isn't one.*" Annabelle waved at the colored threads. "The groups are connected so they can support one another but the connections are local and limited and it isn't hierarchical. The groups are all independent, for safety. Like—"

"Like a terrorist network," grated Kian. "Goddamn it, how did I not see that?" His eyes darted around the network of paper and wool. "That's exactly what it's like."

"So what the hell is it?" asked Aedan.

The whole time she'd been explaining something technical, Annabelle had been confident. Now that she'd come to the end of her knowledge, it was as if she'd remembered she was shy and awkward. "Umm...I'm not sure," she said, flushing a little. She slid down from the tree to stand beside Carrick. "But I think maybe someone built it."

We all stared at her.

"I mean, it's artificial," she said. "A real cult starts because some crazy person believes in something and recruits followers, right? But I don't think the person who started this was crazy. I think they're very, very smart. They're not doing this for ego, they're not interested in being worshipped. It's for something else. I think they took the most effective parts of a cult: the drugs, the recruitment, the intense sessions that bring people under control. And they combined that with the structure of a terrorist network, so it's almost impossible to find the leader. I think they've learned some lessons from organized crime, too: getting DAs and judges under their control. There might be other influences I'm not seeing."

I felt my skin begin to prickle and crawl. This thing had been scary enough before. Now, it was terrifying.

"But who would set all this up?" asked Kian, half to himself. "*Why?*"

Annabelle shook her head. "I don't know. But it means there *is* someone running it, somewhere. Find them, find the heart of this thing, and we can maybe find Bradan. But we aren't going to get any closer from the outside. The whole setup is designed to prevent that." She took a deep breath. "Someone needs to go inside. Someone has to go inside the cult."

24

AEDAN

Sylvie caught my eye across the room and in that instant we both knew. I knew what she was thinking, she knew what I was thinking, we both knew we were going to argue about it.

Everyone else was just staring at each other, aghast at what Annabelle had suggested. "Let's all get something to eat while we think on it," said Kian at last, rubbing his smoothly-shaven chin. He scowled for a second, as if he'd expected to find stubble there.

"I'll join you in a bit," I said. "Need to work out first." I turned to Sylvie, pretending to be casual. "Want to join me?"

"Oh, hell yeah." She stalked past me and out into the garden.

I could feel Kian's eyes on me: he knew there was something wrong but I didn't want to get into it. I just shook my head, grabbed some training pads and followed Sylvie.

She was pacing on the lawn, already fuming. It was still early and the air was cool but the anger was rolling through me, making my skin blaze. I stripped off my t-shirt and threw it to the ground then shoved my hands through the elastic straps on the pads and held them up for Sylvie to hit.

She went into our normal training routine, starting with quick jabs. And as soon as the punches started, the fight began. "You know I'm right," she muttered.

"No. No *way*. I'm not letting you do it." I absorbed two solid blows.

"I'm the only one who can!" She lashed out with a vicious right.

"If anyone's doing it, it'll be me."

"Oh, come on! They already know you! They've got your names and photos from when you were kids. It has to be one of us girls and it's too dangerous for anyone else." Her fists slammed into the pads faster and faster. "I'm the only one who can handle herself!"

I growled. God, she could be so frustrating! I remembered when she'd arrived at the gym for our first day of training, how I'd told her she had no power, no balance, no presence. She'd fixed all those things. When she was fighting for something she believed in, like now, she was the fiercest fighter I'd ever met. But it didn't change the fact she was small. And fragile. And *mine*. I had to protect her from everyone...including herself.

I ripped the pads off my hands and thrust them out to her and she strapped them on. "Didn't you hear what Calahan said?" I asked. "No one has ever escaped the cult. *No one.* Not one feckin' person." I threw a hard left into the pad, then a right, knocking her back with each blow.

Sylvie set her jaw and did her best to hold her ground but I had more raw power. "I want to help!" she yelled.

"If you go in there, you'll not come out again!" I walloped the pad right in the center and she staggered back a good foot.

But then she recovered and stepped forward, chin up, so beautiful it made my heart ache. "I can do it."

I shook my head. It wasn't that I doubted her. I just couldn't risk losing her. "I'm not letting you. Those bastards took my mom. My dad. My brother. I'm not letting them anywhere near you!" I threw punch after punch, driving her back and back....

Suddenly, she threw herself inside my arms, her speed and agility beating my strength. *Feck!* Her lithe body pressed against mine all the way from shoulder to ankle and all the fight went out of me. There were two low thumps as she dropped the pads to the ground.

"You have to let me do this," she said, looking up at me defiantly. "It's the only chance we have of finding Bradan."

I closed my eyes. *Please don't make me make this decision.* I couldn't risk her. Not Sylvie. But I couldn't give up on my brother, either.

No! Tell her no! My chest filled as I inhaled to argue...but Sylvie moved with it, so close I could feel her heartbeat. My angel. My vicious, sweet fighter, willing to do anything in the world for me.

I glared off into the distance, not wanting to accept it. But I knew she was right. *"Feck!"*

"You'll be right there," she told me.

"You're fucking right I will be," I grated. Just talking about the plan, the fear was like an iron band across my chest.

She laid a soothing palm over my heart. "You won't let them take me."

I captured her in my arms and crushed her against me. "Damn right I won't," I breathed.

It was long minutes before I finally relaxed my grip and looked down into her eyes. I stroked a lock of dark hair off her cheek. *I have to marry this woman.* It wasn't just her beauty or the way she saw the good in me. It was *this,* this strength inside her. Who else would do what she was doing? Who else would put themselves in harm's way to help me and my brothers?

The ring was under the bed. I could do it right now. *Sylvie, just wait here a 'sec.* I'd ask her to close her eyes, run upstairs and get it, and when I told her to open them again I'd be kneeling in front of her.

I stared down into her eyes, torn. No. Not now, not just after we'd been arguing. She deserved for it to be perfect. And then, because I couldn't look at those lips a second longer without kissing her, I leaned down and did exactly that.

25

SYLVIE

The kiss was like an anti-fight. Every soft contact healed us, every brush of his lips let us know how much we needed each other. All of our anger rushed out of us, meeting in our lips and cancelling out. The way I opened under him, the way he owned my mouth...it said what we needed without words. He only wanted to protect me; I only wanted to help him.

The anger evaporated but that left behind the adrenaline. Just like when we fought in the ring, all that tension and fight-or-flight edginess had to go somewhere. His tongue swept across my lip and my whole body stiffened, the heat welling up inside me and then searing out to every part of me, making me tremble. I flexed against him, spine arching, wanting, *needing,* to put every inch of me against every inch of him.

He broke the kiss just long enough to look at me again and when I saw how those blue eyes were clouded with lust, I went weak. I took a staggering step back, overwhelmed for a second by the size of him, the brute strength of him.

He followed, pressing up against me, not allowing even an inch of air between us. His hands slipped under the back of my tank top and up my back, rough fingers over naked skin. I drew in a shuddering gasp of cool morning air and when I breathed it back out against his chest, it was scalding hot. I could hear both of us panting, desperate. "Let's go upstairs," I said.

In answer, he leaned down and kissed me again, deep and hot, making me his. He captured my lower lip between his teeth and sucked on it, making me groan.

He looked towards the house. "Everyone else is having breakfast." So innocent a sentence. But the Irish in his voice, the low growl as he said it, loaded each word with dark promise. I knew exactly what he meant and the idea of it made my head swim with fear...and excitement.

Both of us glanced at the swing. Then, before I could say anything, Aedan had put his hands under my ass and lifted me off the ground, my legs automatically going around his waist. He walked over to the swing and set me down on the seat, kneeling down before me as I grabbed hold of the flower-covered ropes. He was so big, we were now almost eye-to-eye.

He knee-walked forward and I spread my knees to let him in, the denim of my jeans rasping against his. He only stopped when he was right up against the wood of the seat, my legs open wide to accept him, the feel of his muscled torso between them making me heady.

Then he started kissing me again and, as my eyes closed, I felt his hands peel my tank top up my body and over my breasts. I felt the cups of my bra flip up and then my breasts were throbbing in the outside air, nipples tightening in the cold for a second before his hot mouth enveloped them and I cried out in delight.

His mouth pressed me slowly back, his size and strength not giving me a choice even though the last thing I wanted was to resist. His tongue swirled around my nipple sending crackling, sparking streamers of pleasure through me. My hands tightened on the ropes and my arms straightened as I leaned back, back.... My ass shifted on the wooden seat, scooching forward until my groin was right up against him. He pressed harder in towards me and I groaned as the hard ridges of his naked abs stroked my inner thighs and the softness between them.

My arms reached their limits but he was still pushing my upper body back. I tentatively released my grip on the ropes, trusting him, and felt his big hands slip under my shoulders to support me. He had most of one breast in his mouth now, the soft flesh engulfed in heat, his tongue circling, making me twist and grind my hips in response. I leaned further and further back, my legs kicking out and straightening to balance me, feet off the ground. Aedan was leaning right over me: when I opened my eyes for a brief second, his hulking body blocked out the sun—

And then I felt my hair go slack and realized it was trailing on the ground beneath me. I was lying flat, supported only by my ass on the swing and Aedan's hands under my shoulders. He held me there, working my breasts slowly and firmly with his mouth. Hard licks that made me quiver right to my core. Soft bites, lips covering his teeth, until I was thrashing and panting, my denim-clad ass twisting on the wood, my outstretched fingers clawing at the grass above my head. "I need to," I said in a strangled voice. "I need *you*."

His hands grabbed mine, hauling me back up to sitting. But he didn't stop there: he jumped to his feet, pulling me to standing, and I gasped as the sudden movement sent cool air washing against my spit-wet breasts. While I was still catching my breath, he pulled my tank top and bra off over my head. Then his hands were at the buttons of my jeans and mine were at his, both of us panting with anticipation.

I couldn't resist running my hand over the bulge at his groin and he growled. Then I was shoving his jeans and jockey shorts down around his thighs and his cock sprang free. He didn't bother taking them the rest of the way off, too focused on helping me pull my jeans and panties down my legs, my sneakers going with them in a tangled mess. Then he was picking me up and twisting around. I realized what he was going to do only a second before he did it.

He sat down on the swing. A good thing it had been built for grownups: his muscled hips only just fit. He pulled a condom from the pocket of his jeans and rolled it on. Then his hands were on my naked ass, urging me forward....and *down*.

I took a deep breath and glanced over my shoulder at the house. No sign of anyone. I put one foot on the seat of the swing and stepped up into the air, grabbing the ropes for support. I gingerly threaded my feet between the ropes and his body so that I was astride him, facing him. Then I lowered myself down.

My eyes widened as I felt the first hot touch of him against my wet folds. We'd never done it quite like this before. We could stare right into each other's eyes as I slowly sank down onto him, using my feet on the ground and my hands on the ropes for support. I rocked forward and back a little, experimenting, then gasping as I got it just right and he slid up into me.

My fingers gripped the ropes hard and then I worked my way down, a finger width at a time, sinking, sinking. Low groans and pants stirred the air between us as I took him, feeling every inch of him: that wonderful stretch. I lowered and lowered, teeth gritted with the effort of holding back, letting him slowly fill me. And then my ass touched down against the hardness of his thighs and I slumped against him, my naked breasts pillowed against his pecs. He was in me to the root.

We kissed, long and slow, our bodies seeming to meld into one. His thumbs found the little creases at the top of my thighs that drive me crazy and I wriggled against him, gasping. Then his palms slid along my legs towards my feet, urging them upward. Urging me to take my feet off the ground.

I lifted...and moaned. I was weightless, sitting completely in his lap, and there was the soft movement like the rocking of a boat as the swing moved. A slow, lazy throb of pleasure strummed through me as my body tightened and relaxed around the hardness inside me. With every breath, I could smell the flowers on the ropes. I could feel the cool outdoor air lapping at our bodies, caressing every part of us save for our fronts. We were so closely joined that not even a breath of wind could get between us.

There was a pause: everything *stopped*. I opened my eyes and found I was staring straight into his. Aedan looked at me with more passion, more *need* than I'd ever seen. And something else, too: a rare second of pure, Irish wickedness. He arched one dark brow.

I realized what he had in mind and my eyes went wide. *Could we? How would it feel?* The blood was rushing in my ears, the pleasure tightening and coiling in anticipation. My eyes answered for me. *Yes!*

Aedan straightened his legs and we lifted. I gulped, clutching at the ropes: it was like that moment on the runway when the plane gathers itself for take-off.

And then we swung.

My hands were already gripping the ropes but now they clutched frantically, working higher and higher. As we swung forward, my weight seemed to increase: I was pushed down on Aedan's cock, grinding there, and as I leaned instinctively forward against him, the base pressing hard against my clit. My whole body trembled, pleasure rushing and soaring inside me, my legs kicking out behind him.

Then we reached the apex of the swing and I was weightless for a second. He fell a fraction of a second before me, his cock drawn from me with satiny smoothness...and then I was chasing him down, the delicious weight and *crush* against his muscled thighs and abs, the swell of pleasure as his angle changed inside me. My hair flew out behind me as we rose. We reached the top of our backswing, me facing up into the sky and him down towards the ground, and then *I* was hooking my legs back beneath us and we were plunging back down again.

Every swing was a glorious, heart-pounding rush of sensation. It was so intense and yet so intimate because we hardly moved, relative to each other. We could stare into each other's eyes as the world sailed past us, experiencing every second of each other's pleasure.

Without words, we kicked harder. Swung faster. We drew our breath in on each swing and panted it out at each apex. His hands reached up and covered mine on the ropes. The tiny movements of him inside me, no more than an inch or so of travel, meant I could focus on every tiny sensation: his heat, his hardness, the twitch of his hips as he got close.

I was barely hanging on myself, the pleasure twisting in on itself, growing hotter and brighter with each pass of our heels over the ground. I'd never experienced anything like it, had never climbed towards my peak so smoothly and steadily. I could feel how wet I was around him, how hard his whole body had become. His thighs, under me, felt like rock. The ropes creaked. The air rushed past our bodies. My naked toes strained for the sky and—

He leaned forward and kissed me, letting go of the ropes to tangle his fingers in my hair, and I groaned and panted my orgasm into his mouth. It was like dawn breaking, huge and unstoppable, washing through every part of me. Aedan kissed me deep and hard, his hips drawing back just a little...and then, when he could hold it no longer, his hips surged forward and he broke the kiss, arching his back and thrusting up into me as he released.

26

SYLVIE

It was strange, waiting to become a victim. It went against every instinct I had. As a woman, I'd learned about avoiding situations that put me at risk. I'd come to trust those gut feelings that tell you to *get out, now,* because someone means you harm. Then Aedan had taught me how to stand up to people and intimidate them, fight them if necessary.

And now all of that was useless. If we wanted to find Bradan, I had to just wander through the crowd, oblivious to everything around me. I couldn't be cautious or alert: if they picked up on that, they wouldn't approach me. I had to be a lamb to the slaughter.

It was early afternoon, two days after we'd decided that I should infiltrate the cult. I was at an alternative spirituality and lifestyle fair, the fourth one I'd visited. It was being held in a convention center, a huge hall filled with hundreds of booths, stalls and tents. Calahan's notes had said that the cult sometimes recruited at them. We'd managed to piece together a very rough idea of what sort of people they were looking for: intelligent, stable but in need of something, looking for guidance or direction. It was a pretty loose description and I didn't know if I was projecting the right image. How do you look like you're in need of something? Especially when you're not.

One thing I knew: with Aedan in my life, I wasn't in need of a damn thing.

I wandered the aisles, getting more and more edgy. All around me, people were offering everything from yoga retreats to crystal healing, from ingredients for casting spells to courses on how to become more "marriable." Some of it was very mainstream, some of it was weird as hell. But I hadn't seen anything that might be the cult.

"Find anything good?"

I twisted to find the voice. The woman was standing to my side, grinning at me. She had long, laser-straight hair the color of corn and was a few years younger than me. "Sorry. Just: I keep seeing you wandering around. I've been here like, two hours? Is there anything *good?*"

I smiled and relaxed. It was a relief to take a break from the mission, just for thirty seconds. "Not much. A lot of *weird.*" I pointed. "There's a really big guy with no shirt and a walrus mustache selling massages back there."

The woman's face fell. "Oh! Um. That's my dad."

My smile collapsed and I flushed beet red. "Oh, *shit.* I'm really— I'm sure he's—"

She snorted and doubled over, laughing, shaking her head. "I'm sorry. Couldn't resist. Your *face!*"

I blinked and then grinned myself. I liked her. She reminded me of myself, before my parents died, when I was still carefree.

"I'm Gwen," she told me.

"Sylvie."

"Nice to meet you, Sylvie." She threw an arm around my waist and we started walking. "So what brings you here?"

I opened my mouth and then hesitated. I figured I should probably maintain my cover, just in case anyone was listening. "I'm not sure," I said at last. "I just sort of feel like there's something missing."

Gwen nodded. "I'm the same. Went to a talk this morning on voluntary work overseas, helping to build schools and stuff, but it didn't feel like my thing." She looked at me with big, concerned eyes. "Does that make me a bad person?"

I gripped her arm. "No! Not at all. I think you've got to find what works for you." I was sure she was a student, now. She really did remind me of me when I was younger, happy and eager but full of self-doubt. I looked around as we passed more stalls. "I've been here for hours and I haven't found anything that grabs me."

Gwen sighed. "Closest I came was with a sort of...I don't even know what you'd call them. A movement? Trying to just sort of...make the world better. Help each other."

"Yeah? What do they call themselves?"

"Aeternus."

I had to work hard to look casual. "So what happened?"

Gwen shook her head. "The guy was really nice and everything. But I think it's more for people a couple of years older. Like, with a job and everything. I didn't want to be the only one my age."

I nodded, trying to contain the swelling excitement in my chest. Maybe the cult didn't recruit anyone under twenty-one, to avoid trouble from worried parents. I looked around. "Whereabouts were they?"

"Way down the other end," said Gwen, pointing. "They're sort of hidden away at the back. C'mon, I'll show you."

I let her tow me along, nodding and smiling as she started talking about the classes she was taking and the party she was going to that night. But I could feel myself gearing up for a fight, physical and mental. This was it. This was going to be the first time any of us had actually met someone from the cult. I straightened my spine, felt my breathing quicken. I realized I was unconsciously forming fists with my hands and had to force myself to stop. *Act innocent! Be the victim!*

That thought sent unease snaking up my spine. Gwen thought she was being friendly and helpful but she was leading me right to people we knew were incredibly dangerous. What if I really did become a victim, just another of the cult's thousands of members?

At that moment, we passed a stall selling palm readings...and when the huge, broad-shouldered man browsing it turned his head, I saw that it was Aedan. He caught my eye for a second. I hadn't seen him look so scared for me since we'd stepped into the hay bale ring to fight each other to the death. He looked as if he wanted to grab my hand, tear me away from Gwen, and drag me home to safety. I had to look away quickly so that Gwen didn't notice. But the fact he was here, watching me, pushed my own fear away. And somewhere here, Sean and Louise, Carrick and Annabelle and Kian were watching, too. Six people had my back. I was perfectly safe.

Just as Gwen said, the tent was hard to find. It was small, only about ten feet across, wedged up against the wall at the very back of the hall. You had to push between the final row of stalls to get to it: if I hadn't known, I would have presumed it was some employees-only thing. "There you go," she said.

"Okay. Hey, thanks."

Gwen beamed. "No problem. I'm going to run: I want to have a last look around and then I have to get back for classes. Nice meeting you."

She gave me a quick, unexpected hug and dashed off. And I was left staring at the entrance to the tent. *Am I really going to do this?* All my fears suddenly came back.

Then I glanced back along the aisle and saw Aedan, then Sean, then Kian, all watching me. If I backed out now, none of them would blame me. When Aedan and I had come in from the garden and told the others our plan, they'd all tried to talk me out of it.

But if I ran, we'd lose our only chance to find Bradan. I took a deep breath and pushed through the tent flaps.

Gwen must have taken me to the wrong tent.

I'd unconsciously developed expectations, a couple of vague stereotypes in my head. One was the old, silver-haired guy in long white robes who'd call me *my child* and would speak in a calming voice and then try to grope me. The other was a young, Hollywood-handsome guy, all white teeth and infectious laugh, who'd talk me into signing away all my possessions.

But this guy? This guy looked like someone's dad.

He was in his fifties with soft, curling hair that refused to lie straight and was thinning on top. He wore a white shirt with his slacks but no tie and he was just a little overweight. He sat behind an office desk and, save for some crates, that's all there was in the tent: no incense or crystal balls or cushions to sit on.

He looked up from his paperwork and grinned at me. It wasn't salacious or predatory, it didn't creep me out. It was friendly and curious. When I just stood there staring, he said, "You look a little lost."

I am definitely in the wrong place. "I'm sorry. My friend said..." I looked over my shoulder, towards the hall, but the tent flaps had swung closed behind me. It was warm inside the tent: the hall's air conditioning didn't reach in here. "I was looking for Aeternus."

He spread his arms wide. This time, his grin was almost sheepish. "You found them!" He glanced down at himself, then around at the tent, as if he was afraid he didn't quite measure up.

I was utterly thrown. This couldn't be them. This couldn't be the same group who brainwashed Aedan's mom, who manipulated the courts and had their dad thrown in jail. Who spirited away Bradan, never to be seen again. I stood there with my mouth open like an idiot until the guy took pity on me. "What made you seek us out?" he asked.

"I..." I didn't know what to do. The plan was for me to sit through whatever talk they gave me, asking questions where I could and finding out as much as possible. Then I'd leave and, if I hadn't gotten what we needed, the guys would come in and we'd damn well beat it out of him. But I couldn't imagine us beating this guy. He was so...*normal. Stick to the plan,* I decided. *Play along.* "I guess...I feel like there's something missing in my life," I lied.

He nodded. "What's missing?"

I wasn't ready for that. "I...I don't know."

"You're not happy?"

"No. I mean, yes, I'm happy."

"You have a job? A home?"

"Yes. Both of those. But...." Even though it was only an act, I started to feel ashamed, like an over-privileged idiot. Why was he trying to push me away? Was I *not suitable,* like Gwen?

"Friends?" he asked.

"Yeah," I said firmly. And then felt a stab of guilt, as if I'd lied. *But I do have friends!* I had Aedan and Alec....

The guy just waited patiently. He must have been able to see something in my expression because he looked sympathetic. My face went hot. *No! I don't need your sympathy! I'm not some crazy cat lady who lives all alone with no friends!* I was *just fine.* I wanted him to know that. But I couldn't seem to find a way to explain.

"You're friendly," the guy said slowly. "There are people you work with, people you say hi to when you go into their store, and people you talk to every day on the internet. But if one of those people says: hey, how are you doing? And actually, something's really wrong in your life? You don't feel you can tell them so you lie and say you're okay. And if you have an emergency, a real crisis, at three in the morning, you scroll through your list of Facebook friends and there's no one you know well enough to call."

My mouth moved but nothing came out for a few seconds. "Yes," I said at last.

The guy nodded. "I know exactly how that feels." For the first time, he gave me a long, steady look, right in the eye, and it felt like he actually did know. He leaned back in his chair, nodding at the one across from him, and I sat. "I'm Martin, by the way."

"Sylvie." I could feel something inside me. Not something new: something that had been there for a long time, but that I'd never admitted to myself until now. A deep, dark chasm.

"You want some water?" He picked up a jug of water from the desk.

Suddenly, I felt myself go straight back onto high alert. *No! They use drugs! Don't eat or drink anything!* I shook my head. "I'm good." I hadn't realized how much I'd relaxed. Why had I sat down? If he'd asked me to, I probably would have said *no* to that, too, but he'd just sort of nodded to the chair and I'd done it. *Stay focused!* I sat up straight.

Martin dropped a slice of lemon into his glass and poured himself some water, then sat back in his chair. "You've suddenly gone nervous," he said.

I flushed and tried to relax my shoulders. Maybe I wasn't good at all this spy stuff: he could read me like a book. I felt stupid...and *hot*. God, it was hot in here: with the tent flaps closed, no air was moving. No wonder he'd wanted the water. I wished I'd asked for one, now: clearly it wasn't drugged if he was drinking it. "Yeah," I said. "I'm just nervous about getting involved with something...." I trailed off but he waited patiently for me. "...weird," I said at last.

He raised an eyebrow as if offended, but he was trying not to laugh, too.

I flushed again. "Sorry, I didn't mean..." *Why am I apologizing?* "I just don't want to be....changed."

"*Changed?*" He leaned forward, concerned. "You think that's what we do?"

I was completely lost. One half of me was screaming that this was the enemy, that these were the people Calahan, even the President had warned us about. The other half of me was telling me not to be ridiculous. "Isn't it?" I asked lamely. I licked my lips: my mouth had gone dry, in the heat. "I mean, isn't that what all, um...movements do? Get you all thinking the same way, so you're all...clones?"

"*No,*" said Martin with what sounded like genuine sadness. He lowered his voice: I had to really concentrate to hear it. "We're the *opposite* of that. We celebrate difference. We think that everyone has something to offer. Everyone has unique skills, you included." He said the last two words with such firmness that I felt a little glow of pride, despite everything. "And we think that we can all use them to make the world a better place." He closed his eyes and smiled. "Does that sound corny?"

Actually it sounded...perfectly reasonable. Nice, even. But I said, "A little."

He shook his head and looked around. "Sorry. This isn't really my department, introducing new people. I'm more of a numbers guy, I help out with the books."

I found myself nodding. I was relaxing again. Every time my alarm bells went off, he said something that quieted them. My mouth was so *dry*. And Martin was drinking his water again, it looked so good. *It's safe. He's drinking it.* But what if he'd somehow made himself immune to it? Or taken some counter-drug first. I cursed inwardly: was I being stupidly paranoid or healthily cautious?

Then I saw my salvation. Sitting in the corner was a whole pallet of Coke, the cans still in their shrink wrap. No way *that* was drugged, not unless Coca-Cola was in league with the cult. "Um...could I have a Coke, please?"

He looked around as if he'd forgotten it was there, then grinned and went over to grab me one. "Sure!" It took him a moment to wrestle one free of all the packaging. "It's pretty warm, I'm afraid."

"Warm is fine." I was grinning, so relieved to finally have something to drink.

Martin opened up an ice bucket, dropped a couple of cubes of ice into a glass, added a slice of lemon and poured in the Coke. "Let me tell you about me," he said, settling back in his chair again.

I took a drink of my Coke. Oh, God that was good. The ice chilled it just enough and I could feel it sluicing through my body, taking my temperature down.

"I thought I was no good to anyone," said Martin. He stopped and looked me in the eye. "You think I'm going to say I was a criminal, don't you? A drug addict, on the street, and then I found Aeternus and turned my life around?"

I felt my face grow hot again. I *had* been thinking it would be something along those lines. "No," I lied. I drank some more Coke to cover my embarrassment.

He threw back his head and laughed: a warm, easy sound. *Comforting.* "It's nothing that dramatic," he said apologetically. "I had a good life. Worked in a nice office. I was an accountant. That's why I help out with the books now: that's my skill. And I knew people. I went out for beers with the guys I worked with. But I worked pretty hard. Didn't have much time to socialize. My close friends took jobs in other cities and we drifted apart."

I nodded. That sounded a lot like me, back in New York. With our parents dead, Alec and I had been too busy working to pay the bills to have social lives. And all of my friends were at college: when I had to drop out, I lost touch with them.

"I mean...I was okay," said Martin. "I don't want to sound like I was sat at home with no life. I *knew* plenty of people. I just..." He sighed. "I had friends but not...*buddies*. Guys you can go and get drunk with when you've broken up with your girlfriend. Guys who'd have your back in a bar fight. Guys you'd tell your deepest secrets to. Friends for *life*. You know? I didn't have *that*."

I leaned forward in my chair and nodded again. That did sound eerily familiar. I had Alec, of course. But we'd leaned on each other so heavily that I'd never found my own tight circle of friends. And now he was off with Jessica. Sure, I had Aedan, but who was I supposed to talk to *about* Aedan, about female stuff, about how I was feeling? Sometimes, I'd type a message to someone I knew on Facebook and then delete it, unsent, because I didn't know them well enough. I wanted women I could sit and talk to, with wine and a tub of ice cream and a movie on in the background that no one wound up watching because we were all getting stuff off our chests about husbands and boyfriends and bosses and life. And I didn't have them. It was worse now I was living in Chicago and didn't know anyone but even in New York, I'd felt alone. And I'd never felt able to talk to anyone about it, not even Alec or Aedan, because not having friends is a problem you're meant to have when you're six. I could feel the chasm inside me more clearly, now, deep and black and spilling out freezing air.

"I guess..." Martin looked at the ceiling, thinking. He almost seemed to have forgotten I was there. "I guess...sometimes, I just needed to know if I'm acting crazy. I wanted friends who knew me well enough to tell me if I was being an idiot. And friends who could reassure me I wasn't going nuts when I got angry or upset or whatever. Friends I didn't have to pretend with, you know?" He looked at me and grinned, sheepish again. "I'm sorry. Is this making any sense at all?"

I nodded a third time. *Yes!* I drank some more of my Coke. *This is just like me!*

"So...I started looking around, much like you did today. And I found Aeternus. For the first time, I was part of something. Something bigger than me, something...warm." He looked down at his desk and went quiet for a while. "*Real* friends. Friends you can share anything with. Friends who'd do anything for each other. And after so long being silently lonely, it just felt..." He shook his head. "It's hard to describe. Can you imagine how good it felt?"

And I could. The chasm was yawning wide inside me, now, chilling me, and I could imagine it filled with light and warmth, with friends who'd giggle and sob and hug. Real friends, not just names in a list of likes on a Facebook post. I imagined all that love and affection radiating out, filling me instead of the loneliness emptying me. "*Yes!*" I said firmly.

Martin nodded. "Why don't you tell me your story?"

And I began.

27

AEDAN

"Something's wrong," I said. My eyes were locked on the door of the tent.

"It's fine," said Kian in my ear. He'd bought some radios and earpieces for all of us so we could stay in touch without clustering together and looking suspicious. Maybe it felt normal for him, being a Secret Service agent, but the feel of the plastic bud in my ear was driving me crazy. "This was always the plan. She needs to talk to them, get everything she can out of them. Then she'll walk out and we'll go in."

I nodded, as much to reassure myself as him. I knew I should trust him: he had more experience than any of us in this kind of thing. But all I could think about was Sylvie. It had been over an hour since she entered the tent. *I should never have agreed to this.* "Is everyone okay?" I snapped for about the tenth time.

What I meant was, *is everyone alert? Is everyone watching?* With six of us keeping the tent in view, there was no way Sylvie could leave without us knowing. Two or three would have been plenty. But I wanted to know we were doing everything we could. Carrick and Annabelle sounded off, then Kian and Sean. But Louise stayed silent. "Louise?"

"Yep!" she said suddenly. "Sorry! I mean: I'm here."

I whirled around, trying to find her. Then I spotted her, staring at a stall that sold birthstones for babies. *Help your baby sleep soundly! Only $19.99!* "Pay attention!" I snapped, more harshly than I meant to.

Kian's voice came over my earpiece, authoritative and calming. "It's okay, brother. I know it's hard but we've got to wait it out."

I was silent for a second. My fists itched with the need to hit something. I hoped to God there were at least four cult members in there, one for each of us. When we went in, I was going to annihilate mine, pound him into a bloody pulp on the floor. *These are the bastards who took our parents.* The rage rose inside me, scarlet and burning, but the fear was still there, coiled around it like a snake, twisting my guts into a tight, hard knot. *They took our parents...and I let Sylvie go in there.* It tightened and tightened until I had to let the words escape. "What if they're— What if they've got her in there and they're...*doing stuff* to her—"

"This is Sylvie," said Carrick. "*Sylvie.* Anyone tries to touch her and they're going to lose the arm."

I knew he was right: Sylvie could take care of herself. But this was worse than when I'd had to watch her fight, back in New York. Then, at least I was right there watching her. Knowing she was in danger, unable to see her or do anything...*is this how the girls feel, when they know we're in the shit? How they hell do they cope?* I was almost panting with tension, now. I wanted to yell, to scream, to charge in there. Just standing still was the hardest thing in the world. "We should have put a microphone on her," I muttered.

"Too dangerous," said Kian. "You've heard what they do to people who try to investigate them. This way, she's just another recruit. And that means they won't hurt her, not here in a public place. The only danger is if they took her away somewhere and we're all watching the tent. So—"—his voice had been growing harder but he suddenly softened, maybe remembering it wasn't some Secret Service guy he was talking to. "So just hang in there, okay, brother?"

And suddenly he was there beside me. He slapped a big,

comforting hand on my shoulder and looked at me, questioning and concerned.

I sighed and nodded, relaxing a little. God, it felt good to be with my brothers again. I looked towards the tent. *Why didn't I propose?* I'd nearly done it just before we left for this place, had actually caught her hand in the hallway and put my hand on the ring in my pocket. But it had felt wrong, then. Like we were promising to be together forever but our very first act would be to separate. I knew that if I asked her then, I wouldn't be able to let her go through with this. So I'd pulled her close and just kissed her instead, letting the ring drop back into my pocket.

Now it sat there scalding my thigh and I wondered why I'd been so stupid. *As soon as I get her home. The second I get her home.*

"Five more minutes," I said darkly, glaring at the tent. "Then I'm going in after her."

28

SYLVIE

I t all just came out. My parents dying, Alec and I trying to support ourselves, his injury and coma, my volunteering to fight in his place. I never normally talked about personal stuff: I'd shared my story with the others, when we'd arrived at Sean and Louise's house, and of course I shared everything with Aedan. But I'd never tell my life story to a stranger.

Now...it was as if I was connected to Martin, in a way I'd never been connected to anyone. It was like basking in the warm glow of a fire when you're cold. All he was doing was silently listening but it felt somehow active, as if he was drawing my secrets out of me. Having secrets from him hurt, like they were jagged little slivers of ice, and pushing them out of me brought welcome relief.

Then he suddenly glanced at his phone and jumped to his feet, collecting his paperwork. "Oh God, I'm sorry. It's been over an hour," he said. "I've kept you way too long."

I blinked and just stayed sitting there. "What?" *No, it's okay. I don't want to go.*

"I'm sorry," said Martin. "I'd love to hear the rest. But I have a thing I have to go to."

I felt this sense of...*loss.* Like I was being dragged away from the warm glow, maybe forever. Martin moved towards the tent door and I looked at it in horror, imagining how cold it would be outside. "Please," I said. "Can't we keep talking? Maybe I could come with you?"

He shook his head. "It's really just for members. Just five or six of us sitting around talking. I shouldn't really—"

"*Please!*" Somewhere, distantly, I was shocked by how forcefully I said it. "I want to. Can I come?"

He bit his lip and I *prayed.* And then he seemed to take pity on me. "Okay," he said. "But we've got to go right now."

I nodded quickly and stood. It was harder than it should have been to push my chair back and get clear of the table, but Martin helped me. And then he led me to the back of the tent and pulled aside the canvas. There was a door there. "This way," he said, pushing it open. Blinding daylight flooded in, dazzling me.

I frowned and stopped for a second. Somewhere in the back of my mind, there was a memory. A sort of warning. Something that I must not do.

"Come on, Sylvie," said Martin. He stepped halfway through the door. "Or I'll have to go without you."

That woke me up: I could feel the warm glow slipping away, the further I got from him. I caught up to him and followed him to his car.

29

AEDAN

"Enough." The five minutes I'd given it were up.

"Wait," said Kian beside me. He grabbed my shoulder but I tore away from him, marching towards the tent. Out of the corner of my eye, I could see Sean and Carrick muscling forward to join me, all of us converging on the canvas door. I was breathing hard, shoulders already pulling back, fists coming up, ready to smash and grab and throw. *I am going to devastate these fuckers.*

I burst through the tent flaps and saw—

Nothing. A table with a jug of water. Some crates. No sign of Sylvie or anyone else.

"No," I said aloud. I heard the others flood in behind me. "No. No, no, no—"

"That's impossible," said Kian, his voice tight with fear. *"We were watching the door!"*

"Is there a second room?!" Sean's voice was incredulous. We all started checking the walls: was there another part to the tent? Was it bigger than it looked?

Then I found the opening at the rear. Swept the canvas aside and found the door. I felt the bile rising in my throat. "Oh Jesus," I whispered in terror.

I pushed open the door and we were looking at the parking lot. Cars. A million cars.

Carrick barreled past me. "I'll get my bike," he said. "They might still be here, or on the street!" He sprinted off.

Sean was next out of the door. "I'll drive up and down the rows, try and spot her." And he ran off to fetch the Mustang. But I knew it was useless. For all we knew, she'd left almost an hour ago.

I turned to see Kian standing there with his hands up to placate me. "She'll be okay," he said quickly. "She's smart. She's strong—"

"*It's Sylvie!*" I yelled. And I just lost it: I took one step forward and punched him full force in the jaw. Even with his size and weight, he lifted clear of the ground and crashed down on the desk, snapping its legs. The glass water jug shattered and the ice bucket spewed cubes across the floor. "It's Sylvie, not one of your fucking Secret Service agents!"

He lay there glaring up at me, furious...but then I saw how pale his face was, underneath the anger. "I know," he croaked.

He was feeling the same fear I was. He wasn't trying to be an asshole. He was just trying to reassure me. I turned away and let him get up. I wasn't up to apologizing, right now. "We need to call the cops," I said and pulled out my phone.

Kian got slowly to his feet. "We can't," he said. He sounded so *calm.* How the fuck did he do that? "They've got people deep in the cops."

I ignored him. My hands were shaking so hard with fear, I hit *8* twice before I got the *9* of *911.*

Kian put a hand on my wrist, catching me just before I hit *call.* His lip was bleeding but he still managed to keep his touch gentle. "If the cops tip them off, if they guess she's trying to infiltrate them, they could kill her."

I slowly moved my thumb away from the call button. Every muscle in my arm was screaming: I was squeezing my phone so hard the casing creaked. *Sylvie!*

Sean's voice on the radio, breathless with panic, the Irish coming through strong. "She's not anywhere in the parking lot."

Carrick, his Harley's engine thumping in the background. "Nothing on the street."

I turned and kicked the nearest thing, a crate of Coke. Cans flew and scattered but the soft canvas walls soaked up the impacts with no sound at all. We'd thought we were being so fucking clever. Everyone had warned us not to do this. *Everyone.* And now they had Sylvie. We were in completely over our heads.

Kian reached for me again but I just shook my head and barged out of the tent, back into the fair. Thousands of people were cheerfully chatting away, buying and selling, unaware anything was wrong. I wanted to scream in their faces. Didn't they realize she was gone? Didn't they realize I'd lost her?

Kian caught up to me. I could see the guilt in his eyes: all those times he'd told me not to go into the tent, all those times he'd said everything was fine. "We'll find her," he told me.

But we had no idea where to even start looking.

30

SYLVIE

The sunset was lighting up the interior of Martin's car in oranges and golds by the time we arrived. I had no idea where we were: it was an upmarket, leafy suburb but I didn't know if we were north or south of the city. But it didn't matter. As long as I stayed with him, I could stay within the warm, comforting glow. The idea of being away from him was *cold*, cold like a lamppost on a freezing day, so cold I was worried that if I thought of it too long, my mind would stick to it and hurt when I tore it away. I'd never felt so desperate to stay in someone's company. Not even....

I blinked.

Aedan. Why had I had to concentrate to remember his name? I must be tired.

Martin showed me inside. It was modern and comfortable and very clean, with couches that looked like they'd wrap you up in a warm hug. Thick blackout blinds were already drawn and the only light came from table lamps spaced around the room on low tables, the walls disappearing into shadow.

Four people were already there, two men and two women. They were in two pairs, their voices quiet. The mood was hard to describe. It was like those moments you get very late at night, when the party's long over and a few close friends sit around having earnest, heartfelt conversations. I was nervous for a second. They must know each other very well, to talk like that. What if me being there was awkward?

But immediately, one of the women jumped to her feet and ran over. She was older than me, with long straight black hair shot through with strands of silver. "I'm Julie," she told me, smiling. I found myself smiling back. "Come and sit down. We're going to be great friends."

Great friends. The words seemed to roll around inside my head, inside my *heart,* and a part of me lit up pink and bright. I smiled even harder and that seemed to please Julie.

I thought I'd be talking to Martin but he started talking to the woman Julie had been talking to and she sat with me. As she asked me my name and we began to talk, I realized that each pair was made up of one newcomer, like me, and one person like Julie or Martin, from...I frowned. From...the cult? That was the word I remembered having in my head, when I came here, but it seemed so silly, now. This wasn't a cult. It was just a group of friendly people. *When I go home, I need to tell everyone how wrong they were.*

We seemed to talk for hours. Julie wanted to know everything about me, so much that my mouth got dry and they had to keep bringing me more Cokes. Sometimes, the three newcomers would talk together, telling our stories. There was a man called Frank, in his fifties, and a woman called Melanie who was a little younger than me, dressed in knee boots and an expensive skirt and top. Most of the time, though, I talked one-on-one with Julie, Martin or the other man, a blond-haired guy called James who had rolled-up shirt sleeves and a nice smile.

Time seemed to go syrupy and thick. It felt as if we'd been talking for hours but I knew we couldn't have been because no one made any sign of winding things up or kicking us out. I told my story, more slowly, this time, and with all the details. When I reached the most painful, personal part—the night when I was nearly raped at The Pit —Julie nodded sympathetically.

And then asked me how it made me feel.

I shook my head. "I've put it behind me." It was the part of the story I always skipped over.

Julie put her hand on my arm. "You need to get it out," she said. "To heal."

I didn't want to. The wounds had closed and I'd have to re-open them. But she was so *nice.* They all were. I wanted them to like me.

So I told her. In detail. Halting sentences became gulping sobs. Warm tears fell into my Coke. Julie nodded and gave me encouraging smiles and I knew she was right: it had to hurt, to heal. But it didn't feel like healing. It felt as if she was mapping every secret little place inside my soul.

When I was finally done, she hugged me. "I know," she whispered. "I know that was awful." She drew back and her hands found mine. Then she knitted our fingers together. "But friends have to know each other, don't they? And that's what we are, now. *Great friends.*"

And I blinked the last of the tears away and felt that bright, pink light shine inside me again, even stronger than before. She couldn't have known I needed friends. I hadn't even admitted it to myself until today. It was lucky, so lucky, that we'd found each other. I grinned.

"Now that we're friends," she told me, looking deep into my eyes, "you can join us. We can *all* be your friends. Friends who'll never betray you, who'll always be there for you, no matter what. Do you know what Aeternus means? *Everlasting.* Come here."

She led me by the hand to the center of the room, where there was a big circular rug that looked hand-knitted. Martin was doing the same with Frank. James was bringing Melanie over. We sat down in a circle. The rug was surprisingly thick and comfortable and the six of us neatly fitted, as if it had been made for just this purpose.

Julie took my hand and, next to me, Martin took my other hand. Their touch was wonderful: warm and smooth and *secure.* When all six of us were holding hands, it felt like the best thing in the world.

"This is The Group," she said. "We can all rely on each other here,

Sylvie. She looked deep into my eyes. "You know what it's like to have people leave you, don't you?"

I just stared at her as a deep, hot upwelling of emotion rose in my chest. My eyes suddenly filled with tears. *Yes! My parents!* How had she known? Had I told her about them dying? I didn't remember.

"Listen to me, Sylvie." She squeezed my hand. "Listen to me very carefully. No one in Aeternus will ever leave you. No one will ever let you down. We will always be here for you. That's what we're about: helping each other, taking care of each other."

I nodded. All three of us newcomers did. It sounded *so good!*

We ate a meal sitting cross-legged on the floor: bowls of sticky jasmine rice and chicken with soy and ginger. I was worried I was being rude, staying there: Martin hadn't even wanted to bring me along, and wasn't it getting late? But Julie said there was plenty for everyone.

After dinner, we talked more. Then Martin was gently shaking me and I sat up, blinking: I flushed as I realized I must have drifted off to sleep, slumped against the side of the couch. I was bleary-eyed at first, but then James pressed a big mug of coffee into my hands and I started to wake up.

We divided into pairs again, one newcomer to one Guide. *Guides are just what we call ourselves,* Julie told me. *We help people when they're joining. One day, you might be a Guide too.*

She asked me questions about my family and friends, writing down my answers. James was doing the same with Melanie and I overheard some of it. Her life sounded much more glamorous than mine: her dad was some sort of rich industrialist who owned skyscrapers downtown. "But I don't want to be like him," Melanie said, tossing her hair back. "I don't think life should be all about money."

"That's right," I heard James tell her, and he gave her a grin, and Melanie sort of giggled and smiled back at him, entranced. "Aeternus doesn't even need a lot of money, because there are so many of us. We all give $100 each month, just to keep things running." He shrugged casually. "Some people give more, if they're rich like your dad, but that's up to them."

I frowned at Julie. "What does Aeternus...*do?* I mean, what's the money used for?"

"It helps us to find new people who want to join, like you," said Julie. "And some of it goes to help everyone: even Outsiders. It helps to bring Beautiful Order." She grinned as she said the last two words. "That's what we call it when we fix things and make the world a better place. But it's not just about donating money. Sometimes, we can help in practical ways, too."

I was about to ask her what she meant by that, but we were gathering into a circle again. We all shared life experiences where we'd needed someone but, because we'd been Outsiders, we hadn't had Aeternus to call on. I didn't want to remember, didn't even want to imagine how life had been before I'd met my new friends. It made me go cold and shaky. But with Julie holding my hand for strength, I told them about trying to make ends meet in New York, Alec getting injured and my deal with Rick to save Alec's life. My heart started to pound...I'd forgotten what it felt like to feel so *alone*—

But then Julie was folding me into her arms I realized that tears were running down my cheeks. I gradually relaxed, the shaky feeling dropping away. "The world is dangerous," Julie told everyone. "That's why we need each other. Most Outsiders don't think like us. They don't care about each other, only about themselves."

I frowned a little because Aedan *had* helped me, even though he was an Outsider. Then I smiled. *I'll have to bring him into The Group.* Aedan could know what it was like to be safe and warm, too.

Julie opened up a big cardboard carton and took out some thick wads of paper, stapled at one corner like an examination paper. The newcomers were each given one. "This will help us get to know you," said Julie.

I looked at the first question. *How strongly do you agree with the following statement: I feel happy and secure when I know exactly what I'm meant to be doing.*

"It won't take long," said Julie.

But it did. The test must have been fifty pages of closely-spaced questions. I started to nod off again, but James brought around more of the delicious coffee and I woke right back up. For a while, the Guides withdrew and it was just us three newcomers sitting with our pads, our pencils scratching away on the paper. I don't think I've ever concentrated so intensely on something in my life.

There was another meal: a dark, home-cooked chili with little crackers. *I can't eat again! I just ate!* But I was surprisingly hungry. James came around with a camera and took a photo of each of us for The Group scrapbook.

There were more questions, this time about our jobs. Melanie had a very junior role at the Mayor's office. Frank was an engineer with a mining company. The Guides seemed very interested in both of those. "There'll be lots of little ways you can help," Julie told them. When I looked questioningly at her, she said, "Everyone can help in some way. Doctors can help get medicine for people who really need it, or make sure someone gets special care. Or, sometimes, the immigration people at airports can harass our people for no reason, but if we have someone who works at the airport, they can make sure our people go straight through."

I nodded. Then frowned. "But I just...." I flushed. "I just teach fitness classes at a gym. That's all I can do except...fight."

Julie rubbed my back. "Everyone is valuable, Sylvie. There will be plenty of ways you can help. People who can fight can even become Primes. But we're getting ahead of ourselves here."

Time seemed to stretch and blur. There were more meals and more sitting in a circle. I felt like I'd known Frank and Melanie, Martin, James and Julie forever. Sometimes, one of the Guides would go away for a little while but there were always two of them there.

Julie told us some stories about how there were some people who didn't trust movements like ours. They didn't like the idea of people helping each other and helping make the world a better place. They wanted to keep the world under their control. Sometimes, they even tried to hurt us. "But we're stronger than them. As long as we work together to Protect The Group." She motioned for us all to join hands: by now, it felt natural. "I'm Julie and I will protect all my friends," she said, looking around at us. "I will Protect The Group."

We went around the circle saying it. Then, after a little more talking, we did it again. And again. It started to get frustrating. *I understand! Enough, already!* But after a while, the words started to sound reassuring and familiar, like the lyrics to a song you love. They seemed to resonate in me. Hearing the others say them felt right and, each time we went round, I couldn't wait for it to be my turn.

"I'm Sylvie," I said. "And I will protect all my friends. I will Protect The Group."

But later, when we were all quiet, I frowned. A memory was coming back to me, hazy and faint. Aedan. Aedan was one of those people who didn't trust Aeternus. And he'd convinced me. I'd even come here to...I suddenly felt dirty. To *spy* on my new friends. *I must tell them!*

"Are you alright, Sylvie?" Julie was looking at me strangely. "Is something wrong?"

I nodded. Aedan and Carrick and Kian and Sean...they were wrong about Aeternus. *So wrong.* They might hurt us by mistake. And we must Protect The Group. "There are some people who don't like you," I blurted. "They sent me here."

Julie leaned forward, suddenly very serious. "Oh?" She led me off to a corner. "Tell me all about them."

At that moment, the door opened and Martin walked in. I hadn't even noticed that he'd left. He'd changed his clothes: is that why he'd been gone?

The door had swung almost shut behind him when it flew open again, so hard the whole room seemed to shake. A man burst in: a big man with very dark hair and heavy brows. I knew him instantly but in that way you recognize an old classmate you haven't seen in years. *Aedan!*

But Aedan was an Outsider.

More men rushed in behind him, with the same dark hair. His brothers. They were Outsiders, too. They didn't understand. They wanted to hurt us.

As if to prove it, Aedan grabbed Martin and slammed him up against the wall, pinning him there by his throat. Melanie was screaming over and over again. Julie, who had been sitting on the floor, was crawling backwards frantically, trying to get away. James rushed forward to protect us but the man in a leather biker cut—*Carrick!*—swung a shotgun up and slammed the butt across James's face. I screamed as he fell to the floor.

"No!" I said, trying to stand up. "They're my friends!" But my legs felt like they were made of matchwood, crumpling under my weight. Why was I suddenly so tired?

Aedan was punching Martin in the face again and again. Kian and Sean ran over to me but I seemed to see it in slow motion. They trampled on our lovingly filled-in personality tests leaving big, dirty boot prints on them. I snatched my test up before it could be trodden on.

Kian grabbed one of my hands and Sean grabbed the other and they hauled me up, supporting me between them. But their hands didn't feel like holding hands with Julie and Martin. These people were Outsiders and their grip was hard and cold. I started to panic. *What if they— No, they wouldn't—*

Martin fell to the floor, his face a bloody mess. Aedan ran towards me and scooped me up into his arms, cradling me with one arm under my back and another under my legs. "It's okay," he said. "It's okay."

And it *was*. All my love for him flooded into my mind, a warm sea that fought against the cold and panic. Everything was going to be okay.

"We're getting you out of here," Aedan told me.

What? WAIT! I tried to tell him that he was wrong about Aeternus, that he didn't understand, but he was looking towards the door. Then I heard a woman's voice, quick and efficient, saying, *911: What is your emergency?*

"There are people in my house!" yelled Julie into the phone. "Armed men!"

"We need to go," growled Carrick.

And suddenly Aedan was moving, carrying me towards the door. Away from The Group.

I took a huge, panicked gulp of air and dived out of his arms. When I landed, my legs were so weak I almost fell.

"Sylvie!" There was real fear in Aedan's voice. He tried to pick me up again, his arm encircling my waist.

"No! I don't want to go!" My voice was shrill, hysterical.

He lifted me.

And I punched him as hard as I could.

His head snapped to one side and there was a sickening crack as his nose broke. He stared at me, dumbstruck. And the fear that had been on his face before was replaced by sheer terror.

The room was silent for a second. I stood there staring, unable to believe what I'd done. The shock of it cleared my mind just enough and a big, hot swell of love broke through me. *Oh Jesus! Aedan!* I ran into his arms.

Kian and Sean and Carrick surrounded me—to keep me safe or to stop me running again, I wasn't sure which. They hustled me and Aedan outside. The Mustang was there and they pushed me into the back seat, jammed between Carrick and Aedan. Sean and Kian jumped into the front and we roared off.

I twisted around to look at the house as it receded. The loss of leaving The Group started to hit and suddenly I couldn't speak, couldn't breathe. Tears started to stream down my face. "Why did you —" I asked. My face crumpled. My heart was broken. I felt like I had when Aedan walked away from me in the rain. "I was *Inside!*" I screamed at them. "I was *Inside* and it was *so good!* Why did you take me away from them? I only got to be with them for a few hours!"

Aedan cradled my hot, red cheeks in his hands. "Sylvie," he said, his face deathly pale. "You've been gone for three days."

31

SYLVIE

No one, including me, realized just how many drugs were in my system, at first. The best thing would have been for me to sleep: that's what my body needed. But the drugs had left me far too wired. So as they began to fade, I got to lie on a bed, wide awake, as all the carefully-engineered fear and loneliness and need flooded through me. I wasn't just withdrawing from the drugs; I was withdrawing from The Group. I cried until the pillows were dripping wet. I threw up five times.

And through it all, Aedan was there with me, holding my hand. Carrick had helped him set his nose and Annabelle had taped it but he refused to go to a hospital until I was okay.

It took forty-eight hours for most of the drugs to seep out of my system. Some would take longer still, but I was able to finally sleep. I curled up in a fetal ball and Aedan curled up around me, a barrier of warmth and strength that would keep anything out.

When morning broke I still felt shaky and tired but I felt more like *me* again. Aedan was already awake, still cuddled around me but half sitting up, looking at something small in the palm of his hand. I tried to look but he hid it away in his pocket as soon as he realized I was awake.

There was a knock at the door. I sat up and, a second later, Kian put his head around the door. It hadn't registered, when they'd rescued me, but one side of his jaw was swollen and bruised. "You okay?" he asked. "You need anything?"

I shook my head, trying not to stare at his jaw. Then, "Actually, could I please try some coffee?" I felt like my stomach was finally returning to normal.

Kian nodded and disappeared, his eyes troubled. "He blames himself," said Aedan.

"What happened to his face?"

"I hit him," said Aedan, looking away.

I put my hand on his chin and gently turned him back to look at me. His nose seemed to be healing okay but I was going to make sure he saw a doctor today. "I'm sorry," I said, looking up at him. "You hitting Kian, me hitting you...I caused a lot of trouble."

"*You* didn't cause anything," Aedan told me, pulling me close. "It's all on the cult."

I gingerly touched his cheek, not daring to touch the nose itself. It was the first time I'd really injured him, despite all our fights in the ring. "Does it hurt?" I asked.

He gripped my hand in his big, warm one. "No."

"Liar."

"Well, it's my own fault. Should have had my guard up."

He meant it as a joke but the memory of hitting him kept playing on loop in my mind. Fresh tears sprang to my eyes. "I'm sorry!" I sobbed.

He smoothed his hand through my hair. "It wasn't you," he said, and crushed me against him. I sat with my cheek against his chest, my tears wetting his skin. I loved this man. Loved him like I'd never loved anyone my whole life. The fact that Aeternus had managed to overcome all that, to hotwire my brain to be so scared of being separated from them that I'd lash out at him...that truly terrified me. I didn't want to think there were people like that in the world. If they did it to me, they could do it to someone else.

And then my stomach twisted. They *had* done it to someone else. Melanie and Frank. And, God, *five thousand other people!* All of them had people they'd loved, normal lives...and Aeternus had turned them against them. I made up my mind, in that moment. This wasn't just about finding Bradan, anymore. We had to stop them.

"How did you find me?" I asked when I eventually felt strong enough to move back from him.

He told me how they'd searched the fair without finding any clues. How they'd eventually had to settle for going to more fairs over the next few days, until they'd finally found one with an Aeternus tent, and then followed Martin to his car and then to Julie's house. "We were going out of our minds," he said. He couldn't look at me for a moment. When he did, his eyes were wet. "Jesus, Sylvie, I thought I was never going to see you again."

He threw his arms around me and hugged me so tight my ribs ached, his arms like bands of iron that were never going to separate again. It was exactly what we needed. Kian knocked again and brought in two steaming mugs of coffee but Aedan didn't let me go. I felt him lift his head, though, and nod to his brother over my shoulder: an apology. Kian put one big hand on Aedan's shoulder and squeezed it in reply.

When he'd gone, Aedan and I sat on the bed and I told my story. I couldn't bear to be out of his arms: if I couldn't feel them around me, I started slipping back to Julie's house. Then everything she'd forced into my mind started screaming at me. That was the problem: with the drugs gone, I knew what was in my head was wrong, but it was still *there,* telling me I needed to run back to The Group. Trying to ignore it was like trying to ignore music blasting at ear-splitting volume from speakers right next to your head.

So Aedan sat with his back against one of the posts of the four poster bed and I pressed my back against his chest. He wrapped his arms around me and that seemed to quiet the memories down. I told him how I'd entered the tent. How something had happened in there, something that had made me receptive and pliable. "I don't understand it," I said, shaking my head. "He must have drugged me but I was so careful! I didn't drink the water!"

And then, replaying it in my mind for about the twentieth time, I saw it: the drug had been in the ice cubes. Martin had put them in my drink but not his. And that realization unlocked everything: I started to see how I'd been played. The room, so bakingly hot. The safe, shrink-wrapped cans of Coke, so temptingly sitting there in my eye line. I'd thought I was being so clever but I'd done exactly what I was meant to.

As I related it all to Aedan, I closed my eyes and put my head in my hands. It all seemed so obvious, now. The balding, overweight Martin, so unintimidating. Not really a cult member at all, just an accountant. Putting me at my ease, always there to disarm me just as I was getting suspicious. He'd probed me gently. He'd asked if I had friends and he must have seen the sadness in my eyes and steered the conversation that way. "He figured out my weakness and used it," I said savagely.

Aedan's arms tightened around me. "What weakness?"

I shook my head, embarrassed. "Doesn't matter." Martin had used every reverse psychology trick in the book on me. Instead of asking me to go with him, he'd said he had to leave...and I'd *begged* him to take me with him. "I feel so stupid," I said, my voice thin.

"You're not stupid. These people are just the best at what they do. I don't know who that guy was, but he wasn't a fucking accountant. Professional con man, maybe. Or they'd trained him up."

I remembered what Julie had said: *one day, you might be a guide.* A few years and they would have had me bringing new people in. I felt sick. I thought back to Gwen, the student I'd met at the fair, the one who'd shown me where the tent was. "God, that poor girl," I said. "She nearly wound up in Aeternus instead of me, and no one would have come to rescue *her.*"

Aedan went quiet, as if there was something he didn't want to say. "What?" I asked.

"We saw her at the fair today, the one we followed Martin from."

I stared at him. "Gwen was in on it too?!"

I felt him nod.

I groaned. It was all so obvious, now. Martin stayed in the tent and Gwen and probably others—patrolled the floor, looking for likely candidates, befriending them. Appearing eager and just a little naive, so the targets felt protective and slightly superior. Telling us how great Aeternus was, a personal recommendation. Marketing companies had a name for it: *social proof.* Oh, but there was always that little bit of hesitance: *I think it's for people a couple of years older than me,* Gwen had said. And of course I'd gotten all excited because that described me. If she'd latched onto a man, she would have said, *I think it's more of a guy thing.*

The whole process was perfect. *Practiced.* Young members like Gwen to spot potentials and bring them to more experienced, trained members like Martin, Julie and James who'd drug them, transport them to the house and then tag-team them for days to break them down. The terrifying part was how well it had worked. I'd always thought of myself as smart and independent and—at least since Aedan—I could stand up to people. But in the space of three days, these people had rewired me.

I pulled myself from Aedan's arms, ran to the bathroom and threw up. When I came out, I told him I was okay but I was lying. I said I needed some space and, even though I could see it killed him to do it, he hugged me and left me alone.

I lay on the bed, facing the wall, and just wept. It wasn't just that they'd violated my mind, or how easily they'd done it. It wasn't that they'd made me relive what happened at The Pit, torn the wound wide just so they could crawl deep inside my head. Those things hurt but they'd heal, given time.

It was that they'd shown me something inside myself. The loneliness, the black chasm where friends should have been, had been growing bigger for years. I'd been hiding it from everyone, even myself, but they'd forced me to see it. Then they'd filled that chasm with The Group...and now that The Group was gone, the chasm felt darker and colder and more empty than ever. It felt like my whole soul was being sucked into it.

Maybe in time I could get rid of all the lies they'd filled me with. But that one truth they'd uncovered...I couldn't escape that. I really *did* need friends. I really *was* lonely. And I had no idea how I was going to fix that.

32

KIAN

I'd been pacing up and down the hallway. I froze as Aedan came out of the room he shared with Sylvie. His eyes met mine and there was a flash of shame: I saw him glance down at my swollen jaw. I shook my head. He'd hit me because he'd been mad and he'd had good reason to be. We damn near lost Sylvie because of me. I was so confident I knew what I was doing, with my suit and my radios and my Secret Service training. And it had gone so horribly wrong.

Our dad's words to Carrick and me rang in my ears. *You two are the oldest. You have to protect your brothers.* He'd warned us not to go after Aeternus and I'd let my love for Bradan cloud my judgment. Never again. We were *done* with this thing.

Another door onto the hallway opened and Sean stepped out, hesitating as he realized he'd stepped into the middle of something. My chest tightened. *Sean!* That whole six months of hell he'd gone through with Louise, not knowing if they were going to raise the money to save Kayley in time. Around that time, I'd been protecting asshole senators and quieting my demons with drink. *This should never have happened.* I should never have joined the Marines, should have stuck around and pulled my family back together. Sean would have never become an enforcer, Carrick wouldn't have joined his MC, Aedan could have kept his boxing legit....

...and he would never have met Sylvie. And Carrick would never have met Annabelle. And Sean would never have met Louise.

And I would never have met Emily.

I sighed and leaned against the wall, rubbing my face with my hand.

"What?" asked Sean, sounding concerned.

"Nothing. What's going on with you?" My youngest brother was looking worried.

Sean shook his head, glancing between Aedan and me. "I don't know. It's Louise, she's acting weird."

"Since when?" asked Aedan. Like me, I think he was glad of something to take his mind off what had happened to Sylvie.

"Since you all arrived," said Sean.

"You think she doesn't want us here?" I asked quietly.

Sean shook his head firmly. "No! She loves having you here. I do, too, and Kayley's loving have three more older brothers."

I had to smile at that. Kayley *was* enjoying having a full house. She'd bonded with the girls over nail polish and movie nights and Carrick had taken her out on the Harley, Aedan had taught her how to punch and I'd shown her a few self-defense moves. If some guy at her high school got creepy with her, he was in for a very, very bad time. "So what is it?" I asked.

Sean sighed. "She keeps looking like she wants to say something. And then, when I ask her, she's all, 'Nothing.' It's driving me feckin' crazy." Sylvie was right, I realized: we *were* all starting to sound more Irish, the more we were around each other.

"You should talk to her," said Aedan. It should have been funny: in a family of men who aren't big on talking, Aedan was by far the most brooding and silent. But I could see the way he was staring at Sylvie's door, wishing he could follow his own advice.

"He's right," I told Sean. "It's difficult to get privacy, with all of us here. Find somewhere quiet and talk to her."

Sean sighed again and nodded. "You're right. I s'pose I should count my blessings." He looked at me sheepishly. "At least I've got her here with me, right?"

I nodded silently. I was missing Emily like crazy. When we came back from the fair without Sylvie I'd stayed awake all night, pacing the kitchen, tearing myself apart over how I'd failed to protect her. Emily had come to be my safety valve, the one person who could stop me turning my anger inward and make me see clearly. And she wasn't there.

It wasn't just that night, either. Often, I'd wake in the middle of the night and lie there half asleep, wondering why she was taking so long in the bathroom and waiting for her to return so I could spoon with her again...then I'd remember she was on the other side of the continent. In the morning, grumpy and exhausted, I'd glimpse her on the TV news. She was always surrounded by the Secret Service but that didn't stop me aching to be there to protect her. I didn't just miss her, I needed her. I'd never needed anyone like that, before.

But there was no way she could be here. After what had happened when we rescued Sylvie, I was worried that the cops were going to arrest us all for assault any second. If Emily was around when that happened, it would be catastrophic for the whole First Family.

It was lunchtime before Sylvie emerged from her room. She found us in the kitchen, where we'd just finished throwing together a lunch of cold meats, cheeses, bread and salad. The room was full: over-full, in fact, with six of us helping. But all chatter stopped when Sylvie stepped through the doorway.

She looked so...*weak*. Sylvie's just a tiny little thing but Aedan had shaped her into a ferocious fighter: ever since I'd known her, she'd been full of fire, ready to take on the world. Now, she moved as if she was brittle, as if the cult had sucked everything out of her and left just a fragile husk.

"I want to tell you what I learned," she said. Her voice was thin and tight, as if she had to hold onto every word lest it get away from her.

We all looked at each other. "It can wait," Aedan said. "Why don't you rest?"

Sylvie shook her head. "I want to piece together what we learned before I forget anything. I don't trust my memory, anymore." Her voice cracked on the last word and we all winced in sympathy.

Louise bit her lip: I could tell she was close to tears. I think all of us had the same instinct, which was to send Sylvie back to bed. But her eyes were pleading with us. I realized she needed this: she needed the hell she'd been through to have been worth it.

"Okay," said Aedan. I was amazed at how gentle he could make his voice. "Grab a plate. You should try to eat something, you're running on empty."

Sylvie nodded gratefully and picked up a plate. "But...can we go outside?" she asked. She looked at us, then looked at the floor. "I need to feel some air on me," she said. "I was in that house for too long."

We carried our plates out into the garden. Even so late in the year, it was still comfortably warm. We sat in a circle on the grass, I dialed Emily and put her on speaker so she could listen too, and Sylvie filled us in. Between her first-hand knowledge, Calahan's information and the structure Annabelle had figured out, we were finally able to get a handle on Aeternus and how they operated. And it was terrifying.

They recruited people into small local groups around the world. Drugs and a whole battery of intense psychological techniques were used to break the recruits down until they'd do anything for "The Group" and for the wider organization.

The drugs made it impossible to resist: even now Sylvie was out, she told us, her mind still kept rebelling. "Every few minutes, I feel this sort of *pull* back towards The Group," she said. She started to say something else but her voice caught and broke. Aedan pulled her close and just held her against him for a moment, her face buried in his chest, while we all looked on. My chest closed up tight in pity and wordless, white-hot rage. Aedan glanced up and met my eyes and the fury I saw there was almost frightening. Maybe it's the fighter's discipline but Aedan's always had a slow burning temper, much slower than mine. But when he *does* go off.... I was mad enough myself, ready to break some heads. But if Aedan came face-to-face with a cult member again, the guy was going to be annihilated.

Sylvie sniffed, wiped her eyes, and we continued. We figured out that the personality tests and the questions about recruits' backgrounds were used to identify how each person could best serve Aeternus. Everyone donated $100 per month but the real value was in the little jobs Sylvie's Guide had told her about. People who worked in the CIA, FBI or police could ensure that an investigation was quashed, or that a 911 call was answered a little more slowly, or even that a suspect was "accidentally" shot. Judges could give leniency to an Insider or even have the case thrown out completely. Prosecutors could ensure that a scapegoat was sent to jail to throw suspicion off Aeternus, just as they did with our dad. A prison guard could look the other way as an enemy was stabbed in the yard.

And by setting hundreds of these tiny tasks each day, Aeternus had them all working towards some dark purpose. Each person's role was tiny but put enough of them together.... It was the perfect system: each person only knew their task, with no idea of how it fitted into the big picture, so it was impossible for them to turn traitor. It wouldn't have worked without the cult-like elements: people would have gotten too curious and asked too many questions. But the drugs and brainwashing removed that weakness: the followers did exactly what they were instructed to, no questions asked, thrilled that they were contributing.

"I started off thinking: what if your job isn't useful to them?" said Sylvie. "What if your job is something boring? But when you think about it, *any* job can be useful. If you work for the phone company, you can eavesdrop on a call for them. If you work in a hospital, they have you stealing drugs or...Jesus, maybe even altering patient records, to cover up a crime."

"Or kill someone," I said darkly. "Delete someone's allergy from their records so they're given a drug that kills them. It gets written up as a mistake or a glitch and no one even suspects."

Sylvie hugged her knees. "If you work in transport—trucking, the docks, airlines—you can help to smuggle stuff or get someone in or out of the country."

"I know why they were interested in the mining guy," said Carrick. "Mining companies have access to explosives. Farmers can get licenses to buy black powder, too." He shook his head. "Jesus, you're right. *Everyone's* useful."

"What about people who just work office jobs? Sales, stuff like that? Or teachers?" asked Annabelle.

"Martin, the guy I met at the fair? I have a feeling he was a salesman, before they recruited him. Anyone who can sell, anyone who's good with people, they'll get them to quit their job and work for them full time, recruiting people. And teachers?" She thought about it and suddenly shivered. "Jesus!"

"What?" asked Annabelle, leaning forward.

Sylvie looked at Annabelle and then Louise. "Teachers have access to thousands of kids. I bet they have them picking the best and the brightest, or anyone with influential parents, and grooming them for recruitment once they're a teenager." Louise went pale and I knew we were all thinking of Kayley.

"There's worse," said Sean.

"It doesn't get any worse than that," said Louise tightly. Her eyes had hardened at what she was imagining, a tigress ready to defend her young.

"Think of people who work in IT," said Sean. "Someone working for an internet service provider. Someone who has access to all your emails, your private conversations, your pictures. The data on your phone." He looked ill. "Or what about the people who write the software for voting machines?"

"The media, too," I said. "I bet they've recruited people at the big TV networks. They can bury a story, or do a hatchet job on a political candidate."

"And some people, they probably just milk money from," said Carrick. "Sylvie said they were interested in the dad of that girl, Melanie, because he was rich. CEOs, high flyers, rich retired people...I bet those people are donating millions. But even if they aren't, even if it's just $100 per person, per month...with five thousand people, that's half a million dollars a month."

There was silence for a moment. Then, one by one, they all turned to look at me. It took me a second to figure out why: I knew about planning operations and organizing things and I'd spent years facing insurgents in Iraq and terrorist groups who threatened VIPs. I was no expert but I was the closest thing we had. "What could you do," Carrick asked me, "if you had a half million dollars a month and all those followers doing your bidding?"

I was silent for a second, looking down at the ground. We'd thought Kerrigan and his plan for a coup was scary, but this was on a whole different level. The power of Aeternus made my skin crawl. I finally lifted my eyes to the others. "What *couldn't* you do?" I said.

All of us were looking pale and drawn as the implications soaked in. The sun was warm but people were hunching their shoulders as if against the cold. The President himself had been worried about Aeternus, but not even he had realized the scale of it.

"There are some parts we still don't understand," said Aedan. "Like: some people seem to be taken away to some other part of Aeternus, based on their personality tests. Like Bradan. What happens to them?"

"And the drugs," said Louise. She looked at Sylvie. "I learned a lot about drugs, this summer. And I've never heard of anything that would do what you describe. It's something not on the market, legal or illegal, and it's pretty specialist stuff. Where did they get access to that?"

"And what son of a bitch set this up?" growled Carrick. "And what's their plan?"

We lapsed into silence again but inside, my brain was working overtime. The whole time we'd been talking, I'd been moving closer and closer to a decision. And as I sat there looking at Sylvie, broken and shaking, a ghost of her former self, I finally made it.

"It's over," I said, standing up.

Carrick blinked at me. "What? It's not—"

"*It's over!*" I snapped. "This is too dangerous. For the girls, for all of us. Calahan was right. The President was right. We're out of our depth. We have been this entire time. I'm going to call Calahan. We can tell him what we found out, then we're going to book flights home."

And I stalked off towards the house.

I didn't think anyone would join me: figured I'd alienated everyone. But just as I was about to call Calahan, Carrick and Annabelle walked in and sat down at the dining table. Carrick gave me a slow nod, like he understood: he wanted Bradan back, but we needed to protect the others.

Sean and Louise joined us next. I wondered if they'd had time to have that talk, yet: *no,* from the worry in Sean's eyes when he looked at her. They sat down opposite me and I got another silent nod. It made me feel a little better about what I was doing: at least I wasn't acting on my own.

Aedan came last, casting worried glances out of the window towards the garden.

"How is she?" I asked.

He looked at me, looked towards the garden, then just shook his head. "Needs space."

Watching him was agonizing. He was actually leaning a little towards the door, trying to resist the urge to run back out there. When you really love someone, the hardest thing in the world is to watch them going through something and be unable to help. But I could understand that Sylvie needed some alone time: I'd been like that, after some of the stuff I saw in Iraq. Your brain needs time to process, without interruptions. Plus, she wasn't just dealing with what had happened to her: she was reacting to my decision to shut us down, too. Not only had they violated her mind: it had all been for nothing.

I stood, put a hand on Aedan's shoulder and led him gently over to the table. He reluctantly sat, still glancing at the window. Sylvie had disappeared from view.

I called Calahan and explained what had happened to Sylvie. To give the guy his due, he never once said *I told you so*. His first question was *how's she doing?*

We all looked out of the window. Sylvie was tying some boxing practice pads to a tree. As we watched, she started to punch the makeshift punch bag. "She's dealing with it," Aedan said.

Next, I explained everything we'd learned. I could hear the grudging admiration in Calahan's voice as he asked for clarification on a point. We'd gotten further than he'd done. Just not far enough to find our brother.

We heard a *bang,* followed by another and another. Outside, Sylvie wasn't just punching the pads, she was intent on destroying them, hammering the vinyl and foam into the trunk of the tree. The whole thing was shaking, branches rustling all the way to their tips, and tears were running down Sylvie's face. Aedan rose but Carrick clamped his hand on his brother's wrist and shook his head. "She needs to get it out," he said.

"We're wrapping it up here," I told Calahan. "It's too dangerous, plus I can't see how we can get any further. Every group is disconnected from the others. There's no way to find out where the whole thing's being run from."

Again, Calahan was big enough to not crow that he'd been right. He just sounded relieved that no one else would get hurt. "Smart move," he said.

Outside, the *bang*s were coming faster and faster. All of us at the table tensed, our shoulders rising in sympathy. All of us could feel Sylvie's pain. All of us would have cheerfully beaten the cult members to a bloody pulp for what they'd done to her. We heard a low howl of rage which rose to a scream. The noises sped up to a vicious, desperate flurry—

And then it stopped, like a switch had been thrown. Outside, Sylvie had dropped her fists and was staring at the ground, panting.

"We should go," I told Calahan, my voice thick with emotion. The others were close to losing it, too: even Carrick looked like he was one step away from tears. "I guess this is the last time we'll talk. Thank you for...everything. We wouldn't have gotten anywhere if it wasn't for you."

"Maybe that would have been a good thing," said Calahan bitterly. He sounded as sorry for Sylvie as we felt.

I couldn't think of a response so I put my hand out to end the call.

"*We're not quitting!*" yelled Sylvie, bursting through the door.

I froze, my finger a hair's breadth above the *end call* button. We all looked at each other, then at Sylvie.

"It'll be okay—" began Louise in a calming voice.

"*No!*" yelled Sylvie. "No, it won't!" She jerked her head at the garden. "I thought what I needed was to pound it out. But this isn't something I can *get out of me*. They *changed* me. Do you understand that? They changed me like it was nothing, in just a few h—"—she closed her eyes, her hands balling into fists. God, it must still feel like it was hours, to her. "*Days,*" she corrected. "In just a few days."

Aedan stood up. "You're safe now," he said, reaching for her. "They can't hurt you."

"*They already have!*" Sylvie's voice was so raw, it made all of us wince. "You don't understand. This is *my mind* and I don't feel like I'm in control of it anymore. Jesus, I went in knowing that everything they told me would be bullshit. I knew it then. I know it now. *But it still worked.* Those drugs they gave me burned this stuff right into my brain. Don't you get it? *I still want to be back there!* I know they're evil and part of me still wants my—my—" She choked on the words. "My *friends* back!"

I've never wanted to kill anyone so much as I have right then. *Just give me one of those bastards.* I glanced at Aedan. He was shaking, he was so mad. *Aedan and me, in a room with a couple of them. That's all I'm asking.*

Sylvie gulped and looked at the ceiling. "I—I don't know when I'm going to feel like *me* again. Or *if.*" She glanced at Aedan, her face tortured. I got it, then, why she kept pushing him away, saying she needed space. I'd felt that same way, when I'd come back from Iraq:

tainted. Poisonous. You want to stay away from everyone, *especially* the people you love. I understood but it tore me apart, seeing the two of them like this. Sylvie drew in a deep, shaky breath. "But I know what I can do. I can stop these bastards doing it to anyone else."

She picked something up off the side table: the thick pad of paper she'd been clutching when we'd brought her home. Her personality test. She slammed it down on the table. "They took this out of a box," she said. "Do you understand? They're getting them delivered *by the box.*" She leaned over the table, hands flat on the surface. For the first time, I saw that her knuckles were raw and bloody. "There were three of us new recruits in that house. And Martin was back at another fair three days later. Do the math. That's well over three hundred people a year they're bringing in and that's just one group. How many more groups do they have around LA? How many more around the whole country?" Her voice was rising. "Even if only one in five stays with the cult long term—and I bet it's closer to four in five—there still have to be thousands upon thousands of people being...*changed,* every year!" She looked around our faces. "This isn't just about Bradan anymore, or about me. We have to stop them."

I felt sick because I could hear the need in her voice. If we stopped now, I was worried she'd never get closure. But... "I can't let anyone else get hurt," I told her.

"People are getting hurt *right now,*" she snapped. "Right now, some single mom is talking to Martin. He's inside her head, getting her to pour out all her secrets, drawing her in. And some truck driver has Julie whispering in his ear, telling him how great things can be, how he can be a part of something that really matters." She turned to Louise. "And some kid only a couple of years older than Kayley is getting all starry-eyed about James, she'll do whatever he tells her to, he's passing her a Coke or a Starbucks and she doesn't realize that—"

"Alright!" yelled Louise. Sylvie stopped and both of them just stayed there, panting at each other, eyes brimming. Louise gave a little nod and Sylvie nodded in return.

There was silence for a few seconds. All of us were in pieces. No one wanted to be the one to say it. In the end, it was Carrick who spoke. "We can't," he said, more softly than I'd thought him capable of. "We can't trace the cult beyond this group. We didn't get anything —"—He broke off as Sylvie's face started to crumple. "No! I mean, you got *plenty!* Jesus, you found out all about them! But...we haven't got anything that lets us find the person at the top."

Annabelle picked up the personality test. "Maybe we do," she said quietly. "All the groups are disconnected, but they all use *these,* right? You said they were delivered in boxes: I bet they're printed centrally and shipped out." She showed us the hundreds of little "check the box" boxes. "These are designed to be scanned into a computer—it's kind of old-fashioned, really. Like, why aren't they just using an app, on a tablet? But anyway: that means the tests have to be mailed somewhere for processing."

Aedan was shaking his head. "If you're thinking of going back to the house and getting them to tell us where they mail the tests to, forget it. It'll be a PO box, untraceable, I guarantee it."

Annabelle sighed, staring at the test. "There must be *some* way." She flipped it over, examining every page. "Like Sylvie said, they need *thousands* of these. Some company must be printing them and they must know who pays for them."

Calahan's voice came from the phone, making us all jump. We'd forgotten he was still there. "There might be a way," he said.

"How?" asked Annabelle. "I've looked all over it. There's nothing to say where it was printed: they're too smart for that."

"I know someone who might be able to help," said Calahan. "She's retired but she does know a hell of a lot about computers and printing...and tracking people down."

33

ANNABELLE

As soon as the call ended, we scattered. Everyone was shaken and we all needed space. I wandered out into the garden: so beautiful, with the trees and swing and the area with the long grass I thought of as *the meadow,* full of wildflowers and butterflies. Back in Haywood Falls, the lawn that separated Carrick's house from our neighbors was an intimidating jungle, probably with some old bike parts buried in there like lost treasure. *When we get back, we're really going to have to do something about that.*

I wound up at the one place I hadn't been yet: the big greenhouse down at the end of the garden. Curious, I opened the door and crept inside. It was like walking through a rainforest in a far-off land: plants hung down from overhead racks and scaled support beams. The air was damp, warm and loaded with exotic scents. All that was missing was the sound of a waterfall: if a snake had slithered past, I wouldn't have been surprised. Huge flowers in bright colors filled a central table and I didn't recognize any of them. I leaned closer to look at a glossy white and pink flower whose petals were the size of my hand.

Then Louise suddenly stood up from behind the table, just a few feet from my face, and I screamed and jumped back. That scared *her* and she jumped back, too.

"Sorry," I said. "Didn't know anyone was in here."

Louise shook her head. "It's okay. I was just...thinking."

I looked at where she'd been crouching. She'd been examining trays of tiny seedlings, each one no bigger than my fingernail.

"This place is amazing," I told her, looking around. "This stuff isn't American, is it?"

She shook her head. "A few things are but most of it's from South America. There are all sorts of laws about what you can import but, once you get past the red tape, you can raise them and sell them to collectors." She suddenly seemed to catch herself and flushed. "You know. It's a hobby."

Why is she embarrassed? "It's *amazing,*" I said with feeling. "I never understood this stuff. I don't...*get* plants." I caught her eye and flushed myself when I saw the curious look she was giving me. "I'd like to. I'd love to be able to grow stuff." I was thinking of Mom and her trailer with the window boxes: I could help her look after them. "But plants are too...squidgy."

Louise blinked. "Squidgy?"

I flushed deeper. "Organic and...imprecise." *God, I sound like such a nerd.* "I'm used to, y'know, numbers and metal."

Louise shook her head. "It's just inputs and outputs." She started talking about sunlight and precision watering and soil acidity. And slowly, the light flickered on in my head: they were really just tiny green machines which told you how they were doing through color instead of noise. I'd had no idea it was *science.* And Louise seemed to genuinely love teaching me about it. We crouched beside the seedlings for nearly an hour as she told me about root systems and moisture in the air. Then she seemed to catch herself again. "Sorry," she said. "I'm just...into this stuff."

And suddenly, I got it. I'd been thinking of Louise as my opposite but she was just like me, geeking out on plants the way I did on machines. I started to get a warm glow inside: I'd finally found a kindred spirit. "We should go out," I said on impulse. "You must know all the good bars in LA. We could have cocktails."

Louise grinned. "That would be great. I might pass on the booze, but—" She cut herself off.

And suddenly it clicked: her staring at the seedlings; the throwing up I'd heard; her sudden cry of shock from the bathroom, the night we'd arrived; the avoiding alcohol. *"Oh my God!"* I breathed. "You're pregnant!"

Louise grabbed my arm, horrified. "Don't tell anyone! I haven't told Sean yet!"

I grabbed hold of both her hands. "He doesn't know?! Does Kayley know?"

"No one knows!"

"Why?!"

"It was unexpected!" She let out a sigh and then it all rushed out of her. "I don't know if he wants a family! And all of...*this* was going on and then Sylvie went missing...there was never a good time and —" She bit her lip and looked at me. "What if it scares him off?"

Part of me wanted to run. This was exactly what I wasn't good at: people and social stuff and girly chat. I'm the last person someone should go to with a problem. But...she needed someone. And just seconds ago, I'd been thrilling at having my first actual proper female friend. Well, this was part of that. I manned up. Or girled up.

"That isn't going to happen," I said firmly. "I've seen the way Sean looks at you. It'll be great. But Louise: you have to talk to him."

34

BRADAN

The blue light came on but it wasn't morning. The alarm was ringing with a different tone, the urgent beeping that meant *See Me: Now.*

I scrambled into my clothes and raced downstairs to his office. Dad always kept it cold, said it helped him stay awake through the long nights. I wasn't sure when he slept or if he ever did.

Two women were just leaving, hurriedly pulling their clothes on as if they'd been interrupted. There were usually women. Dad would select one or sometimes two to be with him for a night. Their partners were Insiders too, so they didn't mind.

Dad was standing on his office's balcony, back ramrod straight as he stared out at the world. When I opened the door, he turned to me and I saw the anger in his eyes. He crossed to his desk in three big strides and nodded down at the photos that were strewn across it.

"There was an attack," Dad told me. "Someone broke into a Group house. Kidnapped one of the Recruits. Beat up some Guides."

I drew in my breath as I looked at the photos. Blood poured from broken noses, bruises stood out dark and ugly on a man's neck. There were action shots, too, taken with the hidden camera. All of the Group houses have them, for security. I could see four men invade the sanctity of an Initiation and begin assaulting people. One man was up against the wall, pinned by his throat. Anger rose and uncoiled like a waking serpent. *How dare they?!* "Did we catch them?" I asked, my voice choked with fury.

"No," said Dad. "We've tracked them down, now. It took us a few days but we found them. But that's not the point. Look at them." He pushed five photos across the desk to me.

The first was of a young woman sitting at a dining table. She was a slender, frail-looking thing, with dark hair tied back in a ponytail. She'd been caught off guard and was looking up at the camera with a big, natural smile. I recognized that she was pretty but only in the same way I'd recognize if the two halves of a picture were symmetrical, or that a puzzle had all its pieces. Beauty, love...I'd learned, when I was chosen to be a Prime, that all those things were weaknesses. The only person I should love was Dad. And I did. And he loved me.

Even if he'd never said it. He'd praised me, thanked me...but he'd never once said he loved me. I was self-conscious about how much I wanted to hear him say it.

The other four photos were a little blurry: they were freeze-frames from the video the hidden camera had shot. Four men, all with black hair. One was in a suit, one was in a biker's leather cut, one was in a hooded top and one was in a tank top. I could see tattoos on one of their backs. That would make him easier to identify: it's exactly why we Primes don't have them.

"Do you know who they are?" asked Dad.

I looked at him in surprise. There was a tone in his voice I'd never heard in all the years I'd known him. A sort of...*fear.* And Dad wasn't scared of anything.

"No," I said.

"You used to know them," said Dad slowly. He was watching me intently. "Before we found you."

My chest constricted: I didn't like to think about the time when I was Outside. I know it was chaotic, without Order. I have memories of it but they're far away, down at the end of a dark corridor where I don't venture. Sometimes I can hear a muffled sound, like someone's banging on the other side of thick glass, but I know to turn away, when that happens. I focused on the photos again but the faces didn't mean anything to me. I looked at Dad and shook my head.

Dad seemed to relax a little. "They tried to hurt us," he told me. "They might try again."

My chest went even tighter, this time with shame. My old life was threatening us, threatening everything Dad had worked so hard to build. "I'm sorry," I croaked, my throat closing up. "What can I do?"

He pushed a slip of paper across the desk. "That's their address. Tail them, see where they go. Keep me informed. If they take any more action against us..."—he looked me right in the eye—"...stop them. Is that clear?"

I nodded firmly. "Yes, dad." The rage was back now, burying the fear. I snatched up the paper and pocketed it. I'd find these four men. And if they tried to hurt us again?

I'd kill them all.

35

ANNABELLE

I opened the door of the diner and let out a little squeak of delight.
The place was out in the desert, just off the interstate. Clearly,
the owners had taken some inspiration from all the tourists heading
from LA to Nevada and Area 51, because we'd parked next to a life-
sized statue of a gray alien with shining black eyes. Inside, it got even
better: the walls and ceiling were painted to look like space and every
booth was an enclosed flying saucer, with curving vinyl seats either
side of a circular table and a doorway either side to let the waitresses
lean in with trays of food. Kian and Carrick both rolled their eyes but
I loved it. We settled ourselves in on one side of the booth.

It was just the three of us: Aedan, Sean and Louise had stayed
home to look after Sylvie. Really, only Kian needed to come but when
Calahan had called to tell us he'd set up the meeting, he'd specifically
requested that Carrick and I be there, too. *Why?*

We'd barely sat down when a man's head poked into our UFO.
Beneath his cowboy hat, I could see curls of soft brown hair and his
eyes were the color of dark, melted chocolate. He put me in mind of
the outdoors, but in a very different way to Carrick. Carrick made me
think of hard, weather-beaten rocks, howling winds and freezing
rain. This guy's deep tan made me think of deserts and big skies, and

his accent sealed the deal. "Here," he called to someone. "They're in here." Pure, unapologetic Texan.

He ducked his head and slid into the booth opposite us: God, he was as big as Carrick! The woman who followed didn't share his outdoor look: she wasn't as pale as me but she had the very dark, shining hair and olive skin of someone with Italian heritage. I've always thought of myself as a little top heavy but her curves put mine to shame and she rocked them in a daringly cut silky blouse and tight jeans. She slid right up to the cowboy, her leg pressed against his just as mine was pressed against Carrick's.

I opened my mouth to say hello but then another woman slid in from the other doorway. She had long, luxuriant mahogany hair spilling down over her scarlet sweater and she was followed by another man. This one was in a black suit and tie and white shirt, and he had the sharp cheekbones I associate with Eastern Europe. He gave Kian's suit an approving nod as he sat down. He was as big as the cowboy and it was a tight squeeze with all four of them crammed around their side of the table.

"Which one of you is the one Calahan told us about?" asked Kian, looking between the two women.

"Me," said the Italian-American woman. Her accent was nothing like the cowboy's: it was straight out of New York. "I'm—"—she exchanged a look with the cowboy—"Mary. This is Luke."

I was pretty sure those weren't their real names.

Mary nodded to the other two. "That's Gabriella. And that's Alexei."

Alexei? Could the big guy in a suit be Russian?

"Thanks for coming," said Kian.

"Yeah, well, Calahan said you were on the level and I trust his opinion," said Mary. "Plus, we owe you."

Kian frowned. "Owe us?"

Mary nodded at Carrick and me. "Owe you two."

A memory started to stir, something that had happened at the end of the whole Volos nightmare, but I couldn't quite connect it. I looked between Mary and Gabriella. Two women. Something about them being two women....

The waitress arrived and everyone ordered coffee. When she'd gone, Mary leaned across the table towards me. "That stuff you went through in Haywood Falls with Volos...remember how he made a call to his boss, in Austria?"

I nodded. Just thinking back to that day made my stomach twist in fear. I remembered hiding in the blood drains beneath the floor, looking up through the grate at Volos. Carrick must have sensed my mood because his hand found mine under the table and squeezed protectively.

"Well, we've been tracking that guy," said Mary. "We're trying to bring him down. And all the stuff you gave the FBI...that brought us a lot closer. So thank you."

I drew in my breath. "You're the Sisters of Invidia!"

The guy in a suit muttered a curse, then poked Gabriella. "I told you we should have changed name," he said in a thick Russian accent.

Mary ignored him. "Most of them," she told me. "Yolanda doesn't come on field trips. Let me have a look at what you've got."

I handed her the personality test.

"We need to find out where it was printed," Kian said. "If we can get that, maybe we can find out who paid for it and track them down. But I don't see how it's possible. There are no clues on there, nothing like a name or the logo of a printing company."

Mary smirked and dug in her shoulder bag. She pulled out a laptop festooned with stickers and a scanner that wouldn't have looked out of place in a CSI lab. The coffees arrived as she plugged the two of them together. "There are all sorts of things that can be hidden in ink," she said. She grabbed her latte and took a drink, then talked to us while the laptop booted up. "See, the government likes control. When there was just one printing firm in a town, if suddenly thousands of pamphlets talking about revolution started being passed around, it was pretty easy to figure out where they were coming from. But then the eighties and nineties rolled around and people started getting printers in their own homes...well, that wasn't good."

She stopped for a second to enter a password, her fingers flying over the keyboard. "Suddenly, people could print leaflets, ransom notes, even fake currency, and the government had no idea where it was coming from. So they made all the printer manufacturers make their printers encode a unique code into everything they print."

Kian frowned. "Really?"

"Yup," said Mary. She opened the lid of the scanner and slapped the personality test face-down on the glass, then hit a key on the laptop. The scanner hummed and whirred, a blinding light escaping around the edges of the paper and lighting up the inside of our UFO. "They can tell that two documents came from the same printer. And if you register your details when you buy the printer, to get the warranty, they know who you are and where you live. Mostly, it was designed to track home users but even big printing firms use commercial printers so...yup, there we go."

She spun her laptop around to show us the screen. Right in the middle of the front page of the personality test, dots that had been invisible to the naked eye had been highlighted and joined together into a pattern. "That's the printer's unique code. All I have to do is look it up in the database."

Kian leaned forward, shaking his head. "But that database...that's a government thing."

"Fortunately, government databases and I have a long and intimate history." She looked across at Gabriella. "Want to do it together?"

Gabriella beamed and pulled out her own laptop. Seconds later, they were both typing furiously while talking in indecipherable hacker speak. Before we'd even finished our coffees, they looked up from their screens triumphantly. "Henderson and Kolbech," said Mary. "They're right here in California. Bakersfield."

Carrick leaned forward. "Can you hack them? Find out who pays them to print all the tests?"

Mary shook her head. "Already tried."

"Their security's too tight?" asked Kian.

Gabriella gave him a look. "Oh, *please!* We were in there in twenty seconds. *What* security?"

Mary nodded. "Yeah, the problem is: there's nothing there. No customer records at all. They must keep everything on paper." She wrinkled her nose as if that was an alien concept to her.

"Maybe that's why Aeternus uses them," I said. "More secure."

Kian nodded. "Maybe." But he was frowning, as if there was another possibility. "We'll just have to pay them a visit."

"Pay them a visit?" I echoed. "You mean *break in?!*" I looked between Carrick and Kian, hoping I was wrong, but they didn't disagree.

I looked at the other side of the table for support but Mary put her hands up defensively. "Hey, don't bring me into it. What you do with the information's up to you. I stay strictly behind the keyboard, these days."

My heart sank and I turned to Carrick with big, pleading eyes. *What if he gets caught? Arrested?* He could wind up in jail, like his dad. But I couldn't ask him *not* to go, not when this was our only lead.

Carrick hugged me close and kissed the top of my head, then buried his nose in my hair. "It'll be fine," he told me. "Won't be the first time I've broken into somewhere. We'll be in and out. No cops."

He smiled at me and I gave him a nervous smile back but I didn't feel any better.

And I was right to be scared. It wasn't the cops we should have been worried about.

36

SEAN

Where the hell was she? I'd checked everywhere but I still couldn't find Louise. I'd even gone to Aedan and Sylvie's room but had stopped outside when I heard their low voices inside: Sylvie's strained and cracking, Aedan's low and reassuring. The door had been ajar and I'd glimpsed them through the crack, her face nestled in his chest, his arms wrapped around her. "No one's ever going to hurt you again," Aedan said. His voice was soft but his face was a mask of cold rage and his eyes were closed. Imagining what he was going to do when he got his hands on one of the cult members.

I'd checked our room, the living room, the kitchen—nothing. I knew she wasn't in the garden because a few hours ago, the heavens had opened and a heavy rain was battering against the windows. So where? This was the first time the house had been really quiet in days. With Aedan and Sylvie in their room and everyone else out, maybe I could finally talk to her.

Talk. Like I'm any good at that. But I had to do something. Seeing her so tense and withdrawn broke my heart. Was she worried about something? *Ill?* I thought of what had happened to Kayley and my stomach lurched. It would be just like Louise to keep illness a secret, too worried about looking after her sister to focus on herself....

I had to know.

But first I had to find her. Where would she go when she was feeling bad? Back when I first met her, she'd used to go up to the roof of our apartment building, where she kept her plants.

I finally figured it out and ran through the rain to the little greenhouse at the end of the garden. Louise was down on her knees, leaning over a tray of seedlings. I stopped just inside the doorway, shaking raindrops from my hair. God, she was beautiful. Surrounded by plants, she looked even more like some goddess of nature: that gorgeous soft, pale skin, the long red hair gleaming against the backdrop of green.

Every time I saw her, every *single* time, I was just so taken with her: that same sudden rush of emotion, that same need. I wanted those soft lips against mine, wanted to lose myself in her sweetness and fragrance. I wanted to feel the soft warmth of her breasts as they brushed my chest. I was desperate for her. Part of me wanted to forget the talking and just kiss the hell out of her.

No. I steeled myself. My girl was hurting. I had to find out why.

She wasn't planting or moving the seedlings to pots. She was just staring at them, stroking each tiny leaf with a fingertip. She didn't even seem to notice I was there until I closed the door. Then she looked up, caught my eye and immediately turned away. *Shit.* I'd never felt so clumsy, so useless. "I know something's up," I said, my voice low in my chest.

She shook her head, copper hair tossing in a way that made me catch my breath.

I bristled, the frustration building. No. No way. I wasn't going to let it go, not this time. We were private, for once, cocooned in the little glass house and then isolated a second time by the rain. No one was going to bother us for a while. As thunder sounded overhead, I walked over and squatted down next to her. "Louise?" I said slowly. "What's going on?"

But she still wouldn't look at me so I lifted her to her feet. She came easily at first and then tensed up, resisting. By the time I got her upright, her body was tight and hard, twisting away like a plant determined to grow in the other direction. "Louise!"

She finally looked up at me and I saw how those moss-green eyes were shining. I was getting mad, now. Not angry with her, angry at myself for being so bad at this. "What is it? What's the matter?!"

She bit her lip, about to tell me. Looked up into my furious eyes and twisted away again. I growled, put my hands on her waist and lifted her into the air, sitting her down on a table top so that she was eye-to-eye with me. "Goddammit, Louise, tell me!"

I saw her chest twitch, that last warning sign before the tears would break free. I'd done it again. I'd made the woman I loved cry. I stayed silent but, inside, I was screaming at myself for being a big, clumsy fucker. I felt like I was made of stone, a hulking great statue come to life, trying not to hurt the fragile human I held in my hands. I'd come here to help but I was just making things worse. *Why am I so bad at this?*

And Aedan's words came back to me. *Talk to her.*

I'm useless at that.

But I had to try.

I opened my mouth to speak but I couldn't find any words. So I did it with touch, instead. I loosened my hands on her waist so that I wasn't pinning her in place anymore. I pushed closer and slid my hands up and around her back, wrapping her up and drawing her to me.

She stayed tense and hard for a moment. Then she softened and her soft arms were sliding around my shoulders, vines entwining my stone statue. But I could still feel the heat of her chest, the damp of her eyes against my neck.

"Louise," I said. And then the words just ran out. I closed my eyes for a second and reached down deep. Trying to connect what I was feeling to my mouth felt like trying to get a pipe onto an oil well. But I finally managed it and then it all came pouring out. "I love you," I blurted. "I'll never stop loving you. And I know I'm not good at this stuff." The Irish was thick in my voice now, brought out by the emotion. "But I've got to know what's up with you. Are you ill? Is someone bothering you? Bothering Kayley? Louise, *whatever it is,* it's okay. There's nothing it could be that would stop me being crazy about you. Tell me. Let's face it together."

I stopped, the words still echoing. For a second, there was just the sound of the rain hammering down on the glass.

Then Louise moved back enough to look into my eyes. "I'm pregnant."

37

LOUISE

He froze. The man everyone feared, the man people used to run inside their homes and slam the doors to shelter from. All that strength, all that muscle and attitude and I'd stopped him dead with two words. I could see the shock change to raw fear in his eyes.

It was my greatest fear, come to life. I'd lost him. And now I was—

I couldn't even think the word: it was too terrifying. I slid off the table and past him and walked out into the rain. It was hammering down and the heavy drops were freezing cold, scouring all the warmth from the air. To me, they were a welcome relief. They chilled my burning cheeks, cooled the eyes that had gone liquid and hot.

I marched through the meadow, where we'd spent so many long, hot summer afternoons. The grass was soaking now, the long stalks soaking my jeans as I pushed through it. It wasn't his fault. He'd changed more than anyone could have expected. He'd put down his sledgehammer and left his old way of life behind. He'd gone straight, got a job, moved in with me and settled down. He'd even become like an older brother to Kayley. And now, by getting pregnant, I'd pushed him too far, too soon. I was—

My stomach lurched: I thought I was going to throw up. I couldn't think that word. I focused on the rain coursing down my face and mixing with my tears. I focused on the swing, the rain dripping from the wooden seat in little waterfalls. But it was no good. I couldn't hold back the thought any longer. *Mom is gone. Dad is gone. I have to look after Kayley and the baby and I'm—I'm all—*

I'm all on my own.

A hand grabbed mine from behind and spun me around. I slipped on the wet grass and almost fell but he didn't let me go: he lifted his arm and took my weight and I dangled there for a second, feet skittering, until I got my balance. I looked up into Irish blue eyes and gulped.

The fear was gone. He was angry, staring down accusingly at me, his chest stretching out his soaked white tank top as he took big, shuddering breaths.

"You daft feckin' mare," he snapped. "Where are you going?"

My breath caught and hitched on sobs. "You—You're scared! I s— scared you off!"

Those heavy brows knitted in a deep frown. "I was *shocked*. You just told me I'm going to be a dad!"

And I realized that I hadn't even considered that part. I sniffed, so much rain coursing down my face that I could barely breathe. "I didn't scare you off?" I had to almost shout it over the rain.

He looked at me as if I'd gone mad. "Scare me *off*? You mean away from you?!" He shook his head, rain droplets scattering. "Louise, for feck's sake. There's not a thing on this earth that could scare me off you."

Deep in my chest, a little flicker of hope crackled into life. But the worry I'd been carrying around pressed in on it, a freezing gray mist, threatening to snuff it out. I had to make sure he understood, had to get all my fears out there. I grabbed hold of his upper arms, looked up into his eyes and...."*We're having a baby!*" Which was at the same time stupid and a perfect summary of all my fears.

Sean cradled my cheek in a big, warm hand. "Yeah," he said. "It'll be great."

That little flicker of hope flared and rose, pushing back the gray.

"But I don't know anything about—it's a *baby!* How do I—What if I—"

He cupped my other cheek. Gave one low command, granite-hard but warm with Irish silver. "*Stop.*"

I stopped.

"Swap all those *I's* for *We's.*"

I did. And then let out something between a hysterical hiccup and a nervous laugh. It all sounded better, with *we's.*

Sean leaned down and touched his wet forehead to mine. "Louise, the only thing you did wrong, the only thing you can ever do wrong, is not telling me about stuff. I've been going out of my feckin' mind!"

I flushed. But I was still jumpy inside, like when you wake from a nightmare and it still feels real. "I'm not on my own?" I asked, voice quavering.

In answer, he pulled me tight into his chest and wrapped his arms around me. Our clothes were soaked but the heat of his body soaked into me and, with his head lowered to kiss my wet hair and his arms hugging me close, I couldn't feel the rain at all. And I let out a spluttering, tear-filled snort of joy and he moved back just far enough to kiss me.

The rain sluiced down our faces and washed my tears away and there was only his lips, hard and strong and *certain,* and his tongue teasing mine, and the solid weight of his body, a warm mountain against me. And I cursed myself for being so stupid, for not trusting him.

I broke the kiss so that I could lean back and look at him. He was gazing down into my eyes with relief and frustration and...*pride?*

"You look feckin' amazing, Louise," he told me.

I blinked. "What?" I looked down at myself. I was drenched and disheveled, my hair plastered to my back. *Wait...does he mean....* "I don't look any different," I said. "Not *yet!*"

But he just shook his head. "Yeah, you do," he said. And his voice was heavy with lust and emotion. "And it's great."

I looked down at myself again and I saw myself through his eyes. I hadn't thought about that part of it, either. I'd been focusing on the nausea and the mood swings. I hadn't seen myself as being.... I blinked. Maybe I didn't *look* any different but I sort of knew what he meant. I felt sort of...*bountiful*. Earth-motherly. And from the look in his eyes, he liked that. I flushed. Then his hand was on my belly, its warmth soaking into me through my wet clothes. And he just looked into my eyes and nodded, and everything was okay. Everything was *better* than okay. Everything was great.

He put a hand under my ass and scooped me up into the air, drawing me against him as he kissed me again, long and slow, and this time I could relax into it and give a joyous little moan of delight because I had my man back...and I realized I'd never lost him at all. We stayed there for a while, the cold rain soaking our backs and each others' heat warming our fronts. And then the warm push of our bodies started to have an effect.

"I s'pose this means no sex for a while?" Sean muttered in my ear, each syllable a little rush of blazing, silver air.

"No," I breathed, surprised at how urgently it came out. I could feel a sudden heat pulling at me: it had been suppressed by all the worrying but now it was rising up inside me, desperate to be released. I shifted position slightly and my soaking thigh grazed the hard bulge at Sean's groin, the wet denim feeling paper-thin. I groaned and swept my hands up his back, tracing his muscles through his wet, clinging t-shirt. "It's fine for six months, at least."

He lifted me a little higher and suddenly started walking through the rain, so suddenly I gave a yelp of shock and anticipation. I was bouncing in his arms and every bounce stroked me against his cock, every brief contact making him grip me a little tighter, walk a little faster. We entered the garage. I could still hear the rain pounding down outside but for the first time in what felt like hours, it wasn't running down my face.

Sean opened the rear door of the Mustang and almost threw me inside. I landed on my back on the soft leather seat and quickly scooched along it to give him room. He climbed in, his knees between my legs. It occurred to me that we'd never actually done it in the

Mustang, despite—let's face it—Mustangs practically being made for separating good girls from their panties.

"Guess I don't need to look for a condom anymore, do I?" Sean panted, hunkering down over me.

"I guess you don't," I said breathlessly

He leaned down and kissed me hard and it was like I'd been hit by a live wire: everything I loved about him rocketed down inside me, thundering through my body and lighting me up from the inside out. It was like coming alive again: I hadn't realized how much the stress of not telling him had locked me up tight. We kissed madly, desperately, we kissed like we only had a few seconds left. When the seat beneath me had melted away and I was swirling somewhere on a cloud, Sean broke the kiss, took my chin between his fingers and glared down at me. "Don't be doing that again—not telling me stuff."

"*Uh-huh*," I panted, nodding.

He grabbed the hem of my tank top and wrenched it up, wet fabric catching and stretching. I levered myself up and he peeled it off me and then my bra came off too in one messy, wet tangle of dripping straps. I fought it over my head, grabbed the bottom of his t-shirt and pulled that off him, hurling it over my head to slap against the window, and then we were skin to skin and I moaned as my breasts stroked against his muscles. Every sense had awoken: I could feel every millimeter of wet skin as it contacted his body. I could feel the tiny crinkles around my nipples and the perfect, hard curve of his pecs as they ground against them. God, I'd missed him. And he'd never even been away: *I* had.

We kissed: slower and open-mouthed with low, groaning breaths. Our hands became frantic on each other's bodies, moving without conscious control, driven by the kiss.

He ducked his head and slid down my body. I grabbed at the leather seat, fingers digging deep into its softness as his chest glided over my breasts. Then his mouth was on me, his hands rough as he squeezed my breasts and brought them to his mouth. "*Christ, you're glorious,*" he panted between licks, and the heat blazed and scalded right down to my toes. I writhed like a mermaid under him, dripping wet and gasping, my heels kicking at the edge of the seat, his knees and lower legs hanging outside the car. The interior echoed with the sound of our panting; the rain seemed very far away.

He lifted his head, my breasts shining and wet, throbbing from his mouth. I felt his hands pluck open the button of my jeans and then he was dragging the wet fabric down over my hips. The wet denim resisted, clinging to me, so he pulled harder and I yelped as I was pulled along, too. I had to reach over my head and grab onto the door handle to give him traction and then he did it, jeans and panties slithering down my calves, my sneakers going with them. I saw his eyes lock on the little patch of copper hair between my thighs the instant it appeared. That cobalt-blue gaze seemed to sear straight into me like a laser, melting me into lava: I ground my hips against the seat in response and *he* reacted to *that,* every muscle of his naked chest standing out hard and primed....

He almost dived back into the car, his own jeans rasping on my inner thighs with delicious friction. I wound myself around him, entangling him with arms and legs. We kissed with him taking his weight on his elbows so he could free his own jeans. I felt him ram them down his thighs, his hips spread mine and—

I cried out and clawed at his back as I felt him enter me. It was my first time without a condom and God, it was so different: so hot and naked and real. He surged up inside me and my knees rose, my toes dancing on the very edge of the seat. *"Oh Jesus God yes!"*

He buried himself inside me and for a second we just stopped, our bodies joined. I slowly opened my eyes and we just stared at each other, utterly connected, both of us getting used to the new sensation. His eyes roamed over my naked body and I could understand the lust in his gaze because I was feeling it, too. He was getting off on taking this...*maiden* that he'd already...*seeded.* And I was looking up at the hulking, brooding warrior who'd...*bred* me. It was so caveman, so primal, and it was turning into raw, urgent heat in my groin, a need I couldn't ignore. I writhed a little, unable to help myself, and he growled low in his throat and pinned my shoulders to the seat, both of us panting.

He began to move: slow at first, hips drawing back and then pressing forward to fill me again. I moaned and tilted my head way back, wet hair squeaking on the leather. God, I could feel every silken millimeter of him, every vein, as he plunged deep into me. It was like being without clothes for the first time, feeling the air on your skin. His hands slid down from my shoulders, tracing my body all the way down to my hips, sending waves of heat radiating inward to join the twisting, lashing fire at my core. I did the same, palms flowing over his back as if sculpting him, thrilling at his hardness, at the way his shoulders and lats bulged under my fingertips.

"God, Louise," he breathed. He brushed damp strands of hair from my cheeks with his thumbs. "You make me crazy. Always have done."

I reached up, grabbed the back of his head and pulled him down to me. We started kissing again as he began to move. It became a smooth pumping, his ass rising and falling between my thighs, the car rocking gently on its suspension. The heat was tightening with each thrust, drawing everything inward, stealing the air from my lungs and making me claw and grab at him. My hands slid down his back and found the hard muscles of his ass, pulling him into me. His hands covered my breasts, thumbs stroking over my nipples, and I gasped and moaned and circled my groin under him, needing to move, delighting in the way he so easily held me fast. It became hard, brutal, a pounding between my legs that was exactly what I needed. We stared into each other's eyes, his fingers buried in my hair, the heat filling me now, cinching unbearably tight—

"I love you, Louise," he panted. And even as the glow from those words rushed through me, I saw in his eyes the exact second he let go. I felt his hips lunge forward, felt the first jerk of his cock deep inside me....

And that sent me over the edge. I knitted my fingers into the short hair at the back of his head and kissed him deep and hard as he shot and shot, my own climax roaring through me as all the tight heat exploded. It rushed through me like a forest fire, blasting away everything before it. I screamed out my pleasure. My shoulders lifted into the air, my heels hammered on the seat and my fingers rasped again and again over the bristly fuzz at the base of his scalp. My groin ground against his as I shuddered through each hot jet inside me. When I finally slumped back onto the seat, breathless and exhausted, I realized all of the stress of the last few weeks had evaporated.

"We need to do that more," I croaked. "We need to do that a lot more."

Sean didn't speak, just hugged me close.

That evening, the others returned from meeting the hacker. Carrick gave Sean and me a curious look as he climbed off his Harley. I flushed and squeezed Sean's hand, trying to look innocent. Carrick just smiled and, as he walked past us, he clapped Sean affectionately on the shoulder as if to say, *well done.* I was embarrassed that people seemed to know we'd been having problems but it didn't matter: I was so happy, it was hard to keep from grinning.

Until, over dinner, the others told us the plan.

The plan was to break into the printing works this Mary person had located. And they would do it straight after dinner, so they'd have the cover of darkness. As soon as the meal ended, I pulled Sean into the kitchen on pretense of needing his help. "You don't have to go!" I told him.

He sighed and stroked my hair. "Yeah, I do."

"It doesn't take four of you to break in!" I was desperate, flailing around for an excuse. "In fact, fewer is better. Stealthier. Burglars don't go around in fours."

"Out of all of us, Carrick and me are most used to paying places a visit in the dead of night."

"But you used to smash your way in, not be all....cat burglar-y!" I reached up and grabbed hold of his shoulders. "I just have a bad feeling. I don't want you away...now."

He looked down into my eyes, then lower, down to my stomach.

He slid a hand down my body and rested his palm there. I could see the battle going on in his eyes: his need to care for me, for the baby; his need to help his brothers. "I'll be fine," he said at last.

"Don't say that! That's what fathers-to-be say in movies just before—"

He gave me a look that quieted me. Then he ran the hand back up my body, stopping on the way to give my breast a squeeze. I gasped and went up on my tiptoes just in time to meet his lips as they came down.

We had a lot of time to make up for.

I felt myself slowly relax as the kiss grabbed hold of me. *God, he's a good kisser.* I moved with it, my body arching and flexing against his, lips gliding and tongue teasing and—

He broke the kiss and I reluctantly sank back down onto my heels. "More later," he promised.

My eyes went wide. "Don't say that! Stop saying things like that, just before you—"

He squeezed me and kissed the top of my head, then quickly turned and walked away. It was only later, remembering that moment, that I realized *he* didn't want to leave, either, that he was doing it before he changed his mind.

I wasn't the only one who was nervous. Annabelle gave Carrick an extra big hug, clinging to him for long seconds before she let him go. Sylvie, still pale and shaky, clutched Aedan close. I could see the determination in Aedan's eyes: after what the cult had done to his girl, he was ready to kill: God, he almost looked as if he *hoped* they'd run into trouble.

And then there was Kian. He was standing awkwardly by the open door of the Mustang and it suddenly hit me that he didn't have anyone to say goodbye to him. He was doing his best to hide it: checking the time, looking impatient. But I knew what he really needed was Emily to run up to him, throw her arms around him and tell him not to go. He needed to know that someone wanted him to come back. *Should I just run in there and give him a hug?*

Too late. Everyone climbed into the car and I was left there cursing myself. Sean gave me a smile from the driver's seat and I had to resist the temptation to run to his window and press myself to the glass.

And then they were gone, the whole street echoing with the Mustang's roar, and the three of us were left standing on the porch. *What happens if they wind up in jail? Or dead?*

I couldn't take my eyes off the car's tail lights as they faded into the distance. I reached out my arms, felt for the other two girls, and pulled them close.

38

KIAN

We sat there in the darkness, not speaking, just watching. Everything looked good. The printing works was on a quiet backstreet. Only a few cars had passed by the alley we were parked in, there was no sign of any cops, no private security cruising around and no glow of a flashlight inside that would suggest a night watchman. It looked easy.

So why was I so tense? Why did something feel wrong?

I looked across at Aedan but he was staring straight out through the windshield, messing with something in his jeans pocket as if he was turning it over and over in his hand for good luck. In the driver's seat, Sean looked like I felt: eager to get this over with but twitchy as hell. And Carrick was his usual grim, stoic self. We'd let him ride shotgun because foregoing the Harley *and* being crammed into the back seat was too much to ask.

The hell with it. Let's just do it.

I climbed out and the others did the same. In front of us, the huge brick building stayed silent and dark. It looked to be well over a hundred years old and it hadn't been maintained well: even from down on the ground, I could see that the roof was ragged in places and the iron fire escape looked like a death trap. Hopefully that meant they were too cheap to spring for decent alarms.

Carrick and Sean went first because they'd at least had experience breaking into places. Aedan and I were just muscle and hopefully we wouldn't even be needed: we'd sneak in, find the paperwork we needed and sneak out with no more than a broken window left behind. But as the moon crept out from behind a cloud and I saw Aedan's face, I realized he didn't feel the same way. He looked like he was just about to step into the ring. He *wanted* us to run into some cult member, wanted revenge for what they'd done to Sylvie. *Aw, hell....*

"Here," muttered Carrick. We all joined him at a window. "Other ones are alarmed but they skipped this one because it doesn't open. So..." He pressed strips of duct tape all over it, turning it into a lattice, and then he punched the pane until it crumpled silently inward. In a few minutes, the window frame was empty and he tossed the mess of tape and glass to the ground. He caught my raised eyebrow. "Had to sneak into a few other MC clubhouses, in my time. Guy called Hunter taught me how."

We climbed through one by one. There were skylights in the roof and just enough moonlight came through to see by. It was one huge room with several massive printing presses down the center, each one the size of a truck. Huge rolls of paper, eight or ten feet across, were already in the machines. It wound around rollers and then leapt across the gaps from machine to machine, stretched tight as a drum skin between them. You could actually walk under it in some places, and it was like being under the awning of a tent. The smell of ink filled my nostrils: that scent you get when you unfold a fresh newspaper, but times a thousand.

Down at one end, some iron stairs led up to a raised area with glass-fronted offices: probably where the boss sat to keep an eye on things. I nodded towards it and we started to move, Sean and me on one side of the presses and Carrick and Aedan on the other.

Dammit, I wish Emily was here.

It jumped into my mind, taking me by surprise. *No I don't!* If she was here, I'd be arguing with her, hustling her to safety. I didn't want her *here.* I just—

I just wanted her close. Not on the other side of the country with no idea of what she was doing. I wanted to kiss her goodbye, kiss her when I got back, wrap her up in my arms at night—

It hit me hard: *I can't do without her.* I couldn't understand it: I'd functioned just fine on my own in the Marines and then in the Secret Service. But either I'd lost that ability, now that I'd seen how much better life could be when you had someone to share it with…or I'd been kidding myself that I'd been fine all those years. I closed my eyes for a split second, imagining the brush of her silk-soft hair against my shoulder, my hands stroking down her naked back to her—

"Christ!" yelled Sean. At the same exact second there was a dull thump as two bodies collided. As I opened my eyes, I saw him crash to the floor, another man on top of him. I winced as the back of Sean's head hit the floor

Fuck. I ran towards them but I knew it might already be too late: I'd missed the guy's silent approach because I was getting all dewy-eyed about Emily. *You moron!*

A knife blade flashed in the darkness: the guy raised it, then brought it down towards Sean's chest.

My little brother groggily raised his hands and caught the guy's hands in his, stopping the blade an inch short of his body. The blade winked in the moonlight as they fought for control, muscles straining against one another. The guy was a similar build to all of us: big, muscles standing out in his arms, their shape visible through the thin hooded top he wore. But Sean had had years of swinging that sledgehammer of his: he could hold his own, even semi-conscious, at least for a few seconds.

And a few seconds was all I needed. With a howl of rage, I barreled into the guy, knocking him sideways. He managed to keep hold of the knife, though, and he was on his feet in an instant, stabbing and slashing, making me jump back. I'd faced people with knives plenty of times in the Secret Service but most of them were idiots who didn't know how to fight with one. Someone had trained this guy.

I had to get him away from Sean, who was still trying to get to his feet, and over to the other side of the room where Carrick and Aedan could help. They were calling to me, trying to figure out where we were in the darkness, but the huge printing presses blocked the direct route across.

I found a point where the paper stretched between machines and ducked under it, backing away from the guy. He followed, the moonlight from above shining through the thin paper and bathing us in a soft glow. He had his hood up and I couldn't see his face but I was betting he was with the cult, sent to stop us.

He suddenly lunged forward with the knife and I only just knocked his hand to the side in time. Then he stabbed up. If I hadn't staggered back at that exact moment, he would have buried the knife under my chin. Instead, the blade stabbed into the stretched paper above us. I grabbed his hands, trying to keep the blade away from my face. But I was off balance and he just pushed me back. God, he was strong as well as fast. The knife slashed a long tear in the paper as we moved, the two halves falling either side of us.

He was moving faster and faster, almost running, now, and I was having to stagger backwards to match him. I had to stay upright because that's the only way I could keep forcing the knife up and away, but sooner or later I was going to miss my footing and then—

As we emerged from under the paper, it happened. I staggered and went down and he fell atop me. There was too much momentum to stop the knife: all I could do was twist to the side and hope. I felt it burn as it whistled past my cheek and then it stabbed into the linoleum. *Jesus, that really hurt.* I was pretty sure I was bleeding. And the knife was already lifting again—

A chain whipped around the guy's wrist and he cried out in pain as it suddenly wrenched him half off me. This time, the knife went skittering into the darkness. Carrick stepped out of the shadows, the other end of the chain gripped in his fist. "Right, you fucker," he growled. He jerked the chain again and the guy was dragged forward towards Carrick's waiting fists.

"Watch it," I panted. "He's tougher than he—"

The guy waited until he had just enough slack in the chain and then ducked under Carrick's punch and drove his shoulder into his stomach. Carrick folded, the air knocked out of him, and the guy gave him a vicious kick in the head. *Fuck!* He really had been trained. He took control of the chain, using it to pull Carrick forward so he could hit him right in the face. Carrick staggered and fell to his knees.

Fuck! I got to my feet but hot blood was dripping down my face and I was still winded. And Sean: where was Sean? He should have been on his feet by now, helping us. Unless....

Unless he was hurt much worse than I'd thought.

My stomach twisted. First Sean, then me, now Carrick. This guy was taking us out one by one. I saw him draw back his fist again—

"Oi." The voice was quiet and utterly calm. It came from the darkness right beside him.

The guy turned just in time to take Aedan's fist right in the jaw. A real Aedan special, strong enough to lift him right off his feet. He went sailing backwards, dropping the chain, and crashed to the floor.

He was up again in an instant. My jaw dropped: I'd never seen anyone take so much punishment and keep getting back up. But Aedan was marching towards him, unstoppable as a freight train.

"You *fucker!*" yelled Aedan, and hit him again.

The guy staggered back, on the defensive, now. He tried hitting back, a quick one-two that would have stopped another man cold. But Aedan just knocked the punches aside like they were nothing. For the first time, I saw a tiny hint of fear in the way the guy shuffled back: he'd finally met his match.

Another punch from Aedan doubled him over. The next one caught him under the chin and knocked him back against a wall and now I saw his head turn: he was looking for somewhere to run. But Aedan wasn't going to let him escape. He roared and hit him again. As he stepped forward into a shaft of moonlight, I saw Aedan's face for the first time. It was a mask of rage, so twisted up with anger that he barely looked like my brother anymore. "My mom," he spat, and that big fist connected again. "My dad. My brother."

A flurry of punches and the guy slumped to the floor. Between the shadows and his hood, I couldn't see what shape his face was in but it must have been a mess. "Enough," I called. "Aedan, *enough!* You'll kill him!"

Aedan ignored me.

He grabbed the front of the guy's hooded top and lifted him clear of the ground. "*Sylvie!*" he spat. "You hurt Sylvie, you fuckers!"

And he drew back his fist for a punch I knew would end the guy.

39

BRADAN

I'd followed them from the house all the way to their meeting with the four strangers. I'd sat in that diner, in the booth behind theirs, and strained my ears to pick up every word of their conversation that I could. When I'd told Dad that they were going to break into the printing firm we used, he was very clear on what I had to do: make sure they never bother us again.

But I hadn't expected *this*. I'd managed to take one of them by surprise but the one in the suit had been trained. The biker had that damn chain and now my head was ringing and the world was going dark as I was pummeled by the one who hit like a prizefighter. I'd always been taught that Outsiders only cared about themselves. But these four were working together, saving each other from me, like—

A memory from that dark hallway in my mind, the thick glass cracked by the pain I was enduring. Running. Running up a hill on little short legs, laughing. Slipping and tripping but hands hauled me back up. A name—

"Aedan, *enough!* You'll kill him!"

The memory dissolved and I was back in the present, being hefted into the air. "*Sylvie!*" the man spat. "You hurt Sylvie, you fuckers!"

He drew back his fist. I tried to twist aside but my whole body felt slow and numb. Blood was trickling into one eye and I suspected a few ribs were broken. *I'm going to die.* But at least I'd die bringing Beautiful Order.

Just as the fist started forward, the one in a suit caught it. He had to put his whole weight into holding back the other guy's arm and even then the fist slowly crept towards my face. "*No!*" he snapped. "Jesus, Aedan, Sylvie wouldn't want this!"

The fighter, as I thought of him now, just shook his head and *heaved,* nearly shaking the other one off. But then the biker put his hand on his shoulder. "He's right. The fucker deserves it but these people own the police: if someone finds a body—"

The fighter was panting through his teeth. For long seconds, I thought he was going to shake off the others and go ahead and kill me. But then he slowly lowered me to the floor. I let my body go completely limp, even when that meant my head knocked against the wall. I needed them to drop their guard.

"Watch him," said the one in a suit. "We can get some answers out of him. I'll go and check on Sean." And he strode off into the darkness.

"You okay?" the fighter grunted to the biker. There was something in their voices. I hadn't really picked up on it, at the diner: I'd been too busy memorizing what they said. But there was a strong accent. I wasn't familiar with it...and yet one for some reason it resonated, deep inside me, as if I *was.*

The biker grunted. One eye was already swelling shut and he was swaying on his feet. He wasn't the threat: the fighter was. "You did the right thing," he muttered. "Kian was right. Sylvie wouldn't want it."

The fighter stepped closer to me. "Let's have a look at him."

As he reached down to pull back my hood, he was off balance for a second. I reached up, grabbed his wrist with both hands and pulled, dropping down onto my back at the same time. He fell forward, cracking his head on the wall, and I slithered out from under him.

"*Shit!*" The biker grabbed for me. Missed. And then I was running down the room. "*Kian!*" the biker yelled.

Three sets of running footsteps behind me. They'd be on me in seconds: I was staggering and weak from the beating I'd taken. The door whose lock I'd picked was in the other direction and so was the window they'd used. But I knew how I could get away: and maybe get them all arrested, to boot.

I ran straight for one of the big, plate-glass windows, wrapped my arms around my head and dove straight through it.

And the room exploded into sound as the burglar alarm went off.

40

CARRICK

Everything changed in a heartbeat. The printing works' alarm was ancient: instead of a shrieking electronic tone, it had an old-fashioned mechanical bell, metal hammering metal hundreds of times a second. We all threw our hands over our ears as it pounded our eardrums. "*Jesus!*" I shouted.

Kian ran out of the shadows. My stomach lurched when I saw Sean: he was awake, but slumped against Kian's body, unable to stand on his own. "Is he okay?" I had to squint to see him: my right eye was swollen almost completely closed.

"I don't know. There's a lot of blood." It was the first time I'd ever seen Kian really panicked. "Aedan?"

I turned and helped Aedan to his feet. He was groggy, too: he'd cracked his head against the wall when that cult fucker grabbed him. We were *all* messed up. I spun and took a step towards the window the guy had jumped through.

"Leave him!" snapped Kian. "He's long gone. We've got to get out of here!"

I looked towards the offices where we thought the files were.

"No! There's no time!"

But I started walking.

Kian grabbed the back of my leather cut. "Carrick, the police'll be here in a few minutes. We don't even know if there's anything in there!"

"That guy was here to stop us," I growled. "There *must* be something here."

But Kian wouldn't let go. "Sean's hurt! We've got to get him out of here!"

I turned to him. Our faces were only inches apart. "It's the only way to find Bradan!" I yelled.

"We can't help him if we're all in jail!"

I looked at the stairs. Looked back at him. "We won't be," I said. "Just me. Get him to the car and get out of here."

And I was off and running towards the stairs at the end of the room. Behind me, I heard Kian curse and start to drag Sean away.

My boots must have made a hell of a racket sprinting up the iron stairs but I could barely hear them: I was closer to the alarm bell, here, and the noise was head-splitting. I burst into the offices and grimaced. The place was *lined* with filing cabinets. *This is what happens when you refuse to use computers.*

I picked one at random and started rifling through it. Customers. And all neatly sorted into alphabetical order. Except...I got a sick feeling in my stomach. I had no idea what name I was looking for. The name was what we needed to find out!

There was one hope: each customer file seemed to have a master copy of what the company had printed for them. Somewhere, there'd be a file with that creepy personality test in...but I was going to have to go through every file to find it.

There was a *bang* from right next to me as a drawer was flung open. I spun around to see Aedan standing there: I hadn't heard him follow me in, with the alarm clanging in my ears. "Faster with two," he said without looking up.

I froze for a second, stunned. When I'd ran up to the office, there'd been a kind of grim familiarity to it: *on my own, again.* I figured I'd get caught but at least I'd get the information we needed.

I'd pass it to the others when they visited me in jail, if need be. I knew guys who'd done time. I'd survive.

And now suddenly Aedan was here. I wanted to grab him and shake him: *what the hell do you think you're doing?* I rode with the MC: getting caught by the cops, even doing time, was an occupational hazard. But he was doing well, he had Sylvie....

And I have Annabelle. The thought of sitting in a cold cell, cut off from her...suddenly, that didn't sound so easy. And just as I admitted *that,* something else crept in: a warm glow. Aedan wasn't going to desert me, wasn't going to let me take the rap on my own. I'd had that feeling before, with the MC. But I hadn't had it from a brother, not for a very long time. The emotion swelled up inside: it was suddenly difficult to breathe.

I grunted and turned back to my filing cabinet, discarding file after file. *Nothing. Nothing.* And now, off in the distance, I could hear the wail of sirens. *Maybe they're on their way somewhere else.* I started the next drawer. *Nothing.* The sirens were getting louder. *Shit!*

The door crashed open behind me and I spun around: if I could tackle the cop to the ground, maybe at least Aedan could get by him. I lowered my shoulder, ready to charge—

But it wasn't a cop. It was Kian. He and I exchanged a look...and then he ran to the filing cabinet next to Aedan's. We all searched frantically, rooting through drawers, leaving them hanging open when we'd finished. *Still* nothing. "What about Sean?" I yelled as I finished the first cabinet.

"In the car, down the alley. Cops'll think he's just a drunk, sleeping it off."

I ran to a fresh filing cabinet and pulled open the first drawer. "You should have left," I muttered. But that feeling I'd had was back, and stronger. It was just like when we were kids again: defending each other, sticking together, one of us down but the family still strong.

I felt a swell of pride. Now we just needed Bradan.

I rifled through the drawer. *Nothing.* And now the sirens sounded like they were right outside. I could feel the mood in the room change. We knew we were going to get caught, now. We were just hoping we could make it worthwhile. I glanced up just as I pulled open the next drawer. The night had turned red and blue outside the windows. *Shit!* I looked down.

I feel happy and secure when I know exactly what I'm meant to be doing, I read. I gave a strangled groan of disbelief. Questions. Check boxes. Yep, it was the test. I grabbed the whole file. "Got it!" I yelled.

We all just looked at each other in shock for an instant. Then we bolted for the stairs. The alarm drowned out the sound of the engines but we could see police cars pulling up outside.

I sprinted towards the window the cult guy had jumped through but, just as we arrived, someone shone a flashlight through it from outside. I backpedaled and we ran the other way, back to the window we'd climbed in through. We were halfway there when a cop appeared in it, silhouetted by the lights behind him. *Fuck!* We were trapped! We hunkered behind one of the huge printing presses, panting and desperate.

"What about him?" asked Kian suddenly.

"Who?" I asked.

"The cult guy. He must have gotten in somehow." Kian narrowed his eyes, looking towards the far corner of the huge room. "He came from over there."

We ran into the shadows. Behind us, flashlights lit up the darkness: unless we could find a way out, they were going to find us in seconds. There was a loading dock. The big doors for trucks were padlocked shut. But next to them was a regular, blue-painted door....

I tried the handle and prayed.

The door swung inward, bathing us in cool night air. All of us gave a groan of relief and we raced outside and down the side of the building to the alley. Sean was in the back seat, belted in to keep him upright. I dived in beside him.

Kian jumped into the passenger seat. Aedan got behind the wheel. "Keys!" he yelled.

Shit. I started going through Sean's pockets. As I leaned across him, my arm brushed warm wetness on the back of the seat. With a sinking feeling in my stomach, I fumbled with the overhead light. The interior suddenly lit up...and I caught my breath. Blood was dripping from the back of Sean's head, coating the seats. *"Fuck!"* I spat, and searched faster. My fingers finally closed on hard metal and I pulled out the keys and tossed them to Aedan. "Hospital!"

The engine roared into life and we tore away into the night.

41

BRADAN

Dad summoned me as soon as I got back. I walked down the hallway to his study, wishing I'd at least had time to wash the blood off my face. I knew he wouldn't have sympathy: the wounds were my fault. They were evidence that I'd made a mistake.

Dad wasn't at his desk, for once. He wasn't doing anything as lazy as sleeping, even though it was late, but he was sitting in a leather armchair with a glass of cognac. *Maybe that's what he does instead of sleep.* There were no women, this time, and that didn't bode well.

He stared at me. I didn't have to speak. If I'd been successful, I wouldn't be all battered. He just sat there glaring, his gaze stripping me down to the bone.

Movies and TV are for the weak, a diversion that stops Outsiders from focusing on the real problems of the world. But occasionally, when I was on a job, I'd have to follow someone into a movie theater, or spy on them when they were at home watching TV, and I'd see what they saw. I could see why it was so addictive. Everyone was so beautiful and the stories were so...*satisfying.*

In one of those TV shows, there was a boy and a father. And the father disciplined the boy but he was kind to him, too. Even when the boy got a bad mark on a test at school, the father still loved him.

It made me so angry. Partly because it was just another example of how TV and Movies lie to the Outsiders: Dad wasn't like that at all, his love conditional and never put into words. And partly because it stirred a memory locked behind the glass in my mind. A memory of another father, one who was *just* like the one on TV.

"*How?*" asked Dad at last.

He was even angrier than I'd thought. The terror started to unwind inside me. The one thing I'm scared of: disappointing him. I took a deep breath, which hurt my bruised chest. "I underestimated them," I said. "One of them was trained, maybe military. Another was a fighter. One had a chain."

"A *chain?!*" His voice struck me like a whip. "Did we waste all our time when we taught you how to fight?"

I thought of those endless years, out in the desert. Running until my legs gave way. Grappling and punching and kicking the endless stream of men they sent at me, ending every single day in much worse shape than I was now, until I gradually became stronger. "No," I said.

He sipped his drink. "Do you have *any* good news for me? Did you at least stop them getting any information?"

The sick fear inside me spread. I closed my eyes in shame.

"*Look at me when I'm talking to you!*" Dad roared.

My eyes flew open. He was glaring at me and the disappointment I saw there made my heart feel like it was tearing in two. If I could have gone back in time, at that second, I would have kept throwing punches at that fighter instead of collapsing like a weakling. I would have kept fighting and fighting, even when my arms failed and had no power, until he had to kill me, because even death would be better than this.

What if this is it? What if he says I'm no longer Prime? What if he throws me out entirely? I couldn't imagine life outside Aeternus, in the same way you can't really imagine death: I just thought of a blank nothingness, unending. I'd done so much to bring Beautiful Order, over the years, but all that counted for nothing. With Dad, you're always on your last chance.

"I had to escape," I said. "They'd caught me. I was outnumbered."

"So you *ran?!*"

I hung my head but his eyes didn't leave me. They burned into me until I was screaming inside, barely able to breathe. *Stop it! I'm sorry! I'll do anything!*

"We have to assume they got what they came for," said Dad. "That could lead them right back here. They could threaten us. They could stop us bringing Beautiful Order."

The way he said those last two words was so perfect, like music in my brain. The idea that everything he'd worked for could be destroyed was horrific; the idea that it would be my fault made me want to throw up. "No!" I croaked.

He went quiet. I didn't dare look up for a long time but, when I did, he was looking at me with great sadness...and a hint of forgiveness. He lifted his hand and I raced forward and clasped it in mine.

"You can fix this," he said. "But it needs to be done right, this time. No mistakes." His eyes looked deep into me. Could they see? Could they see the weakness I'd been feeling, since this whole thing started? Did he know about the memories banging on the other side of the glass?

"No mistakes," I echoed firmly. *I'll make it right. I'll please him.* If I pleased him enough, maybe he'd even say those words I needed to hear so much.

"Go to their house," he told me. "And kill every one of them." His gaze pinned me. "Even their women, Bradan. Kill them all."

42

SEAN

"Follow the light," said the doctor.

I followed his penlight as it went back and forth in front of me. Behind the doctor, Kian, Carrick and Aedan were watching, worried. Kian, especially, had gone white when we'd come into the bright lights of the ER and he'd seen the sheer quantity of blood that had dripped onto my neck and back. I knew where part of the concern came from: he'd always been the responsible one, looking after us all, and I was the youngest. I understood that but it still made me a little mad: when was he going to realize I wasn't a baby anymore?

"He'll be fine," said the doctor at last. "Head wounds always bleed a lot, but there's no damage to the skull."

The others let out long sighs of relief. "You inherited the O'Harra hard head," Aedan told me. "We should have made a boxer out of you."

~

By the time we arrived, it was the early hours. But the girls had waited up for us. As soon as the Mustang's roar echoed off the windows, they flooded out of the door. Almost before Aedan had brought us to a stop, they had the doors open and were pulling us out like anxious mothers. It was chaos for a few minutes: four female voices all talking at once: they told us how worried they'd been, berated us for being in danger, fussed over our injuries...and then they started all over again.

Wait...*four* voices? Then I saw that Kayley was there too, long, long after her bedtime, and was worrying and berating and fussing with the rest of them. They hustled us up the driveway and into the house: Annabelle pulling Carrick, Sylvie pulling Aedan, Louise and Kayley taking one of my arms each. It was overpowering...and wonderful.

Then I heard the car doors slam behind us. Kian had stopped to close them because...my stomach twisted guiltily. *Because there's no one for him to come home to.*

I grabbed hold of Kayley's t-shirt. "Kian needs you," I whispered in her ear.

She got it straightaway and ran off, grabbing hold of him and pulling him to the house, too. She had her sister's caring nature. *I hope our daughter inherits that, too.*

That thought made me stop in my tracks. *Our daughter. Or son. God....* It was the first time I'd thought of it in those terms: not just a pregnancy and a baby but a child to raise. Louise was pulled up short by my sudden stop and turned to look at me in concern, worried I was going to collapse.

I gave her what I hoped was a reassuring smile and, unable to help myself, slid a hand under her tank top and laid it on her smooth belly. She smiled too, blushing, but pushed my hand away before someone saw. *She hasn't told the other girls, then.* I realized that, at some point, I'd better tell my brothers. But first I had to get my own head around the whole thing.

The girls bundled us inside the house and into chairs. The living room became a hive of activity as wounds were cleaned and bandaged. "We need a steak, to put on your eye," Annabelle told Carrick.

Sylvie shook her head. "That's a myth. Just put ice on it."

Behind her, I saw Aedan reach into his pocket and close his fist around something, as if he was about to pull it out. But at that second, Sylvie turned to face him. "Oh, Jesus! Look at you!"

His injuries were nothing compared to how the cult guy must look, but they were still pretty nasty: a cut over one eye and a big, shiny bruised cheek that had swelled up even more since the hospital. "You poor thing," Sylvie said, hugging him. "You're a mess!"

I saw Aedan open his fist and the thing—whatever it was—dropped back into his pocket. "I got him, though," he told her. "I got the fucker."

She laid her cheek on his chest and squeezed him tight, a silent *thank you.* "What happened?" she asked. "Tell us everything."

We filled them in on the man in the hooded top. "Tough bastard," muttered Carrick, gingerly probing his swollen eye.

"He'd been trained," said Kian. "Trained *well.*"

Something connected in my mind. My head was still throbbing and it hurt to speak but I wanted to get the idea out. "Remember they told Sylvie in the cult that people who could fight could become *Primes?*" I asked. "I think we just ran into one of them."

Carrick pulled the folded-up file from a pocket inside his cut. "The personality tests were ordered by a business. *GTRL Holdings.* There's an address and a phone number."

"Probably a front company," said Kian. "Emily's good at cutting through those. I'll fill her in in the morning."

We all looked at each other. As quickly as it had started, the chaos calmed. The wounds were all dressed, everyone was up to speed...and, as the adrenaline wore off, it suddenly started to *feel* like four in the morning. I was utterly exhausted. We all were.

"Come on," Louise told me, dragging me to my feet. "The best thing for you is sleep. None of us have to be up in the morning. It's Saturday: even Kayley can sleep in."

That was true. There was nothing else we could do until Emily had had a chance to look into the front company. We'd all earned some rest. I followed her willingly to the stairs and let her lead me up them. Behind me, I could hear the others doing the same, yawning and cursing about how much their bruises hurt.

In our room, Louise carefully stripped my bloodied t-shirt off me, groaning in horror as she saw the caked blood on my neck and shoulders.

"It looks worse than it is," I mumbled guiltily.

"It better! I knew I shouldn't have let you go!"

I grabbed her shoulders. "I'll be fine. And we got what we needed. I'm glad I was there." I wrapped her in my arms and held her close. But as I stroked her hair, I was inwardly fuming at myself. Once again, my brute strength hadn't been enough to help my brothers. They'd all managed to at least have a crack at the cult member: Kian with his Secret Service training, Carrick with his chain, Aedan with his fists. I'd been taken out of the fight in the first five seconds, too slow and clumsy.

Meanwhile, the rest of my life was about to get even more complicated. *I'm going to be a dad, for fuck's sake.*

When she'd told me, I'd been shocked but then delighted. Motherhood seemed to fit Louise, somehow. And having gotten her pregnant filled me with a weird sort of caveman pride.

But now it was sinking in that the baby would be the first of a new generation of O'Harras. *How the hell did it wind up being me, the youngest?* It should have been Kian or Carrick. And then I realized something else: all my rage, that whole section of my life when I did nothing but destroy...that had all been caused by my foster dad and what he did to me. *What if I do the same to our kid? What if I fuck this up?*

What if the violence was too deeply ingrained in me? What if I somehow passed it on?

"Come on," said Louise, and pulled me into the bathroom. "You can't sleep like that." I stumbled along beside her, still troubled, my head throbbing.

Like the rest of the house, the bathroom was old, with an ancient roll-top tub. She stood me in it, my back to her, and started to sponge me down. Each spongeful of water washed a little blood away, a small pink waterfall. It took forever but Louise was patient and determined. She believed she could get me clean, just like she'd believed I could change.

What if she was wrong? I tried to imagine raising a kid, teaching it how to do right...when for so much of my life, I'd done wrong. For years, I'd been the guy people were scared of. My chest closed up. *What if our kid is scared of me?*

As the water finally ran clear, I turned to face Louise...and saw how worried she was. I cursed myself. The whole time I'd been away, she must have been worrying about how she'd raise the kid alone if I didn't come back. Now I understood why she'd tried so hard to stop me going.

The hell with my worries: I had to look after my girl.

"We're going to be okay," I told her firmly. I slid my damp fingers deep into that mane of copper hair and pressed my palm to her cheek.

She nestled into my hand but her eyes were huge. "How do you know? How do you know I'll make a good mom?"

"Louise, that's the one thing I'm sure of. You're the kindest, most caring person I've ever met." And it was true. It was me I was worried about.

She looked up at me, her eyes huge with fear. "Don't...don't leave me again, okay?" She put a hand on my chest, her voice tight. "Please?"

I nodded but I didn't say *I promise.* I could feel myself being tugged in two directions: my brothers needed me; she needed me....

But there'd be time to think about that tomorrow. Right now, we needed each other. I grabbed Louise around the waist and pulled her into the tub with me. She *mmf*ed and then slowly relaxed into it, her arms going around my neck and her sneakers squeaking on the porcelain as we twisted and moved. Immediately, it felt like a weight had lifted from me. Just touching her made me feel better.

My chest had gotten wet and the water soaked through her t-shirt, then her bra. I could feel the soft warmth of her breasts pressing against me, and I growled, burying my face in that sweet-smelling hair. She yelped again as I lifted her into my arms and stepped from the tub.

And wobbled a little.

"*Careful!*" said Louise, grabbing tight hold of my shoulders.

She had a point. I was still a little woozy and my head was still pounding. I managed to carry her over to the bed, though, and she leapt off me to safety, relieved.

"You lie back," she told me, pushing me down on the pillows and peeling off her tank top. "Let me do all the work."

I nodded weakly and grinned, my problems forgotten for now.

43

BRADAN

The lock was old, its pins sliding into position almost as soon as I started picking. I could have been inside in seconds but I forced myself to wait on the doorstep and listen.

Nothing. The house was silent, save for a weird rustling.

I crept inside and closed the door. Dawn was still a way off and the whole house seemed to be asleep. Now I could see what had made the rustling: a full-size tree, growing up through the house. I stopped for a second. I'd never seen anything like it. At home, everything was functional and efficient. This was...*whimsy*. It was ridiculous: no one had a tree in their house. So why was I standing there, gazing up at it?

I shook my head. *I'm losing it.* I'd already messed up once and disappointed Dad. I wasn't going to do it again.

I crept up the stairs. It was risky, but I wanted to check they were all there before I did this. I made no noise as I climbed. I'd learned to be good at that.

After four years of the water treatment works, training by day and sleeping in the terrifying Room 9 at night, they'd moved me to a different facility. Still underground, but this one had a maze of rooms over several floors. I suspected it was to be some sort of military bunker from the Cold War. I'd slept in a windowless, concrete dormitory with ten other Primes, five floors beneath the ground. Sometimes I'd have nightmares that *this was all there was,* that the world above had disappeared and the few concrete chambers I could see were all that existed. When that happened, the only way to calm myself was to creep silently up five flights of stairs, without being caught by a Guide, to where there was a tiny window. Then I could look out over the moonlit wheat fields and reassure myself that the world was still there.

I reached the hallway and checked the first room. A man with bandages wrapped around his head: the first one I'd taken down. Atop him, her skin creamy-white in the moonlight, a red-haired woman. Both of them were sleeping peacefully.

The next room: the fighter who'd almost killed me. He was with a woman, too, a little dark-haired thing, his arms protectively cradling her.

Across the hallway I found the biker, snoring on his back. A red-haired woman slept next to him, her head on his chest. I hesitated before closing the door. Something about the scene, the way she looked so serene beside him, the way *he* looked so peaceful and happy, despite how vicious and angry he'd been at the printing works...I'd never slept like that with anyone.

But part of me wanted to.

I closed the door and checked the next room. The guy who'd worn the suit, stretched out on his own in the big bed. His sleep was troubled: he was muttering to himself. A nightmare.

I left him and was about to go downstairs when I realized there was one door I hadn't checked. I cracked it quietly open.

A teenage girl.

I stopped, staring at her. I hadn't planned on this. She had short, curly blonde hair. A phone lay next to her on the pillow, right by her hand: she'd probably fallen asleep in the middle of messaging someone, most likely a boyfriend.

Without knowing why, I stepped closer, right up to her bed, and looked down at her. The moonlight coming through the drapes lit up her face in silver.

I can't. Not a kid.

I felt the thought pulling at me, tearing down my resolve. But just as the walls started to fall. I found my focus again.

The world needed us to bring Beautiful Order.

I stared at the teenager's sleeping face, committing it to memory. When I got home, I would hold hands with a Guide and share my sadness and we would remember the girl and her sacrifice.

I retreated into the hallway and closed her door. Then I made a tour of the house, locating each smoke alarm. I opened up each one, took the battery out and dropped them into my left jeans pocket. Then I inserted one of the dead batteries I'd brought with me from my right pocket.

I was good at this. I'd had lots of practice.

In the living room, I picked out the best place: on the edge of a table, next to some drapes. I found a candle and lit it, then held the drapes over it until they caught. I made sure that, as the fabric burned, some pieces fell onto the rug. I kept the door closed so that the crackling of flames wouldn't wake anyone.

I squatted down and watched as the flames licked across the rug and set fire to the old-fashioned wooden furniture. I've always loved fire. It's one of the few beautiful things I get to see.

Far away, in that dark hallway in my mind, I could sense frantic banging on the glass. Some other part of me awoke, a *weak* part, the same part which had stirred when I'd heard the men speak in that strange, foreign accent. It told me I was doing something wrong.

I closed my eyes for a second and *focused,* as I'd been taught. And the certainty of The Group returned. When I opened my eyes, the room was ablaze.

Now I opened the door and watched the smoke start to churn and billow up the stairs. They'd choke to death in their sleep.

The fire crept across the hallway, licking up the walls, spreading from room to room.

I quietly slipped out of the door and drove away.

44

LOUISE

The baby woke me.

Or, rather, *being pregnant* woke me. The thought of it being there sometimes roused me in the middle of the night when I moved and my belly pressed against Sean. I did what I always did: I reached down with one hand and stroked it, and then nestled closer to my man.

I was in that warm, dreamy state when you can still pull sleep up around you like a comforter. I was still half on top of Sean, my legs straddling the hardness of his left thigh, and if I twisted just so, like *that,* I could press against my...I smiled like a contented cat, wrapped my arms a little tighter around him and took a slow, deep breath.

And something filled my throat, like I'd just inhaled mud, not air. It caught in my lungs and I coughed. I gulped in more air but that was thick, too.

I fumbled around and managed to switch the bedside lamp on, then frowned bleary-eyed at the ceiling. The ceiling was moving, rolling and shifting and pressing lower. I focused and the movement resolved into thick white smoke.

I drew in a shuddering, terrified breath so I could scream for help, but that just started me coughing again. And each time I inhaled, it just made it worse: I was taking in heat and roughness but no actual air. Beneath the smoke I could see there must be another, thinner layer. I looked around, still coughing. *It's all around me! I can't breathe!*

I looked down at Sean and had a horrifying thought: with all my coughing, he should have woken up by now. I grabbed his shoulders and shook him. "*Sean!*" I rasped.

He didn't move.

I dug my fingers into his bare shoulders and shook him harder. Nothing.

Already, the room seemed to be getting darker. I felt floaty, like my brain was retreating up into the top of my head. Just shaking him was using up what little oxygen my body had: I felt like a mountain climber struggling to reach the top of Everest.

Something came back to me, a fire safety video I'd seen during a commercial break when I was about six. It had always stuck with me because the little girl in it looked like Kayley—

KAYLEY! My mind thrashed in panic for a moment. I started coughing again. I slumped forward over Sean, holding my chest, and nearly passed out.

Think! What had they done in the commercial?

Gotten down on the floor.

I didn't have the energy to stand: the fear had burned it all up. But I slithered out of bed, down onto my hands and knees, and then put my face right next to the floorboards. That took everything I had. The room dimmed. My lungs didn't want to work, anymore: my chest burned and I didn't want any more pain. Easier to just go to sleep.

Kayley!

I forced myself to breathe in...and my lungs filled with cool, sweet air straight out of an alpine meadow. I breathed out, coughing smoke, breathed in...the fog in my head lifted and I hauled myself up to kneeling.

I couldn't drag Sean's heavy body out of bed so I rolled him instead, doing my best to catch his head as he fell so he didn't hit it on the floorboards. Between the pain, the cleaner air and me screaming in his ear, he came partially awake. Then he realized what was going on and came the rest of the way, fast.

We crawled over to the door. My brain still wasn't working right but somehow, I was hoping that the fire was only in our room and the rest of the house was okay. It was only when we reached the hallway and saw the whole house lit up orange from below that it sank in. We were in a disaster movie, a horror movie. *This doesn't happen! Not here! Not our house!* The smoke was even thicker, here, pushing up against every door.

I screamed what they always scream in the movies. "*FIRE!*" But my lungs were scorched and raw and it came out as a pathetically weak wail. I crawled straight to Kayley's room, Sean beside me. I threw open the door and scrambled across the floor. Grabbed her sleeping body. "*Kayley! Wake up!*"

She didn't wake. Not even when I pulled her from her bed and yelled.

Oh God Jesus God please. I was too scared to cry, too scared to do anything. I started panic gulping air and the room started to fade out again—

"*Outside!*" yelled Sean. "We have to get her outside!"

He hooked an arm under her armpits and we started dragging her down the hallway. As we passed the other doors, he hammered and kicked on them. At first, it didn't seem like anyone else would wake up. But then Kian stumbled out, and he managed to get into Carrick's room and get him and Annabelle up, and together they got Sylvie and Aedan.

Just in those few minutes, the fire had gotten worse. Orange embers were rising in clouds from downstairs and the smoke was so thick we couldn't even see the floor. But we had to get out, had to get Kayley out. She was a dead weight in my arms: all the nightmares I'd had during her illness had come true. As we crawled down the stairs in a line, Sean and I carrying Kayley between us, I could feel the heat on my bare arms. My chest tightened as I realized what was burning: it was the tree, the flames rippling up its trunk and consuming its twigs and branches.

By the time we reached the bottom of the stairs, the heat was agony, scorching my lips and eyes, pushing down into my lungs. Even close to the ground, there was no air, here, and all of us were close to passing out. I fumbled for the handle, turned it—

A flood of cold night air slammed into our faces. It gave us the energy to drag ourselves out. We immersed ourselves in it, panting the coolness down into our chests. Smoke billowed out behind us, chasing us like a monster.

Sean and I rolled Kayley onto her back on the lawn. I pawed at her chest, still trying to get her to wake up, but then Kian pushed me out of the way. He put his mouth to hers and I watched her chest rise and fall. Then he was leaning over her, pressing her chest. Again. Again. The vomit rose in my throat as I watched her lifeless eyes—

She blinked, coughed, and Kian turned her on her side just as she threw up. I clutched her back, hugging myself to her as she spasmed. "*Thank you,*" I muttered, eyes squeezed shut. "*Thank you, thank you.*"

Carrick had somehow thought to grab his phone on the way out and dialed 911. The fire trucks were there within minutes and the sirens brought people out of their houses. But with the house standing on its own on the hill and the drapes closed, hiding the orange glow inside...*God, no one would have known for hours. We all would have died in there!*

The firefighters plunged inside and brought hoses to bear on the downstairs rooms. Meanwhile, a paramedic gave Kayley oxygen, checked her over and declared her okay. "But it might be worth us taking her in," he said. "We could keep an eye on her overnight...."

"*No!*" said Kayley firmly. "I've been in the hospital enough."

She clung to me and I wrapped my arms around her. The paramedic relented when I promised to bring her straight to the ER if her condition changed.

It didn't take long for the firefighters to kill the fire: the flames hadn't reached upstairs. But it was some time before they declared everything safe and we were allowed in to check the damage.

The living room was gutted. The dining area wasn't much better but most of the kitchen was okay. The hallway was scorched and smoke-blackened but the stairs were sound.

But the *tree*....

The trunk was scorched and blackened. The branches had been stripped of many of their smaller twigs and the whole thing looked sick. I hugged my arms around myself. All the fear for Kayley, for everyone, that hadn't had time to come out during the fire was coming out now, tears rolling down my cheeks. Sean came up behind me and hugged me and I pressed back against his warmth, but I still felt like I wanted to be sick. *Our home!* It wasn't just the damage, it was that we'd come so close to death in the one place we'd thought was safe.

A firefighter handed me something: a smoke detector. "Batteries are dead," he told me. He managed to say it without too much anger or disgust. "They're all like that. You were lucky."

I nodded meekly and took it from him.

"How did it start?" asked Kian.

The firefighter shrugged. "Looks like the living room. A cigarette, maybe."

None of us smoked. I looked at him blankly.

"A candle? Maybe you left one burning?"

I frowned. I occasionally lit candles when we were having a romantic dinner, but we hadn't done that since everyone came to stay.

The firefighter shrugged. "Well, *something* was burning in there."

The firefighters filed out and we watched them drive away. Then I stood there staring down at the smoke detector in my hands. *Flat batteries? You idiot!* I could tell it was what everyone was thinking. "I'm sure I replaced them," I said in a small voice. "When we moved in." *Didn't I?* I started to second guess myself. *Obviously not.*

Aedan clasped my shoulder. "It's an easy thing to forget."

But I'm sure I—

Kian patted my other shoulder. "The important thing is, everyone's okay."

Everyone made noises of agreement, which made me feel even worse. Sean's grip on me tightened and I knew he was feeling the guilt, too. But it had been my job to do, I remembered climbing the stepladder, inserting the new batteries....

I frowned. I remembered them so clearly. I'd bought a whole pack from the store. Black ones, the same brand I always bought because they were the only ones my dad had trusted.

I popped the back off the smoke detector. The battery inside was red and white.

"Oh shit," I whispered.

"What?" asked Sean.

I ignored him, hurried into the next room and grabbed a chair. The others followed me in as I stood on the chair, pulled the smoke alarm off the ceiling and popped off the back. Another red and white battery.

My whole body went cold, every hair standing on end. "It wasn't an accident," I said. "I didn't *forget*. Someone's been in here. Someone came in while we were sleeping and changed all the batteries. *Someone started the fire!*"

Everyone looked at me. They wanted to believe me but it sounded so crazy. I started to doubt myself again....

No! I was sure I was right. And if I couldn't convince them, we were all in even more danger.

I jumped down from the chair and marched through to the ruined living room. It took me a while but I eventually saw the pool of hardened, melted wax on the table. "*There!*" I said. "Someone put a candle there. They lit a candle and that started the fire."

I saw the others shift uncomfortably. "It could have just melted in the fire," said Annabelle timidly.

I shook my head, certain, now. "No." I recognized the color but I sniffed it to be sure. Even with all the soot, I could smell the cloying, sickly scent. "It's that strawberry one." I turned to Sean. "The one Stacey gave us. We lit it once and the smell was so bad we couldn't face lighting it again."

Sean nodded, his face going pale. "She's right. But we didn't want to throw it out in case Stacey came round. So we keep it up on that shelf." He turned and pointed across the room.

The shelf was empty.

Sean's voice grew shaky. "Unless one of you took that candle down last night and put it on the table...." They all shook their heads. "Then Louise is right. Some bastard came in, in the night, and did this. Set it all up to look like an accident."

Everyone stared at me, horrified...and a little guilty, that they'd doubted me. I should have felt victorious but all I felt was scared. Aeternus knew where we lived. They'd sent someone to kill us. And I knew they'd try again.

45

KIAN

Dawn was already breaking but we were all still exhausted, having only slept a few hours. So I persuaded everyone to get some sleep while I kept watch in the hallway. I lied and said I'd wake Sean to relieve me in a few hours but I let them all sleep in till noon.

It wasn't like I would have slept anyway. Before the fire, I'd been having a nightmare about Iraq, mixed up with Emily and my brothers until it seemed like everyone I knew was out there with me in the desert. When I bent over the dead bodies of my squad, it was Sean and Emily and Annabelle's faces that stared back up at me. All I knew was that I had to protect them all...and I'd failed.

My normal solution would have been to tell Emily about it. That always made it fade into black and white: it lost its power. But Emily wasn't there.

I somehow got through the morning with coffee and willpower, keeping myself busy by tidying up the place but trying not to make too much noise. The paperwork we'd covered the walls with was gone, countless hours of work reduced to ash and shreds of burnt wool on the floor.

When everyone else emerged from their beds, we started to strip the living room of all the blackened furniture. Sean wasn't happy that I'd lied to him and kept watch by myself: didn't he get that I was looking out for him? He should be resting and healing. It was thanks to me that he'd wound up with a blow to the head that could have killed him: *my baby brother!*

By the end of the day, we'd gotten rid of all the damaged stuff and were starting to think about what needed to be done to fix the place up. "We can just paint over this," I said, looking at the soot-covered walls.

But Sean shook his head and pointed. "This bit, we can." He poked at another section, identical to my eyes. "But that whole section's going to have to come down." I blinked at him, surprised, and he rolled his eyes. "I *do* work construction, you know," he said.

I nodded, a little chastened. I'd had no idea he knew all that stuff.

We ate dinner—well, I pushed some food around a plate, too tired and worked up to eat. I was thinking about how I was going to stay awake for another night to keep watch when we saw blue and red lights through the window. *Shit!* I actually wobbled on my feet for a second before I caught myself: the exhaustion, the fire, the stress. My mind felt like it was shredding. *I can't take any more!*

Carrick and I looked at each other. "You think they got our license plate, at the printing works?" I asked.

"Or the cult went to the cops," said Carrick. "About the guy we beat up, or the guys we hit when we rescued Sylvie." We stared at each other, thinking fast. "I'll go," he said. "Give them someone to arrest. Try to get them to pin it all on me."

There was a heavy knock at the door.

"*I'll* go," I told him, glancing down at my suit. "I'm more likely to be able to talk my way out of it." I headed for the door.

"For fuck's sake," snapped Carrick, chasing after me. "Stop trying to be the hero! If *you* get arrested, it's a scandal!"

I ignored him. On some level, I knew he was right but I was running on adrenaline and coffee, too desperate to think straight. The nightmare was still going around and around in my head: all I could think about was protecting Carrick, protecting everyone.

I took a deep breath and pulled open the door, looking down at my feet while I composed myself. "Can I help you?" I asked in a strained voice, and then lifted my eyes to look.

"Sorry," said Miller. "She insisted."

I had time to blink once. Then Emily *wumf*ed into my chest.

46

EMILY

A bandage was covering what must have been a sizable wound on his head. He was gaunt and red-eyed and stressed out of his mind.

And absolutely the best thing I'd ever seen. I pressed myself even closer, molding myself to him, and felt his body relax.

"Sorry," said Miller again. "As soon as she heard about the fire, she said that if I didn't bring her, she was going to sneak out and get on a plane herself, alone. I think she was actually ready to do it."

"I was," I said, my voice muffled by that wonderful, warm chest. My cheek was rubbing against his soft white shirt and I never wanted to feel anything else, just that hard, solid muscle and the throb of his heartbeat.

Behind Kian, I heard footsteps on the upstairs landing. I lifted my face to see a teenage girl, dressed for bed, had come out to see what the commotion was. On seeing me, her eyes lit up like Christmas. She jumped over the handrail, swarmed athletically down the tree and jumped to the floor. *"Oh my God oh my God oh my God!"* she squealed. I gave her a shy smile. I kept forgetting I was a celebrity.

Kian drew in a huge, heavy breath, as if he was going to protest. I quickly pressed myself to him again and tightened my arms around him. And I felt all the air just huff out of him again in a long, resigned, and very happy sigh. "*How?*" he asked. "I didn't call you."

I separated face from chest just long enough to glare up at him. "No. You didn't," I said pointedly.

"I did," said a voice behind him.

Kian turned in surprise, which dragged me around with him because *hell no* I wasn't letting go of him anytime in the next few million years. A pretty red-haired woman was smiling timidly. *Annabelle!*

"Annabelle called me," I said. "First thing this morning."

For a second, I thought Kian was going to blow up at her. The look on his face was pure *how dare you ignore my authority!* A man in a leather biker's cut—that had to be Carrick—stepped protectively in front of her. I grabbed Kian's arm before a fight could start—

But then Annabelle lifted her chin, unafraid. "It's what you needed," she said.

Kian just gaped at her, then turned to look at me.

I nodded at him.

Kian looked around at his family...and then just sort of deflated, all the fight going out of him.

"Could you maybe give us a minute?" I asked, looking around at everyone. They all nodded and retreated. I took Kian by the hand and led him firmly towards the stairs.

"Wait," he said, shaking his head. "I need to keep watch—"

"No you don't," said Carrick.

"We got it," said another brother, bandages around his head. A third one nodded in agreement.

"And me and my men will be right outside," said Miller. "No one's getting in this house tonight."

I pulled on Kian's hand again and, this time, he followed.

When we got to the bedroom, I gawped at the four-poster bed. "This place is incredible," I told him. "You've been sleeping on *this?!*"

"Wasn't much fun without you," he muttered. His voice was different, the Irish stronger. I'd noticed it on the phone but I'd thought it was just my imagination. It was glorious, like a concentrated version of him...but it wasn't the only thing that was different. We'd been through tough times during the coup but he'd never looked like this, haggard and worn. And he looked as if he hadn't eaten in days.

I pushed the door closed with my ass and looked at him. "You're a mess," I told him.

"*Thanks.*"

"I mean it," I said, moving closer and gently touching the bandage on his head. "What's wrong?"

He sighed. "I just...I'm just trying to do the right thing, keeping everybody safe."

I nodded. "Oh."

"I just feel like—Wait, what do you mean, '*oh*'?"

I slid my hands under his suit jacket and cuddled up to his chest again, sighing contentedly. *This is my happy place.* "You're trying to protect everyone. You feel it's all your responsibility. You can't understand why everyone can't see that. Stop me if I'm close."

I could feel him staring down at me. Then he rested his chin on the top of my head. "You're close," he said tightly. Then, "how did you know?"

"Because you try to do the same thing with me," I said. "But I know how to deal with you."

"Deal with me?" his voice was softening with each passing second.

I looked up and the sight of those blue eyes, so full of pain yet so full of love, sent a tingle right down to my toes. "With me, you know we're a team."

He took a deep, slow breath, and somehow it felt like that was the first full breath he'd taken the whole time we'd been apart. "*Yes.*"

"But your brothers are on your side, too," I told him. "You just have to let them be."

He nodded. And we relaxed into each other. I melted against his rock-like body, my personal shelter against everything the world threw at me. And he clutched me tight, pressing my softness into him as if he wanted to absorb me whole. *"Feck,"* he said at last. "I've missed you."

"I missed you more," I said with feeling.

We rotated, arms around each other as if we were slow-dancing, his lips pressed to my hair in an endless kiss. I could *feel* it flowing out of him like exorcised ghosts, all the bad stuff he'd been dealing with, all the memories seeing his brothers had brought back, all the stress he hadn't been able to vent. And I cursed myself for not getting there sooner.

And then I remembered how many times I'd tried to come, and he hadn't let me. So I punched him hard in the arm.

"Ow! Jesus!"

"You shouldn't have come here alone," I told him.

"It was the right thing to do," he said firmly. Then he sighed, closed his eyes and put his cheek on mine. "But it wasn't *right.* I'm sorry."

And I had my Kian back. Warm and solid and real, not just on a computer screen. He held me close for long minutes, his big palms stroking my back. Then he finally eased me back until we were at the length of our outstretched arms, our hands joined, and he just *looked* at me, drinking me in.

The room was utterly silent...or maybe every other noise in the house just ceased to matter. I've never felt so focused on someone, so entirely connected to them. I looked up into his eyes and I fell in love with him all over again...and it felt like he was falling for me. His fingers squeezed mine once, twice...and then those powerful biceps jerked me forward and his lips descended on mine.

We kissed and I groaned at how good it felt: the hardness of his lips, the way he coaxed me open and then damn well devoured me. We fit together so well, twisting together and chasing each other, his strong Irish will and need to tame me, my softness and quickness and refusal to ever quite be tamed.

We broke the kiss, moved back and just stared at each other again, panting a little, our breathing in time. And a different sort of need started to take over. He didn't move, didn't touch me aside from his hands holding mine. But I could see it in his eyes, feel the heat throbbing through his fingertips.

All the time we'd been apart, it had been building inside me, an ache that was so basic, so primal and raw it almost scared me. I'd been denying it, suppressing it but now—

I saw the realization in his eyes at the same instant, the sudden flash of furnace heat.

We're alone—

In a bedroom—

With a four poster bed—

We flew at each other, meeting in the middle of the room. My head tilted back for his kiss but I kept pushing, desperate to get him *on* something or *up against* something. His lips took mine, owning me, spreading me wide and tasting me, and meanwhile he was pushing me backward, just as determined to pin *me*.

He had the size, the weight and a lot more muscle. It's testament to how much I needed him that, for a few seconds, I actually held my ground.

Then he growled and *pushed,* walking me backward even though my legs were trying to go forward. A second later, my ass hit the wall and he pinned me up against it, his big body towering over mine. I gave a kind of strangled cry of joy and kissed him even harder, letting him know how much I needed it.

Our hands were all over each other and every touch of those warm palms sent a rush of pure fire through me. He stroked my hips through my skirt. Then up over my sides, the warmth soaking into me through my blouse. I had my hands up under his jacket, tracing the muscles of his back and then pushing them up between us so I could feel every hard ridge of his abs and fill my hands with the broad cliffs of his chest. Both of us were breathing in shaky, urgent gasps. "I need you," I panted.

"I need you more." His voice wasn't loud but it filled the room. And that new, stronger Irish accent was something else: it echoed off the walls like flashing silver blades and then turned molten as it hit my ears, flooding down inside me and winding its way straight to my

groin. I think I gave a little whinny of lust and we kissed so hard, so urgently, our teeth clacked together.

His thigh pushed very hard against mine, until my ass was locked against the wall. I automatically pushed back a little and found I couldn't move *at all*. He was like rock against me. *Oh. It's going to be like* that.

He pulled my blouse out of my skirt, bunched the hem of it in his hands and ripped it up the middle with one strong pull, buttons flying and bouncing. *OH! Oh God, it really IS going to be like that.* I panted, suddenly breathless, my hands going crazy on his sides and abs. I pulled his shirt out of his pants and slid my palms up onto warm, naked skin.

He grabbed hold of my bra but there was no way to open the clasp because I was pressed so hard against the wall. I started to arch my back to give him room—

He took one cup in each hand and just ripped the stitching that held them together. The two halves fell either side of my breasts and I let out a cry of joy as his mouth enveloped a breast. My hands tangled in that thick, black hair, my ass grinding against the wall as if I was trying to climb it. I was sucking in huge, quick breaths through my nostrils, shuddering as his tongue licked and swirled, my nipple puckering to hardness quicker than I'd thought possible. The need for him was vibrating through me, now, like I was a violin string being plucked, every inch of me aching and trembling for him.

I grabbed hold of his belt and unbuckled it, then started working on his pants. Kian's hands found my legs and started to run up them, stroking and squeezing them, expert fingers finding every secret place. I gasped and twisted, flexing and squeezing my thighs together in time with his touch. Every brush of his fingers against my skin brought another rush of heat that soaked straight down to my groin. I was frantic, now, desperate. I'd never needed it so much.

His fingers reached my panties and slid around to the front, stroking me through them, and I moaned and ground against him. He grabbed my skirt, wrenching it up my legs inch by inch, baring me. I felt the cool air of the room on my thighs, my upper thighs...God, he had it right up to my hips.

His fingers hooked into the top of my panties. *At least those he can get off pretty easily, if he just—*

There was a pull and a *crack* of elastic snapping and my panties were gone. He wasn't interested in waiting. The heat strummed faster and faster inside me, echoing through my brain, no room left for coherent thought. He cupped me and I grabbed hold of his head and dragged him up for a kiss. Then, as he sucked on my tongue, a finger slid into me, finding me soaking. I had his pants open now, and I was threading my hand inside his jockey shorts—

I groaned as my hand curled around the shaft of his cock, hot and iron hard. He responded by hooking the finger inside me, touching me just...*there*—

"*MMMF!*" I managed through the kiss, desperate to speak. When he let me, I grabbed his cheeks in my hands and stared at him from just a few inches away. "I've *got to have you*," I croaked. "*Right now.*"

His eyes didn't leave my face. I heard the rustle of foil, the rubber sound of a condom. And then—

My eyes widened as he slid up into me, all the way in one long, marvelous thrust. My eyes closed and I grabbed at his shoulders, my long groan turning into a high little squeak as I rose up on my toes. He drew back and it was like a loss: my fingers clawed at his muscles, urging him back. Then another thrust, mashing my ass back against the cool plaster of the wall, my thighs pressed wide as they cradled him between them. I cried out and crushed him to me, my teeth and lips finding the shoulder of his jacket, silencing what would have been a scream of pleasure.

He stayed there for a second, our bodies pressed together. The heat of him soaked into me, his chest like warm rock through the thin cotton of his shirt. Then he slid his hands up between us and captured my breasts. Every squeeze, every expert stroke of his thumbs across my nipples, made me writhe and thrash, and that moved me on him, and *that* made him growl and fondle me faster.

"Christ, I've missed these," he panted in my ear, the hot rush of Irish silver making me grind against him.

His hands slid down my sides, over my rucked-up skirt, onto my hips. He smoothed his palms along my thighs, all the way down to the knees, then back up. "And these," he said, and the lust in his voice made me press myself harder against him. "I love your legs." He suddenly grabbed them and lifted, using his forearms to help, and my legs hooked up and around his waist. I yelped as I fell onto him a little more deeply. Now I was supported only by my legs and the pressure of his hard body pinning me to the wall.

His hips started to move, a steady rhythm that pressed me into the wall. So much better than a bed: no give, no flex that would stop me grinding against him. Every thrust was a silken push of heat and tightness, silver streamers of pleasure swirling out. Then that grind as our pelvises met, diamonds spraying and glittering inside my mind. The heat inside me was strumming faster and faster. I gave a choked gasp and grabbed him hard, heels digging into his ass. The brute power of him was amazing: it felt as if he could hold me there for hours.

His big hands came up to cradle my face, thumbs tracing my cheekbones, as gentle with his touch as he was forceful with his thrusts. I began to pant out my pleasure, a safety valve that didn't come close to relieving the pressure inside. I'd screwed my eyes tight closed in ecstasy but they flew open when he growled in my ear. "I'm never going away like this again," he told me. "I need you. I need to feel you against me or I go feckin' crazy. I need you, Emily."

I wasn't capable of speech so I just locked my arms tighter around his shoulders and pulled him forward for a kiss. Our mouths met in a frenzy of lips and tongue and teeth, riding the hurricane inside us, clinging to each other. His hips moved even faster, pounding into me. Each time he filled me, it was a confirmation that we were reunited, that I'd got him back. The heat was strumming so fast now that I couldn't follow it—

I kissed him hard as I shuddered and exploded, yelling my climax against his lips. My fingers dug into his shoulders, my thighs squeezing him so hard it must almost have hurt. And as he felt my release, as he felt what he'd done to me, he went even harder, faster, drawing out the detonation into glorious slow-motion, and then he pushed deep inside me and shot. We kissed cheeks and lips and necks, our mouths frantic on each other. Then he lifted me away from the wall and into his arms, hugging me there while I recovered.

47

EMILY

I'd always loved watching him sleep. I was an early riser, like my dad: some genetic Texas thing where we had to be up with the dawn, tending to cattle. But Kian was more like my mom, half-asleep and adorably grumpy until he'd had his coffee. He'd sleep until noon if I let him. And right now, he was sleeping like he hadn't been near a bed in a week. I could see the tension releasing: the worry lines around his eyes were gone, the gaunt look was receding. Me being there was good for him and that lit a warm light inside me.

But there was still something wrong. The night before, long after we'd finally moved to the bed, after he'd lain me down and it had been slow and romantic, my legs thrashing either side of his in the moonlight, we'd spooned and talked. He'd caught me up on everything that had been happening: not just the facts he'd told me in our phone calls but the real stuff: how Sylvie was feeling, how he and his brothers were getting on. It made me realize what a poor substitute phone calls, even video calls, were for some face-to-face time.

When I was caught up, he asked me about the White House and my heart just melted: even with the hell he was going through, he still wanted to check I was okay. I reassured him that life was normal and we started planning what would happen when all this was over and we got back. For years, I'd wanted to go to Europe and see the sights, maybe even visit some of the European royalty. And Kian needed a vacation, after this. But—

But I could hear it in his voice. A tension, as soon as we started talking about photo calls and press interviews and security cordons: you know, normal stuff. He smiled and said all the right words. But deep down, I could sense a battle going on inside him. He got a look in his eyes that made my heart ache, a look I'd seen somewhere before but I couldn't remember where.

He wouldn't talk about it, claimed everything was fine and that he was looking forward to going back to DC when all this was over. But when you've been around politicians as long as I have, you get pretty good at reading people. Something was wrong, something that had been wrong even before he came to LA but that had been allowed to grow unchecked while we'd been apart.

I couldn't just lie there brooding on it or I'd toss and turn and eventually wake him, and God knows he needed his sleep. I crept out of the bed but that left me with a new problem: I was utterly naked. Even my panties had been shredded, the night before.

I'd packed plenty of clothes but my bag was still in one of the Secret Service SUVs, unless Miller had thought to bring it in: even then, it was downstairs. I held my blouse up to the dawn light coming through the drapes. Most of the buttons were missing and he'd actually torn the fabric in one place. *Yep, that's not getting fixed.* I couldn't help but give a little smile.

After rooting around in some drawers, I found an old t-shirt and some sweatpants of Kian's. They drowned me a little, but they'd keep me decent while I crept downstairs and tried to locate my bag. I might even have to run outside to where the Secret Service were maintaining a perimeter.

Everyone else seemed to still be asleep, probably catching up after the fire the night before. I started down the stairs....

And stopped, looking at the tree. Having a full-size tree growing through your house...that was the craziest and most fantastic thing ever. And it made me want to—

No. Don't be ridiculous.

I'd seen how easily Kayley had swarmed down it when I arrived. Even I could see it was a good tree for climbing, with thick, solid branches. I could see it had been scorched by the fire, with a lot of the twigs gone, but clearly it was solid enough for now, even if it eventually died.

I took a step towards the handrail.

Come on, seriously, are you nuts?

My whole childhood, my mom had wanted me to be ladylike. Shooting and hunting with my father was just about allowable because that was traditional but climbing trees? No way. *I might never get the chance again.*

I bit my lip. Then I threw one leg over the handrail, stretched out and grabbed a branch. I balanced for there a second, the floor suddenly looking very far away. "Well, this can only end well," I muttered to myself.

I swung my other leg over the handrail and pulled myself into the tree. There was a sickening rush of air and a swaying that took my breath away, and then I was straddling a branch and grinning like a loon.

Where next? I could sort of slither down to the branch below me and then hook around like *this* and pull myself over *there*.... I had my eye on the perfect spot, a nice wide branch from which I'd be able to see the whole hallway. One foot *here* and bend the branch a little so I can reach and grab on *here* and— I slipped and had to catch myself. Then I pulled myself up onto my chosen branch, my heart hammering but an even bigger smile on my face. I felt like I'd scaled Everest. And it was so peaceful. I sat there with my feet idly kicking, listening to the creak and shift of the tree around me...*everyone should try this.*

Eventually, though, I figured it was probably time to go and find some proper clothes. So I slid my ass off the branch, stretched out with my toes and—

Oh.

I couldn't actually reach the next branch down. Well, no problem: I'd go back the way I'd come.

Except...I'd bent that branch towards this one to make the jump and now it had sprung back, beyond my fingertips.

Okay, I'll go up. But even crouching precariously on the branch and stretching up, I couldn't reach anything above me.

I was stuck.

Calling for help was out of the question. No way was I admitting to Kian or anyone else that I'd gotten stuck up a tree. I settled down to think. Straightaway, I was brooding on Kian and DC again. What was it that was bothering him?

About ten minutes later, there was a creak on the stairs. My head whipped around. Kian was slowly descending them, looking highly lickable in a pair of suit pants and nothing else. "Emily?" he called in a half-whisper, not wanting to wake everyone. "Emily?"

I sat there drooling over the wide, rugged mass of his shoulders, the way the dawn light played over each hard ridge of his abs. Then he passed me and I realized he hadn't seen me: he hadn't thought to look at the tree. He was at the bottom of the stairs before I thought to call, "Here."

He stopped and looked up. Blinked. "What are you doing up there?"

"I wanted to try it," I said as if this was the most normal thing in the world.

"Okay. Are you coming down?"

"Yeah," I said. Then, "You know, in a while."

There was a pause. "You can't get down, can you?" he asked, crossing his arms.

I hesitated, then shook my head.

He nodded to himself. And made for the tree.

"What are you doing?" I asked.

He looked at me as if it was obvious. "I'm coming up!"

My heart unexpectedly swelled in my chest.

He put one hand on the tree. Started up. Fell back. "You okay?" I called.

Kian gave me a look. "Fine. It's just...it's been a few years." He selected a different branch and began to climb.

Watching him scale the tree, the muscles in his arms and back smoothly flexing, knowing he was on his way to rescue me, made me melt in a whole new and unexpected way. When he heaved himself up onto the branch beside me, it all threatened to burst out of me: I wanted to throw my arms around him and say *my hero!* But given that we were quite a long way up, and the branch was quite narrow, I settled for leaning in and kissing him. "Thank you," I said.

"My pleasure, ma'am." He stopped to look around for a second and I saw some of the tension slip away from him: he liked it up here as much as I did.

"What's bothering you?" I asked, before I'd even realized I was going to say it.

"What?"

"Something's been up, even before you came to LA. You're not...*happy* in DC, are you?"

"Happy? Of course I'm happy! I've got you!"

I gave him a look. He looked away, exasperated. Looked furiously around him, his gaze going everywhere but me. But there was no escape, not up here. We were alone and private and his defenses were down just enough. He finally sighed, looked down at the ground and said, "I don't know if I'm any good at this."

"This? You mean...us? Relationships?"

"No. *This.*" He fingered the soft fabric of his suit pants. "This whole Washington life. You were born to it. Raised with it. Hell, cut your mom open and she bleeds champagne."

"Not that you want to cut my mom open."

"No." He thought about it. "Only occasionally." He sighed. "Emily, your dad is the President. That's about as high society as it gets. And me, I'm...me. I grew up barely getting by, spent as much time in Ireland as I did America."

I finally realized where I'd seen that look before: in the eyes of a panther, prowling its cage at the National Zoo. My stomach lurched. *Is that how he feels: trapped? Have I trapped him?*

"But you were around DC for years before you met me," I said. "All that time protecting VIPs. We were probably at the same parties."

He turned and looked at me. "I was at the same parties," he said. "But I wasn't a *guest.*"

And suddenly I got it. My panther analogy was just perfect. People like me hired people like him because they were big and scary. We kept them on a leash, used them to protect us...but that wasn't the same, for him, as sitting at the table.

He saw the realization in my eyes and nodded. Took my hand and gently squeezed it. "I can wear the clothes," he said. "Learn what words to say. But I'm just acting. I come from a different world and I'm just a different kind of person. The military: I understood that. Protecting people: I understood that. But *this,* shaking hands and going to parties...that's not me."

"It's not like that's *all we do!*" My voice was fractured, one slip away from angry. But it wasn't him I was mad at: he was being straight with me. It was me who'd put him in this situation. "I'm not my mom. I have my job!"

He stroked my hair, burying his fingers in it. "I know. And I'm proud of you. But that's part of the problem: you have a job but since the coup I've just been freewheeling." It was all coming out of him, now, everything he'd been keeping bottled up. "I mean, what the hell am I going to do in DC? I can't go back to being a bodyguard. That's way too blue collar for your mom."

"Since when did you care what my mom thinks?"

"It's too blue collar for your dad, too. And...for you."

"No—"

"Emily, you're kicking ass in your job. You'll be running the place in a few years—"

"N—"

"I'm not going to drag you down!"

"Would you let me just *speak?*" I snapped.

He went quiet. I took a deep breath. "Do you remember when we first met? You were the one guy in a leather jacket, amongst all those suits. You were the guy who got kicked out of the Secret Service. You were the guy arguing with everyone. And I liked that guy. I fell for that guy. Hard."

We just stared at each other for a second.

"You don't have to try to be something you're not," I told him, laying one hand on a thigh that felt like rock. "If I'd wanted a senator, I'd have found a senator. I want *you*. I don't care if you never come to another party. I don't care if you never wear a suit again. All I care about is that you're the sort of guy who climbs a tree to rescue me."

He blinked, taken aback. God, this is what happens when you're separated by an entire country: he'd forgotten just how much I loved him. "I don't even have a feckin' job—"

"You'll find something! Something that suits you!"

He looked into my eyes and I saw him remember: not just how much we loved each other but how I'd match him every time, just as bull-headed as he was.

"Something that won't embarrass you." He was drawing a line in the sand.

"I wouldn't be—" I saw how determined he was and sighed. "Okay, fine, something that won't embarrass me." I shook my head. "Why do you always try so hard to protect me?"

"It's my job. Ma'am." But he was grinning. I could see how much he'd relaxed in just a few minutes. Sure, he was still uncomfortable with the DC social scene but we could cut back on that. And deep down, I knew this hadn't really been about that: this had been about *us*. About his concern that, if he wasn't right for DC, maybe he wasn't right for *me*.

"You're the best thing that ever happened to me," I told him. "You're my rock. You're the one person who can always make me feel safe."

He cradled my face in his palm. "You're the one person who can see inside my soul. You're sweet and good and you make me want to be better. You *have* made me better." He sighed. "Christ, I love you." And he suddenly leaned forward and kissed me, slow and soft but *oh,* so intense, like he was doing it with every ounce of love. A delicious silver spark went right down my spine and detonated into warmth in my chest and I didn't even realize I was tipping back on the branch, swooning, until his other hand caught me. He levered me gently back to safety. "I gotcha," he whispered.

Both of us were grinning, now. Everything was going to be okay. I shook my head and then blew a lock of hair away from my face. "Besides, I'm from *Texas*. Do you think *I* feel right at a cocktail party?"

He rubbed at his jaw. There was some stubble there, for once, because he'd rushed straight out of bed to look for me, and it looked really good. "Hadn't thought about it like that."

We went silent, just enjoying sitting in the tree for a second. Kian looked down at this pants. "Y'know, Carrick thinks I've gone soft."

I couldn't help it. I burst out laughing. "*You?*"

"I'm not one thing or the other," he said, exasperated. "It was simple, when I was a bodyguard. I don't know what I'm meant to be, anymore."

I looked at him seriously. "Maybe all you need to do," I said softly, "is stop worrying about everybody else and ask yourself what *you* want for a change."

He looked at me for so long that I flushed. "God, it scares me how much I need you," he muttered. He took my chin between finger and thumb and just looked at me, drinking me in. "I forgot how smart you are." Then he laughed and shook his head. "Jesus...you didn't get stuck up here at all, did you? It was all a ploy just to get me up here and make me open up."

I nodded quickly. "Yeah," I lied. "You got me."

He shook his head, leaned forward and kissed me. This time, it was gentle and teasing, as if we were meeting again for the very first time and we were both still teenagers. Our lips just brushed, that magical point where every tiny contact makes your body crackle and hum until you're panting with it. Then we shuffled closer on the branch and it became deeper, hotter, his hands gliding up my sides, feeling my body through the oversize t-shirt, my fingers raking down his neck.

There was a giggle from beneath us. "Kian and Emily, sitting in a tree. K-I-S-S-I-N-G."

We both laughed and looked down to see Louise standing below. She must have crept past us while we were occupied. "You okay getting down from there?" she asked.

I looked at Kian and nodded. "We'll be just fine."

Kian had told me about the huge, chaotic breakfasts with everyone gathered around the table. With the kitchen only half usable and the dining room out of action, it was even more crazy than usual but everyone helped. We ate on the lawn outside, taking turns to run back and forth with jugs of juice, trays of crispy bacon and platters of eggs. Kian wolfed down enough breakfast for three, which was a relief: I could tell he hadn't been eating properly. I insisted on making some breakfast sandwiches for the Secret Service detail, who very much appreciated them.

It was the first chance I'd had to properly meet everyone: the intimidatingly fit but down-to-earth Sylvie and Aedan; Sean—who I'd met briefly in DC—and his warm, friendly girlfriend Louise; Kayley, who had about a million questions about life in the White House, and Annabelle and Carrick. Annabelle I took to immediately: she reminded me of the girls I'd known back in Texas, sweet and direct and refreshingly free from the bullshit and cattiness of DC. But Carrick I couldn't figure out at all. I knew he was meant to be a serious badass, that he rode with a Motorcycle Club and that he'd done some pretty dark things for them. But he didn't seem that way at all, at least not with me. He was polite and gentle and almost...*shy*. He kept going to curse and then catching himself. "What's with your brother?" I asked Kian when I had him alone.

Kian grinned and looked me up and down.

"*What?*" I wasn't wearing anything special, just a fresh suit jacket, blouse and skirt.

"Carrick's never met a lady before," said Kian.

I flushed. *Me? A lady?* But it was sort of sweet.

The best part about having all eight of us together was, we got to feel like a couple. Back in DC, we didn't get to mix with other couples socially: every social occasion was some sort of networking or fundraising opportunity dreamt up by my mother. Sitting there chatting about how all of us met, talking TV and movies and books...it was idyllic. I loved it. And Kian was grinning, too: I suddenly realized how rough it must have been for him, these last few weeks, being the only single one. I slipped my arm around him and he did the same, pulling me into him possessively. *I'm here now,* I thought happily.

After breakfast, I broke out my laptop and went to work on the data Kian and his brothers had brought back from the printing works. As we expected, the company listed in the file was just a front. But between digging into Kerrigan's data during the coup and my new job, I'd gotten pretty good at following the money. By noon, I'd traced it all back to an email address from a private server. Kian looked at it and nodded. "I know someone who might be able to pin that down," he said. "I'll give her a call."

With nothing more we could do on the investigation until Mary, the mysterious hacker, called back, I spent a day with Kian just hanging around the house. We helped Sean measure up for replacement drywalls and furniture for the damaged rooms and I helped Kayley with her politics homework, but mostly we just sat in the long grass and watched the butterflies or swung on the swing, with occasional breaks to run upstairs to the four poster bed when we couldn't keep our hands off each other. It was like a mini-vacation, exactly what we needed after so long apart.

But all vacations have to come to an end.

Late in the afternoon, Mary called and Kian put her on speakerphone. "I got it," she said victoriously. "But...."

"But what?" asked Carrick.

"I've got a rough location but I couldn't get into the computer itself."

We all looked at each other. "Okay," said Kian. "That's fine, as long as I know where we're going. You did great."

"No," said Mary. "You don't understand: *I couldn't get into the computer.*"

We looked at each other blankly.

"I can get into government databases," Mary said. "But I can't get into the PC of some cult leader? Doesn't that seem weird to you?"

"Oh," said Annabelle, catching on.

"The only place I've seen encryption like this is on the FBI's servers," said Mary. "And even that, I beat. This is some serious spy-level stuff. You guys are in over your heads."

Kian sighed. "That much we know. Thanks for the warning."

"Wait," I said. "You hacked *the FBI?*"

"Who is that?" asked Mary. "I don't recognize that voice. She's not with the government, is she?"

"No," said Kian before I could answer. "Not at all. Thanks, Mary." And he ended the call. We looked at each other and I bit my lip. This was good news but I knew what it meant.

An hour later, I was standing beside one of the black Secret Service SUVs. "I'm leaving one car with you," Miller told Kian, dropping the key into his hand. "Figured you could use something less distinctive than that Mustang. Try not to leave it in another city this time, huh?"

Kian pocketed the key and shook Miller's hand, then pulled him into an embrace. "Thanks."

Miller and the other agents withdrew to let Kian and I say goodbye. I tried to swallow the lump that was suddenly in my throat.

"This'll all be over in a couple of days," Kian said. "And then I'll come back to DC. I just can't have you anywhere near here while it all goes down."

I nodded. Looked at the house, the swing, anywhere but his eyes. I understood and I knew he was right. But that didn't stop it sucking and I didn't want him to notice how much I was suddenly blinking. "Promise you'll take care," I said, my voice cracking a little.

He wrapped his arms around me, squeezed me tight and pressed his lips to the top of my head. "Promise."

I cinched my arms so tight around his waist that it must have hurt, but he didn't complain. Then I looked up, kissed him once, and quickly got into the SUV so he couldn't see the tears in my eyes.

48

CARRICK

I was sitting with my back against my bike. The air was cooling as the sun started to set but the engine was still warm and the heat was throbbing through my leather cut and into my back in a very relaxing way. I'd taken Annabelle out for a quick blast around town: back in Haywood Falls, it was our way of saying goodbye before I left on a ride with the club and it worked just as well here in LA. Riding with her pressed tight against my back, we were together in a way few people ever were. I felt the wind in my face and knew she felt the same wind, felt the thundering, growling bike beneath me and knew she could feel it, too. It was about sharing something we could carry with us until we saw each other again. Not many girls would understand that, but Annabelle did.

Kian sat down next to me, throwing his bag down beside him. I glanced at him and then did a double take. The suit was gone. He was in jeans and a leather jacket, the leather worn-in and battered. I suddenly realized he hadn't shaved. And he looked a hell of a lot better than the night before: he looked rested and alert, not burned out and distracted. "What happened to you?" I asked.

"Emily," he said simply.

I nodded. "You want to hold onto that one. She's a classy lady." I could feel my neck going hot: it wasn't that I liked Emily in *that* way: aside from being with my brother, she wasn't my type: give me Annabelle's lush curves and copper hair any time. But whenever I was around her, I came over all tongue-tied, like I was in the presence of royalty. Thinking about it, she and Kian together made a weird sort of sense: he was the most respectable of any of us. But of course I didn't tell *him* that. "Just don't mess it up, you idiot," I grunted.

He grinned, like he knew what I was thinking. "I'll do my best."

Sean sat down on the other side of me. "I've said goodbye to Louise," he said. "But it feels wrong, leaving them. That bastard's still out there, somewhere. That fire could have killed all of them: Kayley, too."

I nodded and took out the photo that showed all of us with Bradan. "These are the people that have our brother," I said, my voice tight. "We can't leave him in there. This is the closest we've ever got: what if this lead goes cold? We might never get another chance."

Sean let out an agonized groan. "I know. But the girls...."

Aedan sat down beside Sean. "Don't worry about that," he said. "I got it covered. Made a call, after we got back from the printing works." He nodded towards the street. A taxi was climbing the hill towards the house.

For a few seconds, we sat there in silence, watching the taxi approach. It was what I'd always wanted: all four of us together, a family once more.

I stared at the photo. *Almost.* We were so close. *Please let us find him.*

The taxi pulled up in front of the house. We all got up as Alec climbed out. Aedan embraced him. "Thanks for doing this," he told him.

Alec slapped his back. "Anyone comes near this house, they're going to regret it."

We showed Alec inside, picked up our bags and climbed into the SUV. I still would have preferred to take my bike but we were a team on this one.

"Everyone said their goodbyes?" Kian asked, looking around. "Everyone got their bags? Anyone need to go pee-pee?"

When no one spoke up, he started the engine. We'd just started to move when Aedan suddenly said, "*Wait!*" threw open his door and ran for the house.

49

SYLVIE

I was just coming down the stairs, having shown Alec where he'd be sleeping, when Aedan burst back into the house. He froze on the threshold and stared at me, eyes wild.

He'd never looked more gorgeous. He was wearing that same hooded top he had when I first met him but now the hood was down, exposing him. Those powerful shoulders almost filled the doorway, his broad chest rising and falling as he panted. His hands were curled into fists. He looked so brutally dangerous...and yet, in that second, he looked so vulnerable.

"Forget something?" I asked. I walked slowly down the last few stairs and he moved forward. We met under the tree.

He looked deep into my eyes and drew in a shuddering breath but didn't speak.

"What is it?" I asked, worried.

He took my hands. "I meant to do this before you went into the cult," he said. His voice was strained, like every rough-edged, silver-dusted boulder weighed a ton. "But then it went wrong and they got you and I thought I'd never see you again. I wanted to do it as soon as you got back but you weren't yourself. I wanted to do it before we left for the printing works but I felt like I was jinxing everything, like I might not come back if I did it. And then when I came back I was a banged up mess—"

"*What?*" I asked. "Do *what?*"

He squeezed both my hands hard. And then he dropped to one knee. I blinked because it was almost like he—

My hands flew to my mouth. *OH GOD!*

He pulled a box from his pocket. Opened it to show me a silver ring with a square-cut diamond that threw dazzling patterns against the wall as the light caught it.

Blue eyes looked up into mine. Desperate. Determined. "Will you marry me?"

I wasn't ready for the emotional response. It hit me like a truck, stealing every breath of air from my lungs and damn near doubling me over. I could feel my eyes huge and staring: *I had no idea!* It was the very last thing I'd expected from him. All the love I felt for him rushed inward to my heart and just exploded into pure happiness because now it could be forever. I couldn't speak. Tears were flooding my eyes: I thought I wasn't like that, thought I wasn't a girl who cried but—

Aedan swallowed. *He thinks I'm saying no!* "I know I'm just a fighter," he said, every syllable echoing through me. "But you complete me. I need you to marry me, not because I want a life with you: because I can't imagine a life without you." He swallowed again. "And—And if—"

I finally found my voice. "*YES!*" I screamed, tears running down my cheeks. "*YES, YES!*" I dived forward and he stood up just in time to catch me. He whirled me around in sheer joy, lifting me like I weighed nothing, my legs flying out behind me. He kissed away my tears, panting in relief, as we spun. As we gradually slowed, more and more of me settled against his body. My breasts pressed against his pecs. My stomach kissed his abs. My groin settled onto his. My feet still dangled off the ground because he was so much bigger than me. I hung there, kissing him, and I never wanted to be anywhere else.

He finally put me down and I staggered, drunk on love. Then he was taking my left hand on his. *What's he—Oh my God!* I'd almost forgotten about the ring part. My chest closed up tight as he slid the band onto my finger. *A man is putting a ring on my finger!* It felt enchanted. It had *power,* tingling and throbbing against my skin, sending waves of excitement right through me. Everything swelled up inside me again and I almost started crying anew: I'd never known what *so happy I could burst* meant until that moment.

Aedan wrapped me up in his arms. Touched his forehead to mine. "I have to go," he said.

And it was okay because I knew he didn't want to: he needed to. I nodded, breathless. "Go." He stepped away but I grabbed his t-shirt, the thin cotton stretching in my fists. "Hey!"

He turned back.

"You're marrying me when you get back," I told him, my voice catching.

He nodded and smoothed his hand down the back of my head. "Damn right I am." He bent and kissed me, his lips tasting me and then his tongue seeking out mine in a kiss that lifted me right up onto my toes, glittering sparkles shimmering right down my body. I'd never felt so light, so *girly.*

He stepped back and then he was gone, marching off down the drive to the waiting SUV. The ring felt so heavy on my finger, weighing my hand down as if it weighed a thousand tons. I kept fingering it, stroking it. I couldn't get used to it, couldn't *not* feel it.

"Come back soon," I whispered to myself.

50

SEAN

We drove for hours, way out into the sticks. The towns grew further apart and there wasn't a light for miles. Eventually, we turned onto a side road and began to climb up a grassy hill. Kian stopped just before we reached the crest and killed the engine. He pointed to the map on the GPS. "If Mary's right about the location, it's on the other side of this hill."

We all climbed out. The adrenaline was pumping, now: this was *it.*

Kian fished in his bag and brought out a huge, boxy handgun that looked like it could bring down an elephant. He shoved it into a shoulder holster under his leather jacket. Carrick brought out the carved, monstrous shotgun he called Caorthannach and concealed it under his cut. The four of us crept up to the top of the hill to look. *We should have brought bolt cutters,* I thought suddenly. There'd be a fence, probably with razor wire....

I peeked my head over the crest...and blinked.

On the other side of the hill, laid out like a picture postcard on the floor of a valley, was an idyllic little town. It was tiny, maybe a few hundred people. Every building was white painted and everything was traditional: there was what looked like a town hall, a big three

story mansion that might once have belonged to the mayor and
streets of perfect little houses with—I squinted—*Jesus!* Actual white
picket fences.

"You put the coordinates in wrong," grunted Carrick.

"It's right. I double checked," said Kian.

Aedan shook his head. "So where is it?" There was no place to
hide a camp full of cult members in the tiny town below. It would
have stuck out a mile.

Kian shook his head. "The co-ordinates are *right*. Let's go take a
look."

Half an hour later, we were wandering through the heart of the town.
It was late but the place was still busy. Some of the stores were still
open, there was some sort of live music playing in the town's one bar
and families were strolling around eating ice cream. It reminded me
of a holiday resort but there was no attraction to come for: this place
was in the middle of nowhere. These were *locals*.

We passed an old man sitting on a bench, doing a crossword
puzzle under a streetlamp. Further along the street, a couple of guys
were playing chess. It was so *quiet*. I realized what I wasn't hearing:
sirens. In LA, there's always a siren blaring somewhere. We kept
thinking that, around the next corner, we'd see a huge barn or
something surrounded by razor wire fences and guys with guns. But
there was nothing that looked remotely shady.

"Maybe only the leader lives here," said Kian at last. "The
compound or camp or whatever, where they take people like Bradan,
is somewhere else. That way, if it ever gets raided, the leader's safe. It
would explain why Mary traced the computer here: it's just one guy
in his house, with a laptop."

Carrick nodded reluctantly. "That makes sense. *Shit!* I thought we
were close."

"We *are* close," said Aedan darkly. "We're going to find that son of
a bitch and make him tell us where Bradan is." He looked around.

"This is the sort of place where everyone knows everyone. Let's start asking questions."

He marched into a diner that looked like it had come straight out of the fifties. In fact, the whole town had that look about it. The town planning committee must be strict as hell because I couldn't see a McDonalds or a Starbucks anywhere. I followed Aedan, the other two behind me.

Inside, it was still busy. People were chowing down on slices of apple pie, coffee and ice cream: late-night dessert must be a *thing,* here. I sat down beside Aedan at the counter and ordered coffee. Kian and Carrick joined us.

"Just passing through?" asked the waitress. She was pretty, with auburn hair pinned up and a pencil tucked behind her ear.

"Yep. Just stopped for gas." I gave her a friendly smile. "Seems like a nice little town."

She smiled.

And I froze.

She turned away and I sat there staring at her back as she poured our coffees, suddenly deeply unsettled. Her smile had been friendly but her eyes hadn't matched. They'd been cold and hostile but also pitying. I'd seen that look somewhere before.

"*What?*" asked Kian, leaning across Aedan to reach me.

I didn't answer. I was still staring at the waitress. In my head, I was back at the house where the cult had initiated Sylvie. The woman there had looked at me while she called the cops and she'd given me the exact same look: I was the enemy, but I was also somehow beneath her because I was an Outsider.

She was one of them. She was part of Aeternus. But what were the chances of us stumbling across the leader of the cult as easily as that?

I turned on my stool and looked at the people in the diner. Then the people walking past on the street outside. The old men. The couples. The children.

I gripped Kian's arm hard to make him listen. "Stand up," I grated. "And walk out."

Carrick blinked. "What? Why?"

I was already sliding off my stool and throwing a few dollars on the counter. "Sorry," I told the waitress. "Change of plan." And I headed for the door without waiting for a reply.

My brothers followed but Carrick was muttering in my ear, asking questions. *"Outside,"* I told him.

On the street, I tried to keep them moving, heading back the way we'd come. But they all wanted answers. "What happened in there?" asked Kian.

"We found them," I said under my breath.

"Where? The diner?"

"The *town,"* I told him in a strangled voice. "That's why we couldn't find it. We're already in the middle of it." I was glancing at each person walking towards us, expecting them to jump us. Everyone had that same look in their eyes: we were Outsiders and they knew it. "Every fucking person in this town is part of the cult."

Kian drew in his breath. I saw his hand twitch, a hair's-breadth from going for this gun. But guns wouldn't help us, here, not when we were outnumbered hundreds to one. Our only chance was to get out of town while they still thought we were just tourists who'd wandered in by mistake.

There was the *woop-woop* of a siren behind us. I turned to see a cop car pulling up outside the diner. Two cops immediately climbed out and started walking towards us. *Shit.* And ahead of us, that short blast of the siren made every head turn.

They looked.

They identified us as Outsiders: ones wanted by the police.

And then my blood turned to ice as every single person on the street started towards us. Young lovers out for a stroll dropped each other's hands and walked towards us. Mothers pushed their children behind them and then started forward. Young men who'd just left the bar, old men who'd been playing chess: *everyone* started to move in our direction. Their faces were stony, their eyes cold. We were the enemy. It was the single scariest thing I'd ever seen in my life.

"Run!" yelled Kian.

We ran, charging down the sidewalk towards the edge of town. The townsfolk grabbed at us as we passed or ran to block our path. We had to shoulder them out of the way but there were too many of them: we were going to be overrun long before we reached safety.

A big guy with a beard leaned in and made a grab at me from the right but I shoved him aside. Out of the corner of my eye, I saw someone else rushing in from the left and I raised my other hand to punch...but at the last second, I realized it was a girl no older than Kayley. I dropped my guard and she barreled into me, tackling me to the ground.

The girl and I separated as we landed but others were rushing forward to grab hold of me. They would have got me if Carrick and Kian hadn't taken a hand each and hauled me to my feet. Aedan pushed back the two guys who were closest but it was like trying to hold back the tide. I saw Kian reach for his gun...but just as quickly, he shoved it back into his holster. There were kids and teenagers everywhere.

Two guys grabbed Carrick around the shoulders and tussled him to the ground, then tried to drag him away. Kian snarled and launched himself at them, shouldering one aside and punching the other so hard he folded silently to the ground. He grabbed Carrick's hand and hauled him up...and I saw something in Carrick's eyes: respect, relief and a little pride.

"What?" snapped Kian.

Carrick shook his head: *nothing.* But I was pretty sure I understood that look. He was realizing his brother hadn't gone soft at all.

We staggered on but there was no way we were going to make it to the edge of town. My heart was hammering. This was terrifying: *everyone* was against us.

"Down here!" yelled Carrick and led the way to an alley. We had no idea where it led, but at least it was free of people. We sprinted down it, legs burning, lungs aching. But I could already hear more people in the street beyond. It didn't matter how fast we ran: we were surrounded.

At that instant, a bright red jeep tore out of a side alley and screeched to a stop in front of us, so close that Carrick had to stumble to a stop to avoid running into it. *Shit!* Now that way was blocked. We all turned towards the side alley it had come from, hoping we could duck down there—

The driver leaned out of his window. *"Get in!"*

We all gaped at him. *What?* The guy was a stranger. And it made no sense: we had no friends in this town. Was he just trying to delay us? I could hear the townsfolk pouring into the alley behind us.

"Get in!" the guy yelled again.

Kian hesitated, as confused as I was. Who the hell was this guy and why was he trying to save us? I checked over my shoulder. A solid mass of people filled the alley behind us. The closest ones were only seconds away.

"For fuck's sake," roared the guy. "It's *me!*"

The face was many years older than I remembered it. But I finally recognized the black hair, the blue eyes. "Oh Jesus," I whispered. I looked at the others, all of us making the connection at the same time.

I'd been wrong. We had one friend in this town. Just one.

We piled into the car and slammed the doors. "Where are we going?" panted Kian.

"Somewhere safe," said Bradan.

The crowd arrived. Bodies slammed against the car and hands pressed against the windows. Bradan floored it so hard that we were mashed into our seats and we were gone before they could get a door open.

We hurtled through the side alley, walls whipping past with only inches to spare. Bradan turned into another alley, then onto a street. This was his town, not ours, so we couldn't do much to help. That gave us time to glance at one another and it looked as if we were all thinking the same thing.

We found him!

I'd been thinking about it for so long. In the last few weeks, I'd been constantly aware of it: self-conscious, almost. I'd been able to feel him getting closer and closer, always just beyond my fingertips. He'd been the first thing I thought of in the morning, the last thing at night. But I hadn't known what we were going to find: would it be an unmarked grave in the desert?

What I hadn't realized until now is that I'd been thinking about it long before that: ever since he was taken from us. I'd buried it inside me so as not to go insane but it had always been there, along with my mom's death, filling me with that rage that had come out in every swing of the sledgehammer. It had been with me for so long, I couldn't believe it was over.

He was here. I could reach out and touch him. *Bradan!* I could see scars on his neck and his forearms were thickly muscled from constant use. He reminded me of Kian: a warrior's body.

And then the guilt hit.

He'd been in the same fucking state as me for years. He'd been through hell while we'd all been living our lives. I looked at the others again, seeing the same realization in their faces. *We looked for him,* I told myself.

We could have looked harder.

Bradan threw the car into a tight turn and we tore down a concrete ramp that led underground. We were plunged into darkness for a second, then my eyes adjusted and I made out a small parking garage. Bradan jumped out as soon as we stopped. Blinking in surprise, we slowly climbed out as well. Why had he brought us here? Shouldn't we be getting out of town?

Five men stepped from the shadows. Four of them were in police uniforms, their guns drawn. The fifth was an older guy, mostly bald but with white hair stretching back over each ear.

The cops leveled their guns at us. We all slowly raised our hands, looking at Bradan in shock.

The old guy embraced him. "Well done, Bradan," he said. "Well done."

51

AEDAN

The cops led us upstairs, which was when we realized that Bradan had driven us to the police station. It looked like it was still being built, or maybe remodeled, because there was construction gear down the hall. They took our weapons and cell phones and pushed us into a holding cell with bare cinderblock walls, the door swung shut and the cops left. As soon as they were gone, the building was utterly silent: I wasn't even sure they'd left someone on night duty. Then it clicked: in this town, with every citizen loyal to the cult, there'd be no crime.

The cell had a tiny, barred window, a toilet and sink, a couple of bunks, and that was it. Kian and Sean sat down on the bunks. Carrick slumped down on the floor, back against the wall. I grabbed hold of the iron bars that fronted the cell and just stood there raging, my knuckles white where they gripped the metal.

How could we have been so stupid? He'd been with them for years. Of course he'd be on their side. But all he'd had to do was show up and we'd trusted him instantly. And then he'd— I wanted to throw up. I understood why. I'd seen what Sylvie was like after just a few days. They'd had Bradan for years.

But he was our *brother*. And he'd betrayed us like it was nothing. Like he didn't even know who we were, anymore.

None of us slept that night. Nobody came for us. *Why aren't we dead?* Why hadn't they just shot us, taken us somewhere far from town and dumped the bodies?

The sun had been up for a few hours before the cops returned. We were cuffed, pushed into the back of a police van and driven a short distance. When they hauled us out, blinking in the bright sunshine, we were looking up at a large, grand house that overlooked the rest of the town. Immediately, I had a pretty good idea who we were going to meet.

He was seated at a dining table, eating breakfast. Apparently, we didn't warrant our own slot in his busy schedule. Rich, golden scrambled eggs were piled in a neat crescent on his plate. Two strips of crispy bacon were stretched out next to it, precisely parallel. A mug of black coffee was at exactly one O'clock. On his left, the day's newspaper, folded back on itself to show just the page he needed. On his right, a gunmetal-gray laptop, the lid closed. It wasn't *posh*...it wasn't bone china cups and silver teapots. Everything looked normal. But everything was *perfect*.

"The famous O'Harra brothers," said the man. "You may call me Mr. Pryce."

Kian stormed forward. "What the hell did you do to our brother, you son of a bitch?"

There was a vicious cracking noise as one of the cops brought his nightstick down across Kian's shoulders. He cried out and fell to his knees.

I immediately stepped forward to help but Sean caught my eye and shook his head, glancing behind me. I turned and looked. There was a cop behind each of us, nightsticks raised and ready.

Kian started to struggle to his feet but Pryce shook his head. "Down there is fine," he said simply. And the cop behind Kian stepped forward a little to make sure he obeyed. Kian growled low in his throat but stayed where he was.

Pryce made us wait while he broke off a hunk of crisp bacon: the room was so quiet, we could hear it snap. He speared it, added a little buttery scrambled eggs and devoured the mouthful, watching us as he chewed. Christ, it looked good. I wasn't sure if it was some psychological trick, making us watch him eat when we were hungry, but it was working: my mouth was watering at the thought of that crispy, salty bacon and the rich roast of the coffee smelled incredible.

"Your brother's been a great aid to me, over the years," he said at last.

"You...changed him," said Carrick. He was struggling to control his rage, too. The temptation to just leap across the table at the guy was almost too much to take. But with our hands cuffed, we wouldn't even get one good punch in before the cops took us down.

Pryce drank some coffee before he answered. "He fought it. For a *long* time. I don't think I've ever seen someone fight it as hard as Bradan did. But you know the funny thing?" He took another sip. "When people break—and they *do* all break—the harder they fought it, the more completely they commit. Bradan is one of my most trusted people."

My stomach twisted. I knew now who the hooded guy at the printing works had been. *He would have killed us. And I nearly killed* him! I glanced at Sean and saw the look on his face, the pleading in his eyes for it not to be true. That's when it hit me: Bradan had set the fire, too. *Louise. Kayley. Annabelle.* He'd tried to kill them all.

He'd tried to kill *Sylvie.* Oh Christ. My own brother!

"You're running it," said Kian. "You're running this whole thing. *Why?* We get that it's not about being worshipped: people in the groups don't even know who you are, do they? It's not about money. So why? We know you have them doing stuff, lots of little tasks. What's it all for?"

Pryce looked down at Kian and, for a second, a smile toyed with the edges of his lips. "This is the part where I tell you my entire plan, so you can foil it: right?"

Kian just glared at him.

"No," said Pryce, as if telling a child he couldn't have chocolate. "Even the people in this town don't know that. They don't need to. Only I do. Me..."—he glanced at the laptop—"and the ones who'll come after me." He waved at the cops. "Put them back in the cell. I'm done with them for now."

The cops hauled Kian up but, as he reached his feet, he roared and tried to twist free. They pulled a nightstick tight against his throat, choking him, and he quieted. My hands bunched into fists, but there was nothing we could do, not cuffed as we were. "Just shoot us!" yelled Kian. "Get it over with!"

Pryce blinked at Kian. Then he gave a huge, wide grin: the smile of someone delighting in being able to deliver bad news. "You think I'm going to *kill* you? Oh Kian. You're not as smart as they make you out to be, are you?"

Kian panted, chest heaving, and glared at him.

Pryce picked up his coffee and took a sip. "One O'Harra brother has been very useful to me. Think what I can do with five."

It was as if the floor had opened up beneath me and I was falling into the unknown. *What?* I felt the same way I had when Rick had told me I'd have to fight Sylvie: it was a possibility I just hadn't considered. I'd lain awake at night thinking about Sylvie being brainwashed by the cult, and Bradan...but *me? Us?*

Pryce looked right at me. "Your skills with your fists will be very useful. You'll be a Prime, just like Bradan."

A cold hand grabbed hold of my heart and squeezed. *No!* I tried to tell myself that I wouldn't do it, that I'd never kill for them. I still had nightmares about Travere, the guy I'd killed in the ring years ago. But I'd seen what they did to Sylvie. They'd turn me into their attack dog, just like Bradan. I'd kill whoever they ordered me to: man, woman or child.

"You," said Pryce, turning to Carrick. "You are going to let us expand into whole new areas. You're our way into the MC world. First you, then your president—Mac, yes?" He grinned. "We'll gradually spread through the chapters. Our own loyal, mobile army. The Hell's Princes are going to be very useful: no one's going to question it if a biker gets caught shooting someone, or shanking someone in jail."

I watched as Carrick turned pale. I knew it was his greatest fear:

that he'd betray the MC and corrupt it, turn it into a twisted version of the brotherhood he loved so much.

"Sean," Pryce said, turning to him. "You're the least useful. But we'll find something for all that dumb muscle to do: we always need manual laborers." He lifted his mug again, drained some coffee and smacked his lips in satisfaction. "But Louise? She's going to provide a very valuable source of income."

Sean went pale. "*Louise?!*"

Pryce grinned. "You thought we didn't know about the drugs? We've learned *all about* you all in the last few days. I called my connections south of the border and they gave me all the details. Once you're Insiders, we'll move Louise somewhere she can grow serious amounts. We own plenty of empty buildings that can be turned into grow houses. There's an underground bunker in Kansas, for example, that your brother is intimately familiar with. Within a year, I think she could be bringing in millions." He paused and read Sean's terrified expression. "Oh, don't worry about Kayley." He allowed Sean a few seconds of hope before he crushed it. "We can find plenty of uses for a teenage girl."

Sean gave a howl of fury and ran at him. A nightstick cracked against his legs and he went sprawling sideways, yelling in pain.

Pryce gave us all a few seconds for things to sink in. The room went very quiet: all we could hear was our own slow panting as we stood there in helpless rage. Then he smiled at Kian. "But *you,*" he said. "*You...*are the ultimate prize. I couldn't believe my luck, when I realized who'd stumbled into my lap."

Kian had always been so strong. I'd never seen him waver. So when I saw him begin to crumble, it was truly terrifying.

"No," he said, his voice hoarse.

"First," said Pryce. "You'll go back to DC and tell the President he's wrong about Aeternus."

Kian was silently shaking his head.

"Then—" said the man

"*No!*"

"—you'll bring in Emily."

"*NO!*"

"Very slowly. Very carefully. But you'll bring her in. And once she's in..." Pryce shook his head in awe. "Our own eyes and ears in the White House. Between the two of you, we'll have influence over her father. It'll be a new era."

Kian gave a strangled cry and lunged forward but the cops grabbed him under the arms, hauling him back.

Carrick was sucking in air through his teeth, trying to control his anger. "Annabelle," he said. "Sylvie. You don't need *them*. Leave them alone."

The man drained the last of his coffee and then shook his head. "We never leave partners or spouses behind. Too many questions. Sylvie already knows how to fight. We can teach her to kill. A female Prime could be *very* useful. And Annabelle? I got hold of her school reports. She has an *astonishing* mind. I'm sure we can find something for her." He smiled. "Besides, it's too late."

We froze and stared at him.

"Oh, Emily will have to be handled very delicately. That could take months. But the others, at your house? We're taking care of them right now."

52

ANNABELLE

"...And then he said?" Kayley was leaning forward across the table, eyes huge.

Sylvie flushed. I could tell she wasn't used to this, wasn't used to girly chats and sharing. But at the same time, she seemed to be loving it. "He said, *you complete me.*"

Kayley *squee*d, grabbed Sylvie's hand and looked at the ring again. "You are *so* lucky," she breathed. "I *so* need to find a guy like Aedan. Or Sean. Or—"

"No!" Sylvie, Louise and I all said together. We looked at each other and grinned, and Louise took charge. "You're going to fall for a lawyer, or a doctor, or if you're *very* lucky I might let you fall for a stockbroker," she told her sister.

Kayley stuck her tongue out at her. "You should all be being nice to me." She nodded towards Louise's stomach. "You're going to need help."

Louise had told us a few minutes ago, blurting it out just after the men had left. Sylvie hadn't had to tell us about the engagement because we'd all been eavesdropping from the kitchen. Only Kayley had missed it, hence the blow-by-blow.

"We'll *all* help," I said determinedly, even though I knew even less about babies than I did about plants. "Haywood Falls isn't that far away. And the others can visit."

Sylvie nodded eagerly. I got the feeling that, like me, she was liking being a part of something, here in LA. Neither of us wanted it to end, when the men returned and we went back to our normal lives.

"Thought about names, yet?" asked Sylvie.

Louise shook her head. "It wasn't *real,* until I told Sean. Now...God, the baby'll be here next summer!" She bit her lip. "What if —" She looked down at the table and went quiet for a few seconds. "What if something goes wrong? I mean, normally you never tell anyone until later on...."

Sylvie leaned across and rubbed her shoulder. "You'll be *fine!* You needed to tell someone, what with...." She jerked her head behind her at the silent, empty house, and we all went quiet. *With all of them gone.*

That's why we were all talking so hard about engagements and babies. They'd been gone all night: not a phone call or a text, nothing. It wasn't even like we could call the police. If Aeternus had them....

I turned to Kayley. "Tell us more about this guy at school," I said firmly. "Jarod?"

"I like him already," said Sylvie. "Good name."

"He's in a band?" asked Louise.

Kayley grinned and leaned forward, loving having two new aunts. Three, if you counted Emily, who she'd already emailed three times.

We heard the front door unlock. All of us jumped up. *They're back!* We hadn't even heard the car pull up. We ran to the hallway. I could hear Alec running from the room upstairs where he'd been dozing: he'd kept watch all night and we'd only just persuaded him to finally take a nap. He was yelling, telling us to wait. "It's okay," I called as the door swung open. "It's—"

I stumbled to a stop as we reached the hallway, the others crashing into me from behind.

It wasn't them.

The first guy through the door wore a hooded top. I remembered the description the men had given of the guy at the printing works. *Oh God....* Behind him were another four guys.

"*Kayley!*" yelled Louise. "*Run upstairs!*"

Sylvie snarled, ducked around me and launched herself at the guy in the hooded top. But he grabbed and threw her, using her momentum against her, and she went sailing through the air to land in the scorched, blackened living room. She landed awkwardly on her hip and gave a howl of pain. The guy stepped towards her—

And that's when Alec, who'd jumped the last ten steps, landed on him with the force of two hundred pounds and a brother's fury. Big as he was, the guy didn't stand a chance. Alec rode him down to the floor and immediately started pounding him in the face. I could see the frustration boiling out of him. He hadn't been here when Sylvie was taken. He hadn't been here when the men were in trouble at the printing works. But he was here *now.* "*That—is my* sister—*you fucking —fucking—*" he snarled between punches.

Meanwhile, Louise and I had dived at the door and were attempting to force it closed. We'd nearly managed it when the three guys outside pushed forward, inching it open. We panted and strained, our sneakers squeaking on the polished floor. Kayley was frozen halfway up the stairs, looking back at us, torn between obeying Louise and helping us.

"*Go!*" yelled Louise. Kayley ran.

Sylvie struggled to her feet and ran to the door, limping a little. She threw her weight against it and we started to gain ground. *Yes!* Another foot and we could lock it. Six inches. Five—

All of my nerves exploded into fire. I couldn't move. Couldn't even feel my hands on the door, anymore. I didn't know if I was still standing or if I was falling: there was no sensation at all other than raw burning, like every part of me was being pressed against a hot griddle.

I hit the floor. The most terrifying part was that I'd lost the ability to think. I could see the door being forced open and Louise and Sylvie being wrestled to the ground by the men. I could see the thin silver wires sticking out of my chest but I didn't know what any of it meant.

Alec stood up and came to help, just in time for one of the men to raise a futuristic-looking pistol. There was a buzzing, clicking sound and Alec crashed to the floor. I realized he'd been Tasered, and that that's what had happened to me. My mind slowly started to come back. One of the men must have reached around the door and fired blindly at whoever was pushing it closed. I was just lucid enough to think, *thank God it wasn't Louise.*

I still couldn't move. My nerves didn't seem to be connected to anything. I watched as the men bound Louise and Sylvie's wrists behind their backs with plastic zip ties. Then they did the same to me. When they'd finished, I was left lying on my side on the floor, my muscles too limp and weak to even roll over. One man went upstairs and, a few seconds later, I heard Kayley scream and the sounds of a struggle. Louise twisted and thrashed, her eyes locked on the top of the stairs.

The man in the hooded top finished zip-tying Alec, stood up and approached us. He was bleeding from his lip and a cut over one eye, but he didn't seem angry or even shaken, just coldly efficient. I frowned. There was something in his face, something I recognized. "Take them to separate rooms and get started," he told the others.

For a second, I had that instinctive fear, memories of Volos and the Blood Spiders and the auction. Then my stomach lurched. There was something even worse than that. I managed to twist enough to stare at Sylvie and saw her face go pale as she realized it, too. They were going to do to all of us what they'd done to her. I started to panic breathe, thinking of my mind being violated, being rewired so that I was just another happy, loyal cult member. *No!*

One of the men stretched out his leg and, using the point of his shoe on my cheek, turned my head to look up at him. "It's not exactly ideal," he said, looking down at me.

I realized what he meant. *We know what they're trying to do to us.* It wasn't like Sylvie, or the other people they initiated, who'd been unknowing lambs to the slaughter. We could resist. We could fight it. *Maybe it won't work.*

Then the man in the hooded top crushed that faint hope. "Use a higher dose," he told them. What was it about him? I'd never seen him before but I swore he looked familiar. "It'll work. It'll just take longer."

And that's when I finally saw it. The blue eyes. The black hair. The jaw line. If the American accent hadn't fooled me, I would have seen it before. "Oh God," I croaked. "*Bradan?!*"

His head snapped up. *I was right.* I heard the other girls give low gasps of horror.

Then one of the men threw me over his shoulder and I was carried upstairs.

53

KIAN

We were back in the cell as if we'd never left. Only now, everything was different. Every time I thought of what they were going to do to us, I wanted to rip the bars out of the wall with my bare hands. Every time I thought of what they were doing to the girls—what they were going to do to Emily—I wanted to throw up.

Emily. They were going to take everything she was, everything she stood for, and twist it. People trusted her. They knew she was one of the good guys. But now she'd whisper whatever they wanted her to in her father's ear...*and I'd help her.*

I'd played a part in saving our country. Now I was going to help to destroy it.

I pressed my forehead against the cold metal bars and tried to shut out the noise. All morning, from down the hall, there'd been the bang of hammers and the scrape of cinderblocks as they were wrestled into position: Pryce had a few of the townsfolk working on the police station. It seemed to be going slow, with a lot of cursing, but I guess Pryce preferred slow progress to letting professional contractors—Outsiders—visit the town.

That bastard. He'd built his own little empire, a secret network spread out around the globe. Thousands of obedient civilians carrying out thousands of tiny tasks, all knitting together into a grand plan. He had a small army of *Primes* like Bradan, trained assassins. And he'd built himself the perfect fortress: a whole town utterly devoted to him, every citizen ready to kill to protect him. It was better than any amount of concrete and razor wire: no one was going to storm in here and start shooting women and children.

But what was his aim? I knew that the key to figuring it out was working out who Pryce was, where he'd come from. But I was too wound up to focus on the problem. And even if I could figure it out, the knowledge was useless unless we could escape.

I shut my eyes. I'd always been taught, ever since I joined the military, that in a crisis calm people live, panicked people die. I knew I had to *think*. But I honestly didn't see how any amount of being cool and rational was going to get us out of this one. They had us. They had the girls. We didn't have a single person left on our side.

This is all my fault. If I hadn't let Sean and then Carrick convince me to put the family back together. If I'd listened to the President, or my dad, or Calahan. Everyone had tried to stop me taking this path, *everyone*. Now we were all screwed: for what? To find a guy who'd turned out to be a hundred percent loyal to the cult. We'd thought we were rescuing him but the Bradan we'd known died a long time ago. *I'm so stupid!*

I kicked the bars with the side of my boot, which did nothing except make them rattle. In the silence that followed, Sean said, "Louise is pregnant."

We all turned to stare at him. Sean just nodded. We hadn't misheard.

So many emotions welled up inside me. My youngest brother: the first of us to be a father! Jesus, I was so proud of him: he'd found an amazing woman, gone straight, saved Kayley, settled down. He was going to have a family!

And then I remembered what they did to families, in Aeternus. By the time the child was born, Sean and Louise would willingly give it up, just as our mom had given up Bradan.

And it was all my fault.

54

LOUISE

The man was in his fifties with thinning gray hair. He had a kind smile: he reminded me, more than anything, of a dentist. It was unnerving, that someone so unthreatening could be so evil. *He isn't,* part of me insisted. *He's no more evil than Sylvie was, when they brainwashed her.* He was just some normal guy they'd sucked in.

But that didn't help me, right now. "Please," I said as he sat me down on the bed. "You can't give me a drug. I'm pregnant."

He blinked just once, taking that in. Then he nodded. "It'll be fine," he said. "It's just something to help you relax."

Except he wasn't *that* good of an actor. He'd probably initiated hundreds of people, had it down to a fine art. But he'd only had to deal with this problem once or twice and I caught the flicker in his eyes. The flicker that said, *shit.*

The flicker that said, *well, that's sad.*

I erupted off the bed. "*Nooo!*"

"It'll be fine!" he insisted, pushing me back down. But he knew now there was no hope of convincing me.

"*No!*" I knew there was no one to help me, no one who could come. But I kicked and screamed for all I was worth. I had no leverage, though, with my hands bound, and he easily wrestled me

until I was sitting on the bed with my back against the headboard.
Then he wrenched my chin up. "Open your mouth," he said.

I saw the pills in his hand and my stomach contracted in fear. I
clamped my jaws shut as hard as I possibly could, hysterical, now,
tears filling my eyes.

The door opened and Bradan walked in. "Problem?"

"Not if you get her mouth open," said the man holding me.

Bradan straddled my kicking legs, pinning them to the bed, and
then gripped my head. I thrashed and twisted, hair lashing at his face
as I tried to avoid looking at him. But his hands were like iron,
locking tight around my skull and slowly turning it. I clamped my
teeth together as hard as I could.

He put his thumbs at just the right place, either side of my jaw,
and pressed. My jaws opened an inch. Tears were streaming down my
face, now. I wanted to beg him but I couldn't speak.

"Pill," said Bradan with terrifying calm.

I tried to press my lips together to seal the opening but then the
other man's fingers were pulling them apart and—

I felt three flat, chalky pills slide onto my tongue. I bucked and
twisted, knowing this was my last chance, but they had me held tight.
Then a bottle of water was pressed to my lips and my whole head was
tipped back. My mouth filled with water and I was coughing and
choking, trying to find the pills with my tongue, fighting my own
swallow reflex—

I felt the pills slip down my throat.

They let me go and I fell on my side, coughing, water spraying
from my lips. I pulled up my legs and pressed my stomach with my
knees, trying to force myself to be sick, but nothing happened.

Bradan got up to leave. The other man sat down beside the bed.

"How can you do this?" I sobbed. "They're your *brothers!*"

Bradan turned and stared at me for a second, frowning. And then
he left and closed the door.

55

BRADAN

I closed the door behind me, leaving the sobbing, red-haired woman on the bed. But I didn't let go of the door handle. I stood there in the hallway frowning, the lie that she'd told me echoing around my head.

It wasn't the lie itself. Outsiders will say anything to try to draw us away from The Group. But down that dark hallway in my mind, I could hear the memories banging on the other side of the glass, and....

I swayed a little on my feet. *And they sounded the same as the lie.*

I stumbled down the stairs. I suddenly needed some air. I passed the tree, blackened and scorched from the fire, and had the front door open when I saw something on a side table. Someone must have dropped it there since the fire, or it wouldn't have survived.

I picked it up. It was a photo of five boys together, in their early teens, all of them with black hair and blue eyes. I didn't recognize them, at first, but then I squinted and started to see familiar lines in the cheekbones, the chins...if it had been only one of them, I wouldn't have got it. But the faces of the biker, the fighter, the criminal and the one in the suit gradually emerged.

Four brothers.

Who was the fifth?

The noise from behind the glass was growing, becoming deafening. I stood stock still in the hallway but, in my mind, I was retreating further and further back into the darkness, hands over my ears. *No!*

I stared and stared at the photo. I could hear Mr. Pryce—*dad*— telling me to stop but I couldn't tear my eyes away.

In my mind, I heard the first crack as the glass began to break. I backed frantically away into the dark. Another crack. A hole opening up. Voices. Boys. A woman. An older man. A *father*.

Deep in the dark, I fell to the floor and threw my arms protectively around myself, covering my eyes and ears.

The glass shattered. A million tiny jagged shards of pain dug into me, opening me up. And waiting behind the glass was an ocean of memory. It swept over me, filling my lungs. I was drowning in it.

I locked up. I just stood there like a statue in the hallway, staring at the photo, my eyes unfocused.

And without thought, all that was left was instinct. I couldn't process, couldn't make decisions. But I knew there was something I had to do, *right now,* or it would be too late.

I turned and marched up the stairs. Threw open the door to the room where I'd left the red-haired woman. The Guide who was going to initiate her looked up in irritation from his chair. "We haven't even—"

I hit him as hard as I could. He and the chair tipped back and he crashed to the floor, out cold.

The woman was lying sobbing on the bed. I rolled her over, took a knife from my pocket and cut the zip tie binding her hands. Immediately, she turned away from me, leaned over the side of the bed and stuck two fingers down her throat. When she'd brought up the water and the pills, she slumped on the bed in relief.

The door banged open again. One of the other Guides ran in. "What the *hell* is going—"

I turned and he met my fist coming the other way. He went crashing back against the wall and slid to the floor. I looked down in surprise at my hand. I couldn't explain where the anger was coming from: I didn't even know what I was doing.

I heard the final two men pounding up the stairs to investigate. I strode out of the room and kicked the first one under the chin just as he reached the top of the stairs. He fell backward and toppled the other one and together they crashed all the way down to the bottom.

And then I just sat down on my ass at the top of the stairs. Whatever instinct had been driving me, it had just run out.

I was only dimly aware of the red-haired woman squeezing past me, her eyes wide and fearful, and running downstairs. She returned with scissors and started going from room to room. The other women appeared, together with the teenage girl and the man who'd fought me. They all slowly approached me, staring into my eyes.

But all I could do was stare blankly back at them. Everything I'd been suppressing since I was a kid was flooding out and I was sinking deeper and deeper beneath the black surface. It wasn't just the memories of my family. I'd learned to lock many other people behind that glass wall: all the ones I'd hurt or killed. And now they were all rushing towards me, an endless black tide, screaming in pain.

My mind sought for something, anything, to shut it off. The truths of Aeternus, the gorgeous simplicity of Beautiful Order: they were like a huge, heavy stone door under my hand. All I had to do was push it closed and the flow would stop. Everything would be back to normal. I placed my palm on it....

But I couldn't bring myself to push. It felt wrong. Those voices inside me had to be heard.

And so I immersed myself in it. I let it all sweep over me and carry me deep, deep down, and I stopped being aware of anything outside my own mind.

56

SYLVIE

"I think he's locked up," I said. "Catatonia...or something like it." It was unnerving, seeing the guy who scared me so much just...sitting there. "What happened?"

"I told him who he was," said Louise.

"You think he didn't *know?*" asked Kayley.

"He was in the cult for years," I said. "God knows what lies they told him."

"And now we...*broke him?*" asked Alec. "By telling him the truth?"

"Or he's processing it all," said Louise uncertainly. "I don't know." She sighed. "What now? This can't be a coincidence, them showing up here. It means—" She bit her lip.

"It means they've got them," I said quietly.

We all looked at each other. "Call the police?" said Louise.

"They have people in the police," I said. "We know that. They'll tip off the cult and the guys will be dead and the bodies gone long before the police show up."

"So what do we do?" asked Annabelle.

I thought hard. What would Aedan want me to do? What would they all want us to do? I could hear Aedan's voice in my head, as clear as if he was standing in front of me. He'd rest his warm hand on my cheek and he'd say, *Run. Go somewhere the cult can never find you.*

They'd want us to hide.

They'd want us to stay safe.

"They've got our men," I said. I looked at Louise, then at Annabelle. "We're going to get them back."

"The three of us?" asked Annabelle.

"Four," said Alec immediately.

"Five," I said, and nodded at Bradan. "We're taking him with us. We need all the help we can get."

Alec shook his head. "When he comes out of...whatever this is, how do you know he's still going to be on our side?"

We glared at each other for a moment, but he had a point. "Compromise," I said at last. "We'll take him but we'll tie him up."

Bradan didn't resist at all when we zip-tied his hands. We'd already tied up the four unconscious men and taken their Tasers. Louise persuaded Kayley to go to Stacey's house and called a cab for her. Meanwhile, I called Emily.

"I'm coming," she said immediately. "I can get on a plane—"

"There's no time," I told her gently.

"I'm the only one of us who can use a gun!"

"I know." I looked at where Louise was hugging Kayley goodbye, then at Annabelle. Alec and I could fight but, really, none of us were cut out for this. "I wish you were here."

I could hear the Texan coming through in Emily's accent, now. *"Goddammit,* I should never have let him send me back to DC!"

"We'll get them back," I told her. And hoped I sounded more confident than I felt.

Annabelle found a large wrench in the garage and then slipped behind the wheel of the Mustang. Louise took the passenger seat and Alec and I climbed into the back with Bradan between us.

I leaned forward and put my hand on Louise's shoulder. "Maybe you should stay here," I said softly.

She squeezed my hand but shook her head. "This baby needs a father."

"Ready?" asked Annabelle, gunning the engine.

I opened my mouth but stopped as I saw her eyes in the rear view mirror. Louise was looking at me, too. And Emily: she might not be with us, but I could feel her. We were together. We were a team.

It suddenly hit me: we were friends. The thing I'd always been missing: I'd found it at last. A deep swell of emotion reduced my voice to a croak. "Ready," I said.

And we roared off.

57

SEAN

Whoever designed the cell had a cruel sense of humor: the one tiny window was too high to see through. But I'd jumped, grabbed hold of the bars and hauled myself up, feet braced on the wall, until my face was up against the little square. The only view was of the alley outside but it meant I could feel a breeze on my face. And that reminded me of nature and *that* reminded me of the woman I loved.

The morning had crept by, the only sound the grunts and curses of the men doing the construction work down the hallway. I figured it was noon. By now, they'd have Louise. They'd have *Kayley.* They wouldn't let us stay together. Louise wouldn't need me to grow and Kayley would only be a distraction. I'd be used as muscle, the only thing I was good for. And Kayley...my stomach twisted as I tried not to think about what use they might find for her.

And the baby. My hands tightened on the bars, my whole body shaking with rage. I'd been worried about whether I'd be a good father, whether I had it in me to raise a child. Now I was never going to find out. There was an upwelling of pain and fury inside me, geyser-strong and scalding hot. I'd worried about Louise plenty of times before but this was different and new. *Paternal.* I was already protective of that tiny life. And I knew, now: if I'd only been allowed to try, I could have figured it out.

But no. We'd give the baby up happily, compliantly. Because all we would care about would be the good of The Group.

And there wasn't a thing I could do to stop it.

"Which one of you works construction?" A voice from behind me, from the other side of the bars. I drew in a shuddering breath, trying to control my anger. But I knew that if I didn't play ball, they'd use their nightsticks on one of the others until I did.

I jumped down from the window and turned to face them. It was one of the guys who was working on the police station, a big guy in his fifties with greasy black hair, his t-shirt stained with sweat and mortar dust. He seemed to be the leader of the crew: the others were clustered behind him, all of them looking sour-tempered and exhausted. Next to them, one of the cops. "You him?" the guy almost spat at me. Kian and the others were getting to their feet, curious.

"I'm him," I said. I had a feeling I knew where this was going.

The guy nodded for the cop, who looked to be about thirty years his junior, to unlock the cell.

The cop shook his head doubtfully. "I could get fired!"

"No one's going to know," snapped the guy. "Look, Pryce wants the damn station finished this week and we're behind. My guys are exhausted. *He* can do some damn work."

The cop sighed, considered...and then unlocked the cell door and waved me out. Immediately, Kian put himself between me and them. The big guy growled and stepped forward but Kian ignored him. He looked at me and shook his head, still determined to protect me.

"It's okay," I snapped. *I'm not a kid anymore! Let me do my part!* Then, more gently, "I'll do it." I didn't relish spending my last few hours of freedom working for the enemy but I wasn't going to watch him get beaten. For a second, I thought Kian was going to keep arguing. Then he seemed to remember something, nodded and stepped out of the way.

I heard the cell door clang shut behind me as they led me down the hallway. When I reached the area where they'd been working, I saw what it was they were doing. The area had been a row of smaller cells. They'd removed the bars and were replacing them with a solid wall, and were knocking down the walls between each cell to make it one big room: probably an office. No need for so many cells when no one broke any laws.

"We'll build the new wall," the guy told me. "You get the rest of the old ones cleared." He pointed me at a wall that was half-demolished: I suspected that had been his job before he'd thrown down his tools in frustration and come to get me.

I stalked over to the wall. With every step, the anger inside me boiled higher and higher. *This is how it ends.* All four of us prisoners, Bradan still part of the cult, our women captured, Kayley and the baby torn away from us...and there wasn't a fucking thing any of us could do about it: not Aedan and his fists, Carrick and his shotgun or Kian with all his connections and experience. And certainly not me, the big dumb lunk who even the cult knew was only good for smashing stuff.

And then I reached the wall and saw what was lying on the ground beside it.

"Well?" grunted the guy in charge. "What are you waiting for? Pick it up."

I just stood there staring at it. *It can't be.*

"We ain't got all day," said the guy.

I ignored him, still staring. Fate was sending me a message. Maybe, just once, *just this once,* my skills were exactly what we needed.

"What's the matter?" snapped the guy. "You never use one before? *Pick it up!*"

I slowly bent and wrapped both hands around the shaft of the sledgehammer. It felt good. *Right.*

"If you insist," I muttered.

58

KIAN

There was a *thump*.

I rolled off my bunk just in time to see a guy fly through the air and crash to the ground on the other side of the bars. All of us ran over to them, craning our necks to try to see down the hallway.

There were more thumps, coming faster, now, as if someone was finding their rhythm. Another guy flew through the air, hit the floor and slid along the linoleum. I couldn't see any blood but there was no question he was out for the count. *What the hell's going on?* I gripped the bars. Whatever it was, I wanted to be ready to take advantage of it. If there was a chance I could save Emily....

Everything went quiet. *What the hell?!*

A thunderous crash shook the whole cell, as if a truck had slammed into the wall. We all looked around, trying to figure out where it came from. On the second impact, we saw one of the cinderblocks that made up the wall twitch and loosen.

On the third blow, the cinderblock tore loose from the wall and went flying across the room, to shatter on the far wall. We only just dodged out of the way in time.

Another crash and two more blocks were torn free. We ducked back against the bars. A third impact and there was a hole big enough to climb through. The brick dust slowly cleared and we saw Sean standing there, a sledgehammer in his hands. His muscles were gleaming with a sheen of sweat and there was a gleam in his eyes I hadn't seen before. "Couldn't find where the cop put the keys," he said.

We all scrambled through the hole. The floor outside was littered with the unconscious bodies of the men who'd been working construction. Carrick stared at Sean in delight, then pulled him into a hug. Then he went jogging down the hallway, looking for something. Aedan hurried after him.

I was left standing there gawping at Sean. My baby brother. The one who'd just saved all of us.

Emily's voice in my head: *your brothers are on your side. You just have to let them be.* It was the only reason I'd let him go with the workers. If I hadn't....

I pulled Sean into a fierce hug. "Thank you," I told him with feeling. When we moved back, my hands still on his shoulders, I gave him a nod. An acknowledgement that things had changed.

At that moment, the main door opened and two cops strolled in. They balked when they saw Sean and me standing there. One started forward towards us, drawing his nightstick. He was halfway to us when Aedan stepped into his path from a side-hallway, his face a mask of vengeful fury. The cop ran right into the punch and was knocked back on his ass. The other cop went pale, grabbed his radio and started babbling into it. Aedan started forward but the cop darted out of the main doors before he could reach him.

Carrick came running back to us. He must have raided whatever locker the cops had locked our possessions up in because he was carrying Caorthannach, that crazy antique shotgun of his, and my handgun. He had something else, too: a police-issue pistol. He offered it to Sean.

Sean shook his head and brandished the sledgehammer. "I'm sticking with this." Something was different about him. For all the ferocious anger in his eyes, he looked at peace with himself.

"We need to get out of here," I said. "They know we're free."

"So what do we do?" asked Carrick.

I went to the main door. I could hear police sirens in the distance: every cop in town was heading our way. *Great.* I looked desperately around, my eyes finally coming to rest on Pryce's elaborate mansion near the center of town. I could see him standing on the balcony like some old-fashioned lord of the manor watching over the peasants....

Old-fashioned. I frowned. Something Annabelle had said came back to me, about the personality tests being on paper. *It's kind of old-fashioned, really. Like, why aren't they just using an app, on a tablet?*

I'm not as smart as Emily, not as good at figuring things out. But finally, it all came together in my head. "God*dammit!*" I said with feeling.

Everyone turned to look at me.

"I know who Pryce was, before all this" I said, my voice shaky with bitter anger. "I know how it all started." And now my mind was racing. That laptop: never out of Pryce's sight, even when he was eating breakfast. He must keep everything on there: every one of the Groups, every cult member. "If we can get to him, maybe we can shut them down for good."

At that moment, the bells in the town's church began to clang. I guessed it didn't see any use for services, since Aeternus seemed to be all these people believed in, but the bells must have been an agreed-upon alarm call because suddenly the streets started to fill with people. They spilled out of every store, every home. Some of them had grabbed improvised weapons: baseball bats, shovels, fire axes. And every one of them, young and old, were moving towards us.

My heart sank. We were no more than a few hundred yards from the mansion but it might as well have been miles. No way could we fight our way past all those people, all of them eager to help capture an Outsider.

Then I looked the other way down the street. The police station we were in was almost at the edge of town and there were far fewer people in that direction. If we ran, we *might* make it.

But then we might never find the girls. By now, the cult must have

them and they could have taken them anywhere. And we'd never get
Bradan out.

I looked at my brothers. They understood what I was asking
because all three of them shook their heads. "Fuck that," said Carrick.

"Pryce needs to get what's coming to him," said Aedan.

"I'm not leaving Louise and Kayley," said Sean.

I felt my heart swell with pride. "Alright, then," I said. "Let's go
start some trouble."

And together, we ran into the street.

We met the cops first: their cars were just screeching to a halt in
front of the police station. But they were expecting a siege, with us
holed up inside, not for us to come pouring out of the doors at them.
Before they knew what was happening, Sean had jumped up on the
hood of one squad car and brought his hammer down on the roof,
crushing it and forcing the cops inside to duck for cover. Two more
blows and the doors were so mangled they wouldn't open, trapping
the men inside.

Two cops ran towards the main doors but met Carrick coming the
other way and were quickly clubbed to the ground with
Caorthannach. Aedan grabbed hold of another cop and laid him out
with one punch. I shoulder-charged the last one as if I was sacking a
quarterback.

We moved fast, before they had time to recover. But while we'd
been fighting them, the crowds of townsfolk had been sweeping
towards us and now they were almost on us. They might only have
fists and baseball bats but, as we'd found out when we tried to escape,
twenty or thirty of them could easily overwhelm us. This was the
whole town. And they were between us and Pryce's mansion. *Shit!*

At first, we only met them in ones and twos: the front-runners
who'd pulled ahead of the crowd. But ahead, they were shoulder-to-
shoulder right across the street, a charging army we stood no chance
against.

Up ahead, I saw a dark opening between two buildings. An alley.
We had to run straight at the crowd and pray we reached it before
they did. "*Run!*" I yelled.

We ran, feet pounding the sidewalk, lungs burning. When one of us lagged behind, the others would grab his shoulders and haul him forward. The crowd rushed towards us horribly fast and the street seemed to extend, the alley telescoping away from us. *Run!* I bawled at myself.

If we didn't make this, I'd never be with Emily again. Not as *me.*

I forced myself to move faster.

We reached the alley a split second before the crowd did and flung ourselves down it. Then left into a side street. *Shit:* not as many people as on the main street but still too many. We shoved them aside but that slowed us down and the crowd who'd poured into the alley behind us gained. The alley shook with their collective roar. It was like being trapped in a city at the center of a riot only much, much worse: riots at least are chaos; this was terrifyingly organized, the crowd like a monster with single-minded purpose. I risked a glance over my shoulder and immediately regretted it. All I could see were hate filled eyes and open, yelling mouths.

We forced our way forward, doing our best to use fists, not guns: ever since I'd realized that it had been Bradan we'd beaten nearly to death in the printing works, I'd been seeing the cult members differently. Every one of them was someone's brother, someone's son.

But they didn't have any qualms about attacking *us.* The word must have gone out that Pryce wanted us alive if possible, because no one was shooting at us. But all of us were soon limping and bruised from being punched, kicked and tussled to the ground. I lost count of the number of times I'd be sent sprawling, only for one of my brothers to pull me up. And every time one of us went down, the stampede behind us got closer.

The constant attacks were taking their toll. Carrick was holding his ribs on one side, Sean had a nasty gash along one cheek and Aedan and I were both staggering from taking so many blows to the head. And the whole alley rung and shook from the thunder of footsteps behind, hundreds of people intent on running us down.

We weren't going to make it. They were going to catch us before we got anywhere near the mansion.

There was a metal door just ahead, locked with a padlock. The alley ran behind the stores that lined the main street so I was guessing it was a service door for one of them.

Carrick saw me looking at it. "We go in there, we're trapped," he said.

I looked around us. The crowd behind us had almost caught up and people were flooding into the alley ahead of us, too. "We stay here, we're finished," I told him.

Carrick gave me a grim nod, leveled Caorthannach at the padlock and pulled the trigger. The gun's roar filled the alley and when the smoke cleared there was a ragged hole where the padlock, handle and some of the wall had been. I pulled the door open and led the way inside.

We were in the town's small department store. Directly across from us, big plate glass windows looked out onto the main street. While Carrick braced a mop against the service door to stop it opening, the rest of us hurried across the store to the main doors. The street outside was still a sea of people: no way out there. I quickly locked the doors: fortunately, the store seemed to be empty: shoppers and staff had all rushed outside when the bells started ringing.

But looking around, I couldn't see another way out. Carrick had been right: we'd gained a few seconds of breathing space but now we were trapped. One by one, we slumped down on our asses beside the racks of clothes, utterly exhausted.

Soon, there was a hammering on the metal service door as the townsfolk outside tried to batter it down. I checked over my shoulder. The crowd in the main street had surged forward and were pressed against the doors and the plate glass windows. We were completely surrounded. In another few seconds, they'd find something to throw through the windows to break them and then they'd be all over us.

"If anybody's got any ideas," I muttered, "now'd be a really feckin' good time."

Everyone was silent. Minutes passed. The store grew dark as bodies pressed up against every square inch of window. They started banging on the glass. Any second, they'd find something to throw through it and then it would all be over.

Carrick slowly got to his feet, one hand clasped to his ribs. He adjusted his leather cut so that it hung straight. "If this is it," he said, "I'm going down fighting. Better than being turned into one of them."

I read the look in his eyes. "They'll try to take us alive."

His jaw set. "I don't intend to give 'em that choice."

I understood what he was saying: fight so hard they'd have no choice but to kill us. I'd never see Emily again. But maybe that was better than being together as Pryce's slaves.

Carrick held out his hand to me.

I reached out, took his hand and hauled myself up, wincing from my bruises. Then I held out my hand for Sean. Blood was running down his face from the cut on his cheek and he had to use his hammer to help push himself up off the floor, but he made it. Then he held out his hand for Aedan. Aedan pulled himself to his feet, rocked unsteadily but stayed standing.

I looked at their faces. "I was wrong," I said.

"'Course you were," said Carrick. "But about what?"

I looked down at my gun. Checked the magazine, even though I didn't need to. "When we were in that cell," I said, "I was thinking we shouldn't have put the family back together." I cocked the gun and finally managed to meet their eyes. "But I was wrong. I'm glad we did."

Carrick put his hand on my shoulder and it seemed like he was about to say something. Then he thought better of it and just pulled me into a hug. Then Sean and Aedan joined in from the other two sides. No one spoke. We just clung to each other.

There was a heavy thump from the direction of the windows. We turned to see a chair from some cafe bounce off the store's safety glass. A big, misty white mark was left where it hit. The guy who'd thrown it picked it up to try again.

"Okay, then," I said. "When the window breaks, we run at them." We all lined shoulder to shoulder.

The guy hurled the chair again, harder, this time. The glass turned into a white spider web. The next hit would take it out completely. Carrick and I raised our guns. Sean lifted his hammer. Aedan put up his fists. We all leaned forward, ready to rush them in one last, suicidal *fuck you.*

"I love you all," I said.

The glass shattered.

And we ran towards the crowd.

59

ANNABELLE

W e crested the final rise and I slowed the Mustang as we got our first look at our destination. *What?!* I'd been visualizing an armed camp, out in the desert, or some backwoods fortress protected by guard dogs. This was a town out of a tourist brochure.

I pulled over and we all climbed out. "The cult's headquarters is down *there?*" asked Louise.

We stared in disbelief. It looked like a place where nothing bad could ever, ever happen. And yet...something *was* happening. Some sort of riot. The streets at the edge of town were all empty and a massive crowd was converging on a shopping street in the center.

"What the *hell* is going on?" whispered Sylvie behind me. I understood why she was whispering: the silence was eerie. In my mind, a riot should be noisy: shouting and chanting and breaking things. But the crowd was oddly quiet and ordered: they moved with purpose. The only sound was the town's church bells, which were ringing non-stop. I scrunched up my forehead. It was like one of those old war movies where a little town rings its bells to warn that the invaders are coming. *Or that they're already here.....*

"Oh *shit!*" I said as I worked it out. "They're in there!" I pointed to the store where the crowd seemed to be focused. "The guys are trapped in there!"

"What?" asked Sylvie. "Why would the whole town be—"

"Because the whole town is in the cult!"

Louise put her hands over her mouth. Sylvie bit her lip and cursed. Alec's eyes scanned the crowd. "Jesus, there are hundreds of them...."

Only Bradan didn't react. He hadn't said a word the entire journey and I didn't know if he was really on our side. He just stood there, hands still zip-tied behind his back, gazing towards the center of town: not at the spot where the crowd were massed but at a large mansion down the street. He was utterly still and quiet.

When I looked into his eyes, though, I could see a battle going on, as chaotic and destructive as the crowd beneath us was silent and ordered. He was being torn in two directions...and I had no idea which would win.

I looked at the town again. The crowd was pressing up against the windows of the store, now, desperate to get at what was inside.

I dived back into the Mustang. The others opened their doors to join me. "No," I said quickly. "Just me."

Sylvie balked. "*What? You can't go down there al—*"

"There are four of them!" I glanced over my shoulder at the Mustang's rear seats. "We can't all go!"

Sylvie hesitated, her hand on the passenger door. I could see she wanted to argue: no way was she going to let me drive into *that*. But she knew I was right. She finally slammed the door and stepped back. "Be careful," she said grimly.

I threw the car into gear and stamped on the gas. The big V8 roared and I picked up speed as I descended the hill into town. Every house I passed looked empty. Many stood with their doors wide open: people must have literally run out into the street when they heard the bells ringing. I passed outdoor cafes with plates of food still on the tables, piles of shopping bags on the sidewalk where people had just dropped them. The idea of a whole town where people were so utterly devoted to a single cause, where every one of them obeyed without question, made my skin crawl.

The idea that I was driving right into a crowd of those people made me want to throw up.

At first, they didn't even notice me. But the Mustang's engine rattled windows and throbbed through the street: you couldn't ignore it. As I drew nearer, I saw them begin to turn around and frown. I suddenly wished I was driving a less recognizable car. It didn't help that I seemed to be the only vehicle moving in the entire town.

And then I swallowed, and my foot slipped off the gas, as I saw it pass like a ripple through the mass of bodies. *Another Outsider.* The front of the crowd stayed focused on the store but the rearmost ranks started to break off and walk towards me.

And then *run* towards me. My blood went ice cold. *Oh Jesus!*

My foot was still off the gas and the Mustang was slowing. A turn was coming up. An empty street. If I hauled on the wheel now, I could be away from the crowd before they reached me.

I thought about Carrick. How he'd made that promise twelve years ago, that he'd be there when I needed him. How he'd kept it.

I was damned if I was going to let him down now.

I stamped on the gas again and blasted towards the crowd. At first, I met the runners who'd pulled ahead of the rest, the townsfolk who jogged every morning. I swerved to avoid the first one.

He jumped right into my path.

I screamed and jerked the wheel. The corner of the hood missed him by an inch. *Jesus, they don't care!* All they wanted to do was stop me. Another two were running towards me, and they were spread out across the road. One was a lean woman in her twenties with red hair, the sort of woman who looked like she ran charity triathlons. She stretched her arms out wide, almost touching fingers with the man running alongside her, blocking the street. My foot came off the gas and went for the brake....

...but I held it hovering there, fighting every instinct that was pulling on me. And then I pressed hard on the gas. I didn't want to kill anyone. But if I stopped the car, they'd have me.

The Mustang shot forward. I instinctively steered towards the man, then jerked the wheel to go around him. When I was six feet away he leapt and I closed my eyes: *God, please no—*

There was a *thud* and the car shook as I hit something. I opened my eyes and slowly lifted them to the rear view mirror, my heart in my mouth....

He was down on the pavement but he was alive, clutching at his hip and twisting in pain. I'd just clipped him. I drew in a shuddering gasp of relief and looked ahead.

The crowd was surging to meet me and the people were coming thick and fast, now. Again, my foot tried to lift off the gas. *Don't lift, don't lift—* I tried to swerve towards the thinnest part of the crowd but they kept moving....

Then a guy right in my path lifted his arm and I saw he was holding hands with someone. A little girl no more than six stepped out from behind him.

I stamped on the brakes.

The air filled with the smell of scorched rubber as the tires grabbed at the pavement. The little girl rushed towards me with sickening speed...but I came to a stop with the bumper an inch from her. A diagonal line burned across my torso where the safety belt had cut into it. I took two panicked breaths and then hit the gas again: I had to get moving before—

Too late. They were all around me, filling the windows, blocking out the sun. A few of them even climbed onto the hood. *I can't see where I'm going!* I was almost to the store, now, but I was only crawling along. They were banging on the windows, palms pressed to the glass....

And then one of them opened the passenger door. *Shit!* I hadn't thought to lock it. I sped up but he was already halfway in: a guy in a suit with a neatly-trimmed beard. He got one knee onto the seat and reached across the car for me. Meanwhile, a woman had gotten the driver's door partway open. I grabbed the door pull and tried to haul it closed but she fought me, running alongside the car and hauling on it with all her strength.

The guy with the beard grabbed the front of my dress and tried to pull me towards him. Then he realized my safety belt was still on so he fumbled for the release. I was now trying to steer one-handed, fighting them off in both directions. My heart was thundering in my chest, tears filling my eyes. There were *so many* of them: all I could see, out of every window, was people intent on grabbing me.

Think!

I pressed on the gas. The car sped up, pushing through the crowd like an icebreaker. The woman on my side fell back a little and the door partially closed. That gave me time to reach down between the seats—

My safety belt went loose. *Fuck!* He'd hit the release. And now he grabbed my shoulder and started hauling me out of my seat. My foot slipped off the gas and we slowed....

I lifted the heavy wrench and brought it down as hard as I could on his arm. He screamed and pulled it back. I dropped the wrench and picked up one of the Tasers we'd taken from the cult members who'd come to the house, then fired it blindly at him. There was a crackling noise and he fell back out of the car.

I lunged across, grabbed the door pull and slammed that door. Then I used both hands to slam the driver's door shut, and finally I hit the button that locked the doors.

I wanted to slump in relief but there was no time. Now that I'd sped up, the store was rushing towards me. The crowd was twenty-deep all around it. If I pulled up outside and opened the door, they'd swarm me.

I looked at the big plate glass windows and my weird mind started to do its thing, calculating forces and structural loads and points of impact...or it tried to. But there were just too many unknowns. What sort of glass was it? Were the supports between the panes hard steel or fragile wood?

As I watched, the crowd managed to break one of the panes further along the storefront and started to run towards the opening. I glimpsed Carrick and the others inside, running forward to meet them.

"Oh, *feck it,*" I muttered. And pressed the gas pedal to the floor.

60

CARRICK

We were halfway to the broken window, all four of us yelling a wordless battle cry, when the windows further down the store exploded into a million fragments and Sean's Mustang came blasting through. We stumbled to a halt and the men running towards us did, too.

The Mustang roared through the store, smashing aside racks of clothing and knocking down mannequins, and came to a stop just before it would have hit the back wall. The driver's door flew open and I saw a familiar face framed by copper hair. "*Get in!*" she yelled.

I just stood there gaping. *Annabelle?!*

"*Get in!*" she yelled again. The townsfolk were over their surprise, now, and were rushing in through the window they'd broken...and in much larger numbers through the big hole the Mustang had left. They were swarming around the car...*shit!* A big guy reached for Annabelle.

That finally got me moving. I bellowed and charged forward, my brothers close behind me. "*Get away from her, you fuckers!*" I screamed, and fired both Caorthannach's barrels over the big guy's head. It startled him enough that he looked around, so I had the satisfaction of whacking him right in the face with the shotgun's stock.

Sean joined me, knocking people aside like toys with his hammer. Then Aedan and Kian waded in with their fists. I managed to clear a path to the passenger door and I jumped in beside Annabelle. The other three squeezed into the back and Annabelle locked the doors.

Annabelle threw the Mustang into reverse and we shot backwards through the store, bouncing over debris. We plowed through the crowd: I think we may have run over a few toes but we were going slow enough that we pushed people out of the way rather than ran them down. Annabelle swung the car in a tight turn and we roared off down the street, picking up speed as the crowd thinned out.

"Where are the others?" panted Sean.

"They're okay. Edge of town," said Annabelle, eyes glued to the road. "Where are we going?"

We all looked at each other. *Away,* was my first thought. Now that we knew the girls were safe....

But then I caught Kian's eye. The cult would still be after us unless we dealt with Pryce. We had to get the girls out of town and then—

"You better not have some plan about getting us out of town," Annabelle muttered.

I opened and closed my mouth a few times. Annabelle glanced up, saw my troubled expression and glared. *"No,"* she said firmly. "We're not leaving you again. Whatever we do, we do it together."

We arrived at the crest of the hill on the edge of town and the Mustang skidded to a halt beside Sylvie, Louise, Alec and—

My whole chest closed up as Bradan turned and I saw his face. *"Him?!"* I asked in amazement as we climbed out.

"It's okay," said Sylvie quickly. "He saved us. He's on our side now...we think."

"Then why is he tied up?"

Sylvie looked down at Bradan's zip-tied hands. *"We think,"* she repeated.

I took a long, deep breath. Around me, the others were doing the same. After the adrenaline rush of our escape, we all just needed to take a second. We were far enough from the crowd that it was quiet, up on the hill. The only sound was the Mustang's cooling engine. The once-gorgeous black paintwork was scraped and ruined, the hood dented and the windshield cracked. But it had saved us.

Sean and Aedan embraced their women. I grabbed hold of Annabelle, picked her up and crushed her against me. I knew the townsfolk would be coming after us but I wasn't going to wait any longer. I'd thought I was never going to see her again. I buried my face in the copper silk of her hair and inhaled deeply, running my hands up and down her back, savoring the feel of her body against me. "Thank you," I said when I finally put her down.

"For rescuing you?" she asked.

I looked at all of the girls and Alec, as well. "For being you," I told them. I glanced at my brothers, who were looking similarly grateful. "What the hell happened?"

They quickly brought us up to speed on what had happened at the house, our arms tightening around each of them as we heard how close they'd come...and how Bradan had saved them, before he'd slipped into this catatonia.

I looked down the hill towards the town. The townsfolk were still mostly licking their wounds but I was starting to see movement in the crowd. They were beginning to head this way.

"So what's the plan?" asked Sylvie. Aedan started to say something but she fixed him with a look: clearly, like Annabelle, she wasn't going to let us go off on our own again.

"Pryce," said Kian. "He's the guy who's running this whole thing. He's the one who's been giving people their orders, I think through that laptop of his. If we take him out, no more orders. Whatever the cult's doing, it would stop."

I was watching Bradan carefully. He'd been passive until now but, as soon as Pryce's name was mentioned, he'd looked up.

"But there's no way we're getting down there," said Aedan. He was looking down the hill towards Pryce's mansion. It was pretty much at the center of town and the streets around it were thick with townsfolk. And...yep, they were definitely moving our way, now. "We have to just go. Steal a car: we can't all fit in the Mustang."

"If we run, they'll never stop chasing us," snapped Kian, his voice rising in frustration. "We have to finish it."

Sean had a protective arm around Louise and was gazing at the dented, ruined nose of his Mustang. "Aedan's right," he said. "Look at that place. There's just no way."

We all looked towards the mansion. Townsfolk were swarming like ants in the streets all around it. I turned to Bradan. Every time I looked at him, the anger rose inside, scalding me raw. It wasn't what he'd tried to do to us: that wasn't his fault. It was what they'd done to him. They'd taken one of *us* and made him into a fucking robot, a *slave*. They'd made him into one of them.

I glanced at the town, then back at Bradan. "I have an idea," I said.

Kian stepped forward, frowning. Then his eyes widened as he realized what I had in mind. "*No!*" he snapped. "Are you kidding? He betrayed us once!"

"And then he saved the girls." I was getting sick of everyone talking about him like he wasn't there. "He's our *brother!*"

Bradan jerked at that. I latched onto the reaction and started to speak to him, gently but firmly. "Yeah, you remember, don't you? I guess they took all that away from you. They took your family and they filled your head full of lies. But you know the truth now." I looked deep into his eyes. "You're our brother."

I saw every muscle in his body tense. He took a staggering step back from me, his eyes flickering. But I grabbed his wrists and wouldn't let go. "O'Harra," I grated. "That's your *family* name. Mom's dead but dad's still with us. And we're still here. It's all waiting for you, brother."

Kian stepped up beside me, doubt in his eyes. But hope, too. Then Sean and Aedan moved in on either side, so that we were in a semi-circle around Bradan. All of us were worried. Hell, all of us were mad: he'd attacked us at the printing works, tried to kill us in the fire, tried to kill our *women!* But that wasn't *him*. *He* was still in there. We just had to reach him.

I could see the battle going on in his eyes. I wasn't surprised he'd gone fucking catatonic. Ever since that moment in the house when he'd figured out who he was, everything he'd believed in had been thrown into question. It wasn't like we were just telling him Aeternus was all bullshit: we were telling him it was *evil*. We were asking him to do a one-eighty and fight it with us.

The only comparison I could think of would be if someone told me that the Hell's Princes were evil, and that I had to help kill Mac. And that was unimaginable.

Bradan looked down at the ground, fists bunching, struggling for breath. Kian put a hand on my arm. "This isn't working," he muttered. "He needs help. He needs...*years* of therapy just to start to undo what those fuckers did to him." He looked over his shoulder and I knew he must be looking at the advancing townsfolk. "We don't have time."

He looked at Bradan but his eyes were closed, his shoulders rising and falling shakily, as if each breath was painful. I could see his eyelids moving: his eyes were going frantic behind them, like he was lost in bad memories. Christ knows what the cult had had him doing, all these years, but I had a sickening feeling I knew, given how efficiently he'd attacked us and started that fire. "Bradan?" I asked desperately.

Nothing. Beside me, Aedan let out a sigh.

Kian turned away. "We need to find another car," he said. "Fast."

"What about Pryce?" I asked.

Kian shook his head. "Aedan's right. There's no way we're getting through all of them. We need to run and hope."

But I could hear the despair in his voice. He knew, like I did, that we'd go to sleep one night and never wake up, victims of a gas leak or a house fire or a "burglary gone wrong." Us...and our women. "*Bradan!*" I snapped.

Bradan just stared at the ground.

"Carrick!" said Kian, pulling me by the shoulder. "We have to *go!*"

But I suddenly grabbed Bradan's arm and held on with a death grip. "*NO!*" I snarled.

Everyone froze.

I turned to look at my brothers and my voice shook as I spoke. "We made this mistake before. All of us." I looked at Bradan. "We gave up on you too soon. We should have kept looking, all those years ago. We should have believed in you. Well, I fucking believe in you now."

Bradan opened his eyes and looked at me. But I'd run out of words. I could see him in there but I didn't know how to reach him.

And then to my astonishment, Kian moved in close, his voice soft but with a core of steel. "He's right," he said, catching my eye. "We should have found you sooner. And we should take this slow. Unpick every last change they made in your head. But we can't. We don't have time." He put his face close to Bradan's. "*We need you*. We need you to be one of us. We need you to be an O'Harra, *right now*." He took a deep breath. "And there's only one way I know to convince you we're the good guys." He turned to Annabelle. "You got a knife?"

She pulled a multi-tool from her pocket and passed it to him. Kian stepped behind Bradan and there was a snapping noise as he cut Bradan's bonds. Bradan brought his hands in front of him and looked at them in shock. Sean, Aedan and I took a half-step back, trying to resist the urge to raise our fists. We knew how tough this guy was.

Bradan opened his mouth. It was the first time we'd heard him speak. His accent was perfectly neutral East Coast American: the cult must have stripped his accent from him, along with everything else. "Okay," he said. "What do you want me to do?"

61

CARRICK

By the time the townsfolk reached us, all eight of us were sitting on the pavement next to the Mustang, hands on our heads, while Bradan stood guard over us with Caorthannach, Kian's gun tucked into his pants and Sean's sledgehammer safely behind him. "Get a couple of vehicles," he snapped as soon as they came within hearing distance. "I'm taking them all to Mr. Pryce."

The townsfolk nodded, wide-eyed, and ran to do his bidding. Clearly, being a Prime carried a lot of weight. In just a few minutes, two SUVs had been rounded up and we were on our way to the mansion. A couple of cops rode with us, one of them scowling and bruised from our run-in with him at the police station. I was pretty sure they didn't completely buy our sudden submission...but they weren't going to question the word of a Prime, either.

We all kept our eyes on the floor as we trooped into the mansion. We'd discussed whether the girls should pretend to already have been initiated, but discounted that plan: Bradan said the process normally took a few days, not a few hours. Plus, there were the missing Guides to explain. So we decided to stick to the truth as much as possible. Of course, if any of the Guides the girls left zip-tied at the house had gotten free and gotten to a phone, Pryce would know Bradan had turned and we were all royally fucked.

Pryce's private guards—more Primes, I presumed—checked us for weapons and then took us upstairs. Bradan still carried Caorthannach and Kian's gun but he'd passed off Sean's sledgehammer to one of the guards. My heart sank when more guards joined us with each floor we climbed. By the time we were up on the third floor, we had nine escorting us. *Great.*

I could feel the tension building in my chest as we approached Pryce. He was standing on the balcony, looking out at his empire. When he turned to us, he tried to make it casual. But I could see the rage in his eyes.

"We really messed up paradise," I told him, nodding at the crowds in the streets, the smashed store front, the police car Sean had wrecked.

"We'll rebuild," he said. "Everyone will help. Everyone will cooperate. Order will be restored." He turned to Bradan. "What happened at the house? I haven't heard from the others."

"They're dead," said Bradan smoothly. "Shot." He pushed Alec forward. "This one was lying in wait for us. I let myself be captured: I knew they'd bring me here. Then I escaped and caught them all as they tried to flee town."

I held my breath...would Pryce buy it? But Bradan made it sound eerily convincing. I almost believed it myself. Pryce studied Bradan's face for a second...and then something that was almost a grin spread across his face. "Good," he said. "Well done, Bradan. Well done."

I froze. Something had flickered across Bradan's face. It happened so quickly, I wasn't sure if I'd imagined it. But even that split-second made my guts twist...because it had looked like *doubt.*

Pryce motioned to the guards. "Bring the women forward."

Everyone tensed. I had to fight the urge to lunge at him. But the guards were still too cautious, too alert, and none of us were close enough to Pryce to grab him. We'd have to wait and pray we got the opportunity we needed.

Louise, Sylvie and Annabelle were pushed to the front. Pryce's gaze flicked between the two redheads. "Which of you is Louise?"

Louise stepped forward, chin held high.

Pryce grinned. "The growers in Mexico are in awe of you. Once you're Inside, we'll put your skills to good use." Then he frowned. "One's missing. Where's her sister?"

Shit. We hadn't thought of that.

"She tried to escape, in the confusion," Bradan said. "I killed her."

Somehow, Louise managed to force tears into her eyes.

Pryce tilted his head to one side and gave Bradan a curious look. "She was a teenager," he said slowly. "Almost a child. It didn't bother you?" He glanced between Louise and Bradan, watching them both, probing for weakness. Bradan didn't reply. The room went utterly silent. My heart nearly stopped: if he suspected Bradan was lying....

"It was necessary," said Bradan tightly. "For Beautiful Order."

Louise whirled around. "*Bastard!*" she snapped, tears running down her cheeks. "*Fucking* bastard!" A guard grabbed her arm before she could run at Bradan.

Pryce nodded, staring into Bradan's eyes. "Yes," he said slowly. "It was. I can always rely on you, Bradan."

And to my horror, I saw that flicker in Bradan's face again. I was certain, this time. He was conflicted, doubting what he was doing. *Shit. Shit, shit—*

Pryce moved on to Annabelle and my chest constricted as he laid his palm on her cheek. This was the first time we'd seen him around women and a different side of him was coming out. He was smirking and I realized he was enjoying the power trip of having a woman terrified into submission instead of her simply being willing and compliant. I wondered how many of Aeternus's women he'd fucked, over the years. *You son of a bitch....* "The engineer," he said. "The thinker. I have great plans for you. What we're going to be able to accomplish, now that the technology is here...."

Annabelle looked defiantly up at him. "I'll cut my own throat before I work for you," she hissed.

"Once you're Inside," Pryce told her, "you'll do anything I tell you.

And you'll delight in it." He glanced at me and I didn't miss the little gleam of triumphant lust in his eyes. Maybe that hadn't been his plan before but, now that we'd messed up his creepy little town, he was going to have his revenge—

Aedan put his hand on my chest and I realized I'd been leaning forward. *Wait,* said Aedan's eyes. We still didn't have the opening we needed.

Finally, Pryce turned to Sylvie. "And you," he said, his eyes sad. "The one we lost." He leaned close and whispered, but he made sure it was just loud enough for all of us to hear. "*I know you miss it,*" he told her. He glanced at the rest of us. "You haven't told them that part, have you? That part of you *wants* to come back? That part of you can't wait? You haven't told them that being Inside gave you something you'd never had, your entire life. That's what we do. We fill in the missing piece."

Now Aedan was leaning forward and I had to restrain him. I didn't do it fast enough, though. Pryce caught the tiny movement and glanced at Aedan. And again, I saw the lust burn in his eyes. "You'll slip back into it, Sylvie. All the way, this time. And when you're completely loyal to us?" He paused for effect. "*I might even make your boyfriend watch.*"

Sylvie had lowered her head as if beaten. She muttered something.

Pryce stepped right up to her. The guards automatically stepped back to give him room: after all, there was no threat from such a tiny, frail woman. "What?" asked Pryce.

Sylvie lifted her head. Glanced at the other girls. "I've already found my missing piece," she said, her voice ragged with anger. She looked at Aedan, then back at Pryce. "And he's not my boyfriend. He's my fiancé."

And she drove her left fist into his cheek with all the force in her body, with all the hurt and fear and shame the cult had made her feel. Her diamond engagement ring ripped his cheek open, blood spraying, and the power of the punch knocked him staggering back.

The guards turned to level their guns at us but we were already moving. Kian, Aedan, Alec, Sean and I all took one guard apiece, raining punches down on them and getting in close enough that the others didn't dare shoot. None of them thought to look at Bradan, so he grabbed two of them by the hair and whacked their skulls together. As they crumpled to the ground, he threw Kian's gun to him and Caorthannach to me.

That left two guards. Kian and I swung around to point our guns at them but—*shit!* We both picked the same one. He dropped his gun but the other guard grabbed Sean by the head and put the barrel of his gun to his head. "Stop!" he snapped. "Both of you put your guns down!"

I winced and looked at Kian but he shook his head. Neither of us could whip around and aim at him before he killed Sean. *We were so close!* Slowly, reluctantly, we lowered our guns.

And then we heard a click. And saw that Louise had quietly pulled a gun from one of the unconscious guards and was pointing it at the armed guard's head. "*You* put your gun down," she said.

The guard paled but hesitated. She was directly behind him, so she had the upper hand. But she was a woman....

"Don't think I won't do it," she said, as if reading his mind. "That's my man and I'm *very* fucking hormonal right now."

There was a clang of metal as the guard dropped his gun. All of us started breathing again...and turned to Pryce, who'd backed up against his desk, blood streaming down one side of his face. All of us advanced on him. But he still didn't show any sign of fear, only disgust.

"You don't know what you're doing!" he snapped. "You don't know what Aeternus really is!"

"Actually," said Kian, leveling his gun at Pryce. "I've got a pretty feckin' good idea. Right from the start, I *knew* there was something familiar about this whole thing. I just couldn't see it, at first." His face darkened. "I didn't *want* to see it."

I frowned at him. "What the hell are you talking about?"

"It all makes sense, when you put it together," said Kian. "The stealthy assassinations, made to look like accidents. The worldwide network, able to mess in other country's affairs. All those connections to people in power, and yet also connections to the drug cartels in Mexico. Highly secretive. Hidden agendas. High-end encryption on your computer, better than the FBI's. And access to mind-controlling drugs no one else has. Now who does that sound a lot like?"

I blinked as the pieces fell into place. "You're telling me.... No. *What?!*" I jerked Caorthannach at Pryce. "He's *CIA?!* This *whole thing* is run by the government?"

Pryce let out a sneer. "Oh, *please.* The CIA is run by a bunch of bitches in suits, now, who do what Congress tells them."

"Back in the seventies," said Kian, "the CIA was running all sorts of programs to do with mind control. My guess is that Pryce ran one of them." He glared at Pryce. "Only they shut you down, or you got fired. So you liberated some of those classified, experimental drugs and stole the personality tests and started your own organization." Kian's voice was tight with rage. "That's why the tests are still on paper: the tech is from fifty years ago! But it still works just fine. And you knew all the tricks. You knew how to condition people. You knew to dress it up like a cult so no one would suspect its real purpose. You built yourself your own little shadow-CIA, a network that would do your bidding and that doesn't have to answer to anyone."

"Order," said Pryce. "The world needs order."

"Not your kind," snarled Kian. What's the endgame, Pryce? All the little jobs you have them do: what's it building towards?"

Pryce ignored my question and looked right past us. "Bradan. Protect me."

All of us looked around in surprise. To my relief, Bradan just stood there. I relaxed slightly.

Pryce spoke again. "Protect your father."

Oh, fuck. I hadn't considered that. I'd thought of Bradan as being the cult's prisoner, *Pryce's* prisoner: conditioned to be loyal, sure, but not—

Bradan's eyes grew wide.

"No," I said aloud.

"Protect your *father,*" said Pryce.

No! The son of a bitch. All those years, he'd raised Bradan like a son. Suddenly, all those flickers of doubt I'd seen in Bradan's face made sense. What better way to instill total loyalty? He'd made Bradan think of him as his—

"Dad?" said Bradan in a shaky voice.

I could see the battle going on in his eyes again. I could see him slipping away from us. And then he was looking at the floor, his gaze jumping to the nearest gun.

"No!" yelled Kian as Bradan crouched and grabbed a gun. But Bradan didn't hesitate. He and Kian swung their guns up to point at each other. "Don't!" screamed Kian, his voice raw with panic. "*Don't fucking do it!*"

Bradan's hand trembled. He was opening and closing his eyes, squinting as if trying to figure out what was real.

"Bradan, *this is not your dad!*" I yelled. "You don't owe him *shit*. You have a real dad, he's sitting in jail right now because of this son of a bitch, we can all go visit him. *I swear to you!*"

Bradan's lips parted. His teeth were locked together, his chest heaving as he panted for air. His eyes went to me and my heart tore in two to see the pain he was going through. *I'm right here,* I thought, praying he could see it in my eyes. *I'm right here, brother.*

Bradan's gun lowered a half inch. I dared to think we'd won.

And then Pryce said, "Bradan? *I love you, son.*"

And Bradan snapped his gun back up and fired.

62

BRADAN

Everything happened so fast. I squeezed the trigger, just like I'd been taught, and then the one who usually wore a suit —*Kian*—

The memories hit me like a wave, making me stagger sideways. Kian on a beach, age seven, giving me his ice cream because I'd dropped mine. Kian in the dark alley behind our school, lying in wait for the kid who'd been taking my lunch money—

Kian was lying on his back, blood spreading across his chest. The others all ran to him, falling to their knees and surrounding him, blocking my view. There was a howl of fear and outrage from Sylvie, a choked sob from Sean.

Carrick had swung his shotgun up to point at me. He was a threat to me and to Dad, so I automatically turned to point my gun at him.

But I didn't fire. *Kian. Kian on Christmas morning, a soldier's helmet and a water pistol. Mom disapproved, Dad told her not to be silly—*

Dad.

I looked at Mr. Pryce. *Not this Dad.*

My mind was tearing in two. *What have I done?!*

Mr. Pryce was staring at Kian. "He was going to be our most

valuable asset," he muttered. Then he sighed. "We'll make it look like he had a fight with his biker brother. Kill him, Bradan."

My grip hesitated on the trigger.

"Bradan," said Mr. Pryce, and his voice had *that* tone, the one I always needed to hear, soft and caring. "Pull the trigger."

He said he loved me! I heard it! Every time I thought of it, my heart swelled, filling my chest. I'd been waiting *so long* to hear that.

The trigger moved. I felt it creak.

Carrick's eyes locked on mine. That foreign accent was strong in his voice: so alien and yet so familiar. "I know it wasn't you. I know it was *him,* in your head. I know what it's like to have someone feel like your father. I know how you'll do *anything* for them." He took a deep breath. "So I'm not going to kill you, brother. I'm going to put my gun down. Because I love you."

And he dropped the shotgun to the floor.

My eyes went from him to Sean. To Aedan. And then, as Sylvie moved aside a little, to Kian. His face was pale and with each slow breath, blood was pumping from his chest, spreading across the floor in a lake. But all of them, even him, had the same mix of emotions on their face. Anger. Hate. And love.

And suddenly those words that Da—*Mr. Pryce* had said seemed empty and hollow. They fit perfectly into the hole in my heart, made it light up just like I always knew they would. But then they disintegrated, crumbling to ash. I snapped my gaze across the room to him and caught his look of disdain before he could change it.

I dropped my gun to the floor. And when it hit, the noise seemed to set everything off in my mind, a chain reaction of detonations. All the memories I'd been suppressing. Everything I'd ever been taught to lock away or replace or gloss over. The lies all came crashing down. I saw the damage I'd done. *Jesus God, how do I fix this?*

Across the room, I heard Mr. Pryce curse. He'd gone around behind his desk and pulled open the drawer. When he brought out his hand, he was holding a gun: and that's when I realized no one else was armed, anymore. "I'll do it myself," he muttered. And he started walking towards Carrick.

And that's when I knew what I had to do, to put things right.

I started to run. I opened my mouth and *howled*. I let out everything that was welling up in my mind: the years of childhood I'd suppressed, the years I'd wasted since, the lies he'd told me, the lives I'd taken.

Mr. Pryce panicked and fired, but it went harmlessly over my shoulder. He fired again and I felt the bullet burn a path across my upper arm, but the anger made me unstoppable. I rammed into him and my momentum carried both of us towards the balcony.

"No!" I heard Carrick say behind me.

And then we hit the balcony rail and went over, tumbling into space three floors up.

63

AEDAN

I ran to the balcony...but they were gone. Carrick and Sean reached me a second later and the three of us just stood there in stunned silence. *He's gone.* After everything we'd been through, we'd lost him.

Feeling sick, I leaned forward over the rail. Three floors below, right outside the front doors of the mansion, Pryce's body lay in a crumpled heap, a lake of blood slowly flowering out from it. And Bradan—

I looked around. *Where's—*

And then I saw the fingertips clinging to the wooden carvings at the very bottom of the balcony. I gave a strangled cry. Then his fingers slipped and I lunged forward. *"Hold my legs!"* I yelled and slithered forward over the rail.

Carrick and Sean barely had time to grab hold of me. The ground rushed up to meet me and then I jerked to a stop. And now I could see him, hanging almost directly beneath the balcony, his own swinging body loosening his grip. I grabbed his wrist just as he let go and then we were swinging together, staring into each other's eyes.

Together, Carrick and Sean muscled us up over the edge of the balcony and back onto safe ground. I staggered over to Kian. "How is he?" I asked the girls.

"We need to get him to a hospital," said Annabelle. She had a wad of fabric torn from her top pressed against Kian's chest but it was already soaked through with blood. "*Right now.*"

Carrick and I looked at each other. "How the hell are we going to get out of town?" I asked. "How the hell are we even going to get out of this *house?*" We'd never stopped to think about that, in our hastily-constructed plan. We were still in a town full of cult members, and we'd just killed their leader. I sat down heavily on the floor. "They'll kill us."

"No."

All of us slowly turned to look at Bradan, who was standing on the balcony.

"Come and look," he said.

Annabelle stayed with Kian. The rest of us trooped over to the balcony, unsure of what we'd see.

Pryce's body was still where it fell. But the townsfolk were quickly gathering: even as we watched, five became ten became twenty. And as they saw Pryce's body, they didn't descend into rage, or come running inside to see who'd killed him. They just...stopped.

It was the same catatonia we'd seen in Bradan. The rest of the cult, spread out around the world, just received their orders: they didn't even know Pryce's name. But here, in this town, Pryce was essentially their god. Now he was gone...and their world had stopped turning.

We ran back to Kian. "Come on," I said. I grabbed his arms and Bradan took his legs: it wouldn't be elegant, but we could get him downstairs and then into a car. Carrick grabbed his shotgun and Sean his hammer, just in case, and the girls did their best to control Kian's bleeding. By now, Kian was delirious from blood loss, muttering something about a laptop. "*Hurry!*" I snapped, my chest tight with worry at how pale he was.

Together, we ran for the stairs.

64

EMILY

K ian opened his eyes. "Don't try to move," I said quickly.
He ignored me and tried to sit up...then grimaced and collapsed back onto the pillows.

I let out a sigh and stroked his forehead. "Told you," I said, mock-sternly. But I couldn't even pull off *mock*-stern. It was too good to see him awake. I leaned down and kissed his forehead. He let out a groan and reached for me, fighting with the covers, and finally managed to get an arm around my waist and pull me down to him until my breasts squashed against his chest. It was terrifying to feel him so weak but I could still feel the muscled solidness of him: he was still my rock. He'd just had the life drained out of him for a while.

When I moved gently back, he tried to speak. That's when he realized he had an oxygen mask on his face. But I strained my ears and managed to translate the mumbling. "Yes," I told him firmly. "Everyone's okay."

I filled him in, piecing it together from what the others had told me when I arrived. How his brothers had carried him out of the mansion and stolen a couple of cars to bring him here, the nearest hospital with a trauma unit. How the cops and the FBI were now swarming over the town, freed at last from Pryce's interference in their investigations. The cult's greatest strength—that its members were absolutely loyal—had turned out to be its greatest weakness. Without orders, the members who'd wormed their way into law enforcement and the government had gone dormant.

By the time Louise called me, I was already on my way aboard Air Force One, unable to wait any longer without news. I'd arrived to find Kian still in surgery and I'd been sitting by his bedside, his hand clasped in mine, for three hours since it finished.

"Laptop," whispered Kian.

I blinked at him. "Laptop?"

Kian licked his lips. "Pryce had a laptop. Important."

I nodded. "I'll tell the cops to keep a look out for it."

Finally, reluctantly, after checking on everything else, he croaked, "How am I?"

I sighed. "The bullet pierced a lung and you lost a lot of blood." I ran a hand through his hair. "But you'll live. *Don't ever scare me like that again!*"

He mumbled something else.

"What?" I leaned closer.

"Take this damn thing off me," he croaked.

I looked over my shoulder to see if the doctor was coming, but he wasn't. "Just for a second," I warned. I stretched the elastic straps and lifted the oxygen mask off, the quiet room filling with the sound of its faint hiss.

"Come here," he told me. And grabbed the front of my blouse.

I didn't need telling twice. My eyes fluttered closed, my lips parted and I kissed him.

65

LOUISE

I clutched Sean's hand as Annabelle gently opened Kian's door and stuck her head round. We'd thought we heard voices from inside and needed an update.

Annabelle pulled her head back. "He's awake!" she whispered. "Talking. Kissing." She poked her head around the door again for another look. Then she pulled it quickly back and closed the door, her cheeks flushing. "He's *definitely* okay."

We all relaxed...including Miller, Jack and the rest of Emily's Secret Service detail. They were antsy enough, having one of their charges shot, never mind that they had to share the hallway with the guy who shot him.

Everyone else seemed to be okay. Sean and the other men had more bruises from all the fighting than I wanted to count and Annabelle had picked up a few from when the Mustang had gone through the window, but otherwise we were fine. And it was *over*.

I was sitting on Sean's lap, his arms around my waist and crossed protectively over my stomach: protecting me *and* the baby. His chin was resting on the top of my head and he kept leaning down to kiss the top of my head. Carrick was standing alongside Annabelle, his arm snugging her to him, their sides pressed so close from ankle to shoulder that not even a sliver of wall showed between them. Sylvie and Aedan were sitting cuddled on a couple of chairs, his arms around her and her feet drawn up so that she could nestle sideways into his chest. Alec strolled off down the hallway to call his girlfriend, Jessica, back in Chicago, and tell her the good news.

That only left Bradan standing on his own. His head was down and he seemed to be lost in his thoughts. We were only now starting to get a sense of what he'd endured, since his mom took him off in the car that day. He'd been lied to, turned into a killer and had his memories sealed away from him. He'd missed out on an entire life. Everything, since being a kid, had been about training, being loyal, protecting the cult. While we'd been waiting for Kian to wake up, I'd thought out loud about getting something to eat and then asked what sort of food he liked.

He *didn't know.* Food was fuel, to him. He ate in whatever restaurant his target was eating in.

He hadn't lived...or loved. How do you even go about healing that?

The doors at the end of the hallway burst open and Kayley came running in, followed by Stacey. I'd called them a few hours ago, when the cops swept into the town and we started trying to explain everything that had happened. I knew that all of us were going to be giving statements for a long, long time and I wanted to give Kayley a hug while I could.

I jumped up, swept Kayley into my arms and spun around with her. "Tell me it's over," whispered Kayley in my ear.

I squeezed her tight. "It's over."

Sean came up behind me and hugged both of us, then pressed his cheek to mine. Our weird, wonderful little family...soon to be one larger. We stood like that for a long time before I finally remembered I hadn't even spoken to Stacey, yet, and that I should thank her for taking care of Kayley.

But when I turned to my friend, she was staring off across the room, her lips parted and an expression I'd never seen before on her face. Stacey, the unstoppable, hyper-organized, empire-building businesswoman, had been....*stopped*. Her pupils were huge, her cheeks flushed and there was a look of confusion on her face, as if she didn't quite understand what was happening to her.

I frowned and turned to follow her gaze. And saw Bradan, leaning against the wall. He'd lifted his head and was looking right at her.

EPILOGUE

Six Weeks Later

Kian

Ｉt was the day before the wedding. I was sitting in the long grass—
the part of the garden we affectionately called the meadow. Emily
was by my side, her head resting on my shoulder. We were watching
Aedan's gull fly in lazy circles around the house, descending each
time I threw him a scrap. We'd shipped him here by road, having to
pay the pet-moving company extra due to the immense size of the
thing. They'd had to use the cage normally reserved for things like
buzzards and eagles. So far, the gull seemed just as happy here as it
had in Chicago, as long as there were plenty of scraps available. If
there weren't, he'd already learned to voice his disapproval by
rapping his beak on our window.

Aedan and Sylvie had made the decision to move to LA after
shuttling back and forth while planning the wedding and finding
more and more to keep them in California and less and less to keep

them on the East Coast. Both of them had told us how Chicago had never really felt like home and they were in love with the warmer weather. There were gyms and fighting circuits everywhere, so they could easily get jobs out here.

Sylvie had become firm friends with Louise and Annabelle and Emily and I visited regularly. Aedan got to see his brothers: including Bradan, who for now was living in one of Sean and Louise's spare rooms. Aedan and Sylvie had moved into the house as well, although their plan was to look for a place of their own close by, once they got settled. With the baby on the way, Louise and Sean were glad of a little extra rent money, so it all worked out pretty well. Alec had chosen to stay in Chicago and was moving in with Jessica: after years of living with his sister, it was about time he had his own space.

And me? I'd taken some advice from the smartest woman I knew. A woman I intended to make my wife, at some point in the not-too distant future. I'd retired my suit, apart from when I really needed it for a White House function. I'd let my stubble grow back. And now that I'd figured out what Emily needed me to be—*me*—I'd started to think about what I wanted to do with my time.

"I've been talking to Miller," I told Emily. "There are opportunities available. Private security."

Emily looked worried. "Like Rexortech, Kerrigan's company? Military contractors?"

I shook my head firmly. "No. The *opposite* of Rexortech. Just a small group of people, former military. We'd do things the government can't do, or isn't allowed to do."

"Sounds shady," she said. But she was smiling.

"I'd be in charge of it," I told her. "I'd choose the jobs. I'd make sure we were on the right side, working for the right people. We'd be the good guys. Or not the bad guys, at least."

She thought about it. "Okay," she said slowly.

Now came the difficult part. "I'd be organizing...mostly. But I couldn't promise...I mean...."

"It might sometimes be dangerous?" she asked quietly.

I hesitated. But I couldn't lie to her. I nodded.

She looked away, staring out over the city. We sat in silence for a few minutes while I tried to put it into words. Then with a sigh, I said, "I just need to be doing something, you know? What Annabelle and Carrick went through with that Volos guy. And Kerrigan. And that fight promoter Aedan had to deal with, Rick. The human trafficker the Sisters of Invidia are chasing. The cult. There are too many bad guys, not enough good."

I leaned forward until I could see her eyes. *Dammit!* They were huge and scared, exactly what I'd wanted to avoid. I gently took her chin between my finger and thumb and turned her head so she was looking at me. *"But,"* I said. "If you don't want me to do it...I understand."

She put a hand on my chest then silently ran it down over the place where I was shot. I was healing well, but it would be a while before I was running any marathons and I'd carry the scar for the rest of my life. "You could get hurt," she said. "Or worse."

I wasn't going to bullshit her. She deserved better than that. "Yeah. I'll try my best. But yeah."

She thought about it for a long time. "It'll *mostly* be desk work?" she asked.

I nodded.

"And you'll have good people watching your back?"

"The best," I said with feeling.

She took a deep breath. "Then do it," she said, nodding to herself. She turned to me. "It scares the hell out of me. But seeing you change into something that isn't you, watching you die inside while you go to another cocktail party...that scares me, too. And knowing those people are out there without people like you to stop them...that scares me even more."

I leaned forward and brushed her soft, mahogany hair back from her cheek. *God,* I loved this woman. "Thank you," I whispered. And kissed her deep and true.

We were still kissing when a black Mercedes pulled into the drive. "She's here," I said, getting to my feet. "Come on. She's here for Bradan but I want to be there to back him up."

Bradan

I don't know what I expected the head of the CIA's Special Activities Division to be like. But Roberta Geiss wasn't it. She was a small woman in her early fifties with a voice that was both soft and firm, and she seemed to have zero capacity for bullshit.

She, Kian, Emily, Stacey and I were sitting in the newly-refurbished living room. Roberta had requested it be just me for this debriefing but I'd insisted they be there. I was still too new to this world: I still thought of it as *Outside*. I needed their experience. Especially Stacey.

Louise's best friend had been crucial in helping me to adjust. She'd taken me shopping, to a movie, to the beach...all the fun things I'd missed out on. The cult had taken so much of my life that normalizing me was a huge job, but Stacey's organizational abilities were legendary. She introduced me to new foods each day, compiled lists of TV I should watch and books I should read and was even talking about helping me to find a job.

I had no idea why she was helping me but I was grateful. And I loved being around her. Right from the first moment I'd seen her at the hospital, there was something about her that fascinated me. All that ambitious energy, everything so sleek and efficient, from her glossy black hair to the glimpses of long, elegant legs beneath her skirt. She'd shared with me that men found her success intimidating. I couldn't understand that at all: I thought she was incredible. Sometimes, she'd look at me *just so,* a smile that was half excited, half nervous, touching her lips, and it was all I could do to stop myself pouncing on her. I didn't want to start something: I knew I was still messed up. But resisting got harder with every moment I spent with her.

"Leonard Paul Mackenzie," said Roberta, tossing a large black and white photo on the table.

I stared down at a younger version of Mr. Pryce. The man I'd called *dad* for so many years.

"He was CIA?" asked Kian at last.

"Back in the seventies, he was program manager on something we called *Songbird*." Roberta looked uncomfortable. "It was researching the use of hypnotic drugs and religious indoctrination techniques to recruit field agents."

"The CIA wanted to create its own cult," said Kian coldly.

"We did a lot of things back then that I'm not proud of," said Roberta. "It was long before my time. It was *shut down* long before my time. Mackenzie quit. A few years later...." She trailed off.

"A few years later *what?*" I asked savagely. I could hear the Irish in my voice. The accent the cult had suppressed was gradually coming back.

She sighed. "There were rumors. Just rumors—"

"You *knew?*" Kian looked like he was ready to explode.

"No!" Roberta shook her head. "I don't know. Look, I'm trying to piece this thing together, just like you. We're talking about things that happened decades ago, CIA staff who have long since retired. But *yes,* I think that back in the eighties, during the Cold War, there were some people who remembered Mackenzie, and they heard about this new cult that was around and...it's possible that they guessed what was going on." She swallowed. "It's possible that they even protected him, a little. Thought that he might create an asset they could later control." She glanced between us guiltily. "Look, this was the eighties, we were desperate for any edge over the Russians and there was a lot of loyalty between the old guard. They weren't going to turn him in. Then, later, when the cult grew more powerful, those people started getting scared. It was too big to control, by then, and they started getting worried they'd be held responsible, so they covered it up. And by then the CIA was compromised: the cult had started to turn some of our people."

"What about now?" I asked.

She looked at me levelly. "Truthfully? I don't know. We're interviewing everyone, trying to clean house. Taking out Mackenzie threw a big, big spanner in the works: the members are operating on their own, now, without orders. That means it's harder for them to cover things up or derail investigations. People aren't scared for their lives anymore if they look into the cult. But these people aren't robots. They'll still protect themselves and try to cover their tracks. You stopped the machine working for now, but we can't guarantee we've dismantled every piece...or even most pieces."

"What do you mean, *for now?*" I asked.

Kian sighed and rubbed his stubbled cheek. "The laptop," he said bitterly.

Roberta nodded. "Kian had a theory that that's how Mackenzie was sending out the orders. Could be email, social media, something else...doesn't matter. If he's right, that laptop is like the magic sword that makes the holder king. Whoever has it controls the cult."

"Mackenzie—Pryce—he said something, when we first met him," Kian told me. "He talked about *the ones who'll come after me.* I think he wanted the cult to outlive him: Aeternus means *everlasting.* He was going to pass the laptop onto a successor."

"And now we can't find it," said Roberta. "We've searched every inch of the town. Now it may just be that he stored it in some secret safe, somewhere we haven't found. But it could be that he had some sort of emergency plan in place. It could be that he had someone with standing orders to spirit that laptop away and pass it on to someone, if anything ever happened to him. And if that happens...the cult's taken a body blow but it's not dead. Most of the members are still in place, waiting for orders. And we still don't know what Pryce was working towards. He saw it as bringing order but we don't know what world he was trying to create."

Kian let out a despairing sigh. "Goddammit!"

"Hey, go easy on yourself," Roberta told him. "It's only a theory. The laptop could still show up, safe and sound. And even if it doesn't, you've crippled them. They sure as hell won't be coming after your family again, and you got your brother back. You freed hundreds of people in that town: we have psychologists working with the police now to rehabilitate all of them. It's going to be chaos for months: no one's ever had to deal with anything on this scale before, but we'll get it done."

"I assume the CIA's involvement isn't going to make the news," said Stacey darkly.

"We're trying to fix things set in motion by a CIA that no longer exists," Roberta told her. "Having people mistrust today's CIA isn't going to help. But people *do* know that the town was at the center of a dangerous cult. If they do try to start up again, they won't be able to recruit as openly. They'll have to go underground."

"That could make them even more dangerous," muttered Kian.

"All the more reason to help us," Roberta said smoothly, turning to me.

I nodded reluctantly. "What do you want?"

Roberta leaned forward. "Come to Langley," she said urgently. "You've spent more time in the cult and you were closer to Pryce than anyone. You understand its workings. Let us fully debrief you: give us every detail."

I went quiet for a long time. "I'll think about it," I said at last.

Out of the corner of my eye, I thought I saw Stacey smile. As if she hadn't liked the idea of me disappearing off to Langley for weeks.

Roberta nodded, stood and smoothed down her skirt. "Do you have any idea what you're going to do, now?"

"I might have a suggestion," said Kian thoughtfully.

"I figure there's no hurry," I told both of them. "I've had a lot of years of always doing something, always being on a mission. Right now, I want to just take some time." And this time, I was sure I saw Stacey smile.

As we walked Roberta out, I looked up at the tree in the hallway. It had lost a lot of twigs and small branches and the trunk was blackened in places, but it was starting to grow back, stronger than ever.

Annabelle

I leaned over Carrick's shoulder, raising my voice over the throb of the Harley's engine. "We're going to be late!"

He shook his head, grinning. "Will you quit your worrying? We'll be fine."

I settled back on the saddle. He was probably right but I was pretty sure it was a woman's right to be anxious, on her way to her best friends' wedding. Friends *plural*.

"There they are," Carrick muttered, and accelerated, threading his way through the traffic ahead.

We'd come out to the freeway to guide the others in, because the little church wasn't the easiest place to find. Mostly, though, I think Carrick had just wanted an excuse to get away from the orgy of estrogen that happens when two women are preparing for their wedding day in the same house on the same morning. You couldn't move for dresses, flowers and women in momentary floods of tears.

We saw Mac first. He cut across traffic to swing in next to us, drawing angry beeps. He winked and blew a kiss at a blonde in a big Mercedes SUV and I saw her blush and look away, then surreptitiously look back.

Ox appeared next. There was a school bus in front of him and the kids were all glued to the rear window, awed by the muscled giant on his oversize bike. Then Hunter, sitting straight and tall as if he was riding a horse, the bike almost part of him.

We formed up and Carrick led the way down the off-ramp and through the twisting, wooded streets towards the church. The trees broke the sun into gorgeous shafts of golden light: my bare arms would get a little blast of warmth as we passed through one of them, then refreshing cool as we plunged into shadow again. It was idyllic and I'd never seen Carrick so happy. With Bradan safe, his family back together and his demons laid to rest, it felt like he'd let go of a ton of baggage and all we had was a clear road ahead.

Emily met us outside the church, already in her bridesmaid dress. "Hurry, hurry!" She pulled us inside and then together we pushed the men into a side room to get into their suits while she zipped me into my bridesmaid's dress. "Where's Stacey?" I asked.

"I have no idea," she panted. The zipper had stuck and she was struggling to free it. "I can't find Bradan, either."

That was weird. I'd gotten to know Stacey quite well recently: Carrick and I had been visiting Sean and Louise a few times a week and Stacey was always there, helping Bradan. She was normally super-reliable.

The door suddenly opened and I yelped...but luckily, the zipper picked just that moment to come free and I was pretty much decent when Kian walked in. "*Knock!*" Emily told him. "What is it with you and not knocking?!"

"Sorry," said Kian. "Sean and Aedan are ready. Where's Carrick?"

Carrick, Mac, Hunter and Ox chose that moment to stroll out of the side room. My lungs filled, my hands suddenly going to my mouth. They all looked good but Carrick looked *amazing!* I'd never seen him in anything but a t-shirt or a leather cut before. With his broad chest stretching out the snow-white shirt and the flawless lines of his gray suit accentuating those wide shoulders and his narrow waist...I flushed and pulled him close. "*You look like a badass freakin' billionaire,*" I hissed in his ear.

Kian crossed his arms. "So how does a suit feel?" he asked.

Carrick grinned, turning his arms this way and that, examining his cuffs. "You know what? Not as bad as I thought."

The other Hell's Princes looked great too. Mac looked like some gentleman rogue about to tell some rich girl to stand and deliver. Hunter looked like a brooding lawman from some old west frontier town. And Ox—who'd had to get his suit specially tailored—looked like the doorman on the gates of hell.

Kayley ran in, using both hands to lift the skirt of her dress so that she could sprint. "*They're coming! I just saw the car!*"

We all started hurrying down the hallway towards the church hall. "Has anyone seen my bouquet?" asked Kayley. "I can't find it!"

Emily nodded towards the storeroom we were just passing. "Stacey has them all lined up in here, with names and everything." She pushed open the door—

Bradan had Stacey pressed up against the wall, her head tilted back, his mouth covering hers. One hand was stroking her neatly-pinned hair, the other was gliding up her side...over her breast. Stacey let out a moan.

The light from the hallway hit them and they broke the kiss, heads snapping round in shock. Stacey flushed when she saw us all standing there.

"Time to go," said Emily, fighting to keep her voice even. A massive grin was spreading across her face.

Stacey fled past us, eyes on the floor. Bradan followed a second later, adjusting his tie. He looked more determined than embarrassed, as if he was counting the seconds until he could get her alone again.

"Stacey and Bradan?!" I asked in disbelief as Kayley grabbed her bouquet.

Emily giggled. "You didn't wonder why she's been spending so much time with him?" She looked at my blank face. "Oh God, I love your innocence. The rest of us have been wondering when it would happen."

"But she runs like fifty bakeries! She wears a suit! She's all...*controlly.* And he's—" I tried to think of the right words. *Irish? Dark and brooding? A barely-reformed criminal?* I looked at her helplessly.

"And he's an O'Harra," said Emily. "Exactly."

Sylvie

Why am I so nervous? I'm never this nervous going into the ring. My heart felt as if it was going to hammer its way right out of my chest.

And then a big, comforting hand curled around mine and gave it a squeeze. "For what it's worth," said Aedan's dad, "he'll be just as scared as you."

I looked across at him and grinned. On the far side of the car, Louise looked exactly like I felt: nervous and flighty and drunk on adrenaline. I was very, very glad Michael was here to give us away.

With the cult in disarray, Kian was able to get a sympathetic DA to take a new look at his case, free of their interference, and the result had been an early parole. We'd all met him at the prison gates and watched as he took his first deep lungful of free air. That very evening, I'd asked him if, since neither my dad nor Louise's were still with us, he'd walk us up the aisle. He'd been a rock of cool confidence amidst the chaos.

He kept telling us to call him *Michael* but Louise and I were both still stuck on *Mr. O'Harra.* And in just a few minutes, it would be *dad. Ulp.*

The double wedding had been something we'd settled on from the start. Sean had proposed to Louise the day after we all returned from the cult's town, as soon as he'd bought a ring. Both of us were eager to do it and neither of us wanted to steal the other one's thunder by being first.

So we decided to both get married at once and spent the next few weeks browsing wedding dress websites together while Carrick and Stacey organized the bachelor and bachelorette parties, both in Vegas. The guys were tight-lipped about what happened on theirs but I'd seen evidence of one thing they got up to: a few days after they returned, I'd run into Bradan emerging from the bathroom, topless after his shower. As he walked away, I'd seen his back...and the tattoo of a shamrock that now lay between his shoulder blades.

The car pulled up. Outside, the photographer started clicking. I took a deep, shaky breath.

Aedan's dad squeezed my hand again. "You look beautiful," he told us. His Irish accent was so much thicker than Aedan's, every syllable like jagged black rock cleaved with an axe to reveal a shining silver core. "Both of you. My sons are lucky men. Now shall we do this?"

I nodded. Adjusted my veil. And the three of us stepped from the car.

Louise

I felt as if I was walking on clouds. It was a good thing Michael was there to hold onto because I was in danger of floating right off into the sky. I'd never felt such a mix of fear, excitement and fluttery joy. *OK*, I told myself firmly as we approached the doors of the church. *It's just a room full of people. Nothing to get all weird about.*

The doors opened and the opening bars of The Wedding March rose up to meet me. Immediately, any notion of staying calm went right out the window.

It was a sea of faces, all grinning at us. Our joint bridesmaids: Emily, Annabelle, Stacey and Kayley. Carrick and Kian, the best men. Alec and Bradan, our ushers. Jasmine, Aedan's friend from New York, and her boyfriend Ryan. Three bikers from Carrick's MC. Jessica, Alec's girlfriend. And too many more to count.

And there, right at the front, two men in suits. They turned at the same moment and I caught my breath.

From the very first moment I saw him in our old apartment building, Sean had always had a powerful effect on me. Just the sight of those smooth tan muscles, the shining black ink of his tattoos...so much *badness,* so much brooding power. I hadn't been able to visualize at all how he'd look in a suit. Would it hide what he was?

Not at all. If anything, the smart clothes just threw all that attitude and brute determination I loved so much into sharp relief. I couldn't take my eyes off his shoulders, off the glorious X-shape of his back, waist and hips, all that barely-restrained power. Other men wore a suit and looked ready for the boardroom. Sean looked ready to smash the boardroom table in two. And with his tattoos and muscles hidden, all that intimidating resolve had to come out through his eyes, a burning gaze that told anyone they'd better think twice before messing with his family.

Then his eyes met mine and the hardness in his eyes just melted, replaced by such an urgent, deep love that I felt my eyes grow hot. It was the same look he'd given me when he'd taken me into the garden, the day after we got back from the cult's town. When he'd gone down on one knee, showed me the ring and asked me if I'd make him the happiest man alive.

Do not cry, I told myself sternly. I risked a glance sideways at Sylvie. Oh God: she was looking at Aedan in the same way I'd just looked at Sean and I could see her eyes shining, too. I swallowed hard and faced front before she set me off.

We moved slowly down the aisle. *Walk slow, walk slow!* If I hadn't been clinging onto Michael's hand, I would have raced down the church in huge strides, heels or no heels, I was so nervous. And then I was there, at the front, and Sean was beside me and *Oh God* it was real. *I'm getting married!*

Everyone looked so amazing: we'd gone for light grey morning suits for the men and deep green for the bridesmaid's dresses, with simple, matching ivory gowns for Sylvie and me. Kayley was beaming proudly, ecstatic. And Stacey was...wait, Stacey was biting her lip and flushing every time she glanced at Bradan. *What did I miss? Did they finally...*

But there was no time to think about it. Everything moved so fast: the service seemed to whip by in a couple of seconds and suddenly we were at the vows. I managed to keep it together until the part where Sean repeated *to have and to hold* and then I gave a kind of jerk, a shudder, and had to blink back tears of pure happiness.

When he slid the ring onto my finger I could feel it in a way I never expected to. It connected us: a bond that had started months before in a graffiti-covered elevator in a run-down apartment block. One that had been strengthened by everything we'd been through and was now unbreakable forever.

"You may kiss your brides," a distant voice said. And then Sean's lips were coming down on mine. I could feel his hard abs press lightly against my belly. I was showing a little and Sean never got tired of touching me there, feeling the new life inside me. When he'd come back from the cult's town, the trace of fear that had been in his eyes was gone. He was ready—*eager*—to be a father.

And me? Weirdly, it was Sean's dad, Michael, who'd finally helped me relax about motherhood. He'd found me pacing the house in the middle of the night, a few days ago, and taken me into the kitchen for some warm milk and a pep talk. "There's just so much to do," I'd told him. "Diapers and feedings and baths and burping and I'm meant to play it Beethoven to make it smarter and *what if I get it wrong?*"

He regarded me, utterly calm. "You'll be fine, Louise," he said in that hard, silver-lined accent, so thick I struggled to understand it, at first. "You and Sean are strong together. That's all that matters. Beyond that, it's just about being organized."

I started to argue and then blinked. "Wait, *what?*" No one had said that to me before. I'd been thinking of a baby as some huge, nebulous that I couldn't get a handle on. "I can *do* organized!"

And I had. I'd already bought breast pumps and bottles, diapers and a changing mat. I'd learned about feeding schedules and we'd converted a room into a nursery. Sean and I had even done some practice diaper changes on one of Kayley's old dolls. Once I had it all planned out in my head, it seemed a lot less intimidating. Not all of the fear went away but now it was firmly overshadowed by excitement. And what made me feel even better was that I had so many people willing to help me.

Sean grudgingly broke the kiss and looked down at me with a look of devotion that nearly started me crying again. Next to me, Sylvie was in a similar state.

Sean and I walked down the aisle hand in hand, Sylvie and Aedan right behind us. Outside, the photographer stopped us for just one photo before we left for the reception. All four couples in a line, each of us embracing.

The photographer moved to take the shot but we shook our heads: *not yet.* Kian grabbed Bradan and pulled him and a blushing Stacey in as well.

Sean sank his fingers deep into my hair and leaned down. And five Irish brothers kissed the women they loved.

THE END

The story of how hacker "Mary," (Lily), met cowboy "Luke," (Bull), is told in *Texas Kissing*. FBI agent Calahan also plays a role.

The story of how fellow hacker Gabriella went on the run (and fell in love) with Alexei, the man sent to kill her, is told in *Kissing My Killer*.

FBI agent Kate Lydecker, briefly glimpsed in Central Park, is stranded in Alaska after a plane crash and must trust her life to a prisoner and former Navy SEAL in *Alaska Wild*.

Finally, if you missed one of the brothers' stories and want to catch up, you can find them in:

Punching and Kissing (Aedan and Sylvie)
Bad For Me (Sean and Louise)
Saving Liberty (Kian and Emily)
Outlaw's Promise (Carrick, Annabelle, Mac, Hunter and Ox)